The FRESHOUR CYLINDERS

The
FRESHOUR CYLINDERS

SPEER MORGAN

MACMURRAY & BECK

DENVER

Printed and bound in the United States of America

1   2   3   4   5   6   7   8   9   10

Library of Congress Cataloging-in-Publication Data
Morgan, Speer, 1946–
The Freshour cylinders : a novel / by
Speer Morgan.
p.   cm.
ISBN 1-878448-84-6 (cloth)
ISBN 1-878448-99-4 (paper)
I. Title.
PS3563.087149F74   1998
813′.54—dc21   98-26668
                                 CIP

MacMurray & Beck Fiction: General Editor, Greg Michalson
The Freshour Cylinders cover design by Laurie Dolphin.
The text was set in Janson by Chris Davis, Mulberry Tree Enterprises.

For Bob Allen Kuykendall

Editor's Note

I first heard of the recordings in a telephone call from Betsy Hillen, an old friend with whom I grew up in Fort Smith and who still lives there today. Her husband, Marshal Hillen, a bank executive, had discovered the boxes of wax cylinders while cleaning out a superannuated vault in the Mercantile Bank. After inquiring among others on the bank's staff about the cylinders, with no luck, Mr. Hillen decided to throw them away. He had actually moved them to the front sidewalk to be hauled off when the only longtime employee he had not questioned, a janitor named Darius Jones, recognized the cylinders and told him that the previous bank president (deceased) had promised Mr. Tom Freshour that bank officials would put them in the right hands when the time came.

Unable to get any further information about the recordings and not having a Dictaphone on which to listen to them, Marshal Hillen took the boxes home and stored them in his garage. This was in 1988, and the boxes sat there, largely forgotten, until 1996, when Betsy did "the mother of all cleanings" and promptly sent the cylinders to me. As she put it, I was the only historian she knew.

Historian or not, a very dependable allergy to dust has eroded my sentimentality about old things. When people eagerly tell me about a bundle of yellowing letters in their attics, my reflex response is to ask them to burn them, please. I was a little piqued by my old friend calling to inform me that she had already sent me these things. However, I'd known Betsy since we were in first grade together; we had a lifelong habit of presuming upon each other, and possibly it was her turn.

When the recordings arrived I made no particular effort to listen to them, aside from making a couple of inquiries to try to find a recorder of a model that used this type of cylinder. Many years ago, when writing my first book, I had used such a machine in Britain when transcribing accounts of World War I, so I was familiar with it. Having no luck initially, I did what Marshal Hillen had done: set aside the boxes and went on about my business. I am a bachelor, and one of the pleasures of bachelorhood is being able to leave things lying about. They remained stacked in a floor alcove of my dining room, three boxes containing forty-six cartoned cylinders, each neatly labeled "Spiro" in a cursive script that I later identified as Tom Freshour's. I assumed that the recordings had to do with some kind of bank business in the Spiro region, and, fascinating though that might be to someone studying regional financial history, such material would hardly be of interest to me.

A month after receiving them, while eating dinner, I idly slit the tape of three of the smaller boxes and found at the bottom of one of them, under one of the cylinders, a handful of photographs. They were black-and-white snapshots, partially faded, of what appeared to be items from an archaeological dig. Three were photos of seashells with complex engraving on them; a fourth was a wooden deer mask; another was a shot of four eye masks, apparently made of a lustrous dark mineral, lying side by side on a table; and another pictured what appeared to be a cloak or coat of some kind. The coat was spread out and appeared to have feathers in it.

I finally put two and two together—"Spiro" plus archaeological items—and realized that the recordings might concern the famous mound located just east of that town. Despite having grown up fifteen miles from the site, I knew little about the Spiro Mound except that it existed and was considered important. Somewhere, decades ago, I had seen pictures of Spiro shells but could recall nothing about their significance.

The last snapshot was of a man sitting behind a desk, glancing up toward the photographer with a distracted expression, a tangle of dark hair down over an eyebrow and his hand on a telephone. He was a handsome man of middle years, caught unawares, preoccupied, in full mental stride, and one could almost see his next movement in the still photograph. He seemed oddly familiar. I had a feeling that I had seen him, conceivably a number of times, during my childhood.

The photographs led me to renew my efforts to find a Dictaphone. Dr. Wesley Miller of the Smithsonian Institution—who has been unfailingly generous in this project—e-mailed me to say that I was welcome to come to Washington and use one of theirs. Unable to do so immediately because of university obligations, I showed the photographs to an old friend from the archaeology department, Jim Kimpole. Jim is an Old World archaeologist and a knowledgeable generalist as well. I've known him for twenty-five years and trust his judgment.

He sat at his desk looking at the photographs for some three minutes, at first taking off his glasses and looking at them from very close range, then getting out a magnifying glass, lingering quite a while over the shell work.

"Creepy, aren't they?"

"Is that your learned opinion—'creepy'?"

He was still thinking. "Warriors, serpent tongues coming out of mouths, severed heads in hands. Death imagery. On first glance, you'd almost think Mayan. . . ." He pursed his lips and frowned. Beneath the oblique exterior, he seemed oddly excited.

"What does a bank vault in Fort Smith have to do with Mayan?" I asked.

"Oh no, it's Spiro all right. There's no question about that." He laid down the photographs picturing the masks and the coat, side by side, as if organizing his thoughts. Eventually he got up from his chair and paced to his window, glancing out at Old Main as if to confirm, on this gray winter afternoon, that it was still there; then he came back and bent over the images a while longer before perching his glasses back on his face. "A bank vault in Fort Smith . . . Anything else? Anything written?"

"Forty-six wax-cylinder recordings made on an old Dictaphone machine."

"Concerning what? Have you listened to them?"

"They're labeled 'Spiro.' All I know is that the person who dictated them apparently was someone named Tom Freshour. I assume that's him." I pointed at the snapshot of the man at the telephone.

He frowned at it. "Never heard of him. Are the recordings brief? Lengthy?"

"There are several boxes of them. I haven't listened to any, so I have no idea. They may be blank; they may have all melted. They're numbered sequentially and labeled 'Spiro.'"

"Well you'd better carry along these photographs." He pointed at his desk. "These two you'd better take very good care of. Store them in a lightless place. They're already faded. They'll have to be worked on."

"I don't have time."

"Oh yes you do."

"Don't be gnomic, Jim. It's too near the end of the semester."

"If they're what I think, these are artifacts that are missing and thought to be doubtful."

"Doubtful as in thought not to exist?"

"Exactly. There are no other photographs or drawings or verifiable listings of them. This one," he pointed at one of the snapshots, "is . . ." He seemed momentarily at a loss for words. "Well, it could be among the more valuable items in North American archaeology. It was thought to be the product of some collector's overheated imagination." He moved the photograph and looked at it under the glass once more. "It's the full feathered cloak. You may have evidence here that it's not just a legend."

I stared at him, trying to take this in. Jim can be histrionic in the classroom, but he is generally restrained with colleagues.

"It's pre-Columbian, reported to have been in flawless shape. A priestly or kingly robe, suggestive of a well-developed economy and of certain religious beliefs. It was disputed—possibly lost, possibly never existed. Anyway, the reasonable contingent decided it was only a rumor. You just don't find textiles or organic products in decent shape after seven or eight hundred years in North America. A few fragmentary baskets and sandals in dry caves was about the extent of what was thought to be possible. But there were other textiles at Spiro that are in excellent shape."

"What kind of textiles?"

"Whole kilts with the dye still vivid. The best collection of them is in New York at the Museum of the American Indian. They're gorgeous. If you know the odds against their having survived, they're breathtaking. When I saw those kilts, the very first thing that occurred to me was that maybe the full feathered cloak did exist."

I was not quite sure how to proceed. "So it's rare?"

He shook his head. "If it exists, it's unique. Which makes it priceless." He moved his head closer to the photograph and said, as if thinking aloud, "Of course, I'm only making guesses. But you've got solidly identifiable Spiro materials in this shellwork, and this thing—" He pointed at the snapshot of the wooden deer mask. "Ever seen it before?"

It did look vaguely familiar, but I had no idea where I'd seen it.

He got up and went to a bookshelf and pulled out a paperback, *The Power of Myth* by Joseph Campbell. There, on its cover, all by itself, was the same eerily evocative deer mask.

He set the book down on the corner of his desk. "It's one of those poster-child artifacts—you see it all over. So. You've got several well-known Spiro items in the shells, along with what appears to be a feathered cloak. You've also got one of the other legendary groupings." He put his finger on a second photograph. "These look like the four masquettes, also declared to be fantasy." He bent down and looked at them again. "And perfectly worked. Those little items were made seven hundred, a thousand years ago. They look almost Chinese."

I was beginning to feel a kind of dread. I let out a little laugh. "I obviously need to turn this over to you, Jim."

He thought a moment, then shook his head. "Don't tempt me, Carl. I'm Old World. A person has to organize his life somehow. I have never done a minute of real New World research. Nothing beyond introductory courses. You don't become a temple-mound scholar by teaching it in Arch 10."

"Well, I'm not an archaeologist at all!"

"Lucky you. If this is a bunch of recordings, it must concern the discovery of the mound. That's history, not archaeology. You're a good editor of primary materials. And you're from the area. You're the natural person to do it."

"If you won't take it, do you have a New World colleague who would?"

Jim looked somber. "Sure, we've got them, but they're all chasing their own little rabbits at the moment. Penis sheaths, dog mites—I know these things matter. They just fail to give me that old thrill."

"And this does?"

"Oh, indeed," he said, lifting his eyebrows.

"No one deserves more than you—"

He waved a hand at me. "That's a nice thing to say, Carl. Truly. But you carry on with it. I couldn't take the excitement. I'm retiring next year; I've got my landing gear down and too much to do before then as it is. Go to Washington. And call me from there. I'll want to know how it proceeds."

That night, I e-mailed Dr. Miller at the Smithsonian, telling him Jim's hypothesis and asking if he could listen to sample cylinders to ascertain whether the recording was intact. He agreed to do so, and I sent the cylinders that according to the numbered labels were the first and last. Three days later, Dr. Miller responded that the recording indeed was in good shape. He recommended that I come as soon as possible. At the conclusion of the note, he said, "I don't quite know what to make of them—since you have sent me only the bookends—but I get the impression that Dr. Kimpole may be on to something. I strongly recommend that you not check these cylinders in airline luggage. Have them packed by a professional at your museum and send them by the most secure transport, well insured.

"You've got them buzzing here. I assure you that you will be welcome. Let me know when you'll be arriving so I can reserve a listening room for you."

Experience and common sense tell me that this story has, or had, a written text behind it. If Freshour did write the story before recording it, the physical manuscript might offer further clues to how literal his tale was meant to be. Such proof would be particularly useful considering the implications of the story and the skepticism that it has already aroused.

In any case, the following is a transcription of the Freshour narrative, divided according to the cylinders. From what he says, Tom Freshour made the Spiro recordings sometime in 1960, when he was in his seventies. The recording medium is the helical wax cylinder designed for a 1933-model Dictaphone. The cylinders are all labeled "Spiro" and are successively numbered beginning with 6. Whether Freshour recorded an initial five cylinders is not known, but the story does appear actually to start on 6. A few of the numbers are actually two physical cylinders labeled a and b. I have taken the liberty of labeling each of these as a single cylinder. Dubbed tapes of the original recordings are available to qualified researchers at the Smithsonian Institution.

Carl Penfield
Fayetteville, 1998

Cylinder 6

I first heard about Lee Guessner and the Indian mound on a hot Wednesday of a hot summer, in the third week of July. I had a trial closing that morning on William Jefferson Goback, a.k.a. "Bill J." or "Jay," for assault and the attempted murder of his wife, and I wanted to drop by the office on my way. When the kitchen door flapped shut behind me, I had less than an hour before court.

It was 1934. Prohibition was over; the New Deal was on hold after its first big spasm. Roosevelt was on a one-month vacation, floating around on the USS Something-or-other in the Caribbean, flashing an occasional well-tanned smile for the photographers. I was a forty-eight-year-old widower who thought of myself as a seasoned, middle-aged man in the afternoon of life, with certain things behind me. I toiled in the trenches—sometimes latrines—of county prosecuting. From my current exalted perspective of years, I wonder if by that summer I had not become a haunted, austere sort of man. The kind who every day has his nose a little too close to the grindstone, trying to fit expectations to accomplishments, categories to facts, beginnings to ends.

I should mention at the start that I am telling this story twenty-six years later to an old wax-tube recorder, which is a formidable instrument of time travel with its pointer riding down a ruler, telling me exactly how many inches I have remaining on each tube. The day the Dictaphone man laid it on the desk of my boss, Bernie Pryor, he said, with the oracular, fumy gleam of a good city salesman in his eye, "Here it is, Mr. Prosecutor, the dick machine. Your life won't be the same." Indeed, the boss's life would change, but not in ways anybody could have imagined.

The machine, in fact, was bought not by the county but by the prosecutor himself. Bernie was the beneficiary of coal money and could indulge his enthusiasms about new kinds of office machinery. He bought the recorder and enough of these cylinders to set down the Encyclopedia Britannica, imagining that we—meaning the secretary and I—would use them up in a fury of efficiency.

On the morning that the Goback trial was to end, I was supposed to be twenty-four hours away from a long-delayed fishing trip to Florida. It had been four years since my last vacation, and getting ready to go had been like swimming through molasses. I was out of practice at arranging vacations. The trial had been postponed and drawn out for a month and a half longer than it should have taken. The defense lawyer, Smiling John Gillis, knew about my upcoming trip and had tried to delay the proceeding until I'd be forced to hand it off to somebody else. Now, finally, it did promise to end, and I was determined to get out of town the next day. But when I pushed the starter button, I discovered there was something else to worry about.

My Ford wouldn't start.

I remember exactly the way I felt at that instant, in 1934, with my finger on the little rusted chrome button and the starter not turning over. Sitting there in my little black clunker in the two-path driveway staring through the windshield at a row of dried-up crimson clover alongside the sun-bleached garage. I remember that moment—when nothing happened—almost more clearly than the strange doings later that day. I felt cranky. I was fed up with the sun looming every day like an incinerator in the pale sky. I was doing my work all right but frankly had gotten a little sick of it. I punched the starter again, and it flashed through my mind that Jay Goback, out on bond, may have wired dynamite to the motor, and this was the slice of time before my fiery demise.

My car didn't need dynamite to make it a bomb, however.

I'd bought it after my wife, Laura, died, from the Ford dealer. Jim Forrest was his name, and he served on the school board, went to the First Methodist Church, for what that's worth, and I guess tried to be as honest as the next businessman. Because of the car Mr. Forrest had sold me, he and I had nearly gotten into a fistfight in his repair garage one day. Lately the car had been under the care of a mechanic named Harlan Jones. The wheel bearings had gone out three times, cables had busted, the brake shoes had to be replaced every few months, the crankshaft proved to be slightly off, causing the valves not to seat perfectly, the carburetor got asthmatic in particularly hot or dusty weather, which that summer was every day, and I could go on with other things that were wrong with it. Many times I had been in a mood to drive this malignant automobile someplace where I had enemies and unload it for ten bucks, but I kept thinking that once you've replaced everything, you've got a new car. There could be no such thing as a modern, mass-produced machine with a curse on it.

I stripped to my undershirt and opened the hood to see if I could find what was wrong. Because I was due in court, I hedged my bet and called Melody Parker, the secretary in the prosecutor's office, and asked if she could come get me. By the time she drove up and gave me her usual sunny 'lo, I was very glad to see her. I'd gotten the grease washed off but was still carrying my tie in my hand.

She was wearing a white blouse, red lipstick, and a canary skirt that matched her yellow Chevy sport coupe. This was well into the Depression, and the jazzy weeds of the '20s were out of fashion. Those who could afford to follow styles were wearing plain clothes or even imitation bum outfits with discreetly arranged fake patches. Not Melody. She stayed intrepidly bright.

She gave me the once-over, wrinkling her nose at the smell of the borax soap I'd used to degrease my hands, then backed into the street and raced off toward the courthouse.

Mel had a generally defective sense of danger. Heavy breathers sometimes called the prosecutor's office and threatened to burn down our houses, skin us, nail us to the wall, and so on. Such calls didn't seem to faze her. She might casually mention them at the water cooler. I had served in an ambulance unit in the war and worried about threats more than she did.

Above the clattering of tires on the brick street, Mel said, "Good thing your car broke down here rather than on your vacation."

"Hadn't thought of it that way," I said, trying to get the knot of my tie straight without a mirror.

"Do you want me to drop by the moron's garage for you?"

"Just call him. Tell him he might have to tow it. And please, don't call him a moron."

"On the phone I could call him anything. He doesn't listen anyway."

One of Harlan Jones's quirks, we both knew, was that he seldom responded to telephone calls. He had a telephone at his garage, which he did answer, but he didn't really believe in telephoning. He regarded all phone talk with limp, ironic amusement. "Oh? You don't say! I'll be." Even a simple request over the phone he would later seem barely to remember, as if it was something you might or might not have mentioned to him twenty years before.

We were sitting at a stoplight when Melody said her phone hadn't stopped that morning.

"Some of the rags called about the trial," she said. When Mel broke bad news gently, it always made me nervous. I was sensitive to her expressions, and she had that look.

"Oh?"

"Three of them. All Oklahoma. Mostly just checking to see that today was closing statements."

I was already well aware of the newspaper coverage. No surprise there. Particularly during the last few days of the trial, the eastern Oklahoma newshounds had been thick as weeds in the courtroom, and a few of them were headlining the case. People had gotten bored with the national news. A sea change seemed to be under way, and no one knew which direction things were going. There'd been a passel of investigations in the U.S. Congress, with about twenty-five committees looking into various high crimes and misdemeanors—Communists in the closet, Nazis under the bed. But people had gotten bored with congressional inquisitions.

Newspaper readers were tired of a lot of things—tired of tax foreclosures, tired of strikes and bankruptcies, and even tired of bank robberies. About a year earlier, Pretty Boy Floyd had waltzed into his home town, Sallisaw, Oklahoma, twenty miles from Fort Smith, and robbed the local bank, taking bows like a movie star making an appearance at a premiere, but there had been too many machine-gun massacres since then; the general mess and confusion of the country had gotten too thick. Crime, even against bankers, was losing its entertainment value.

A little wife-shooting by a colorful local character, though—now, that might still be fun.

I didn't talk to newspapers when I was prosecuting a case. Area reporters were used to me and didn't waste their time asking me questions. My boss, Bernie Pryor, the prosecutor, did most of the talking to the papers when he was in town.

"Judge Stone called," Melody added, then hesitated a beat. "So did the prosecutor, long distance. Said he was cutting short his vacation. Said he'd be back tonight."

That—and the green flatbed truck we were about to run into—got my attention.

"Damn, Mel! Slow down."

She zipped around the flatbed.

"Did you say Bernie's coming back?"

"He called less than an hour ago."

I couldn't see the prosecutor cutting short his annual "big vacation" (Bernie had all sizes and grades of vacations) unless his wife had thrown him out. That wouldn't have been unprecedented. Berenice Pryor was a very demanding woman, something of a drinker, and she occasionally got openly sick of Bernie. Their "big

n" was always taken in her old family home on one of the
r islands off Georgia.

arely Bernie wouldn't be rushing back to brag about the
ㄴㄴ ıck case, no matter what kind of splash it made in the newspapers. He hadn't even been in town during the trial.

"Did he say why he was coming back?"

"No, he did not."

"Then why'd he call?"

"I really don't know. It sounded like he was in a train station.
All he said was 'Don't worry, tell Tom I'm on my way back.'"

"What am I supposed to not worry about?" I asked, and she just
shook her head. More to the point was how any worry I might have
could be alleviated by Bernie coming back, but Melody and I had
an unspoken pact to talk as little as possible about such things.

I fell into my usual mood about my job and the boss. Bernie was
five years younger than I, had vague political yearnings, and enjoyed a trust fund that was large enough or safely enough invested
that the Crash hadn't visibly crimped his style. Officially I had no
status except that of a month-to-month employee. Without doubt,
any work in 1934 was good work. There were lawyers in town who
would have polished Bernie Pryor's saddle oxfords and mixed his
wife's highballs for my job.

A couple of other lawyers occasionally handled cases for us, but
Mel and I hired them and really ran the office, while the prosecutor showed up now and then and made a nervous pass at playing
executive. He sometimes went with me to the courthouse and sat a
while at the prosecutor's table. He also had a knack for talking to
newspaper reporters, but that was about all he seemed to get a kick
out of. The bread and butter of prosecuting is lining up witnesses,
and Bernie couldn't be bothered with such details.

All this is Bernie before the campaign, before the change—
Bernie B.C., as Mel and I later called it. But there was no way to
anticipate what would happen to Bernie, no hint except his rest-
lessness. He was not an unhappy man. He had a family. He had
money. He took pleasure in certain things. In a town full of drunks,

he was not one himself. He was fidgety, he was absentminded and a little insecure about whether others esteemed him, and he was evasive toward authorities and obligations. On that Wednesday morning I knew I had a rich, lazy, uninvolved boss—a decent man who had not found his purpose in life and who showed no sign of ever finding it.

I had worked for the Indian Agency in Muskogee and practiced law for a while on my own in the '20s, and I knew that no job or boss—or lack thereof—was ideal. Bernie did have his qualities. He made sure you got paid, which in 1934 was no small virtue. He wasn't a nitpicker. He'd been to college (a good one) and law school, unlike a lot of lawyers in those days. And he was pretty smart about making arrangements. I was a good assistant because I'm part Indian by blood and could never have replaced him as prosecutor: my skin was dark enough that Bernie didn't have to worry. And Melody was a good secretary because she didn't mind her boss being perpetually absent. She regarded Bernie's absence as a simple fact of life. If somebody asked where he was or how long he would be gone, she'd tell them. She never offered excuses for him, while I occasionally felt that I needed to, and it became something of a game among the lawyers to taunt me about the prosecutor's laziness, the idea being that if Bernie went down, I would too. And he did dance on thin ice, it was true: he occupied an elected office and elections were coming up, and he was paid by public money during a time when they were routinely having to delay schoolteachers' salaries for months at a time, while he, bless his rich soul, did barely a lick for his salary.

I didn't register Melody's other piece of news until she'd stopped in front of the courthouse. Its front steps were already beginning to wiggle with heat.

"Judge Stone called too?"

She nodded and looked at me directly, eyebrows raised. Mel had brown eyes flecked with gold.

"He wants to see me before session?"

"Didn't say. He did sound a little upset. Maybe he was the one who called Mr. Pryor and asked him to come back to town."

With my hand on the door handle, I asked, "What's going on, Mel?"

Mel shook her head. "I don't know, but LaVerne in the sheriff's office said there was a murder out in the county. Probably has to do with that."

"Boy, you really did talk to everybody this morning. Who got murdered?"

"Somebody the judge knows. His name is Guesser or Guessner or something like that. He was apparently an artifact collector. On the Spiro Mound, I think."

I had heard of the Spiro Mound. Barely. A short newspaper article about it had appeared some months ago.

"The Indian mound? Arrowheads?"

"I guess."

"Did you learn anything else?"

"That's about all LaVerne said. She was just calling to pass the word. You know how it is over there."

Mel was referring to the fact that the only person in the sheriff's office who was even slightly interested in communicating with the prosecutor's office was LaVerne, and she did so out of sheer human decency—at times, I felt, endangering her own job. The sheriff himself operated with complete disregard for the prosecutor.

Mel was still looking at me. She wasn't afraid of settling her eyes on you and letting them stay a while. I stared into her young face, taking this in: the prosecutor rushing back to town, the murder of somebody the judge knew.

"You know, Mel, if I don't get out of town pretty fast, I'll never make it. I think maybe it's a better idea for you to drop by Harlan's in person and tell him about my car. Tell him I'll pay him extra if he can get it running today."

"I'll try," she said skeptically. In the seat between us was a newspaper, and she handed it to me as I got out, adding, "You might want to look at that."

I flapped open the newspaper, the *Sallisaw Chieftain*, and saw the headline:

INDIAN LEADER PROSECUTED
BY INDIAN LAWYER

William "Jay" Goback, a leader in the business community of Eastern Oklahoma, is on trial in Fort Smith for inflicting injury to his wife in a domestic dispute in early May of this year. The wife reportedly was engaging in extramarital affairs.

The prosecutor in the case is Tom Freshour, an adjunct to the County Prosecutor in Fort Smith. Freshour is a half-blood Indian.

Freshour is currently employed as a bulldog for the Fort Smith prosecutor's office. Previously, he was employed for twelve years by the Combined Agency in Muskogee, where he gained quite a reputation as a litigator for allotment holders, particularly for the Negroes in the Glenn Pool and Cushing areas. Freshour was fired by the agency because of repeated disagreements with county judges, county governments, and county guardians, according to Dale Cotton, a lawyer at the Combined Agency. "Mr. Freshour was a competent lawyer at one time but got too radical," said Cotton.

I looked up at Melody. "An incompetent nigger lover. Smiling John's getting creative again."

"And a radical," she said. "Don't leave that out."

"That's me," I muttered.

The clock on her dash said three minutes until nine when I got out and walked up the hot steps of the courthouse. A couple of days before, the temperature had reached 112 degrees. It hadn't rained for months, and the little courthouse lawn gave off an odor of well-done grass.

Cylinder 7

The defendant was out on a ten-thousand-dollar bond, and I noticed his car parked down the street. It was a red 1933 Series 90 Buick with a rubber-mounted straight eight, chrome trim on the running board, and an enclosed spare on the rear. It ran through my mind that in a better world, when you convicted somebody you'd get your choice of their earthly goods.

Hank Twist, court bailiff, was standing outside the front door. Hank was an imposing man with white hair and a handsome, aged face who'd been a law enforcer of one kind or another since the horse-and-buggy days. He had been one of Judge Isaac Parker's deputies in the late '90s, and he had a couple of bullet scars on him from those years at work. Hank still wore a pair of fancy revolvers, pearl handled, that matched his hair, although he probably hadn't used either of them in the line of duty for years.

"Gettin up there again," he observed, staring off into the heat.

I looked through the glass door at the crowded hallway. "You have a lot of customers today, Hank."

He almost smiled. "Yep."

I occasionally had a beer with Hank, who was a widower like me, and he was very capable of talking, but during working hours at the courthouse he was closemouthed. My theory about Hank was that he was one of those unusual people who, for whatever reasons of good fortune and biology, managed to be a happy man. There was something about the look in his eye and the way you felt when you were around him. He'd lived a good life, regarded every added day as gravy, and was now more than happy to serve as a functionary in the courthouse.

Inside, I saw that the crowd really had increased since yesterday. There'd been a growing number of regulars at the courthouse since '29, but this trial had gotten unusually popular. Some of them were carrying sandwiches and jars of water so they wouldn't lose their seats if we went to noon recess—which I earnestly hoped would not be the case. I walked into the courtroom right on the hour, hoping to lessen my chances of talking to the judge. I didn't want to get involved in any developing murder cases. Now that my vacation was finally set up, I wanted to take it. I put the newspaper Mel had given me on the table in front of me.

William Jefferson Goback didn't look very worried on the last day of his trial. He was a forward-leaning bull of a man with a muscular chest and arms. He normally sported a big diamond ring, which John had talked him into not wearing during the trial. Today he had on a stark white shirt with a tie pulled up awkwardly at his throat. A number of times during the trial I'd seen people flocking around Goback during recesses, kowtowing and nodding. Mostly they were folks from across the river, around Moffitt, Oklahoma, where he employed a large crew at his livestock sale barn in a blend of legit and illegit operations. Moffitt was and still is a place without law. It was unincorporated, and the only kind of police coverage it got was the LeFlore County sheriff dropping by the roadhouses for payments. If he had beaten up and shot his wife at home it would never have made it to any court. The stockyards in Moffitt were home to bootleggers, fencing operations, harboring, money laundering—and Bill J. Goback was in the middle of it.

I turned and saw his wife, Nora, in the front row, with her sister sitting beside her. Nora had bleached-blond hair, Jean Harlow style, and dusky skin. From a prosecutor's standpoint, she wasn't the best victim in the world. Young and good featured, she scarcely limped from the bullet wounds. Despite a swollen nose and lingering bruises over both eyes, she held her head high. She had a tinge of flapper about her but also the ragged, somber demeanor of east-side Oklahoma. As she came into the courtroom, the cameras popped and sputtered, and I was a little worried that the four matrons on the jury would get envious of all the attention to her. One good look at her haunted, bruise-shrouded eyes, though, and you knew there'd been too much liquor, too many disappointments, too many blows to the head and body. The pretty lady was a moth, and nobody could see it better than the middle-aged dames on the jury.

Goback had used a fireplace poker on Nora, fracturing a bunch of her ribs, and he'd shot her twice in the right thigh, close to the hip, just missing an artery. A few of the smaller Oklahoma newspapers were taking his side, saying that the trial concerned a domestic dispute sparked by the wild behavior of a reckless wife.

Smiling John Gillis, Goback's lawyer, was going around the room shaking hands like a politician. John had droopy, sad eyes but a grin so permanent that you worried his face might break apart like a china plate. He could actually display other expressions, including a frown, on top of this permanent grin. John's face had been useful in this trial because it distracted jurors from the murky, lowering expressions that his client cast around the room during the trial, particularly at the woman, his wife, whom he had attempted to murder.

John gave me a little glance with his soulful eyes that, if I hadn't known him better, I'd have interpreted as a small plea for mercy. *Don't kill me*, he appeared to be saying. It was true that a loss on the attempted murder charge would put him on the wrong side of a brutal man who definitely had ways of reaching out from the pen.

Getting people who were willing to risk life and limb to testify against Goback had been hard. He was an intimidator and arsonist. Arson was a tradition in Oklahoma, handed down from the Indian Territory days. Fire was generally a bigger part of life back then.

Lamps got knocked over. Gasoline stoves blew up. People driven off their land for delinquent taxes sometimes fired their houses before wandering on. Almost everybody had a fire in their past or their family's past. You got mad at a person, you burned them out. You failed at business, you burned yourself out. You had to escape and you didn't know how, you burned it, whatever it was. Whole towns burned down and were abandoned. Fire insurance rates were so high in Oklahoma that just buying it made you a suspicious character. Law enforcement was not very good at arson cases—one reason why somebody like Jay Goback was so successful at intimidating people.

The defendant was a burner, and he wasn't shy about people knowing it. A couple of men who worked at the stockyards had told me that Goback often crowed about taking over the cattle-auction market by burning out competitors.

Regarding Nora's shooting, I had furnished only three witnesses—a doctor at St. Edward's Mercy, a nurse, and Nora's sister—but they'd all been convincing. Goback had showed up at the hospital a couple of hours after the attack at Nora's sister's and had to be thrown out when he started yelling and threatening his then unconscious wife with the same pistol he'd used on her a few hours earlier. Nora's sister, who was an eyewitness, was absolutely solid—motherly, believable, and nobody's fool, least of all her bully brother-in-law's. John had pecked away at Nora's sister's testimony, but it did him more harm than good because she'd answered him with a vivid description of the blood all over her living room.

Smiling John had sniffed the wind and given up early on the idea of denying that his client had done it. He'd used the old standby in wife assault—the wife was a whore and deserved her treatment. He'd run through a half-dozen people testifying to what a floozy Nora had been to this decent, generous, long-suffering, hardworking husband. The total sincerity of all these witnesses wouldn't have filled a half-pint bottle. Most of them had sounded like grade school kids fumbling through lines in a school play. All of them made references to ailments that the defendant claimed to suffer—bad back, headaches, stomach problems—as if these were reasons for a man to shoot his wife.

All in all, John appeared to be hanging his own client, and my instinct was to give him all the rope he wanted. I'd made only a few hearsay objections, cross-examined defense witnesses with questions that established or implied a financial relationship to the accused, and bothered with little else. The jury could put two and two together. Basically, it was a stripped-down prosecution, which fitted what I had to work with and contrasted to the defense's line of bull. Bare facts: man beats the holy hell out of wife, shoots her twice, leaves her to nearly bleed to death, then tries to finish her off in the hospital.

The case appeared to be winding toward a conviction. Smiling John was smarter than he looked, though, and anything but lazy. He looked weak with his little country-lawyer bow tie and his silly smile, but he'd do just about anything to get his client through the door. He rehearsed witnesses. Most of all, he tried to get at you personally, get under your skin, break your medicine.

I glanced back again and saw that people were standing in the doors and sitting in the aisles, women with dusters around their hair, men in threadbare cotton jackets, some unwashed and unshaved. A lot of these people wouldn't have been here if they'd had the dime to go into a water-cooled movie house, but the thick limestone walls of the courthouse held the nighttime cool better than most places. Judge Stone looked on it as a kind of public service to let them into the courtroom. That summer we'd already had a few people faint during trials, but the judge hadn't yet taken the step of shutting the doors after the room was full.

When Judge Manfred Stone—Manny to his friends—walked in, he fixed his gaze on me over his half-glasses. The buzzing in the room lowered. The judge was in his fifties, a brisk, graying man, veteran of thirteen years on the bench. Hank started to call to order, but Stone waved him off and gave me a little nod. When I approached, so did John. Closer, I saw how tired Stone looked.

He said quietly, "I need to talk to you about another matter when this is over. Could you come by?" He glanced at John, who was now beside me at the bench, and said in a different tone, "Defense wants to bring another witness."

"What witness?" I said directly to John.

He hunched his shoulders down around his bow tie, looking almost contrite behind his smile. "The defendant, Tom. I'd like to put him on the stand."

"You're asking me to cross the defendant without any preparation?"

Smiling John looked as if he was brimming with sympathy. "I did try to call you. I think the man needs to speak for himself."

We went back and forth for a while, playing out our roles in front of Judge Stone, but calling unscheduled witnesses was a common ploy, and I was hardly surprised.

"Why didn't you schedule him?"

"Look, he is the defendant. . . ."

"You've been delaying this case, counselor. You know I'm supposed to leave town tomorrow, and you want me to choose between crossing him unprepared or putting off my vacation."

I was speaking to John but hoped that Stone was listening about not preventing my vacation.

The judge said, "If you aren't comfortable doing it today, I'll delay. It's up to you."

I wanted to say, "Hell no, I'm not prepared; he wasn't on the defense list," but John's grin inspired me to grin back—all teeth, not friendly—and say I'd take my chance. Turning to leave, I added quietly, "By the way, John, that business in the *Sallisaw Chieftain?* About me being an incompetent radical who got fired from my job at the agency? How much did you pay for that?"

He pretended to be shocked. "Tom, you know I can't influence what newspapers print."

The courtroom was beginning to heat up by the time Hank had called it to order. When John stood up and made his motion, formally asking to bring a final witness, I watched him—his expression and posture and the way he was acting—and I watched Jay Goback walk, slightly bent over, to the stand. He gave off a little theatrical wince as he sat down in the elevated witness chair and fixed his eyes ten feet in front of himself on some imaginary spot. John suppressed his smile to its lowest level and began asking his client routine questions establishing who he was and what his work was and how many people he employed, and I got the creeping feeling that defense wasn't just shooting in the dark. He got to the point fairly quickly.

"Mr. Goback, can you tell me what happened on the night of May fifth?"

Cylinder 8

"I come home after workin twelve hours at the barn, and my wife wasn't there. She'd gone off to her sister's. I didn't have no dinner and no wife. My back was flarin up, so I took some whiskey. I've had a backache here, last five years."

"A backache for years, did you say?"

"Yes sir. About five years. It comes from wrestlin cattle."

"Have you seen a doctor about this backache?"

"I seen an old root doctor, works there at the stockyards."

"What do you mean, root doctor? Some people here may not know what that means."

"Indin doctor. Old man knows the old cures." Goback glanced at me again.

"Did this . . . Indian doctor help you with your back problem?" John asked solicitously.

"He give me some powders to take. Told me to drink some whiskey with it."

There was a stirring in the courtroom audience, and someone laughed; sudden smiles on several jury members. With so many people packed in, you could feel the hunger to be entertained bouncing off the high plaster walls.

Goback winced again, as if suffering the back pain, although his delivery was otherwise deadpan. "It was worse'n usual that night. So I was lookin around for another bottle. Looked in my wife's top drawer, and I found somethin. Found somethin . . ." He hesitated and frowned. "Proved she'd been foolin around again. It wasn't even hid. There it sat, right on the top."

"What did you find in your wife's dresser, Mr. Goback?"

"I ain't sayin."

"Mr. Goback," John said, dripping with concern, "it would help the jury better understand if you would specify—"

"I ain't sayin."

Goback's refusal to answer his own lawyer started a buzz in the courtroom. There was more stirring around and nervous laughter.

"May I ask why you won't tell us?"

"Because it ain't right to talk about."

The courtroom went quiet.

"All right, sir. Let's say for the moment that you did find something in the top drawer of your wife's dresser proving what you already suspected, that your wife was having an affair with some other man."

John was begging me to object. He wanted me to demand that Goback specify the thing in the drawer (rubbers?) so it would appear to be forced out of him, and therefore true. I wouldn't take that bait.

"Do you know who the man is?"

Goback squinted his eyes and put on a great show of controlled fury. "I can tell you I better not know who they are."

"They?" John repeated, as if bewildered.

Another buzz, tentative laughter. John was getting them going, dramatizing the wronged husband by making a story and a joke of it. He and Goback had practiced well.

"Your wife was having affairs with more than one man?"

"I already knowed it," the defendant said flatly. "It just proved it."

"What did you do after you found this . . . evidence?"

"My back was seizin up. I went to the liquor store over by the bridge for a bottle, and when I was there, it hit me. My wife was doin wrong. I work hard. I'm a good husband. I drove crost the river to talk to her. She didn't do nothin but deny it. I went crazy, I admit it. But it was because of what she done."

"Let me understand you, Mr. Goback. You don't deny that in the process of rebuking your wife you injured her?"

"It ain't me sneakin around tryin to hide what I'm doin."

The judge leaned over the bench and said, "Answer the question directly."

Goback looked at his lawyer, blinked several times, and admitted grudgingly, "Already said I done it."

"Mr. Goback, I have to ask you a question that refers to what you said earlier. You said you saw an Indian doctor for your back problems. Why didn't you see a regular doctor?"

"I believe in the old cures."

"So you are an Indian yourself?"

"Well, I sure ain't Irish," Goback said without a smile.

More laughter, and some of the tension seemed to go out of the room. I saw a flash of grins in the jury box. A couple of the men were shifting around, as if they were beginning to enjoy this.

"Would you describe yourself as a traditionalist?"

With a little flick of his eye toward me, Goback said, "I'm on the rolls."

"The Cherokee tribal rolls, you mean. But would you describe yourself as a traditional Indian?"

"I wouldn't know what you mean."

"Do you believe in the old ways? The customs and ethics of your tribe." John sounded as if he was talking to a child.

"Yessir. I sure do. I said that already."

"And are you a Christian, Mr. Goback?" John asked softly.

"Hell yes I'm a Christian. What else would I be?"

Laughter again. Judge Stone was irritated but didn't intervene.

"As a Christian and a traditional Cherokee Indian, do you believe that a wife—yours or any other—should be true to her husband?"

Goback hesitated.

"Go on," John coaxed.

"Well sure a wife ought to be true to her husband. What else should a wife be?"

There was an eruption of talk in the courtroom, and Judge Stone whacked his gavel down so sharply that it made even me jump. When Stone got mad he looked thicker, as if he was gaining weight in front of your eyes.

Smiling John went on, "You have stated that you are a Cherokee Indian. But your wife isn't an Indian?"

"Damn right she is."

Judge Stone used his gavel again. "Witness will refrain from cursing on the stand."

The audience kept murmuring and twisting and looking at the blond-haired woman. Nora was unmoving and expressionless with her dark-ringed eyes. Fleetingly, she reminded me of my wife, Laura—why, I don't know, except that she looked fragile, as if it wouldn't take much to make her vanish.

Pretending delicacy, almost simpering, John said, "I'm sorry, Mr. Goback, but your wife hardly looks like an Indian."

"She's got just as much Indin blood as I do. She colors her hair."

This caused a few titters, and one of the women jurors showed an open look of disapproval.

"Why does your wife color her hair?"

"I wouldn't know," Goback said grudgingly. "But she's ashamed of her blood, tryin to pass for white. And I know she's ashamed of me."

"How do you know that?"

"She told me. More'n once."

"I want to be absolutely clear about this. Your own wife told you that she was ashamed of you, personally, and that she wanted to pass for white."

"Yes sir."

Smiling John looked surprised at this. "And how did you respond?"

"I bought different clothes and a new car, but I can't keep up with her. I ain't nothin but an old cattle wrangler. I can't change that. Can't help what I am. But I figure I deserve to have a faithful wife like any man."

"That's all, your honor. Defense rests." Smiling John Gillis went around and alighted on his chair with a little flurry, like a church organist.

I didn't get up immediately. My unexpected fear about defense having something had proved unfounded. This was definitely applesauce, but he had scraped together enough scraps of this and that—bigotry, half-jokes about infidelity—to get some of the jury to relax and join the picnic, feel more comfortable with Goback, who wasn't such a bad guy after all. A simple type, an Indian, hardworking, plain-spoken, tortured by this honky-tonk hair-coloring whore of a wife. My internal meter was saying one or two of the jury might balk on the attempted murder.

Still hesitating to get up, I had a sour taste in the back of my throat. Losing the attempted-murder charge would be bad prosecuting. The man was a well-known thug. He'd barged in on an unarmed woman, beaten her up, fired two bullets close to the middle of her body, then showed up at the hospital to try again. A loss here would be failure. The other thing going through me was anger at the defense. Buying ten-dollar articles in newspapers, calling an unscheduled witness, messing with my vacation, playing the race card—it added up to crossing the line.

The courtroom was hot; handkerchiefs were out. It was one of those moments when what was normally just a day's work began to feel burdensome and personal. I glanced over at John's nonstop smile.

"Is there a cross-examination?" Judge Stone finally asked.

Cylinder 9

"Mr. Goback, you've stated that on the night of May fifth you drove to Fort Smith and beat up and shot your wife. Is that right?"

"I didn't say that."

"You did it, though, is that correct?"

"You'da done the same if your wife—"

"What did you use to beat Nora with?"

"She was runnin around on me."

"Answer the question I asked you."

He shot me a look that suggested I'd better upgrade my house insurance. Oh, he badly wanted to say it aloud.

"I did it," he finally said, raising his nose.

"I know that, Mr. Goback. We all know that. My question was, what did you beat your wife with? Did you use a fireplace poker?"

"I hit her a couple of times with it." He glanced toward the evidence table. "But it wasn't like I carried it in there."

"Can you answer the question directly, please?"

"What question?"

"Did you beat your wife with a fireplace poker?"

"I hit her with it."

"Did beating this woman with a fireplace poker break three of her ribs, among other things?"

"I wouldn't know."

"Objection, your honor; the prosecutor has gone over all this already."

"Overruled."

"Did you then shoot your wife twice with a pistol?"

"You'da done the same."

I walked over to the table and picked up the fireplace poker and walked back toward the witness stand. I stopped three feet in front of him. "And did you bring the gun into the house with you, or was it already there?"

Defendant looked at me cunningly but didn't answer the question. I repeated.

"It's my gun. Why not?"

"Why did you carry the gun into the house?"

"What d'ye mean?"

"Mr. Goback, you are a successful businessman. Why do you keep pretending not to understand simple questions? The question is: What did you intend to do with the gun that you carried into Nora's sister's house on May fifth?"

"I always carry it when I'm out at night. You can't tell what might happen."

"So you just happened to have a gun when you pushed in your sister-in-law's front door, and you just happened to beat your wife, breaking several bones, with this two-and-a-half-foot-long piece of iron, and you just happened to shoot her twice with a gun that you just happen to always carry around with you. Then you went to the hospital, where you happened to try to do it a second time and had to get thrown out. That's a lot of just-happened-to's, Mr. Goback. You just happened to try to murder your wife, didn't you?"

"I wasn't tryin to murder nobody. Been tryin to do that, I'da done it." Goback flashed me a fierce, quick, malicious look, as if to demonstrate his certainty on that point.

I got very close to him and slowly raised the fireplace poker over my head. "When you beat your wife, did you raise the poker over your head like this, or did you do it this way, baseball-bat style?"

"Don't know, I was so put out at her for what she done." Goback still showed no obvious fear.

I went over and laid the poker on the evidence table and took up the .38 revolver, flipping open the cylinder and checking it. The room was quiet when I turned and walked back, quickly, to the same position in front of the stand. I cocked the hammer and aimed it at his groin. "Did you know what you were doing when you did this?" I pulled the trigger. The hammer snapped down and made him wince, which was what I wanted.

The courtroom audience exploded in spontaneous talking. Smiling John yelled above the noise, "Ob-jection, your honor! The prosecutor is physically intimidating the witness."

"Please confine it to questions, Tom."

Nobody but the defendant and I could hear Stone in all the noise, but I was surprised by his use of my first name. In chambers, he was as informal as the next judge, but in trial transcripts he definitely wasn't a first-name kind of judge.

The courtroom audience kept up the commotion, a flashbulb went off, and I knew what would happen next. Hank Twist stood up and walked over to a position in front of the judge's bench, right hand on his gunbelt. A drop of sweat went down his jaw. Hank had ridden down some bad men in his time, but even if you didn't know that, the old man had a surplus of natural authority.

"Settle down or I'll clear the court," he said. He pointed at the photographer and told him to give him the camera. The photographer did so, and Hank walked over and thunked it down on the witness table so hard that the bulb popped out onto the floor. He moved his chair so it faced the audience, which by then had quieted.

"You have testified that you are a part-blood Cherokee Indian. Do I understand you further to have said that something about being an Indian—your training, or culture, or something like that—made you more likely to beat up and shoot your wife?"

"Objection. He's putting words into the defendant's mouth."

Stone looked down on me wearily. "Can you explain this line of questioning?"

I was surprised that he didn't overrule. Was his mind drifting?

"Your honor, defense asked the accused if he subscribed to the customs and ethics of his tribe. Apparently his meaning was that any good Indian man worth his salt would be predisposed to shoot his wife when he didn't like the way she was acting."

"My point," John said, "was that Indian men have very strict standards regarding their wives—"

"Calm down, counsel." The judge appeared to be thickening again, and I felt reassured. However hot and frazzled he might get, Stone didn't like messy proceedings. He overruled the objection.

Before I could restate the question, Goback said darkly, "A woman ought to be true to her husband."

"And should a man be true to his wife?"

"I ain't sayin he shouldn't."

"Have you been true to your wife, Mr. Goback?"

"Yes I have."

Nora's sister, who had restrained herself to this point, snorted loudly from the audience, and another buzz passed through the room. Hank Twist sat up a little straighter.

"Mr. Goback, your Indian background is so important in your defense, I'd like to ask you which particular Indian authority influenced you in these matters? Was it the chief of the Cherokee Tribe?"

"That's a dumb question."

He got a laugh for that, but I stayed on it. "Who trained you in what you called the old ways? Was it Geronimo?"

Now I got the laugh. Even Hank almost smiled.

"Objection! Your honor! He's goading and mocking the witness. The prosecutor is an Indian himself."

Stone sighed. "Rephrase the question, please."

I repeated, leaving out Geronimo.

Goback looked at me with the kill-and-burn glint in his eye. "Who trained you how to be an Indin?" he said.

Stone didn't call him on it, and I almost lost my composure. I told myself, don't let him beat you with two deuces, because that's all he has. People like Jay Goback and his lawyer work the school-yard by counting on you being easy to shame and afraid of a scene. I moved up close to him again and asked, in a falsely confidential tone, if he happened to recall who the chief of the Cherokees was.

"Don't know him by name."

"Would you recognize him if you saw him, Mr. Goback?"

"Know him when I see him. Sure I would."

I turned briefly to John, whose smile had gone thin, and back to the defendant. "That's odd, Mr. Goback, because there is no chief of the Cherokees. There hasn't been for many years. The federal government disassembled the Cherokee government some time ago."

Smiling John was up again. "Your honor, this is a cross-examination, not a history lesson."

"Confine to questions," Stone said.

I was finished with him and moved to make closing statements right away. Stone, sitting under his black robe in the steaming room, waved me on.

I dabbed the sweat off my face and took a breath, walked over to the jury, standing my usual respectful distance away not quite at the middle of the box, and gave the sermon. I said that by his testimony, the defendant was asking them to believe he was not guilty of attempted murder because if he had intended to kill his wife he would have succeeded. I asked them to consider, each of them, whether if a man shot them twice in the lower part of their body, he should evade a charge of attempted murder by bragging that he had shot them exactly where he intended to, one inch from death. Defense counsel was asking them to excuse Mr. Goback for shooting his wife because he had to work hard and had a sore back. He was asking them to excuse Mr. Goback because he was a little drunk when it happened and decided his wife was provoking him. In his most ingenious argument of all, defense was asking them to excuse Mr. Goback because he was someone who believed in tribal ways—whatever that might mean in 1934—and therefore knew no better than to beat up and shoot his wife. I started to say that was a whole lot of excuses, but instead I just looked at the floor and, strangely, ran out of words. I shook my head and looked back up at them with a deep sigh.

I later realized that it was my best moment in a flawed prosecution, and it was unintentional. I actually felt weary to the point of sudden wordlessness. Unintentional or not, at least for that moment I had them. Every eye was on me, but I suddenly felt so dry mouthed and tired that I could barely finish. I ended with something like, "Ladies and gentlemen, William J. Goback went a fireplace poker and two bullets over the line. In Sebastian County we don't like men breaking their wives' bones and trying to murder them. Defense is trying to throw a bucket of ashes in your faces. You should return a verdict of guilty of assault and attempted murder."

I sat down and hardly listened while Smiling John went through his closing. I felt as tired as Judge Stone looked. Stone in fact looked to me like a candidate for medical attention. The heat had built up like a boulder in the room. When Smiling John finally sat down and the judge sent out the jury, I followed Stone to his chambers. He pulled off his robe, threw it onto the edge of his desk, went into his little bathroom and washed his face, came back, and flopped down on the end of his couch. I knocked on the door jamb, and he smiled dimly at me and invited me in.

"Want a glass of water?"

I went into his bathroom and quickly filled and drank two glasses. The water system of Fort Smith was an oasis in a desert that summer because a new pipeline brought in pure water from a lake in the Boston Mountains, and it wasn't yet in short supply despite the general lack of rain. I came back in and sat down, perching on the single slat-backed chair across from the couch. For a while we both just sat there drinking in the stirred air from his blessed ceiling fan. Stone was trim, good featured, not a big drinker, generally a fit man. His color seemed to improve.

The trial was over and neither of us felt like talking shop. I asked him if the heat was getting to him. He shook his head once, slightly, and said, "Ever wonder about the past, Tom?"

I said sure, I did my share of wondering.

He gazed at me a while longer. Stone was normally businesslike, even brisk. The heat, I thought. The heavy black robe and the surplus of spectators lapping up the oxygen.

"You were in the war, weren't you?" he asked.

"Ambulance service."

He nodded. "That's right. . . . I was overseas all of two months. They kept me stateside until it was over. Then they sent me to England for a couple of months. Never saw a German. Now whenever the election comes up, the county committee puts 'war veteran' on the newspaper advertisement for me. I tell them that's an exaggeration, and they print it anyway. People think I was breathing mustard gas and rooting out machine-gun nests when all I did was chase a certain individual named Francis in Bristol, England, for a while and didn't even have any luck at that. . . . I worked in a censorship office with Francis before they shut it down and shipped me back home."

Stone reached over, took his glass of water off the table, and drank, setting it down heavily. He blew wind out of his cheeks. "That's my war story. Being horny and two months of reading letters looking for signs of pacifism." He aimed his face upward, toward the fan, and sighed. "Half of what you read and hear is bullshit, Tom. Three-fourths . . . People lying about themselves and being lied about by others. Gossip."

Stone glanced at me wryly, and I wondered if he was referring to the article about me in the *Sallisaw Chieftain*, or if perhaps he'd heard rumors about my brief time in Fort Smith as a very young man, before I'd gone back to southeast Oklahoma. On a number of other occasions I'd had this feeling—that the judge knew something about me, or had heard stories—but only from looks that he gave me. I had the same feeling about Hank Twist sometimes, but Hank was too circumspect to show anything like that. Hank was an old-fashioned country man of a certain fine breed who didn't bring things up that didn't concern him.

The judge stood up. "Anyway, the reason I called this morning, a friend of mine got murdered yesterday. I've asked Bernie to come back to town. When he gets here, why don't you two come over. I'm not in court this afternoon. Good luck on the attempted, by the way."

I walked out of chambers a little puzzled, not knowing whether the judge had just shared a moment of sympathy with me or given me a quick glance at his map of where the bodies were buried.

Cylinder 10

The prosecutor's office was near the bottom of the town's main avenue, three blocks from where the Arkansas River bridge crossed to Oklahoma. Up and down the avenue powdery sand dunes built up in the doorways as western wind blew Oklahoma topsoil into Arkansas. Our building had seen its glory days forty or fifty years before, when it was occupied by a newspaper. Inside, the faint smell of ink still came from the walls. It had an ancient switchboard with plug-in connections that one of the business tenants operated for a reduction in rent.

Three or four lawyers were still making enough of their office rent to not be evicted, along with several businesses that specialized in selling questionable items—a muscle-building system, a goiter remedy, twelve aids to beauty—all of which were fitting cotenants to the exalted work of county prosecuting. The one first-class tenant, on the ground floor, was the front office of a rayon manufacturer, located several blocks away from the plant in case it blew up (which it later did, in fact, on the night the Wehrmacht rolled into Poland). Also on the first floor was a wholesale jeweler that distributed gold watches mainly to points southeast of Fort Smith—Mississippi, South Carolina. Gold watches were big, Depression or not, the owner told me, because there were more women working in cotton mills who had a little disposable income those days. Out of twelve bucks a week, they would eventually save enough nickels and dimes to buy a watch.

It was called the Elevator Building from the time when it housed the *Fort Smith Elevator* newspaper, and it did have an elevator, run by an old man named Thurman Gale. Mr. Gale talked aloud to himself and was generally considered to be off his hinges. His conversations actually seemed fairly reasonable to me; he just saw both sides of every issue and wanted to discuss them by himself, and at more length than most people. And he didn't like to be interrupted by much more than a hello. He stayed on his elevator stool, even when he had no customers, underneath his little black fan, reading a newspaper or debating quietly.

About two o'clock that afternoon—after a quick lunch and a trip to see the mechanic—I rode up with Thurman in the slow, cramped elevator, paying no more attention to him than to a radio.

Our office was somewhat cooler than the hall. We had an air conditioner, one of the first in town. In a twenty-four-hour period this air conditioner was supposed to be able to give off as much cool air as three-eighths of a ton of ice. When left running all day at top speed, it made the office almost as cool as the first-floor offices (rayon, jewelry, goiters), which were without air conditioners. Bernie had paid for this four-hundred-fifty-dollar machine himself, as he paid for many other things, out of sheer enthusiasm for new and marvelous devices.

Bernie wandered out of his office, rumpled and buggy eyed and blinking as if he hadn't gotten much sleep on his long train ride up from the Georgia coast. He had a magazine in his hand. He looked at me and broke into his famous lopsided grin. For Bernie, the office had always been an informal social event, and showing up there was like dropping by the country club for a game of poker.

"Hi, Tom. Surprised to see me?"

I said yes, but that I knew Stone had called him and asked him to cut short his vacation.

"Well, the world's falling apart, have you heard? Jehovah pointed his finger at me, all the way down in Georgia. Do you know what the problem is?"

"I was hoping you did."

"Some friend of Manny's was murdered. That's all he said—that and get your worthless butt—excuse me, Melody—back to Sebastian County."

"Nasty man," Melody muttered, not looking up from her typewriter.

"Sorry, Mel. I keep forgetting you're a modern girl. I'll bet you have a short bathing suit, don't you?"

"I'll never tell," she said.

Bernie waved the magazine at her. "See. She is. She's a totally modern girl. That kind of thing puts Berenice in a terrible mood. The girls on the beach are wearing short bathing suits this year, and it drives her crazy. First they were putting on lipstick in public; she figured that would bring down modern democracy. But these bathing suits—you know, with the whole legs hanging out. And look at this."

He thrust the magazine at me with a page folded back. It was a car-wax ad, with a woman in a flesh-colored bathing suit sprawled fetchingly over the hood of a car and the caption YOUR CAR'S NO NUDIST! PROTECT IT WITH SIMONIZE.

"If she sees this, I won't hear the end of it. It'll be breakfast and dinner for the next month. She's gotten very sensitive. And this business about the universe expanding into ultimate gray lifeless death, it all worries her. I mean, she takes it seriously."

Melody glanced up from her typewriter and asked me if the jury was back in.

I told her I didn't know; I'd just been seeing Harlan about my car.

Bernie looked back and forth between us. "Do you need a car? I can loan you our extra one."

I appreciated it but didn't think he wanted to loan me his LaSalle to drive to southwestern Florida.

Bernie changed the subject. "Well, I heard you bared your teeth in court today. I hope the jury comes in for you, Tom. That son of a bitch"—he pointed a thumb vaguely in the direction of Oklahoma—"has burned out more people than Sherman's army."

"He and his wife aren't clicking like they used to either," said Melody.

"The man's a complete brute!" Bernie hastened to agree. "He needs to go make license plates for a while. Absolutely. No question."

I was gratified that Bernie even knew I'd been in court that day. I suspected, however, that he'd talked to the judge at greater length than he was admitting and that he knew even more certainly than I did that my vacation was off. The closer I came to being roped into staying in town, the ornerier I felt about it.

The phone rang, and Bernie eagerly grabbed it, causing Melody to frown at him.

"Yes, yes, hello, Manny, judge, yes, I just made, yes, yes . . ."

Bernie rolled his eyes, but his yeses became increasingly grave. Hanging up the phone, he looked a little furtive.

"Jury reported yet?" I asked him.

He shook his head. "His majesty is ready to see us."

We jammed ourselves into the elevator with Thurman Gale and didn't speak on the way down. The best I could tell, Mr. Gale was now discussing whether the Nazis would conquer the world. On the street, Bernie's LaSalle, as usual, was spotless. He called it his "work car." His wife had another seven-thousand-dollar car—a Lincoln. As we motored the few blocks to the courthouse, I looked down its long gray hood, wondering whether I could drive this car without feeling self-conscious. I loved cars. I'd even loved the cranky Ford ambulance that I drove in France, mainly because it was my first.

Bernie glanced at me. "You know about the judge's interest in these Indian things? He collects them. It's not just arrowheads but all kinds of items. I guess he trades and sells the stuff. Maybe even makes some money at it."

"I've seen the arrowheads in his den," I said dully.

"It's a hobby. He thinks this mound is a very big deal." Bernie sounded as if he was trying to convince himself.

I gazed at the golden needle on his luxurious airplane-style speedometer, hovering around twenty, and thought about other job opportunities. My savings account consisted of $165 in an old metal ammunition box in my shed. Clients of the paying kind weren't growing on trees in 1934 except in the oil fields and mineral and land rackets in Oklahoma. I'd already made two escapes from Oklahoma in my life and didn't want to have to make another. Seriously tempted though I was, quitting and starting my own office would have been about like jumping overboard into an icy sea.

We walked down the marble floor toward the judge's chambers, and I saw Hank Twist through the glass door of the recorder's office, at his desk having his usual late lunch of sardines, crackers, and a shot of whiskey. Hank always had a dollop of whiskey for lunch, even during Prohibition, right there in the courthouse, and no one ever questioned him about it.

"Jury in yet?" I asked him, and he looked up and shook his head. Bad sign. They'd been deliberating for over three hours in a jury room that had to be stifling hot.

Judge Stone's secretary was a sour man by the name of M. Parfit. Thin shouldered, with an improbable pompadour curled around a receding hairline, Parfit wore a vest, watch chain, and small round tortoiseshell-framed glasses. He had the expression of someone who'd just bitten into a green persimmon. Parfit scrupulously avoided telling anyone what his single initial stood for. He was Stone's Cerberus.

"Judge in, M?" Bernie asked, walking by his desk. I admired Bernie's easy use of the "M." I had stumbled for some time over what to call Parfit and settled on "Mr. Parfit," while Bernie just casually threw out "M." Bernie was good with names. Whenever he dropped by the office for a half-hour's work, he always made sure everyone knew everyone else's name—bootleggers, thieves, secretaries, whoever happened to be around. He was always completely democratic about it.

"The judge isn't here," Mr. Parfit announced with some satisfaction.

Bernie was taken aback, since he'd just talked to him on the phone, but decided he must have just slipped out for a minute, and so we waited. Parfit had a habit of answering questions with mincing, sometimes misleading accuracy, like a mean eleven-year-old, and he seemed to take pleasure in milking exasperation out of people, so I questioned him further to make sure he really didn't know where the judge was. Bernie lasted for twenty minutes, then decided he needed to go home. If the judge showed up, he said, please call him.

I stayed around for almost an hour beyond that, reading a newspaper, pacing the murmuring halls of the courthouse, sniffing five-for-a-nickel cigar smoke coming under the door of the jury room. They were hung on the attempted-murder charge. If they pinned him only for assault, he'd be out in less than a year. After fidgeting around a while longer, I used Parfit's phone to call Judge Stone's house and got no answer.

I suggested to Parfit that he'd better check on the jury, since they might have all fainted by now in that oven, and I walked the few sweltering blocks back to our office, where the secretaries of the muscle-building system and the twelve aids to beauty were hovering around smoking Spuds, soaking up the cool wind of our overworked air conditioner. Melody greeted me with a triumphant smile. Harlan Jones had fixed my car and actually communicated this fact over the telephone. Would wonders never cease. I asked if she'd heard from the judge.

"Weren't you just there?" she asked.

"He ducked out."

"Did you check under his desk?" she said. "Maybe he melted."

"You ain't kiddin," said Barbara Jean Killen, the muscle-builder secretary. Barbara Jean was well built herself, at least in the sense of being well fed, and she wasn't one to mince words. "It's cool compared to Missouri," she added. "People dyin up there, I heard."

The twelve aids to beauty closed her eyes and rolled her head around in the swirling cigarette smoke. "Somethin's out of whack, for sure. Radicals. And them talkin about killin hogs and burnin crops. I'm tellin you. I sure do love this cool wind."

Cylinder 11

After supper I sat down with a bourbon and water and turned on my Grunow All-Wave radio, which was capable of worldwide shortwave reception—Berlin, Moscow, London, Sydney, Rio de Janeiro. I loved the idea of being able to listen to London and Sydney but as usual was listening to KFPW, three hundred watts, located one mile away. "Ramona, Girl of My Dreams" was just about to inspire me to pack my clothes and get out of town. I'd heard nothing from Bernie, nothing from the judge, and nothing from the jury. No one had actually instructed me to cancel my vacation, after all.

My Ford, knock on wood, was ready to go. Why not that night? I could drive to Little Rock and take a morning train from there. The place where I stayed in southwest Florida was an old fishing hotel, with guides and good food and its own boats, and it was the owner's eccentricity to not mind economy-class guys with dubious skin color like me. Swabbing out my dusty suitcase, scrounging up fishing clothes from the corner of my closet, I worked up quite a feeling of relief—adventures on the open road, the soft Florida ocean—when the phone rang. It was Bernie, who said Stone had called and really did want to see us now.

I was sitting on the steps of my front porch, drinking a second bourbon with less water, taking no pleasure in the distant sound of children streaking through the evening, when Bernie pulled up. The deep finish of his LaSalle glowed with the last reddish light of day. When he eyed me across the yard, I could see that he was in no better mood than I was.

I slipped onto the mohair seat, and he held out a pack of Lucky Strikes. I told him no thanks. Bernie refused to remember that I didn't smoke.

He pushed in the dash lighter as we glided off. "I hate empty houses," he said. "How do you stand living alone?"

"My house isn't as big as yours," I snapped.

"Bigger it is, the emptier it gets."

"You may have something there."

Bernie smiled a little. He was used to me making little digs at his wealth. But then he relapsed into seeming gloom. "My family won't be back for four weeks. I forget how used to them I am. My boy's going off to college. The girls soon after . . . They'll all be gone, blink of an eye. Poof." He glanced at me. "Damned expensive to go to college these days, you know. Someone told me it was up to seventeen hundred a year for Dartmouth."

We pulled up to a stoplight. The cigarette lighter popped out, and he didn't notice. He looked both ways and ran the red light.

"Ever wish you'd gotten married again?"

I now wonder whether I'd have appreciated questions like this if Bernie hadn't been my boss. Bernie did surprise you. He did venture out and try to really talk. In fact, he was one of the few men I knew who did. Men in our part of the world talked about business, hunting, fishing, and practical details, not complicated feelings or matters of the heart. Here men stuck out their chins, told you everything was just fine, real good, thanks, and dared you to make something of it. When they told stories it was usually to make fun of other men, or to elevate themselves, however slyly. But that's me commenting twenty-five years later. At the time I only thought, Married again? To somebody like Berenice, perhaps?

I changed the subject. "Have we heard from the Goback jury?"

Bernie glanced toward me as if he was a little stung by my avoidance of his question. "I'm afraid they're stuck. They put them up at the Commercial Hotel."

"Where'd Stone disappear to today, did he say?"

"Said he had to pick up somebody at the train station. Somebody Davis; she's related to the dead man, I think."

The town was unusually quiet after the assault of heat. We were cruising out Free Ferry, the street of the rich. It was that time of the summer when people who could afford it moved to the Ozarks or the Gulf Coast, so the houses were quiet. I liked nice houses. I found them reassuring. Only a few houses down from the judge, Bernie himself lived in a palace of thirty-six rooms, including, I'd heard, a billiard room and ballroom.

We pulled up a curved drive to the horse-and-buggy-sized portico at the side of the judge's house. Stone's house was Southern style, a stocky central box fronted by tall pillars and graceful one-story wings going off in a couple of directions. Bernie turned the motor off and, taking the still unlit cigarette out of the side of his mouth, looked at Sheriff Kenny Seabolt's Ford, parked in front of us. Suddenly energy was radiating from him as if he were a bird dog sensing a covey of quail.

"Seabolt?" he said. "Why's he here?"

Bernie had strong feelings about the sheriff: he was unintelligent, he was a crook, he probably belonged to the Klan—impressions Bernie seemed to get from gossip rather than from any interaction with Kenny. His low opinion was justified, but his details were blurry. In fact, the sheriff was no part of dumb. His businesses on the side changed with the times as efficiently as any good businessman's. Three years earlier his racket had been protecting the bigger players in the whiskey trade; now one of his main activities was taking graft on forced estate auctions. He rigged cheap sales and got kickbacks from certain buyers—people who bought forty acres here and two hundred there at twenty or thirty bucks an acre. That subject probably wasn't discussed in Bernie's social circle since some of those people were the ones doing business with Kenny.

I never talked to Bernie about it because he would have been outraged, or acted outraged, dropped it into my lap, then gone on an unusually long vacation. Bernie was a frustrated idealist who had no end of courage when it came to assigning jobs to other people, and knocking over Kenny Seabolt by myself would have been about as easy as uprooting a fifty-foot oak tree with a teaspoon. Although I did keep an eye out for special opportunities, I wasn't up for doing it solo.

We were soon in Judge Stone's den, standing on his Brussels carpet, surrounded by several large mounted frames of flint arrowheads, with the faint aura of dinner still lingering in the house. Stone introduced Mrs. Lorraine Davis, making no mention of whether or how I might know her. She squared off and stood up very straight when she faced me, looking me directly in the eyes, a bearing that seemed eerily familiar. But I was pretty sure I'd never met her.

Her accent sounded slightly British. She struck me as a city person. Dark hair pulled into a simple bun, well-tanned skin. Her clothes were plain in the extreme, a light brown skirt and white blouse, which only heightened the overall effect. Bernie was suddenly delighted to be here.

Sheriff Kenny Seabolt, tall, spare, looking younger than his years, with a balding head and sideburns, acted uncomfortable from the start. In Stone's den he was out of his territory. He kept looking disapprovingly at Mrs. Davis's canvas shoes. He and Bernie didn't speak to each other. Oil and water.

Kenny had been county sheriff for over twenty years, and he regarded other public officials as transients. For him, the sheriff's office was where things started and stopped. When there was a problem in the county, he talked to people, threatened them, and if they didn't do what he wanted had them beaten up or run out. But Kenny was not the typical good-old-boy sheriff. He was grim, cold, colorless. He could have been a sheriff in Pennsylvania. He didn't drink or smoke; he wasn't sociable; he showed no moments of pleasure or friendliness on his face. He didn't waste time with the courts except when it was unavoidable. He was completely uninterested in helping build cases, finding witnesses, or talking to people for the prosecutor. If a case went to court, it was the prosecutor's job, not his, and that was that. On several occasions I'd had to threaten him with subpoenas in order to get him to court for routine testimony.

For a moment, though, the sheriff, the prosecutor, and I were in the same boat—all wondering why we were in Manny Stone's den at nine o'clock in the evening with a woman named Lorraine Davis. Stone apologized to Bernie and me for leaving his office today. He'd had to go pick up Mrs. Davis at the station. She was an artifact collector and heir of Lee Guessner's estate, and she had been kind enough to fly from Chicago to Little Rock and take a train.

Elizabeth Stone rushed in with a tray of iced lemonade and chided us for standing. She gave us each a glass and then quickly disappeared in a cloud of lavender perfume. I had been acquainted with Elizabeth Stone for several years and never had a moment of real conversation with her. She was always in a hurry, bouncing away like a billiard ball.

We all found seats except Bernie, who made elaborate gallantry of taking Mrs. Davis's drink from her and guiding her to a chair, then handing the drink back to her, which earned him only a look of mild puzzlement. He stood beside her chair. She looked at me, and kept looking at me while Stone talked. Her widely spaced green eyes were my second clue, but I still didn't get it.

Stone went right to the basic facts of the case: Lee Guessner had lived in Fort Smith for the last seven years. He'd rented a little shop downtown but kept most of his important artifacts at his house, beside Lake Wofford, a few miles south of town. Lake Wofford is bisected by the state line, and his house was actually in Oklahoma. A neighbor had found him in his panel truck on Wofford Road, apparently bludgeoned to death. A tote sack with a few broken artifacts was found in the truck with the body, but most of the things at his house had been stolen.

"So these are the Spiro artifacts we've been hearing so much about," Bernie said brightly, as if he was thinking about buying some of them. He put one hand on the back of the chair where Lorraine Davis sat and his other in a pocket, in a casually hovering pose. Apparently he was beginning to see the possibilities in the miles currently between Berenice and him.

Judge Stone gazed at him over his half-glasses. "Why don't you find a chair, Bernie? You're making me nervous."

Bernie came over and sat between me and the judge's desk but kept glancing at Mrs. Davis.

Stone leaned over a shaving-filled box on the floor and picked up a large polished seashell with carvings on its outside. He held it in both hands in his lap and spoke slowly, as if to make sure we listened closely. "I bought this from Lee at his house the day before he was murdered. He didn't say anything about selling the collection. His body was found the next day. I drove there as soon as I heard about it. Kenny was already there when I arrived. We went to the house together. The door was jimmied; the place had been stripped. Twenty-four hours before you could barely get through the house because of all the stuff from the Spiro site. The place was filled with boxes. It would have taken several panel-truck or flatbed loads to carry it all out of there. They got everything."

"So you knew this man—this collector—pretty well?" Bernie said.

The judge gave Bernie a look suggesting that he just listen. "I bought a half-dozen pieces from him over a period of time, but we both felt that the Spiro material should be kept in a single collection. He was very concerned about that. I had done some initial work to help him form a trust. I suppose you'd call us friends in a cause. . . ." Stone said this a little hesitantly.

He handed the shell to the sheriff, who looked at it as if it was a piece of well-hardened dung, then passed it to Mrs. Davis as quickly as possible. She felt its heft and held it up and turned it slowly in her hands, her green eyes traveling slowly across the carvings.

"How many of these were there?" she asked.

"I don't know, but the shells were only part of the collection. He had a lot of other things. I didn't see it all. He'd been buying since the diggers started selling last year."

"Approximately how many of these?" she repeated quietly.

"Maybe a hundred unbroken shells like that one, plus several crates of fragments. That's a guess."

"Were they all carved?"

"Every shell is carved, and the designs are all unique."

"Are they all in this good shape?" she said.

"No. But a great many of them are."

Her expression clouded, eyes still on the shell. "Lee told me that the shells were all different. I took it as an exaggeration. It's pretty unusual. . . ." She trailed off, uncertain or skeptical, I couldn't tell which. Finally, after studying it top to bottom, holding it at different angles close to a lamp, she got up and handed the shell to me, her fingers briefly touching mine.

Cylinder 12

The carving on the shell depicted two men, facing away from each other, apparently dancing. They were almost identical except for wearing different belts. Coming off their backs, like cloaks, were snake bodies that curled up and around each other, intertwined, connecting the two dancers. They danced on a third rattlesnake that was tightly wound in a circle. Both dancers had pronged headdresses and ponytails. They also had what looked almost like flames coming out of their opened mouths.

Indian relics had never particularly interested me. I had plowed up so many arrowheads as a kid in South Oklahoma that I grew up thinking of them as commonplace. This image, though, was arresting: dreamy yet explicit, as if it conveyed something very definite.

Bernie leaned toward me and looked at it. "Their tongues are hanging out. Are they tired?"

"Those are speech scrolls," Mrs. Davis said dryly.

"Speech what?"

"Scrolls. They're like cartoon captions. It probably means they're speaking or singing."

"And three-day-old beards? Did Indians have beards in those days?" He glanced up at my jaw.

Her eyes were still on the shell in my hands, almost as if it worried her. "That's a falcon mask," she said.

I handed it over to Bernie.

Judge Stone asked her, "Do you recognize the kind of shell?"

She shook her head. "Not even dimly. It looks more Mayan than North American. . . ." She sounded either worried or dismissive, as if she didn't want to know about the shell, which seemed odd to me. A collector, I thought, should be excited by a thing she'd never seen.

"I mean the shell itself," Stone said. "The thing it's carved on. Did Lee tell you his theory about the shells?"

She took a long, deep breath and finally lifted her eyes away from the shell as Bernie put it carefully down on the judge's desk.

"Yes, he did. It's a rare species of shell. The whorl pattern goes counterclockwise—backward from most shells. He said they came from the Gulf of Mexico, probably around Veracruz."

Stone's head was canted downward as he looked over his glasses at her. "Do you agree with him?"

She made a little gesture of dismay. "I have no idea. I haven't really looked into this. I only know what the man said. Veracruz to here was a healthy distance seven or eight hundred years ago. Unless the people at Spiro were awfully powerful traders."

Bernie jumped back in. "And were you related to the deceased, Mrs. Davis? Was he an uncle?"

"I wasn't related to him at all. I met him on a pyramid in Guatemala in May."

Bernie appeared now to be truly impressed. "Honestly? This May? On a pyramid? That's a stitch."

She didn't smile back. "We happened to be at Tikal at the same time. I knew Lee for less than two weeks."

"And he left you his estate?" Bernie grinned incredulously. "It must have been a wonderful two weeks."

"What do you mean?" she said flatly.

"I mean, this is Charles Dickens," he hastened to say. "Surely there was some kind of former contact between you."

She let her gaze rest on him a while before responding. "We had things in common. We'd heard of each other. We'd both done work in Egypt. Lee was known for putting together collections. He was an amateur archaeologist, not just a dealer. It's a fairly small world, I guess. . . . But we hadn't met or corresponded."

The sheriff was swiping at the side of his nose with the back of his hand, his nervous gesture. He didn't like being in the judge's den, and he didn't like this world-traveling woman. I noticed by the way Stone was looking down at his desk that some of this was new to him. He was practiced at not showing his feelings, but I was equally practiced at Stone-watching. Something about the situation deeply perturbed him.

That was the moment I began to get interested. I can't say exactly why, but it wasn't the story of the dead collector or the carved shell or the sheriff's nervous lack of interest or the judge's openly expressed interest. It wasn't even this intriguing woman but rather the judge's not quite hidden frustration.

Bernie offered her a cigarette, she shook her head, and he took one himself and this time lit it. "You were in Egypt? Tell me about it."

"I worked there for several years. Lee and I were there at the same time but in different parts of the country. We heard of each other because our projects turned out to be similar—minor collections sold to the British Museum, the whole lot at once. Tikal was where we met, though. First time."

Bernie smiled blandly through an exhalation of smoke. "So you got to know each other quite well? There must have been some kind of special . . . something. People don't leave their estates to just anyone they meet on a pyramid."

She actually smiled a little at this. "I tried to avoid the man, Mr. Pryor. I was there to relax, and he was following around after me. I couldn't see why he was so excited about something in Oklahoma. He did most of the talking, and it was all about Spiro. The story eventually did get interesting, but the man was obsessed. I was putting up with him for the first few days—and not being too nice about it."

"What did he look like?" Bernie asked. "I'm trying to place him. Surely I met him."

The sheriff, as if hoping that a contribution might let him out of here, said, "Five-eight, about one-eighty, glasses. Early forties."

Still looking down, Stone said, "He was a recluse around here. I wouldn't be surprised if you never met him, Bernie. As far as I could tell, he had no social life." Stone then looked up directly at Mrs. Davis, with a tightly pleasant expression. "In fact, it's hard for me to picture him being as forthcoming as you describe."

Her eyebrows shot up. She almost looked amused. "Have you been to Tikal, Judge Stone?"

"Can't say that I have."

"It's in the middle of the Peten Jungle in Guatemala. The trees are two hundred feet tall. Sunlight and deep shade. It's like night-fall with ragged spots of brilliant light moving through it. You have to guard campsites against the monkeys. The birds are overwhelm-ing. Jaguars scream at night. Collectors there tend to stay together in one camp. They huddle and talk. There were about a dozen in camp when I met Lee. Most of them were picking up stuccos, some pottery, jewelry, jade beads. It was a pretty low-key bunch, with the usual couple of drunks. Lee and I were the only ones not buying, it turned out. I was sightseeing, and he was just there to look at the glyphs. I met him the day I arrived—"

The sheriff, unable to stand it anymore, tried to cut her off and change the subject. "You know, Judge Stone, if something was stolen from this man's house, it being in Oklahoma, we're going to have to work through LeFlore County. It was probably vagrants out there, anyway. Squatters all over the hills, more of em on the Oklahoma side. Anyone could have killed him."

Stone looked at Kenny for what I called a long Stone minute, then said bluntly, "I've talked to LeFlore. We're handling it. We've got jurisdiction."

Kenny was taken aback but managed to say, "I figure we could use their help."

"The LeFlore County sheriff is useless, and you know it, Kenny. He's crooked, and he's useless. Mrs. Davis, I'm sorry. Please go on."

There was a moment of embarrassed silence as everyone took this in. Kenny's eyes narrowed a little. He wasn't used to people being this direct with him. Even judges usually deferred to Kenny, or at least politely worked around him. I felt another surge of interest.

"My only point," Mrs. Davis said, "was that I didn't know Lee Guessner, and he said nothing to me about making me heir to his estate. I went away thinking the man probably disliked me for being so uninterested in his obsession."

Stone was still puzzled. "Did you correspond with him after meeting him?"

She shook her head. "No I did not. Not so much as a postcard."

"Well, he knew you by reputation," Stone said, as if thinking aloud. "And there was the Fort Smith connection, with your family . . ."

She didn't respond to this, but it was my next hint, and I could almost hear a coupling in my mind like a dim sound from some distant train yard.

She glanced out the window, and her expression momentarily softened. "The fireflies are still thick, aren't they? I used to sneak out and play in them late at night."

"You had family in Fort Smith?" Bernie asked.

She smiled a little at him. "I grew up here. Not far from here, as a matter of fact."

Before she'd finished what she was saying, I knew who she was, and it caused the hair to stand up on the back of my neck. I'd seen some strange things in my life. I'd seen enough and lived long enough to know that the hair doesn't play wolf too often, but this was reincarnation, and I was suddenly awed at how much of her mother I could see in her—the eyes, the way she held her shoulders, the confidence. It was like seeing her at nearly the same age as when I had met her thirty-some years ago. The most peculiar thing was that I hadn't recognized her at first sight.

Bernie was suddenly in his element, asking enthusiastic questions about her past: growing up here until she was eleven years old, her father, her family, mutual acquaintances. Oddly enough, I wasn't particularly interested in the details—the fact that there was no longer a Mr. Davis (he had died of an illness in his late twenties), even one brief mention of her mother—some of it registered, but mostly it flowed around me like water. Knowing who she was, I wanted nothing but to feast my eyes on her.

Meanwhile, the sheriff continued making quick swipes at the side of his nose and ostentatiously looking at the clock on the bookshelf as if he was about to jump out of his skin listening to all this chitchat.

I tore my eyes away from her and noticed Stone watching me. He gave no sign of detecting my self-consciousness. He interrupted Bernie's questioning, finally, to lay out his reason for calling us together. He wanted to make sure that we'd all met and were fully aware of the situation and, he hoped, all in agreement. He said he wanted the sheriff to be cooperative, Bernie to run the details of the prosecutor's office (a radical suggestion), and me to devote my complete attention to this case until we found out who had murdered Lee Guessner and what had happened to his collection. Despite the fact that I was still tingling like somebody who'd gone into the electric room at the carnival, I was impressed by Stone's resolve in calling Bernie back from the seashore, inviting the sheriff here, and putting us all together face to face.

The sheriff didn't seem to give that much of a damn, as long as he could get out of here, and he said good-night and slipped out the door faster than a coon through a chicken fence. Bernie was already hedging, already saying sure, okay, that's fine, but he would also love to be whatever help he could in this obviously important case.

Stone had a couple more surprises. He brought up the matter of my vacation and asked if I minded putting it off. I had spent all day minding a great deal; now I thought, What the hell, I can catch fish in September. Still I paused for a horse-trader's minute. "Right now I'm more worried about the Goback jury than my vacation."

The judge sighed. "The last I heard, Hank had to put them up at the hotel. I'm afraid they're hung on the attempted murder."

"Would it be possible—"

Stone finished the sentence for me. "I'll talk to them tomorrow morning and remind them of their obligation to reach a verdict."

Stone and I were so used to each other that he could tell by the way I was still looking directly at him that I hoped for more, and, eyebrows raised as if to emphasize that he was sweetening the deal, he added, "Of course I intend to remind them that this is not a lawless county in which men can beat or try to murder their wives and that a failure to come up with a verdict would be very grave indeed."

I nodded slowly, looking at the floor. I was a little surprised at the "try to murder." If anything, it was more than I was asking for. I told him that my vacation was no big deal; I could put it off.

As we were about to leave, Stone mentioned casually to Bernie that he wanted to show him a new duck gun he'd bought; did he have a second to look at it? His guns were in his bedroom, he said, come on back. Bernie, obviously a little puzzled, said sure, he'd like to see it. That left Mrs. Davis and me alone. We talked for five minutes, and her remarks implied that she knew nothing about her mother and me, for which I was thankful. I wasn't prepared to look into those eyes and try to make small talk about her mother.

My relationship with Samantha King (her mother's name then) was so strange and so brief that I sometimes wondered whether it had happened at all. It had occurred when she was in her twenties and I was fifteen or sixteen. Because of things we'd done, things we knew about each other, I could never talk about her with anyone, and a memory that can't be aired is like something locked in a trunk in the attic. After a few decades you aren't sure it's really there, or if so, what it really is.

We established that I should call her Rainy. I asked nothing about her mother. I already knew the basics—that Samantha had later married someone who was originally from Memphis, where they'd moved before the war, and that she had recently died, in her fifties. I knew the day she had died. I'd overheard someone at a lunchroom mention her death and found a *Memphis Commercial Appeal* with her obituary. I hadn't cut it out, only read it. I didn't need to know anything else, really. She was gone.

While the judge and Bernie remained in the bedroom, Rainy acted preoccupied, walking around the room gazing distractedly at the arrowheads that were mounted in solid oak cases on three walls, and I got the feeling that she was trying to decide whether to stick around. The situation seemed to worry her. I asked her a couple of questions, like what she thought about visiting her old home town, which she answered indifferently. As she spoke I was trying to remember the sound of her mother's voice but couldn't really. We lapsed into silence. She wasn't anxious to make small talk. She wandered around staring, seemingly deep in her own thoughts.

"So, are you going to stay here a while?" I eventually asked.

"Judge Stone wants me to see the will tomorrow. For some reason, he couldn't bring it here." She looked slightly perturbed. "Anyway, I have to look at it, I suppose."

I changed the subject, asking her how she'd ended up working in Egypt at such a young age. She told me that she'd gone there on an archaeological dig the summer after her junior year of college and just stayed there, never graduating.

She leaned against Stone's desk and finally looked at me. "The professor in charge wasn't really doing archaeology. He was brokering pyramid goods. He left the students on their own. Since there was no dig, really, I ended up mucking around with the grave robbers. I stayed there. Quit college. Eventually got married."

"Well, you must be brave." I tried to sound avuncular—cheerful, a little brisk.

She gave me a mocking look. "About getting married or being in Egypt?"

"Beg pardon?"

"There's no bravery involved in buying goods. If you've got money, they treat you like a queen."

The judge and Bernie came back from the bedroom, Bernie looking somehow stunned. Stone said to me, "Tom, could you call me and let me know what you find out? I'll fill you in on some more details later. I know you like to get out and scratch around without a lot of preconceptions."

Bernie offered to give us both a ride—Rainy was staying at the Goldman Hotel—but he remained subdued during the whole drive downtown. All of his previous talkativeness and flirtatiousness were gone. The judge obviously hadn't taken him into the bedroom to look at a shotgun. Maybe he'd cornered Bernie to tell him something that he didn't feel comfortable telling Mrs. Davis or me, or maybe he'd just repeated, man to man, that he wanted Bernie to take care of work at the prosecutor's office and free me to work on this case.

I sat in the back seat with the warm wind blowing in the windows, gazing at Rainy's head when she half-turned to me and gave me a little smile, almost a knowing smile, the upcast dash light soft across her cheek. "It looks the same," she said. "This time-machine business is eerie, isn't it?"

I had the sudden powerful, foolish urge to lean forward and grab her around the jaw and smell the crown of her head.

Cylinder 13

At seven o'clock Thursday morning I was standing in front of an abandoned two-story clapboard building near the railroad tracks along Front Street. Set back from the street, perched above a drought-diminished Arkansas River, the building was overshadowed by a larger brick structure that stored railroad equipment. According to the city telephone directory, this was the shop of Lee Guessner, Antiquarian, although no sign confirmed it. Until twenty-five years before, Front Street had been whorehouse row, and this was one of the three original houses that still stood, all similar in style—handsome buildings with modest Greek-revival decorations. But its location and current shabby condition would not attract customers for antiquarian goods, or, for that matter, any other kind of customers.

Sand from across the river had accumulated a couple of feet deep against the rear wall. A window that was broken out, frame and all, allowed me to climb into what appeared to be the old kitchen, which was also covered in ripples of fine dust. In it were footprints made by someone—apparently more than one person— with no shoes. They were broad, square adult feet, the prints lightly obscured but recent. I wandered up the stairs to mostly empty rooms, finding nothing stored in them. Downstairs, the front parlor had a small glass display counter, a coal stove that smelled as if it hadn't been fired for a long time, and a desk that was empty of everything but one broken arrowhead rattling around at the back of a drawer. I looked through a window southward over the river, feeling the cool flint between my thumb and forefinger, wondering why people were interested in such things.

At the Armstrong orphanage, when I was ten or eleven, we played war with arrowheads like this one. Six of us secretly coordinated our field and house jobs so we could meet in the woods, and we divided up and fought as "Greeks" and "Persians," our model of war being taken from Herodotus's book on the Persian Wars. We shot crude arrows toward each other—reenacting Thermopylae, Salamis, Plataea—by amazing luck never seriously wounding anybody. The arrowheads themselves had been only tools of our fantasy wars, with no more interest or magical authority than the ash saplings we stripped and made into bows, but I remembered that feeling of being transported to another place and time, becoming a wholly different person with what seemed like a wonderfully simple job: kill the Persians.

I thought I'd seen a trace of that in Rainy Davis's eyes when she was looking at the carved shell the night before—traveling into a magic past. I dropped the flint into my pocket.

At the assessor's office I found out that Miss Hettie Weeks owned the building at 92 Front, which used to be called the Athenian Hotel. I knew Hettie, and knew that she'd worked in one of the Front Street hotels years ago. Maybe she'd saved her money and eventually bought the old place. She currently owned the Ozark, a "modern" hotel and whorehouse located farther uptown. In Fort Smith the law generally put up with prostitutes as long as they followed certain rules, like sticking to their neighborhoods, although sometime before the World War there'd been a citizens' committee to banish all of them. These virtuous men managed to run out a few women, including Pearl Younger, Belle Starr's daughter, but the way the story was generally told the citizens' committee looked worse than the whores by the end of it, and now the town had fallen back into its tradition of not interfering with them. The unspoken rule was that they had to stay orderly and cooperate in crime investigations.

The Ozark was a brick building that sat on a small but oddly elevated lot, a little hill with the top shaved off. The hotel's wide front porch hung out close to the sidewalk path and the brick street. I met Hettie Weeks backing onto that porch with a coffeepot and a platter of sweet rolls, eggs, and bacon. She sat down at a little table, and I joined her and accepted her offer of a cup of coffee. Somewhere inside the building I heard a stirring voice on the radio announcing the real-life drama of Helen Trent, who fought back bravely, successfully, to prove what so many women longed to prove in their lives—that because a woman is thirty-five—or more—romance in life need not be over. . . .

Hettie was a large German woman of fifty-some years with wide cheekbones and a florid color. She was wearing a blue satin robe and had her gray hair tied loosely back. She had helped me find witnesses in a few minor fracases over the years, but only when she had to. I had never much liked Hettie. She was both pushy and guarded, and she always complained about being in dire financial straits, as if she was afraid that I was going to ask her for protection money.

When I asked if she'd heard the news about Lee Guessner, she said without hesitating, "Sure I did. He was my last paying renter."

"How'd you end up owning the old Athenian?" I asked.

"Honey, I got seven pieces of real estate on this side of the avenue I can't pay the taxes on. I'd trade em all for one five-star whore. Everything I put money into except beds and whores and naughty underwear goes south, and you can't even count on them anymore. That's the story of my life." She frowned and shook her head and took a big bite of egg. "I've had some five-star whores in my life. I had some legends, bring men like iron filings to a magnet. Back in my day we had clients come on trains from New York City, and that's the God's truth. And you think there wasn't whores in New York City." She chuckled through her nose at my presumed ignorance.

I changed the subject back to Hettie's dead renter, but she leaned over the table, her bosom almost touching her sweet rolls, and said, "Know what makes a five-star whore?" She widened her eyes and paused dramatically. "She wants it, can't get enough of it. Floats out of the mist and uses that thing the best way she can. Um-hum. Now you're talkin."

With a piece of bacon between her thumb and forefinger, Hettie made little up-and-down motions and fluttered her eyes. "Ain't a lot of them girls around. They're born, not made: they was playing with that little red onion when they was in their momma's arms. Nymphos. They don't show up here cause they can't get no job at the telephone exchange. They just are what they are. Born that way. And I'll tell you a secret. It don't matter all that much what kind of looker she is. Long as she's presentable. A man looks at her and something about her, the light around her head, only thing he can think about is crawl in her window. And that's the truth. Five-star is a whole different class, like royalty."

She popped the piece of bacon into her mouth.

I asked her what she could tell me about Lee Guessner, and she said about all she knew was that his fifteen-dollar check came like clockwork right up through this month.

"But the building looked unused," I said.

She shrugged. "I never talked to him, but he used the place all right. He paid by mail. I left him alone."

"How'd you meet him?"

She knitted up her eyebrows, chewing on a sweet roll. "Usual way. I offered it in the paper, and he called. That was a good while ago."

I sat there sipping the coffee, looking through the steam, waiting for her to tell me more. "That was no place of business, Hettie. It looks like he had a desk down there, but you don't pay fifteen dollars a month to sit at a desk."

"I don't know," she said vaguely. "Maybe he had a soft spot for old whorehouses. He did ask me a bunch of questions about the good old days in the rowhouses."

"Did you have him under a lease?"

She scowled. "Leases ain't worth the paper they're written on. I don't fool with them."

A young woman—maybe eighteen years old—appeared in the front door about that time: thin, wearing a dead-black dress that bared her chalky shoulders, creature of the night blinking her eyes and wavering uncertainly in the sun, arms hanging limply at her sides. She came over and unceremoniously plopped herself down.

"Up early, ain'tcha, honey," she said, casting me a bitter, flirtatious smile.

"Go on back in, Amy. We're talking."

"Ain't botherin you," she said childishly, her gaze drifting into the street.

As Hettie scolded her back inside I noticed needle marks on the girl's arm. I took another sip of coffee. "So, Hettie. You providing drugs for these girls again?"

She sighed deeply. "Amy's from Memphis. She's been using that old hypodermic since she was fourteen. I'm doing her a favor letting her work here. She'd be dead if I hadn't took her in. I thought we were talking about my renter."

"That's what I'm here for. I'd appreciate it if you'd give me something to go on."

Her scowl transformed slowly into a sly smile. "You know something! You get better-looking every time I see you. Especially when you're a little bit mad."

"I'm not mad yet, Hettie."

"You don't believe me, do you? You probably figure I'm looking at you, thinking half-breed. Brown-face. Let me tell you, Mr. Tom, I'm in the bidness of dealing with men, which lets me say some things other women can't. I'm looking at you in the fresh sunshine thinking you are one of the most gorgeous men I ever done saw. In my life. And I have seen a few."

"Your renter was beaten to death, Hettie. I'm assuming you had nothing to do with it. Tell me what you know about him. Anything."

She weighed her options and decided to give me a half-ounce of information. "He did call me and mention he'd been robbed. Said it wasn't no big deal, a couple of things stolen. Didn't say what it was. Probably kids breaking in to piss in the corner."

"When did this happen?"

"Three, four months ago. I don't know."

"March? April?"

"Early April, I think."

"Did he say he thought it was kids?"

"No," she said defensively.

"Why'd he keep paying rent, then, if he wasn't using it?"

"He intended to fix up the place. Put up bars on the windows or something. Hadn't got around to it."

"Was he trying to get you to pay for these repairs?"

"No." She shook her head slowly. "He didn't ask me for a thing. Not that I recall."

"Hettie, I'm putting it to you as a favor. Give me something to go on. Why'd he rent that dump? Did he know you already?"

"I don't know," she said, pretending to be insulted. "Now, he did say that if anybody comes around asking about the place or who was renting it, don't tell them nothin'. And he'd appreciate knowing who it was. That's all he asked me to do. He liked it being out of the way. Said he felt safe there."

"Safe from what?"

She shook her head. "It was just an office. That's what he called it. His office. He wasn't trying to bring in no trade off the street."

"Do you know what he collected?"

"Antiques, I think. He was a pretty fancy dresser. I did notice that about him."

I stood up. "I'll be back. If you remember anything else about him, I'd appreciate a call." I pointed my thumb at her front door. "On the matter of the drugs—"

"All right, Mr. Tom. All right."

Hettie glumly chewed her roll as I left.

I'd seen a look pass through her eyes, as if she was deciding not to tell me something, but Hettie was tougher than she acted. She would dumb up if I pressed her too hard. She was a canny old poker player. I'd give her time to mull it over and maybe visit her again.

Back at the prosecutor's office, Melody was sitting behind her Burroughs Electric Carriage Return typewriter looking unusually satisfied with herself.

"'Lo. And what happened to your vacation?"

"What're you grinning about?"

"Judge Stone talked to the Goback jury at nine o'clock; they reported at nine forty-five. The unofficial word from Hank is guilty on both charges."

I went over and sat down in front of the air conditioner, held out my palms toward it, and took a few deep breaths of coolish air.

She looked over her shoulder at Bernie's door and lowered her voice almost to a whisper. "Bernie's at work. He was here at nine o'clock. What happened last night?"

"Stone called us to a meeting at his house. He wants me to find out who killed this collector, and he wants Bernie to take full control here."

She rolled her eyes. "The jury officially reports at eleven thirty. You'd better get to court."

"Bernie can go."

"It's your conviction," she said irritably.

"It doesn't matter who sits there while they read it, Melody. That's just a formality."

"It isn't a formality to Nora Goback. She may want to thank you."

"Bernie's good at that kind of thing."

She looked daggers at me.

I walked over and knocked on Bernie's door. There was a brief flurry of action before I walked in to find him looking sleepy. I told him they were coming in with guilty on the attempted-murder charge and asked if he'd sit in for the verdict. He smiled vaguely. Yes, he'd already heard, be glad to sit in. Bernie usually managed to at least act as if he was happy about convictions, but something else was on his mind today.

"What did you think about last night?" he asked me.

"What in particular?"

"Kenny Seabolt. Why was he at Stone's house?"

"It's Kenny's turf. The murder happened out in the county."

"And?"

I shrugged. "Stone wants him to know what's going on so he won't throw a monkey wrench into it."

"Why would Kenny throw a monkey wrench into a murder investigation?"

I wanted to tell him that the sheriff would be anxious about any investigation in the county until he knew for sure that it didn't concern him. But getting Bernie agitated over the sheriff would only confuse matters. There were only so many things I could do at once. Bernie had an instinctive and justified distaste for Kenny Seabolt, but he also had a fatal tendency to lose interest in things, usually sooner rather than later.

I shrugged and said, "Stone just wants everybody to know that this is important. Make sure we understand it."

Bernie looked skeptical. "This whole thing is damned odd. It's as queer as it can be. Do you know Lorraine Davis?"

"Never met her."

"Is she sticking around town?"

"Don't know. Why?"

"She inherited this so-called collection of relics, but it's gone, stolen, whatever. Far as I can tell, all she really got out of the estate is a fishing shack on Lake Wofford. Why should she stick around? She's a goddamned world traveler."

I shook my head. Bernie seemed to be working himself into being interested in this case, and one had to wonder why, since he'd never shown genuine interest in a case before. Was it because it was the first time he'd been asked not to involve himself? Anger at being bossed around by a man with one-tenth his net worth? An interest in the attractive young widow with the slightly British accent? Whatever his motives, I suspected that in order to get anything done, I'd have to avoid him.

Cylinder 14

Although still wet from the last mopping, the checkered tile floor of the Goldman Hotel was already covered by a fine grit blowing across the river and up the whole length of the avenue. KFPW's red lightbulb glowed on the mezzanine level. The shoeshine man sat forlornly alone at his stand against a wall. The lobby, surrounded by handsome thick white columns, was palatially open and empty except for a cluster of leather chairs and couches in the center, where Rainy sat reading. She seemed a little puzzled and, I got the impression, was digesting something that wasn't altogether pleasant.

She was wearing a fitted cotton blouse and checked yellow dress. As I came over, she looked up and without a word handed me two pieces of paper: the Last Will and Testament of Robert Lee Guessner. While it included the usual three or four standard paragraphs, it was a stripped-down will of the kind usually written by country lawyers for poor clients. It named Lorraine Davis, with her address and phone number in Chicago, as both executor and single recipient of all his worldly goods, property, assets, and estate, including his entire collection of artifacts. There wasn't even a predecease paragraph naming another inheritor if she died before he did: it was her or the state.

Judge Stone had apparently served as Guessner's lawyer, since he and M. Parfit had signed the will, which explained why he'd known its contents. She looked up at me as if to ask what I thought.

I sat down in the chair next to hers. "Pretty simple will. Looks like he trusted you."

She looked a little paler today. She squinted and put her lips together in a slight pucker. The lobby was oddly quiet, and for a moment all of us—clerk, shoeshine boy, Rainy, I—were staring at the square of furious sunlight coming through the opened front door, walking across the tiles.

"I don't know whether he trusted me or not, but the judge doesn't. He informed me that Lee had had a different will in the works, but he changed it suddenly—against the judge's personal recommendation."

"Oh?"

"The other will called for delivering up the Spiro collection to a trust. Apparently they needed money to set up this trust but hadn't gotten it yet. Lee ran out of patience and changed the will to this. The judge isn't happy about it. He hinted that he wants me to turn over the collection to a trust."

"You mean the stolen collection."

She turned her eyes to mine. "Pending its recovery. I believe he suspects that I influenced Lee. Seduced him or something. Would you like a cup of coffee, by the way? Have you had your breakfast?"

"No thanks. I'm fine. Did you influence him?"

She smiled at me. "You know, I'd forgotten how un-Southern this place is. How direct people are. It's the West. You drive from Little Rock to this town, and you've gone from South to West. Bam. Did I influence Lee? Apparently I did, but I don't know how. Maybe he just needed somebody to listen. He seemed to think he couldn't talk to people around here.

"I thought the man was a bit of a lunatic at first. If you're stuck in a camp with people like that, you learn how to tune them out. For three or four days I scarcely listened to him. Maybe I didn't say that last night."

I gave her a smile and handed back the will. "You said it. You just put it more delicately."

Rainy and I were soon kicking up a roostertail of dust down a winding dirt road through the hills of the county's south township. I glanced over at her, feeling almost smug at my lack of nostalgia today. No overpowering urges. No questions that I desperately wanted to ask about her mother. I didn't hope, ever again, to be as I had been with her mother—helpless, floating on seas and currents, ecstatic candidate for suicide—as if that were even a possibility at my age.

In Hackett, I pulled up in front of Carr's General Store. For lack of a courthouse, Carr's was where they held municipal court in Hackett, and I'd done some cases there, substituting for our municipal prosecutor in misdemeanors involving loose cows and pigs, dog trouble, fights. They had local justices of the peace in this and other little townships surrounding Fort Smith but not enough money to pay prosecutors, so our city prosecutor had to drive a circuit serving four courts. Sometimes he got overloaded and asked me to fill in for him.

We went inside, where two ceiling fans stirred the air in the dark, ropy-smelling room. Alfred Carr, with a handmade sumac-and-tobacco cigarette hanging out the middle of his mouth, was going around straightening his barely stocked shelves. The Crash had knocked out the last of the little coal mines they used to have in the south township, leaving nothing but subsistence farming, and Alfred's store appeared to be hanging on by its fingernails. Alfred was a bachelor, a thin, neat, careful man in a storekeeper's apron, with a perfectly formed face, skin darker than mine, and a swatch of shiny black hair that fell down across his brow. Born in North Africa, he'd somehow ended up in Arkansas when he was a child.

He took the blazing cigarette out of his mouth. "Hello, Tom. We ain't having court today, are we?"

"Not that I know of. Lorraine Davis, this is Alfred Carr."

He said hello with his alert, sad smile and asked if we'd like a soda.

"Love one," Rainy said.

He pulled three RC Colas out of the ice chest and snapped off their lids.

I took one of them. "We're trying to find out about the man killed on the lake road Tuesday."

Alfred tensed and looked away. "He bought his groceries here sometimes. Lee, right?"

"Yes. Did he mention any kind of trouble he'd been having? Thieves, feuding with neighbors?"

Alfred shook his head. "Nothing but getting his groceries bought. He didn't run an account. Paid cash. He just dropped by for odds and ends. Hurry in, hurry out."

"What's your theory about how he was killed?"

Carr shook his head.

"Just a robbery, you think?"

"Don't know."

"They stole a bunch of Indian relics from him. What's a thief going to do with that?"

"I really wouldn't know." Alfred chugged some more of his soft drink. His expression signaled uneasiness or irritation.

"You see a lot of people on the fritz around here? Hobos?"

"Some."

"The Klan?"

"Sometimes. A couple of carloads came through a few nights ago, sheets flapping in the wind."

"Lee Guessner wasn't having any trouble with them, was he?"

Again he didn't know. He dropped his bottle into the case as if to signal that the conversation was over.

We talked for a couple of minutes longer but got no further. As we were leaving, Rainy asked him, "Are you from Egypt?"

Alfred was so surprised by the question that it took him a moment to respond. "I was born there. My parents brought me to this country when I was very young. Why do you ask?"

She gave him a smile straight from her mother's face, thirty years ago. I almost had to turn away. "I spent some time in Luxor and Cairo. It's a magnificent country."

"Well, I was born in Cairo," he said uncertainly. Alfred's handsome, trim face looked aloof. He would appear friendly at first and then seem to lose confidence, go remote. If I hadn't seen him act this way before, I would have thought he was being evasive.

"Do you have memories of it?"

He shook his head. "Not really."

She appeared to want to ask Alfred something else but changed her mind. As we left, I dropped fifteen cents on the counter. I waited until we were on the road to ask her how she'd known where Alfred was from, and she said that Lee had told her about an Egyptian who lived near him with whom he'd become great friends.

I turned down the lake road, and we were immediately surrounded by deep oak and hickory forest on a rutted lane with turnouts.

"So Alfred was lying, saying he barely knew him?"

"I'm just repeating what Lee said. He may have been exaggerating."

"What do you mean?"

"Well he did go on about the man. This great friend he'd made in the most improbable place, how they reminisced about the sunsets in Egypt and so on."

"Why does everybody have lockjaw about Lee Guessner?"

We bounced slowly down the dusty lane. I glanced at her. She looked at me thoughtfully—as if something was on her mind that she wasn't sure she wanted to talk about.

Nearing the lake, we passed the cabin of Guessner's only immediate neighbor, the caretaker. A couple of cotton-tic mattresses for hot-night sleeping were set out on the front porch, a summer kitchen under a rusting tin roof, an unsplit pile of stove wood spread around the front yard, and—close to the lake and shaded— a part-acre of corn. A boy with a floppy hat stood by the woodpile, his ax resting on the ground, watching us go by.

Lake Wofford was a pond arising from a spring, clear and beautiful in its cup of oak and hickory forest. Sometime in the '20s a group of the better-off sportsmen from town had had a rock dam and spillway built that widened it to about four hundred yards across. I had been there fishing with Bernie a couple of times during the brief period when we'd tried to socialize. Guessner's cabin was on a hill above the spillway, up a precipitous, gravel-popping driveway. A panel truck was parked nearby. The house was Ozark stonework—every rock different, all patiently fitted together, with a wood-framed Cape Cod second story. I parked nearby, and Rainy and I got out and wandered around the yard. We stood for a moment near a sturdy retaining wall below the house, paying homage to the lake. Even this far above it, we could feel the coolness of the spring water in the air. Across the lake, on the south side, was a long backbone ridge running straight east-west, like a scar welding Arkansas and Oklahoma.

Cylinder 15

"This place is so beautiful," Rainy said softly. "It makes me think I've been here."

"You may own it. All of his worldly goods, property, assets, and estate. That covers real estate. That truck too, if you want it. Didn't the judge talk to you about all this?"

She stared out over the lake. After a moment she said, "I don't blame Stone for being suspicious of me. Why would Lee leave his estate to a near stranger?"

"Plenty of estates are given to distant relatives."

"But that's blood," she said.

"When you were with Lee, did he mention having any family? Nephews, nieces?"

She shook her head.

"Maybe he felt like you were his true sister. He seemed to care more about his work than anything else anyway."

Eyes still on the lake, she said hesitantly, "You were wondering why people hold back when you ask about him. I've told you how he was at Tikal: busy, exasperating, going on endlessly about this mound. He acted a little like an invert as well. I didn't mention that."

"A what?"

"A homosexual. Maybe that was why I put up with him. He obviously wasn't interested in me in that way, so I didn't mind his hovering around quite so much. He had the lisp, and everything was fantastic and amazing and gorgeous. He was flying the flag. You know—flamboyant."

I wondered why the judge wouldn't have clued me in on this. For that matter, Hettie Weeks could easily have said something about it. It was the kind of thing she wouldn't miss.

I wandered away from Rainy, back toward the house, and she followed me. The front door had been kicked open, and we walked into a room with pine walls and broad-plank floors; beyond it was a sun room of many-paned windows looking out over the lake. There was a sulfurous smell in the house, a little like bad Oklahoma well water. I was used to that smell from living in Muskogee, with its sulfur cloud hanging over town in the summer, but this odor was different, more piquant. The one easy chair in the living room had been cut with three neat slices, and the stuffing was hanging out. In several places along the walls, the pine paneling had been crowbarred loose, exposing two-by-fours. The paneling was laid aside. Only a few pieces had even been broken. Near the center of the house, planking had been pulled up from the floor. Rainy drifted around the empty house looking but then went back outside, and I went into the small, hot upstairs, where there was one empty bedroom and one with a mattress that was split in the same efficient manner as the chair downstairs. The house had been thoroughly and carefully searched.

I kept walking from room to room, thinking that something was wrong with Stone's picture of what had happened here. In the sun room I wiped my finger across a window seat and saw only the slightest dust on my fingertip. All the rooms, the floors, everyplace but where there was immediate damage from prying up wood, was clean. Would thieves clean a place after they ransacked it? Why should they?

I heard something outside and went back out. Rainy called me from some distance across the hill, and I pushed through drought-thinned brambly bushes. I came out of the bush into a clearing where she was near a cliff's edge, standing in a little square of loose foundation rocks. There were only rocks, no sign of logs. It had probably been a Choctaw cabin seventy-five or a hundred years ago. From there we could see for miles into the hills of Oklahoma. Despite patches of brown, it was quite a view.

"You took the hard way," she said, pointing. "There's a trail."

"You already knew about this?"

"Lee told me there was an old cabin site by his house. . . . Why would somebody build this high, this far from the water?" she wondered aloud.

"Mosquitoes," I said. "Floods. Safety."

"But on a cliff edge? That doesn't seem safe. What about children?"

I stepped inside the square of rocks. "Maybe it was more dangerous to be close to the spring because a lot of people used it."

She continued to look for a while over the forested hills. Beads of sweat ran down her face, but the heat didn't seem to affect her. "There's a mantle over this place," she said quietly.

"A what?"

"A softness. The landscape. It's a perfect scale. Everything about it . . ."

My memories of the territory west of here had little to do with softness, but I said nothing. We were looking out across one of the poorest counties in the United States, in a year when the competition for that award was high.

Her eyes narrowed a little. "Lee had an idea that Spiro was a religious center. But he couldn't figure why it was located here. All he had to do was walk out in his yard and see it. It's beautiful."

This seemingly harmless remark aroused a welter of strong feelings in me. Most people on the east side of Oklahoma were too poor even to move. Famine was menacing. They were living on cornbread and gravy, if they were lucky. And the politics across those beautiful hills—oh, one definitely didn't want to think about that. My nearly twelve-year job at the Indian Agency. It was a waste of one's brain to think about it. Driving into county seats and talking to judges who threatened to throw me into jail the minute I told them I was from Muskogee. Lawyers blowing their stacks, pulling guns. Indians on 128th shares of oil properties whose forty-dollar annual royalty check ended up with a negative net payment because the five lawyers and judges and guardians who lived on them had received good annual takes in previous years and by God weren't going to take a decrease, and to hell with this nonsense about the oil market. And I had seen a few rich Indians, yes indeed I had, the ones who made it into *Life* magazine. The quaint, curious, ridiculous, oil-rich savages. I had a store of bitterness from those years. It came less from disgust at the county machines, less from the race hatred—which I assumed simply to be part of the natural world, like fire and insects—than from my own inability to do much about any of it, my own inept bosses and crooked fellow investigators. That was what caused me to quit the job and leave Muskogee.

What she said about the landscape stirred up feelings about my own past. But the past was a dream to wake from, ghostly and gone and useless. Why fool with it? Give me the radio. Give me a book. Give me Claudette Colbert, swimming in milk. Give me *Frankenstein* and today's *Post-Dispatch*. Give me a new car. Or, short of that, dreams of a new car. Anything now or ahead, not behind.

In the unpredictable alchemy of emotion, I felt a sudden maddening attraction for Rainy, despite the heat and sun in our faces and my urge to tell her how wrong she was. It wasn't a slight attraction but the sharp, physical, man-for-woman kind, and it hit so fast it made me feel almost dizzy. I stepped outside the low, ruined wall of the cabin and kept my eyes on the west and said nothing. But she seemed more comfortable with the silence than I was.

"Your accent sounds English," I eventually said, changing the subject.

"That's from being abroad so long. There are a lot of Brits around the Mediterranean. My husband was from London."

"Tell me about him."

"Oh, you wonder about my husband?"

"Sure," I said.

We wandered over to partial shade and sat on a moss-covered outcrop.

"His name was Eric. He was a Cambridge-trained archaeologist. A very serious archaeologist."

"What do you mean?"

"He disliked other archaeologists, except for a couple of safely dead pioneers. He could give you excellent reasons why they were all pitiful failures. Eric didn't do a lot of work himself, but he had the measure of everyone else's insignificance. He was a shit, Mr. Freshour, all seven years of him. Nine, actually, if you count the whole time I was with him."

I laughed. "That's pretty harsh."

"I was hardly an angel; I did my share of drinking and slandering. When you're young, you know . . . The '20s were a fog anyway. A wasted decade. Eric didn't live long enough to mellow, poor soul, but he did have his qualities. He was a dancer. That he did beautifully."

"What kind of dancer?"

"Oh, night-club dancing. Just having fun. When a dance got from the States to Cairo, or wherever we were, he picked it right up. The first time he saw it, even in a movie, he could do it. Shag, black bottom, whatever. Charleston. The old dances—waltzes, Irish jigs. Ethnic dances. Eric was a physical mimic. He could even imitate someone dancing awkwardly—which he did a lot when he was drunk. He'd tell his pals to watch this and go out on the floor and pick some poor clumsy soul and dance near him or her—usually her—with an exaggerated, foolish expression. Caricature. Mockery. He was so good at it that you couldn't help but be amused."

She frowned at an ant walking down her arm. "Really, the women swooned over Eric. Rumored to be wealthy, danced well, good at flirting, fun to talk to at a party—as long as you kept off his line of work. What else could you ask for? And quite good-looking. Eric should have given up on archaeology and worked as an actor or dancer. You look good, Mr. Freshour." She blew the ant off.

"Beg pardon?"

"You are quite an attractive man," she said lightly, almost smiling. "I am cauterized against attractive men, though, so don't worry. They have no effect on me anymore."

This is my lucky day, I thought. Two compliments in one day— the first from a woman trying to get me to change the subject, the second from one trying to get herself to change the subject.

"So pyramids was your line of archaeology?"

"I wasn't an archaeologist, not so long as Eric was part of the show. At least, I couldn't claim to be. He hated amateurs worse than professionals. I was only a pyramid collector, nothing more. Eric was the archaeologist. He did synagogue and early temple sites. For some reason, he was fascinated by the Jews. A lot of his pals were rabid anti-Semites, and they'd argue this way and that. Eric didn't really like digging. He didn't really like archaeology. He just somehow got caught in it. It brought out the worst in him."

Rainy dabbed at her forehead with a sleeve. "But I'm the one doing all the talking. I trust your marriage was happier?"

"My wife's name was Laura. We had a good marriage. . . ." I wanted to change the subject. "So, have you been to this mound yet?"

She looked puzzled.

"The Spiro Mound."

"I just got here yesterday."

I pointed northwest to a single conical hill that looked like a small volcano. "Well, that's Round Mountain. It's not far away."

"Would you mind taking me there?"

"No problem," I said. We walked back toward the house on the trail and were met by a man carrying a shotgun, standing by my car. I almost grabbed Rainy by the arm but then recognized the caretaker. He had sloping shoulders and a sagging face and didn't look you in the eye. I introduced myself and Rainy and told him our business and asked him some questions about Guessner. Yes, he had been the one to find him. No, he hadn't noticed any cars except Guessner's and those of fishermen, and he had no idea how the house had gotten cleaned out. He said fishermen were always coming and going, and he didn't watch the road that closely.

I asked him what he figured had happened to Guessner, and he shook his head and briefly looked directly at me. "Somebody done a job on him is all I know." He glanced away as if asking me not to go into the details.

"Was he still in his truck?"

"Yes sir, he was. That's it." He nodded at it. "The sheriff asked me to clean it out and park it here. Key's in the floor."

"Was he beaten to death?"

Sighing and looking uncomfortable, the caretaker half-shook his head. "I couldn't tell. I went right on to Hackett and called the sheriff. They hauled him away that afternoon. They asked me to clean out his panel truck. I parked it over by his house."

"Have any suspicions about who might have done it?"

"No sir. I didn't know the man. He kept to hisself. Never come down to the lake fishin nor none of that. Only time I run into him be when he was takin things to the root cellar."

"What root cellar?"

"There's an old cabin site on the bluff—"

"We were just there."

"There's a little cave below it by the creek. I seen him carryin boxes to it, safekeeping place, I guess. When I seen him I offered to help, but he didn't want no help. I ain't sayin he was unfriendly, but he sure didn't want no help."

"Can you show us this place?" Rainy asked.

The caretaker led us down the driveway and across the grassy edge of the lake toward the spillway, a cascade of spring-fed water that went into a round pool with flowering lilies around its edge. The lake and spillway pool were like an oasis in the dry forest. We followed him down a seldom-used path beside the creek to a small cave mouth in the cliff, which Rainy scrambled into without hesitation. A couple of bats flew out, and the caretaker flinched. He kept looking around uneasily. I stuck my head into the entrance, which opened into a space about as big as a small kitchen. Rainy was standing with a match held out, moving it around the room. As my eyes adjusted I couldn't take them off her face. She lit another match and called me.

"Tom," she said, holding the booklet of matches toward me. "Would you help me? I found something."

Cylinder 16

What Rainy had found was a single wooden box full of carved seashells like the one Judge Stone had shown us the night before. Under them, in the bottom of the box, was a ragged notebook with five pages of pencil scribblings. There were thirteen shells, and she set them out on the plain, scarred wooden table in Guessner's kitchen and took up each one individually, turning it slowly as if to memorize the dark, etched lines of birds, spiders, cats, raccoons, snakes, animal heads on human bodies, humans with painted faces. One of the carvings pictured three men surrounding a small rectangular enclosure, brandishing cleavers and holding what looked like human heads by the hair.

"What are those?"

"In Mayan art they call them trophy heads, but they usually have jagged lines along the neck."

"So these people carried around severed heads."

"Your ancestors. Think of it."

"They aren't my ancestors. I'm a civilized Comanche."

She held up a shell. "Don't worry about it; they probably cut off people's heads only on holidays. My ancestors put them on spikes and decorated downtown with them every day of the week."

"Where was that?"

"Oh, Britain, I suppose. Don't know much about my distant ancestors, truthfully. Severed heads were civic decorations all over Europe."

I leaned over and pointed at the marked eye of one of the etched figures. "Is that a falcon mark?"

She glanced at me sharply. "Know more about this than you've been letting on?"

"You mentioned falcons last night."

"There are a lot of them in late prehistoric American art."

"Why?"

She leaned back in the chair, shaking her head. "Unfortunately, they didn't leave any explanations. Maybe it's because falcons are fast and fatal, the warrior's ideal. Who knows? I'm skeptical of flat answers to questions like that. Icons change, gods change. Sometimes they become their opposites."

She pointed at a place on one of the shells. There were four swastikas surrounding a curving geometric pattern.

"You find these in a lot of places. Almost worldwide. It's quite strange. India, the Mediterranean, the Americas—and usually they seem to mean friendship or unity or something like that. Now we have this little spitting man in Germany who goes around wearing swastikas on his arm. Changes in meaning can defy common sense. Icons can be appropriated. So these may not be trophy heads. Perhaps they used to be trophy heads, and by the time this artist carved them on this shell they represented the spirits of ancestors. Or maybe they represented special powers."

"Special powers?"

"I don't know. Lee babbled about that. About trophy heads transforming to symbols of powers. He had mucked around with this stuff so much that he had a quite arcane sense of it all. He believed that these people were definitely priests. Unfortunately, I wasn't listening to half of what he said. My only point is, beware of easy answers. That's your first lesson in archaeology."

She looked at the torn-up notebook that had been in the box with the shells, and I pushed my chair over beside her. The notebook's few remaining pages contained what looked like part of a working inventory, with a list of items going down the left side. Other writing was scattered at various angles: dates, names, words and phrases, question marks.

> *Two facing a serpent staff, three pronged tongues (chunkee? vomit?) . . . Splendid bird man!! . . . Trust date: Sept 1, 1934, Nov 34, . . . Pocola Mining Company . . .*

"Chunkee?" she said. "I've heard of it. . . ."

"It's a game," I said. "One side rolls a chunkee stone across a field, the other throws a lance and tries to hit it where it rests."

She seemed surprised. "How do you know about it?"

"I've seen it played."

"Where?"

"Okemah, a few miles east of here, was the place I saw it. But it's about faded out now. I saw it being played at the Old Hickory stomp grounds." I pointed at Guessner's notation of "vomit." "An old man told me that when they used to have big games between towns, they took medicine to purify themselves before playing."

"Emetics," she said, frowning at me and chewing her lower lip. "So these things I've been calling speech scrolls could be the ceremonial upchucking before the big game." She tapped Guessner's notes. There were droplets of sweat on her face. The house was thoroughly hot. She picked up the shell carved with the swastikas. "Lee wondered about whether these people were ancestors of a Creek or Caddo tribe or what. But the Creeks are from the Southeast. They only shipped them here—what—a hundred years ago?"

She glanced at me and turned back to the notepad. "Your ancestors were Comanche?"

"I'm half-joking. I don't really know. I was an orphan. Some kind of mixed breed. Comanche and white maybe, or Caddo and white. Southeast Oklahoma, that's about all I know."

"Ah." She nodded, an odd look shooting across her face as she kept it fixed on the pages. "He lists pearls, metal ornaments, arrowheads, spearpoints, maces, axes, masks, cloaks, textiles. . . . Under textiles he lists seventy-five fragments, thirteen complete pieces. Thirteen complete pieces of pre-Columbian textiles?" She sighed. "Have you got a cigarette?"

"Sorry."

"You don't smoke," she said glumly. "How very unsociable of you."

I pointed to the word *trust*, with the marked-out dates following it. "Stone said something about a trust last night. Did Guessner mention it when you met him?"

"All he talked about was the collection itself, nothing about the business side of it." She pointed at a notation on one of the pages: *What language do they speak?*

I just shook my head. She frowned intently, looking back and forth between pages. Finally she gave a little frustrated sigh and stood up, walked over to the sun-room windows, and looked down at the lake. "That water looks too good. I'm going swimming." She turned from the window and walked past me.

"It's spring fed. Pretty cold . . ."

"I can use it." She disappeared out the door. She was obviously without a bathing suit, and I didn't know whether to follow her or stay here. From the window I saw her drop her clothes—all of them—onto the grass and walk into the lake. She hesitated briefly going in and turned around, the water just covering her breasts. Looking up in my direction, in the widening circle of ripples on the calm surface, she smiled up toward me. She knew I'd be watching.

I walked down the hill and sat on a rock next to her clothes.

She was dog-paddling. "Come on in. It'll change your outlook."

"I'm afraid the caretaker will get upset. He's supposed to keep this place for fishermen."

"I'm a fellow owner now. You told me yourself." She disappeared under the water and stayed gone a while, then popped up, spitting out water. "God, this is wonderful! I'm going to stay here. It's too hot in that bloody hotel. I love this place."

"Not sure that's a good idea. The last person here was killed a couple of days ago."

The sun had just descended behind the ridge. She paddled quietly, seeming to glower at me across twenty feet of still water. "Thanks for the warning," she said, and sank out of sight again.

"You're welcome," I said to the lake.

She came back up and pushed the black hair out of her eyes. She took a few strokes and started walking out of the lake directly toward me. For some reason, I didn't think to get up and walk away. It was like the night before, when I'd wanted to smell her head. I just sat there, wordless, with her walking right toward me, on those long legs from here to anywhere, until she was within about five feet of me. This lady was not afraid.

"So you've seen a naked woman before, then?"

What was I supposed to say to that?

"I'll bet you have. Well, here's another one. Now get that silly grin off your face and move. I have to put my clothes on."

I took a deep breath, stood up, and looked around the lake, worried that someone was watching.

I gave Rainy and her box of carved shells a ride back to the Goldman Hotel.

Later in the evening at my office, I read that day's *Post-Dispatch*, a ritual I normally performed in the morning but had missed the last couple of days. I found it calming to read a good newspaper, no matter what was in it. *NRA Price Codes Collapse, Heat Wave Continues, Nazis in Control After Reichstag Fire.* I opened the window in my office and looked down the street to the old Laflore Hotel, which some agency of the government had taken over to house unemployed men. There were about twenty loiterers outside, sitting around shooting the breeze, smoking, and one of the sheriff's cars prowled by, watching them. The smell of the stockyards was blowing across the river, reminding me that I hadn't talked to anybody about the jury's official verdict on Jay Goback. Sentencing lay ahead, and it would be a good idea to see what Stone had in mind. He had asked me to keep him informed—enough of an excuse to call him at home.

Elizabeth Stone answered in her chipper but breathless way, as if the phone had interrupted a race she was having around the house. The judge came on the line sounding like he'd had a good dinner. "They delivered for you, Tom. I'll probably sentence him to twenty. He'll be inside eight to ten if he's a good boy. How'd it go today?"

I reported what we'd found at the lake cabin and asked if he knew anything about the dates that Guessner had written and marked out regarding the trust.

"Where are you?" he asked. I told him, and he said he'd come down immediately. As the air conditioner struggled to make headway against the accumulated heat of the day, I finished the newspaper and went down to meet Stone on the street. Neon flickered in a few places on the avenue. Somewhere a drunk was singing. When the judge arrived, we ended up sitting on the running board of his car, looking toward the men hanging around the Laflore.

"I didn't want to talk on the phone too much about this," he said. "We still have a party line out there. You asked about the trust. Lee and I never got beyond the talking stage on it. We went into details but didn't reach the point of filing any papers. Part of it was to avoid a bunch of income tax. Lee wanted to set up a trust, donate the collection to it, and be hired at a fixed annual salary for a term of five years. Then he'd manage handing the collection over to a major museum. That was the idea, but we didn't have any money for it yet. Writing his will to donate the property to a trust was to be done as a demonstration of intent in case the income-tax boys questioned the salary arrangement later. I wrote a version of the will, but it never got filed—and then he came in and changed it."

"Whose idea was it?" I asked.

"The trust? Lee got it from another collector who'd made a big sale that way. It was workable—delicate but workable."

"What changed his mind?"

Stone stared up the avenue toward the men around the Laflore—one group clutched together pitching dice, others just out in the night, making a few lonely, glancing encounters up and down the block.

"I don't know why he changed it," Stone said. "Maybe because we weren't coming up with the money."

"His will looked to me like something written for a farmer with ten acres and a mule."

"You saw it?"

"Rainy showed it to me. She's as confused about this as you are."

"All I know is that Lee went to Central America and within a few days of getting back barged into my office and waited for me for three hours while I was in court. Even Parfit couldn't get rid of him."

"It must have been urgent."

Stone raised his chin and hinted at a smile. His gray eyes were almost blue in the neon. "The minute I walked in, he demanded that I write this will. He was pretty worked up. He wouldn't take no for an answer. To tell you the truth, I wrote it just to get him out of the office. People already wonder enough about my hobby without this guy following me around in the courthouse nagging me to rewrite his will. Lee could be very persistent."

"A pain?"

"A big pain."

"How much money was he hoping to make in this trust arrangement?"

"We were discussing a figure in the range of ten thousand dollars over five years."

"Two thousand a year?"

"Ten thousand per."

I looked at Stone for a minute. "Get me a shovel; I'm in the wrong business."

"It's no joke, Tom. You can go out there tomorrow and buy a single shell cup for a few bucks, but that whole collection—if it still exists—you couldn't put a dollar sum to it."

"Where was the fifty thousand going to come from?"

"Oil money. We had a man interested—Jim Mackey."

"Jim Mackey," I echoed, feeling a funny taste on the back of my tongue.

"You know him?" Stone asked, as if surprised.

"Afraid so. I had to deal with him on some guardianship cases."

"This guy contacted Lee and invited him to Tulsa. I guess he has offices in Tulsa."

"Mackey has an office building in Tulsa. What does he care about Indian artifacts?"

"I never met him face to face, but I know he's a practical man. I'm sure he had some reason."

"So Jim Mackey declared his interest in the collection, and Guessner got you involved?"

"To protect his claim." Stone sighed. "It was all very informal, Tom. At the start, Lee and I got acquainted when I bought a few things from him. He asked my advice about how to set up this thing with benefactors; one thing led to another. I did some pro bono research for him mainly because I was curious. He'd already talked to this oil man several times before I had any contact with him. I called Mackey on the phone, and he acted . . ."

Stone quit talking. I looked in the direction he was looking and saw nothing up the darkened street.

"You called him on the phone, and he acted what?"

"He acted vague. I got the impression he was thinking about funding the collection but hadn't figured out his pound of flesh. Either that or he wasn't sure he wanted to deal with me. I am a judge, after all, and I'm outside the east-side network. He couldn't push me around."

"Could he be the person behind this?"

Stone looked at me. "You mean the killing? I have no reason to suspect that. Do you know something about him?"

"Mackey's a typical oil-field bigshot. Cheats on royalties. Has goons beat people up and forces them to sign over property. Probably killed more than a few. He used to be in the guardianship game, but I imagine he's got enough oil wells now to be out of that."

"So you do already know about him?"

"Oh yeah. If you wanted a character reference, you should have asked me."

He shook his head and stared.

"I'm going to Spiro tomorrow, by the way," I said.

"Want to take Hank with you?" Stone asked.

"Do I need Hank?"

"I don't know. Hank calms people down. I'm just offering."

"Rainy Davis is going. Maybe she'll calm them down."

Stone said nothing to this.

"One last thing. I'm trying to get a better picture of Lee Guessner—what his personality was like. Rainy says he had a flamboyant way about him."

Again, silence. He was looking up at this point, his eyes and expression very still.

"I'm looking for any kind of lead I can find. Some handle on the guy. Where he socialized, who he knew . . ."

Stone remained silent as a black sheriff's car glided slowly by. "What are you getting at?" he finally said.

"Could he have been a homosexual?"

Now he laughed—one expulsion of breath. "I wouldn't know, Tom. I never asked him. He didn't particularly act that way in my presence. Why—did Rainy Davis tell you he was a queer? Remind me not to give my estate to a woman with a British accent."

"She didn't know for sure. She was just commenting on his manner. Al Carr told me today that he's been seeing the Klan down around Hackett—"

Judge Stone narrowed his eyes. "The Klan? All they know is skin color."

"When they called you out to the lake—after they found him—did you see Guessner's truck or the body?"

"No. They'd already taken him away and towed the truck. The caretaker looked shaken up, though. I got the impression it wasn't a pretty sight. I haven't seen Don's report yet. I don't think he's written it."

I stood up. "I'll keep in touch."

Cylinder 17

The Sebastian County coroner in 1934 was a kindly but annoying alcoholic named Don Campbell. Don acted painfully shy whenever he was on the witness stand, and he disliked talking about unpleasantness, which made him a terrible witness given what coroners have to talk about. In testimony Don had to be squeezed like an empty toothpaste tube. He was always laboring to hide his drinking. Why or how Don ended up being coroner I never knew, except that he had worked for a while as a general practitioner, quit that, and somehow got elected and kept getting elected to the office. He stayed at home unless he had a body. That Friday morning it took about twenty rings to get him to answer.

To all my questions he beat around the bush. Even for Don, the reticence was unusually thick. It was a little early in the morning to be talking about corpses, I realized, and Don had to be given ample time to get his brain working, but I finally put it to him directly.

"I was supposed to be on a train to Florida today, Don. I'm putting off a vacation to work on this, Stone's orders. I need to know what the corpse looked like. Was he beaten?"

"Oh yes. He was beaten . . . with something. Maybe a club." Don shut down his voice as if to suggest that that was all, ready to end the conversation now.

"Any other wounds? Had he been shot?"

"No, no. No. No bullet wounds that I could see."

"Is that all?"

"Yeah. Well. The beating was probably the cause of death. That's all . . . pretty much."

"Was there anything else?"

"There had been the use of a knife," Don said tentatively.

"The use of a knife to do what?"

"The head . . . theheadhadbeensevered."

"The head had been what?"

"That's correct. Severed. Right. It was. . . ."

"Where the hell was the head?"

"Oh it was in the cab right there, in the cab. Near the trunk, you know . . . of the body." Don's tone implied that we could be thankful for this consolation.

"Did you tell anyone about this? Did you tell Stone?"

"I haven't finished the report yet. This only happened two days ago, Tom."

"I want to see the report, and Stone does too—soon."

Picking up Rainy a half-hour later, I was still in a murky frame of mind. For some reason, Don's news made me mad—but then, Don's stumbling, embarrassed reticence almost always made me mad.

Rainy was in a subdued mood herself and became even more subdued when I told her what I'd just learned.

"Like the carvings," she said. "There are an awful lot of loose heads on those shells. I spent half the night looking at them."

We fell silent as we drove through the manufacturing sector of town, which had become almost a ghost town that summer. Hitting the dirt of Highway 9, however, we found ourselves in traffic. Farm families from the other side of Arkansas—the eastern cotton delta—were cashing in what chips they could and heading west in rickety cars with possessions tied all over them. The wind was unusually quiet that day, and a thick tunnel of dust lay over the highway. We rolled up the windows but still coughed and choked. I had a handkerchief that I gave Rainy to tie around her nose and mouth, making her look like a bandit. We were both getting dirty fast. A few miles out of town going west, the land begins to lift and the trees to thin, as if exactly there—around Pocola, a mining town then nearly defunct—the forests end, the skies open up, and the great plains begin.

"Pocola!" Rainy said through the handkerchief, pointing at the sign.

I nodded, remembering "Pocola Mining Company" from Guessner's notes.

I stopped at a filling station that seemed to be all that remained of the town. Three furniture-burdened cars were parked at the station, and families sat around dejectedly beneath the scant shade of two nearly leafless trees. A mangy dog with bedslat ribs was racing around in a circle, ceaselessly barking—the running blues, probably gotten from drinking water contaminated by the little mountain of car batteries nearby.

The station attendant didn't hesitate when I asked him how to get to the Spiro Mound. He'd apparently directed others there. Just after a burned-out road joint, a couple of miles west, we were to turn right on Fort Coffee Road. We chugged back onto the dust-boiling highway with a full tank of gas and soon angled right down the unmarked road, where puddles of fine, dry silica powder nearly bogged us down as we approached the river.

The few houses along the road looked as if they belonged to blacks—tarpaper shacks with less junk around them than most Indian houses. Many of the Negroes who lived in eastern Oklahoma were the descendants of Indian slaves who had been declared members of a tribe by the Reconstruction government and had tribal land parceled out to them. Some of them still hung on: there wasn't any oil in LeFlore County, and coal ran only in small veins here and there, so mostly the land wasn't worth stealing.

Our first sight of the mound was five trucks parked at some distance from the road in a field. Behind them were three overlapping stairstepped hills, the largest a little over thirty feet high. The fields around the three-hill mound appeared to have been planted in cotton right up to the mound's base in previous years, but this season they'd been left to grow a thin scour of weeds. At some distance across the field were an old barn and a farmhouse with a shake roof that looked like it was about to fall in. A half-dozen visible tunnels were cut into the side of the mound, and surface pits surrounded it. When we pulled up, Rainy, covered top to bottom in a veil of dust, sat squinting at the sight, totally absorbed.

"Big enough for a temple mound all right," she breathed, taking down the handkerchief and opening the door.

We brushed ourselves off as we approached a camping tent near the larger of the three connected hills. A pack of red hounds came bounding toward us, barking. Pinned to the big tent was a mining permit for the Pocola Mining Company. In front was a big rough-made table covered with points, clubs, shells, pieces of fabric. Beside the table, lying on a cot, was a naked, partly mummified corpse with a cheap, gaudy sombrero thrown over its head. I stared at it—kneebones, gray skin, shrunken genitals.

A man crawled out of one of the mine holes and walked briskly toward us; I guessed he was in his midtwenties, although it was hard to tell through the grime.

"Do for ya?" he said.

I was taking in the scene, feeling a little disoriented, with the dogs still barking, circling, showing us their gums. Rainy spoke up: "I'd like to take a look at your goods here."

He chuckled. "Why sure. We're always lookin for buyers."

"What's that?" I said, indicating the corpse.

"Git on out of here!" he finally yelled at the dogs, and they slouched away. "That there is a genuine Indian mummy, mister. Fresh out of the ground. I'll let you have him for fifty dollars. Throw in the hat. You could sell that little fella to a museum for ten times that much."

"You should get him out of the sun," Rainy said pleasantly.

"Oh, he made it this long. Little sun won't hurt him."

"He'll rot," she said, still smiling.

A stab of suspicion went across the man's face, but he kept up the sales pitch. "Well, help yourself! Look around! We've got pearls, pipes, shells with carvin on em, arrowheads. We're just old country boys tryin to get a decent day's pay, but we've got the best. People been tellin us that. And don't go past that table."

"Mind if I ask you some questions?" I asked.

The salesmanly smile melted when I told him who I was and that I was looking for information about Lee Guessner.

"Lee who?" he said.

"Lee Guessner. He bought from you."

"The old boy from Fort Smith, you mean. Pointy-toe shoes, bow tie? He comes around here quite a lot."

"He won't be coming around anymore," I said.

"Why's that?"

"Somebody cut his head off."

"Do what?" he said dimly.

"Somebody killed him. It happened this week."

His smile now was a sickly parody, convincingly shocked-looking, and he turned heel without another word, went back to the tunnel entrance, and crawled inside.

"I think you scared him off," Rainy said.

From the table of artifacts I noticed a familiar smell, and it seemed to be coming most strongly from thin sheets of rusted metal that lay in a stack. "Take a sniff of that," I said to her. "Remind you of anything?"

She smelled the greenish plate, then touched it and tasted her fingers. "These are copper," she said.

"The sulfur smell is like Lee's house."

"It's copper sulfate. Copper rust." Her eyes played across the table. Two big wooden crates sat nearby stacked full of other items. She picked up a piece of fabric and laid it on the table. It was in several colors of black, brown, and yellow—richly beautiful even at a glance.

Rainy looked at me, her eyes wide, and said quietly, "This is a big find."

The digger squeezed out of the tunnel mouth, and another soon followed. A third man came around the mound and joined them; the three talked briefly, then came toward us. They were all completely dirt covered. One of them was a little older, fat, and walked like somebody belly-deep in cold water. Another had the short legs and big chest of an Irish track-layer. He took the lead— thick hands, eyes blinking beneath a dirty felt hat.

"Hep you?"

I started to introduce us, but he interrupted.

"You tell my brother somebody cut the man's head off?"

"Afraid so."

"When'd this happen?"

"Wednesday."

"We don't know much about him. He come here every few days, had his own jug of water. Paid cash. We didn't have nothin against him. Once he got too close to the mound, but after he learned the line, it wasn't no problem."

"What line?" I asked.

"Right where you're standin. That's it. Nobody goes beyond the tent."

Another man, wearing a pistol, ambled over from the mound, making four, all of them looking out from their dirt masks with wary eyes. And of course they couldn't stop looking at Rainy, who was gazing at the mound with a dreamy expression.

The man in charge adjusted the brim of his floppy hat and said, "Anythin else we can do for you?"

"I'd like to see inside that mound," Rainy said.

He gave her a tight, intentionally false smile and turned back to me. "We got a job to do here, mister."

There wasn't a chance that he'd respond to me or to Rainy unless he knew what her interest was, so I decided to take a chance.

"Your name is?"

"My name? McKenzie."

"Mr. McKenzie, Mrs. Davis here inherited Lee Guessner's collection of things that he bought from you. We're trying to find out what happened to that collection. That's why she's with me. We're trying to find out who else might be interested in these items."

"What did happen to them?"

"They disappeared from his house, we think stolen."

"Well now that's too bad." His eyebrows knitted slightly.

"All of your good work down the drain," Rainy added.

McKenzie openly bristled. The one with the pistol grinned with country-boy malice. Still, I had the impression, from the way they watched us, that Guessner's death really was news to them.

"Could you tell me who's been buying your artifacts?" I asked.

McKenzie laughed. "No offense, mister, but no. We been selling these here curios to a lot of people. Illinois, New York, I never ask names. They come from everywhere. We deal spot cash. Ain't got time for makin lists or keepin no credits."

"Was Lee Guessner the biggest buyer you had?"

"He was the most regular one. Wouldn't know if he bought the most."

A fifth man appeared on the crest of the tallest mound, holding a rifle. He didn't look as if he'd been digging, like the others.

"Mr. McKenzie," Rainy said, "do you own this property?"

He narrowed his eyes and went so still for a moment that he looked like a lifelike statue, despite the rivulets of sweat on his face. "I think that's my bidness. Now, if you two ain't here to buy, we'd appreciate you move on."

Rainy didn't seem to notice that she'd been put in her place. "I only wanted to offer to buy the property and save you all this hard labor. If that's out of the question, what would you take for the curios you've got out today?" She nodded toward the table.

"Which ones?"

"All of them," she said.

"A thousand dollars," McKenzie shot back, plainly angry at her.

The one with the pistol snickered. The fat one glanced toward the crest of the hill.

Rainy reached into one of the deep pockets of her shapeless dress and pulled out three loose C-notes. "I only have three hundred. Will that do?"

McKenzie and the others all looked at what she was holding out, their sneers melting.

"Add two more of them and you've got a deal."

"That's fine," she said breezily. "Please set these things aside. I'll be back to pick them up. I've already looked through them, by the way. I know exactly what's there. If anything's missing, the deal's off."

"Beg your pardon, ma'am, but are you sayin I'm not on the square?"

"No I'm not, Mr. McKenzie. But we don't know each other, do we?"

He hesitated over whether to be insulted and decided not to be. The others glanced at each other with nervous elation, as if they had a real sucker here.

As we were leaving I noticed that about half of the truck license plates were the black on yellow of Oklahoma—one from Tulsa County. The others were the white on red of Arkansas. I stopped at the farmhouse on the edge of the property. It had inside shutters, all closed, and no one came to the door when I knocked.

We were scudding back on Highway 9 when she asked me to stop. I pulled over where there were a couple of cottonwoods, wondering if she was sick to her stomach. She pushed open the door and just stood there for a minute, looking back in the general direction of the mound. I got out and asked across the hood if she was okay. She smiled at me with almost a look of tenderness. "Just getting my breath."

She walked over and sat against a barely living cottonwood tree.

I sat beside her, our backs toward the hot afternoon wind that was now picking up, coming up out of Texas, the plumes from occasional cars drifting away from us.

"It's like Egypt out here. Those men make me feel right at home."

"Be careful with them."

"I know all about diggers, Tom. Believe me, I have an advanced degree." Rainy raked at the sand with her fingertips. She squinted northward toward the mound.

"I should tell you the truth."

"The truth?"

"A place like that brings it up in me," she declared. "I said I wasn't an archaeologist, only a collector. That's not the truth. I was an archaeologist, whether I finished my degree or not. I was born to it. If I was born five hundred years ago, I'd have invented the word. And I had a rich English boy hanging about for nine years telling me that I wasn't an archaeologist and couldn't be an archaeologist. Funny the things one does."

She was quiet a moment, eyes locked into the past. "He started in quite early, but with maximum charm at first. All full of that carelessness and mockery women think signals protection. Rich and careless in a care-filled world, you know. I'd give a lot to have him back."

"Oh really?"

"Yes. So I could tell him that he failed to ruin my life."

"You're really on the outs with this dead man?"

"I didn't say I wanted him back to torture him, I'd just like to tell him something—" She gave me a quick, wicked smile—"then send him back to hell."

A couple of cars rattled by, and then there was just the sound of the wind.

"Why are we sitting in the dirt?"

Elbow on her knee, she pointed in the direction of the mound. "That's a major site. When the word gets out, they're going to be coming from all directions. The kilt I was looking at—if it's pre-Columbian, and I think it is, it's unique. It shouldn't have survived at all, much less in a floodplain. I was at that table, looking at the stuff, and I could hardly see it. My mind was racing. I was thinking that in the rest of my life, no matter what I do, I'll never see anything like this again. Not fresh out of the ground. And those men are tearing it to pieces."

"Did I hear you offer to buy the whole place?"

"Oh, you wave money to impress them. Get their attention, then show them you're not a fool: those are the first steps. You don't have to be very clever about it, you just start that way: flash money, do some bargaining. Never show them you're afraid. It's a dance."

We fell silent, and I noticed a strange feeling, almost a sense of intimacy with her, as if we'd known each other a long time. Maybe living so long with the idea of her mother made me imagine it, since I obviously knew little about Rainy. We sat quiet for a few moments longer with the sun blazing toward the horizon over our left shoulders, the wind blowing her dark hair across her cheeks.

Cylinder 18

On Saturday I made a trip to Poteau, Oklahoma, the LeFlore County seat, where I found the clerk at home and for a small fee got him to lend me his courthouse keys for the morning. I could have requested this information through the office, but routine paper had a way of gathering dust in Oklahoma county seats, whereas a couple of bucks opened doors immediately. The clerk didn't care whether I was working for a prosecutor or a coal company. He was a short fellow with a surly, suspicious twist to his mouth and eyes that remained cold as we talked. He took my two dollars, then had me "take a little walk" while he put the courthouse keys in his mailbox; I then came back and "borrowed" the keys. I had investigated a probate case here fourteen years before, and the clerk, a different man then, had used exactly the same little ceremony, almost the same words, for renting his keys on weekends.

The courthouse itself, gloomy, empty of all but mice and spiders on Saturday, was weathered, badly in need of paint outside and inside, its walls and floors tobacco stained, smelling of smoke and urine and sweeping compound and the accumulated dust of a thousand courthouse sorrows. A light wind whispered through the walls. The records weren't in the same places they'd been when I'd rummaged through them years before, but I tramped around and found what I could and took them to the courtroom, where one of the tables was near a window.

The Poteau courthouse was known for shifting arrangements and cabals and feuds among the local good old boys, who in this county included all skin colors except black. They bought and traded justice mostly outside court in diners, pool halls, lunchrooms. When Fort Smith lawyers went to Poteau, they came back talking about how disgusted they were by the corruption, the open-necked shirts and casual, "Indian" ways allowed by the judge there.

I found it amusing when a Fort Smith lawyer told me, with a straight face, that LeFlore County was corrupt because of Indian ways. It was true that Indian law was less concerned about guilt or innocence than with keeping things in balance. White law was more moralistic: you did a bad thing, part of the idea was to punish you, regardless of consequences. To Indians the idea was more practical: if you committed manslaughter in a drunken fight, say, either you paid a negotiated price to the dead man's family or your own family was responsible for delivering you to the killing tree at an appointed time. The price had to be paid, but there were sometimes alternatives. And it generally did get paid, or a feud could start that might last for years.

There were still a few killing trees in the '30s, and a few groups of Indians here and there who took care of their own legal problems, but only in those places where nothing was at stake for anybody else. Whatever problems there were in this courthouse, they sure didn't have anything to do with "Indian" law.

I slapped the records I'd found onto a table under a shaft of dust-swirling sunlight and hesitated, feeling a moment of uncertainty before the past—that sigh and slipping of the clutch.

Mineral-rights files showed that the Pocola Mining Company was an officially registered company in the state of Oklahoma, county of LeFlore, currently mining "Indian curios and other marketable items" on the property of Helen and James Craig of Spiro. Maps and titles gave me the basic history of the property. It was partly as I'd guessed: allotted to "Negro Choctaws" in 1905. In 1930, "Aunt Rachel Brown" had sold it to William Craig, who died within a year, bequeathing it to two grandchildren, Helen and James. Both were still minors, and their maternal grandfather, George Evans, was now their guardian.

Those were the basic facts. After refiling the records, I walked the keys back to the clerk's mailbox and went looking for an old Poteau acquaintance, Bill Hagglund. Bill had been making a living in LeFlore County as a self-declared lawyer since before statehood, and in my former job at the agency I had occasionally hired him to do title work on restricted lands.

I found him at Martha's Roadside Diner a little after noon, lingering with two cronies at a table spread with the remains of an impressive lunch—potato salad, fried chicken, biscuits, pinto beans, cucumber pickles. Hagglund had perfected the art of sitting around drinking coffee (whiskey-laced when he could afford it), making a modest living on gossip and conversation and bits of information from here and there. He was lazy and had a drinker's nose and gut but sparking cold blue eyes and a memory that matched them: he was a walking morgue of courthouse fact and gossip.

He saw that I was there to talk business and cleared his pals out with a glance. I ordered a cup of coffee and a sandwich from Martha, and before she'd given me a refill Hagglund had told me a few more details about the Craig property: over a year before, George Evans had been asked by the treasure hunters to approach the county judge to ask permission to lease it. A hearing was held, Hagglund recollected, before Christmas of 1933, and the lease was drawn up. The lease price was in the neighborhood of a hundred dollars for a two-year lease. One of the minors who actually owned the property was rumored to have tuberculosis.

Hagglund didn't know anything about the other hunters except that they weren't from this immediate area. He said he'd be glad to investigate them, but I resisted the offer. Hagglund was great for quick information, but on a retainer he'd string it out forever. Besides, what he couldn't find out between here and the courthouse, he wouldn't go looking for—which made me suspect that he already knew more.

"What are you working on?" he asked me, putting a toothpick in his mouth.

"Murder case," I told him. "A collector who was buying artifacts from the Spiro Mound. He was killed, and the stuff he'd been collecting was stolen. I've heard that Jim Mackey has some interest in the mound. You know anything about that?"

Hagglund's expression went from blank to evasive. He moved the toothpick to the other side of his mouth and said he wouldn't know for sure.

I asked it a different way: "Has he done any business here lately? Him or any of his people?"

He seemed to think for a minute, staring at his coffee cup, then he spoke in a lowered tone. "I'd have to check around."

"Bull shit, Hagglund."

He looked at me innocently.

"Nobody comes into this town without you finding out, especially not a bigshot like Jim Mackey."

"Yeah, and asking questions about his type can get touchy."

"I'll pay you right now for the asking you've already done."

He leaned back with that little lightening of the face that implied, okay, now we may be bargaining. He named his price the sly country way. "What I know ain't worth ten bucks."

"I'll pay you what it's worth."

He glanced toward the couple of other men in the shabby little diner and leaned toward me. "I wouldn't know about your Indian mound—I can't imagine why he'd give a damn about something like that—but Mr. Mackey owns property in this county that he's paying property taxes on, and he's doing some guardian business here."

"Guardian business?"

"Goddamnit, Tom, I ain't the one who told you this."

"Why would Jim Mackey be chasing guardianships in LeFlore County? Doesn't he have enough to do with his oil wells?"

"If all you have to do is establish a legal residence, pay the judge, and cash the checks—that ain't too much work," Hagglund said.

"He must have a big fish on the hook if he's going to all that trouble."

He glanced out the window. "Ever hear of Levi Colbert?"

"Levi Colbert . . . who lives in Tulsa?"

Hagglund nodded. "He moved to this county three years ago. Lives down south in the mountains. Mackey was his guardian in Tulsa County, and I don't know whether Colbert was trying to get away from him or what, but moving here didn't help him. Mackey stuck to him like bark to a tree. Followed him here and bought a big piece of property near Colbert's, like he was saying, I'm right with you, buddy."

"So Jim Mackey kept guardianship over Colbert by bribing the judge here?"

The toothpick went to the other side of his mouth as Bill looked out the window. "Way I heard it, Colbert tried to get a hearing in Tulsa County to be declared mentally competent. Of course Mackey had the judge in his pocket, and there wasn't no hearing. That could be why Colbert moved here. Maybe he hoped he could get declared fit here. But it never got to court."

"I wonder what that cost Mr. Mackey. Who's your county judge now—Spellman?"

"Randy Spellman," Bill said, letting out a little sigh as he said it. That little sigh was local sign language for: me and the son of a bitch don't get along, but he's a fact of life.

"So Judge Spellman is personally doing very well, considering the county has no revenue," I said, not even making it a question.

Bill stirred a little more sugar into his coffee and looked up at me from beneath his eyebrows. "You know how it works. He spreads it around just enough until nobody puts kerosene on his house."

"You making any money off this, Bill?"

He smiled. "Would I be talking to you if I was?"

"You'd think Jim Mackey would stick to his oil wells."

Hagglund leaned forward and raised his eyebrows at me. "Jim Mackey can drive around in any kind of limousine he wants to, and he can have a little army following him to keep everybody toeing his line, but Levi Colbert's got more mineral property than Jim Mackey ever thought about, bigshot or not. Some of it may be played out, yeah, but that old Indin ain't small time. And you know what a tricky business Mackey's in: he's sunk a lot of dry wells in the Seminole fields. He needs a good milk cow. You ever met Mackey?"

"Not really. I dealt with some of his lawyers when I worked at the agency. Never face to face."

"He's the type that'll do anything not to lose—a deal, a lease, game of cards, it don't matter. Only thing he hates worse than losing is admitting it. He'd follow that guardianship to hell if he had to. He figures that old Indin belongs to him."

"You say Mackey's paying property tax here?"

"That's the way they do it around here with guardianships. You want a guardianship, you pick your target, you have to be a taxpaying white man, and you pay the judge to get the incompetency ruling. I guess I don't have to tell you that."

"Does Mackey ever reside in this county?"

"Not that I know of. He rolls up in a train of sedans, does his business, rolls out. I imagine he's paying cash to the judge. Nobody knows exactly how much. There's considerable speculation about that."

"Do they keep records on Colbert's estate in the courthouse?"

"Not a chance. This ain't something you can rent the keys for, Tom."

"So you don't know anything else about the Indian mound business?"

"Sure don't. Nothing but what I told you."

I put a ten-dollar bill under the edge of Bill's plate and got general directions from him to Colbert's place. There was only one highway through that part of the mountains, so it shouldn't be hard to find.

"Keep this between you and me, Tom. I don't want to get any more crosswise of Judge Randy Spellman than I already am. And I sure don't want to get into it with Jim Mackey." He gave me a crooked smile. "And say hello to your boss, Mr. Pryor, for me. He used to own five coal mines around here. One of my Polish uncles died working for him. Keeled over with a goddamn shovel in his hand."

I grinned back at him. "You tell me that every time, Hagglund. It was his father who owned the mines."

"All the better: he never had to wash his hands. Watch out in them old outlaw hills, Tom. You can get yourself lost in the Winding Stair. I wouldn't go down there at night if I were you. I hear old Colbert's about half-crazy."

"What do you mean?"

"Oh, I don't know. You just hear rumors. I never laid eyes on the man, but I heard he's got some strange types living on his property."

Cylinder 19

Heavener was even more pitiful and dead than Poteau that Saturday afternoon. A couple of miles past town, I stopped in a one-pump station and topped off my gas tank and filled an extra water canister with rank-smelling well water. I opened the cowl and looked at both sides of the motor, making sure nothing was about to fall off. After paying the attendant, I walked into the road and stared toward the mountains hulking off to the south, reconsidering whether I wanted to try to find Colbert this late in the day. Against the last of the red sky, looking like a hunched-over animal with one claw, a farmer with his shucking peg was working his way across a field, looking for cobs to strip in a field of stunted corn. A broom of wind swept dust into my face.

The night was coming on, but I decided that if I went back to Fort Smith I wouldn't be able to sleep anyway, waiting to come back out here. I got into my car and drove on toward the mountains. The potholed dirt road was good for about fifteen miles an hour. It rose into scatter-rock hills that soon grew precipitous. I had traveled this road on a horse before it was called a "highway" on the map, and it hadn't changed much since then.

Hickory and chinquapin trees were already dropping shriveled-up dusty fists of leaves. The only signs of habitation were a few double tracks leading to what might have been, mostly in the past, little settlements. Unlike most other mountains, the Winding Stair run east-west, and the northern slopes are mixed hardwood, the southern slopes pine. They're rocky, in some places with great rivers of rocks, cliff-edged, and honeycombed by caves—a natural place for fugitives. Jesse James and the Daltons hung out there between jobs on a few occasions. Belle Starr lived just north of there for much of her criminal life and rode into these mountains when she had to hide out. The dirt is too poor for farming except in tiny pockets. The people who lived in these remote mountains were mostly outside the system, people without birth certificates— mixed-breeds, squatters, citizens of no country, living God knows how.

Levi Colbert had to be desperate to be living here.

He probably wouldn't remember me, but I'd met him once years ago. When the superintendent of the Indian Agency pro- moted me to the probate division, he had me tag along with one of the other lawyers to visit clients. At that time Colbert was living simply in a modest house south of Tulsa, smack in the middle of the Glenn Pool, surrounded by his oil properties. Years later a newspa- per called Colbert "the World's Richest Indian," and a picture monthly ran a three-page spread of ridiculous photographs of him sitting on the back of a seat in a convertible wearing a headdress (a Creek Indian might as well wear a fez as a headdress), standing with his arms crossed, legs spread, flashing a fake scowl, and so on, look- ing generally like a fool. I wondered at the time whether Colbert had changed since I'd met him (when he'd seemed modest and shy) or a photographer had just suckered him into playing the dim- witted rich Indian.

There was no question about the fact that Colbert really had been a lucky man in terms of money: as the only surviving member of a large family, he had inherited a big hunk of prime land in the Glenn Pool, one of the earliest oil fields, before mineral-rights buyers were running all over the state getting people to sell out. During the Tulsa boom, money from Colbert's royalties poured through probate at the agency; the man who had helped raise and educate him as a foster parent was a lawyer, apparently an honest man who kept him from being fleeced. Colbert went to school, even through a year or two of college. An honest foster parent, land in a lucky spot, mineral rights unsold, not having been bitten to death by the thousand horseflies that swarm an Indian with money—he really had been fortunate. But Jim Mackey getting him declared incompetent and latching onto him as guardian was definitely the other shoe falling.

With my puny headlamps I feared that I was going to get stuck there for the night, slapping mosquitoes, trying to sleep in a gritty, hard back seat. I carried a half-pint of bourbon in the glove box for such emergencies, but that wouldn't make it a fun time. I stopped the car and gazed into lengthening shadows. I didn't want to have to turn around and come back here the next day. This place reminded me of my own past, my own secrets, although, oddly, I didn't think about that until the darkness had fallen.

At age fifteen or sixteen I had ridden through these mountains on a plow horse in a blizzard, with ice-burdened trees exploding around me, and if I hadn't gone to sleep on the horse's back and fallen on the leeward side of the roadbed I'd have frozen to death in the bitter wind.

In the middle of the previous night, I had killed the principal of the Armstrong Academy orphanage and burned the orphanage to the ground. Although it had been self-defense, I would certainly have been charged with murder and hanged if they'd caught me. The principal of the orphanage—Reverend James Schoot of the Kentucky Presbyterian Missionary Church—deserved to die: he was what people now call a sexual pervert, a sadist, although at the time he was called a stern principal. He beat his pupils daily, sometimes the same boy five or six times in a day, for every excuse from failure to learn conjugations to impertinent posture. I had personally known at least a half-dozen who died from infections caused by his beatings. One boy was essentially beaten to death over a three-month period because he did not know English and was too frightened to learn it. The principal seemed to take particular pleasure in beating people who were already ill.

My subsequent nightmares were less about killing him than about burning the building. Forty boys were in it when I set the fire, and it was only by unlikely good fortune that they all got out. Instead of helping, or even making sure they did escape, I stole one of the plow horses from the barn and fled the place. I knew they were awake because I heard them yelling, but still I made no effort to help. It didn't occur to me to help. It did not even cross my mind. In one mindless moment of terror, I could have caused more harm than the principal had caused in his whole wretched life. In the confusion of the moment, and of the days following, I did not clearly remember setting the fire. It took me weeks to fully realize what I had done.

Three people had known that I killed the principal of the Armstrong orphanage, including Rainy's mother, Samantha King, and in 1934 they were all dead. By then, few in Fort Smith had even heard of the Armstrong Academy (ninety miles away in nowhere, Indian Territory), yet I occasionally got the feeling that a rumor of my crime had survived, ambling along after me through the years like a mangy dog. I particularly had that feeling at times with regard to Manny Stone.

My progress along the road was slowed by years of unrepaired washouts. I concentrated on the little tunnel of light, avoiding the rock-strewn ruts. Over the racket of my Ford I heard the rising and falling of cicadas. Bumping through a dry low-water crossing and maneuvering around a switchback, I saw a man materialize out of a shadowy place in the road, squarish, broad backed, wearing denims. His appearance was so sudden that I braked to a halt to see where he'd come from. There was a rocky outcrop, and I guessed that he had hopped down from it. Now he was walking in the middle of the road away from me, and when I got close behind him he didn't turn around and didn't seem to hear me. I blew the horn, and he moved just enough for me to drive alongside him. I said hello and asked if he happened to know where Levi Colbert lived.

He stopped walking but remained sideways to me, looking down, and said something I couldn't hear. He seemed disinclined to speak more loudly, so I turned off my motor to the sudden silence of hot, powdery night woods.

He slowly turned his head toward me, looking in the direction of my face. His left eye was whited, and there was an erupted vertical scar down his cheek. He had long hair in a ponytail with a piece of hair in front tied off and going down his forehead. He gave off a slight perfume that I couldn't identify but assumed was some kind of liquor, and his hand didn't stray far from his knife. Something about him beyond the obvious fact that he was a knife fighter made me uneasy. I felt as if I'd met him before. He had that look of someone living according to the old ways, his eyes glazed over almost as if by the onset of cataracts. When I was a hopeful young lawyer, knocking on doors, out to save my corner of the world, I'd sometimes been met by eyes like his, aware of me but only as a thing from the outside to be dealt with, a force, whether I brought good news or bad.

"I'm looking for Levi Colbert," I repeated.

"What you want?"

"I just want to talk to Mr. Colbert. He knows me."

"Better go back." His voice had a peculiar timbre to it, almost an echo.

"Colbert does live around here, doesn't he?"

His expression went completely blank, his black eyes fixed just below mine and his body quite still.

I told him thanks anyway, hit the starter button, and watched him in the mirror as I pulled away. He didn't hurry after me, but at the pace I had to drive, I could see him for a while walking along behind, shadowing me until there was a brief stretch of straight road.

Upward through the dark hills, I had gone perhaps four miles farther, squinting into the aura of my headlamps, when I went around a curve and suddenly there, to my astonishment, running alongside the car with his head practically sticking in the window, was another man waving what at first glance looked like a huge pistol. Instinctively I put on the gas. I'd gotten past him when something went over me that exploded ahead in a ball of fire. I was well acquainted with signal guns from the war, but it happened so fast that at first I felt only the rage of being shot at, the shocked anger at incoming fire. In the mirror I saw another signal, this one shot straight into the air.

In less than two minutes, car lights were coming down the hill toward me, barreling around the switchbacks, and without even thinking about it I took an old two-track lane off to the right, getting off the road, where I killed my lights and motor and sat for a moment with my heart pounding. There was enough moonlight for me to feel my way a couple hundred feet away from the road. I heard the car going by, slowly, as if trolling for me. I got out quietly and stood there for a minute, uncertain of what to do. To the south, beyond a hill, the sky glowed almost as if there was a forest fire, and I could hear what sounded like diesel motors.

I walked into a run-off bottom and bushwhacked up the hill through the strangely short trees pruned by mist and freezing rain, eventually finding a perch on a flattened hilltop boulder. The next hill was about the same elevation as this one, several hundred yards away. Along its eastern slope was a mostly cleared space with a bunch of small fires, apparently campfires, illuminating what appeared to be round-shaped houses made of wood. The sound of a baby crying occasionally drifted across the valley, and I could smell human waste. Unable to see the people clearly, I counted fires—twenty-three of them. Two heavy-equipment trailers were parked at the bottom of the hill, and up a driveway, behind a house, two bulldozers were working under headlights.

The house, just under the crest of the hill, was surrounded at regular intervals by blazing oil smudgepots set about twenty feet apart. It was a clapboard bungalow-sized building with what looked like red shutters, a broad front porch, and designs on its outer walls. I watched the bulldozers, trying to guess what they were doing. All I could see was the outline of a hill of rocky dirt that they seemed to be steadily adding to.

The scene made no sense to me.

A car crunched up the driveway, with a couple of men riding on the rear bumper, and when it stopped several more piled out. Other people drifted up the hill from the campsites and began to collect in front of the house, and someone emerged from it. I couldn't tell much about him except that he seemed to be wearing a long, dark-colored coat or robe. The people drew nearer, lighted by the smudgepots. I saw him raise his arms, and I caught a trace of his voice on the slight evening breeze. He seemed to be delivering a speech to them.

I was about to move closer when I heard a shattering directly behind me, then a bunch of crashes and shouting, and I gave up watching and picked my way down the hill. Heart catapulting in my chest, I squatted behind a boulder and watched through the brush as a pack of men—shadows to me—tore my car to pieces, grunting, crashing, as fierce as dogs on a kill, smashing the car's windows with rocks, slashing tires, tearing hoses out of the motor. When one of them tore a headlight off the hood, I decided it was time for me to get out of there.

I backed out and circled down the hill to the road, where a car sat idling—a convertible with a dark form standing beside it. I found a heavy, weather-hardened stick and walked straight for him and was probably lucky that he was leaning over the back seat picking something up when I approached him. When he turned I was already swinging and hit him on the side of the head with enough force to knock him off the road. I got into the car, rammed it into first, and took off.

Cylinder 20

I'd had plenty of daydreams about trading my Ford for something better, but none of them had gotten quite this imaginative, with a pack of madmen tearing the old car to pieces and me clubbing somebody and driving away in a four-door touring Cabriolet Chevy with a straight eight and a winged ornament on the radiator cap. Pitching back and forth between ruts, I steered with the old ambulance-driving abandon but was beginning to get the creeping sense that the situation was driving me, as if this big Chevy convertible had picked me up and was taking me wherever it wanted me to go. I kept running what I'd seen through my mind but couldn't make sense of it. The one clear image was the knife fighter's face, seen in the reflections of my lights; the rest were only distant figures, shadows. But bulldozers working at night? The fires had made it look vaguely like a Klan meeting, but there wouldn't be any Klan meetings out here. It was too far from anything.

Instead of going home, I found myself pushing straight north toward Muskogee, where I wanted to take a look at the Indian Agency records on Colbert, but after sixty or seventy miles the Chevy was running out of gas, and there were no stations. In Braggs I found a closed station and pulled around back to wait out the night. Too jumpy to sleep, I felt around the car and discovered a bottle of sugar jack—cheap, fast, bad whiskey—to wash the taste of silica out of my mouth. I walked around the car a couple of times, looking it over. It had no license plates. After stretching my legs and taking a few slugs, I settled into a corner of the seat and tried to rest. I found myself thinking, and then dreaming, of Rainy. The dream was an exact recounting of what she had done at Guessner's cabin: walking out of the lake naked, straight toward me. . . .

I woke up with sun on my face, thirsty, dirty, fuzz brained, my mouth feeling like a vent out of hell. Eventually I located the station attendant at his house. Through the open doorway I could see a pile of quilts gray as a rat's belly and walls papered with newspapers. Tin signs were tacked up to cover holes in the siding. He stood in his dirt-bare front yard, with his hair still glued by sleep to one side of his head, scratching himself, hemming and hawing about blue laws until I overcame his moral qualms about pumping gas on Sunday by giving him a fifty-cent tip. With a full tank, a hot Coke, and a candy bar, I got on the road.

Sometime before nine o'clock I ascended the hill to the agency, hoping that nobody'd be there today, but a bicycle leaned against the front stairs and a shiny new black Plymouth was parked in the lot. The bicycle belonged to Peely, the old man who cleaned the building. I parked near the solid rock building under one of the oaks: it was a well shaded and generally breezy yard—one thing about working at the agency that I missed. A big camp pot still sat beneath one of those great oaks, remnant of days when people actually came here in numbers and had to be fed. I went straight for the stand pipe, washed my arms and face, and drank about a quart of water.

Peely had left the door open, and when I walked in he wagged his hand at me from the other end of the broad hallway. "Wet floor, watch out!" Peely had looked and acted old when I first went to work for the agency, and now he really was old. He complained constantly of ill health but seldom missed a day of work. If you told him he was looking good, it greatly irritated him. Glancing at me down the quiet hall, he showed no more surprise than if we'd last seen each other a day or two rather than ten years ago.

"Still working on Sunday morning, Peely? How you doing?"

"I feel like shit," he said, continuing his mopping.

"You still riding that old bicycle?"

"Yeah, and still walkin on the same damn legs too, and neither one workin right."

"Is the probate office in the same place it used to be?"

"I take care of the cleanin," he grumbled. "Don't know about the offices."

I walked up the wide stairs and opened the door of my old office. There, hunched over a desk, was Dale Cotton, the man quoted in the *Sallisaw Chieftain* as saying that Tom Freshour was a radical who'd been fired from the agency. When he looked up, he seemed confused. He had lost most of his hair since I'd last seen him.

Dale and I went way back. We had been hired at about the same time—both of us young bloods with new law degrees who should have liked each other but decidedly didn't. Dale had a guarded, intentional manner even in casual encounters. He always seemed to be deciding how to act, modulating his voice and chuckling and smiling with his superiors and acting arrogant toward people he considered beneath him. He generally favored guardians and mineral interests against rightsholders. How he had kept his job through several superintendents I didn't know, since there'd been a couple of them who were serious—or at least intended to be— about enforcing the law.

I dispatched the friendly greeting and told him I was here to see if I could find out something about Levi Colbert's guardian.

He looked as stunned as if a talking catfish had appeared in front of him. Maybe it was my windburned, reddened eyes, but I'd definitely caught him off guard.

"Can you tell me who Colbert's lawyer is here?"

He was still trying to get me in focus.

"What are you . . . ? What does this concern?"

He shut the file he had been reading and tried to appear only mildly surprised, but his face was slowly flushing from the neck up, like a boy caught elbow deep in the cookie jar. I figured that my only chance of getting anything out of him was to calm him down. I told him that it had nothing to do with agency business, that it was a case I was working on, a murder in Fort Smith. Colbert's guardian might have some information about the dead man.

"If you have questions about agency clients, you can ask through the proper channels during regular hours. It's out of order for you to come here on Sunday. I'm locking the office now."

He stood up and collected the file he'd been reading and stuck it under his arm. Dale would probably act this way whether he had any answers to my questions or not, but he seemed awfully anxious to leave.

I leaned against the door jamb and crossed my arms. "By the way, Dale, I read your comments about me in the *Sallisaw Chieftain*."

"I had nothing to do with that," he said. "I only told them that you no longer worked here. They made up that entire statement."

"Fair enough. The lawyer who paid for the article lost in court anyway, so no harm done. Why don't you write them a letter setting that straight?"

He looked at me suspiciously, and I could see the gears clicking in his head. He would never say yes to that, I realized, even if he were telling the truth. Dale seldom did anything except for immediate self-gain. He smirked at me and said in a falsely confidential tone, "Why did you come here on a day when the agency is closed?"

"It's a murder investigation, Dale. And I'm not asking for secret information."

"I'm taking my family to church, if you don't mind." He pushed against me to get to the door, and I pushed him back into the room. Anger usually causes a funny thing in my head. An observer pops up and watches the situation, takes notes, makes little comments: I can be very angry, and this little observer is sitting there almost laughing at the whole situation. I sometimes worry that he won't be there, that he'll be otherwise occupied and leave me to become the anger, the walking blackout of rage, the thing that gets you into trouble—I know about that too.

He was with me now, although I definitely was mad. Dale Cotton, with eyes going this way and that, tried to get around me again. "Get out of my way! I'm calling the police!"

I pushed him back against the table. "Maybe you can tell me why Levi Colbert is living in the mountains and what's going on down there."

When he came up again and pushed against me, I snatched the folder from under his arm. He started swinging like a boy who hasn't learned to fight yet, hitting only my forearms, then he gave that up and ran to a telephone.

When I got to the bottom of the stairs he had changed his mind about making the telephone call and came clattering down after me, following me to the car. "That is agency business! You are stealing government records! You will go to jail for that. I'm calling the FBI."

"Do that, Dale."

Walking close beside me, breathing down my neck, he said, "Look, look, what information are you trying to find out?"

"Who's his agency lawyer?"

"I am."

"Who's his guardian? Is it Jim Mackey?"

"That's right. He has a good relationship with his guardian. There have been no complaints. None whatsoever. It's a model case. Now give me back my file."

I got into the Chevrolet and put the folder under my right thigh, and Dale started to look truly desperate. For a moment he seemed to be thinking about taking a swing at my head, but instead he said breathlessly, "Wait a minute, wait a minute. . . ."

I started the car. "As soon as you really want to talk about this, let me know."

When I revved the engine it looked as if his eyes would pop out of his skull. "What else do you want to know?" he wheedled.

"Why's he living in the mountains?"

"He wanted to live there. He can live wherever he wants. It was his choice. Tulsa . . . Tulsa got too big for him. He believes that he can help people. Poor people. He's building some sort of shelter for them. He buys bulk foods. That's all I know. . . ."

"He had to move to the Winding Stair Mountains to give out food? Come on, Dale. Was he trying to get away from his guardian?"

"Look, I said they get along well." Dale was leaning on my door, anxiously eyeing the folder, calculating whether he could snatch it back.

I gunned the engine and pulled away, calling back to him, "I'll send this back to you as soon as you get that retraction printed."

I made the mistake of stopping by the office after I got back to town. It was Sunday afternoon, and to my astonishment both Mel and Bernie were there. Mel's 'lo was decidedly unsunny. Her electric typewriter was broken, and Bernie appeared to be in some kind of frenzy of looking at files, having her find things and bring them to his desk; he wandered out of his office as if in a daze, hair disheveled, tie askew, unshaven, and gave me a vague hello, then disappeared back inside. Mel looked at his door with distaste and up and down me with something of the same.

"You been out birdwatching or something?"

I told her I'd been doing some investigating in Oklahoma, leaving it at that, and asked why they were here on Sunday afternoon.

"You should probably ask Bernie that question," she said with forced reserve. "He seems to want to find out something about the sheriff."

"Something about the sheriff?"

"That's what I said." She put her palms on the typewriter as if she intended to push it off her desk.

"What's wrong with your typewr—?"

"I don't know what's wrong with it, but I hate electric type-writers. If I'm going to be sitting here Sunday afternoon, at least I'd like to get something done."

This was the third time that Mel's remarkably expensive type-writer had broken, and its problems were prone to the dramatic: the electric motor had caught fire one afternoon, and Barbara Jean Killen, first-floor secretary, visiting the office for a smoke, had come to the rescue by dousing it with a Nu-Grape soda.

Mel stretched out her fingers and asked quietly, "Have you heard about the coroner's report on the judge's dead friend?"

"I talked to Don on the phone. He told me the details."

She reached into her top drawer and handed me the three-page report, making a face at it. "Who'd do a thing like that?"

While scanning it, I cocked my head toward Bernie's office. "Has he seen it?"

She shook her head. "It's your case. We've been having enough confusion around here, thank you."

"So what does the typewriter do?" I asked, still glancing over the coroner's report.

She turned on the motor, which sounded as if it was running at two or three times the normal speed, hit a key, and the carriage return threw so hard that the typewriter jumped three inches across her desk. She stood up and sighed.

Bernie appeared again with an unlit cigarette hanging out the side of his mouth. He looked disapprovingly at the typewriter and at both of us. Mel said, "I'm taking this to the dealer's house and get a real typewriter so maybe I can get something done next week. I'll be back."

"This country has gone to hell," Bernie announced, as if he hadn't heard her, and walked back into his office.

I went to his open doorway, still carrying the coroner's report. "What's going on?"

"Those men out there, standing around . . . more of them every day. Half the cars going across the bridge look like furniture stores. A weird thing happened last night: I had four different parties knocking on my door asking for handouts. Two of them were women carrying babies."

He flopped down into his chair and lit his cigarette. Files were stacked all over his desk.

"In the past we've only had a couple of people, and now I get four in a single night."

"Maybe your house usually scares people who're broke. I get four or five a week."

He squinted at me through a cloud of smoke. "I thought about it. I lay awake thinking about it. The sheriff's been patrolling our street. Somebody's been paying him to keep people off Free Ferry."

"It wouldn't surprise me. A lot of your neighbors have trespassers-will-be-prosecuted signs up."

"This is the prosecutor's office," he said, widening his eyes. "Have you ever prosecuted anybody for asking for a handout?"

"Municipal has slapped a few vags, but they really have to ask for it."

"I don't think they ought to be prosecuted," Bernie said. "The poor shits are just trying to stay alive."

I held up a hand. "I haven't prosecuted any vagrants, except the ones who get caught burglarizing. Even in municipal, you've got to wave a knife in somebody's face or set up a tent in their front yard to get charged."

"Well, they ought not go to jail just because they're hungry!" he said hotly.

"If you drive past the police entrance at the courthouse right now, you'll see twenty people standing around asking to be put into jail overnight so they can get a couple of meals. They're trying to break into jail, Bernie."

He exhaled a cloud of smoke. "Why did four different people come to my house in one evening?"

"I don't know. Law of averages?"

"The sheriff stopped patrolling. Maybe he even sent people to my house."

"Ask him to start patrolling again."

Bernie looked at me in disbelief. "I hear that he takes people to the county line and beats them to within an inch of their lives—that he's even killed several."

I didn't respond. He was trying to draw me in. "I hear that he's been involved in the Klan. We haven't had much Klan stuff in this county, but we're going to. I'm telling you, Tom, we're going to."

"I wouldn't doubt it," I said.

"I've been looking at our case files, and the sheriff never helps even in routine cases. We're county prosecutors, and the county sheriff never cooperates? He doesn't help with witnesses?"

I resisted mentioning that Bernie didn't either.

"He's a goddamned racketeer. He needs to be taken out of office." Bernie glanced away from me. "I also think that Manny's dead collector is a waste of time. He was Manny's friend, and it's Manny's little hobby, but that doesn't mean we should throw out everything else and hop to it. It isn't the judge's business to tell the prosecutor what to do."

Bernie was half-right, but he was also telling me to not do what the judge had clearly assigned me to do. Also, suddenly, inexplicably, he was trying to butt in and tell me what to do. Too suddenly. I had heard stories of men losing interest in their jobs at Bernie's age, but he was doing the opposite. Either that or launching into one of his one-day enthusiasms.

"Stone told me to investigate," I said. "You were there. The only thing I threw out was my vacation. If you don't want me to investigate, you and the judge work it out. I can tell you, though, that somebody will have to do it."

"It's Oklahoma business. That man lived across the state line. All of his interests were across the line. It's a matter of speculation whether he even was killed in this county."

"He was," I said.

"How do you know that?"

I reached over and dropped the coroner's report onto his desk. "Either he was killed in this county or his truck was driven across the line with him splattered all over the cab."

"What do you mean?" Bernie crushed out his cigarette.

"Read the report." I walked out of the office and took the stairs.

Bernie and I seldom talked this way, and I was surprised at the sudden lightness of my mood.

Outside, Mel had just gotten into her car, and I walked over. She squinted at me in the sunlight. "What are you so happy about?"

"I'm not happy. Bernie and I just had a small disagreement."

Mel's face broke into an expression of agony or agonized relief, I couldn't tell which. "Tom, he's never been in the office before for more than a few minutes. Now he's waiting for me on the telephone when I come home from church. 'Can you work today?' he says. I thought something terrible had happened, so I come here and he's like the ancient mariner, off on this jag about the sheriff. He keeps wandering in and out asking me strange questions. I don't know what's going on."

I leaned in her window, and the metal was so hot I pulled back. "He's just finding out about some things, and it's bothering him."

She gave me a tight smile. "He's a decent boss, Tom. He really is. He's not an ass-pincher. He's really very decent. But he's just so . . . so disorganized." She blushed as if she'd called him a son of a bitch.

"I know," I said. "I know."

"He wanders out of his office looking like last year's bird's nest and asks me how hungry I think the men on the street are. I'm typing a court form and he asks me whether I think the New Deal will ever get to this area. When I start to answer him, he interrupts and starts talking about how he's missing his family. This is Sunday, Tom. I want to be sitting under a fan reading a magazine. I'm sorry. But I do not want to be sitting up there listening to how he misses his family!" She glanced around anxiously, still blushing. Mel seldom complained, and it embarrassed her to do it.

"Stone asked him to handle the office while I'm working on this thing," I said. "He's just doing what the judge told him to do."

"He's not handling the office. He's turning it upside down. And you know the worst thing about it?" Her eyes widened.

"What's that, Mel?"

"He's right. The sheriff is crooked. He's out for his own good and nobody else's. I just don't see how Bernie can handle this."

"He is the duly elected prosecutor, Mel. And he is the person who hired us."

She stepped on her starter. "I just wish his wife would come back to town and comb his hair."

"Drive carefully, Mel."

Cylinder 21

I went home intending to study the folder that Dale Cotton had so desperately wanted me not to read but instead fell into a stupefied and rather long nap filled with wild dreams. Later that afternoon I was sitting in my bathtub with the folder when I had a severe craving for a gin and tonic. Gin and tonic is one of those things that on certain occasions can hit the bull's-eye, and I got out of my bath and, dripping all over my kitchen, made a particularly fine example of one. Nero enjoyed no greater pleasure. In the relative cool of early evening, I sat on my front porch, my new Chevy parked in the driveway nearby, listening to the Metropolitan Opera with Milton Cross and making another pass at the folder. It contained only two sheets of paper, not official forms but working sheets jammed with what appeared to be lot numbers followed by dollar amounts.

There were 313 lot numbers in all, suggesting that if they were the mineral property of a single client (many of them appeared to be contiguous) they probably belonged to the very man I had gone there to find out about, Levi Colbert, which might explain why Dale was so astonished by my questions. I'd caught him in the act. The two sheets were jammed with numbers. Initially I thought that they were notes of oil-lease amounts, but the dollar figures appeared too low for any ordinary leasing periods. More likely it could be a list of kickback amounts paid by lessors to Dale himself that he had dropped by to fondle on the sabbath morn. If his desperation was any measure, that was probably the story. The amounts varied, suggesting that they were based on well production, and none was huge, only twenty dollars here, thirty there, but multiplied by 313, the total was at least three times Dale's annual salary.

After being informed by Ry Krisp that I could eat their product, lose weight, and achieve new fame and by General Electric that a man's castle was a woman's factory, I wandered in and turned off the radio. My neighborhood was quiet, and when a sheriff's car went by I watched through the front window—two deputies rubbernecking my house all the way by. They were taking special note of my new Chevy. At moments like this I shared Bernie's feelings about the sheriff. I knew more about Sheriff Seabolt's games than Bernie did because I was in town hearing things, but I had no clear grasp of why he sent his deputies around like a private squad of watchers, spies, and mischief makers.

I called the Goldman Hotel in search of Rainy, who'd never been quite off my mind. She had moved out of the hotel and left a message for me to come to the lake cabin.

It was twilight when I drove alongside the cool lake and up her driveway. Parked in front was a well-dusted sedan delivery truck. Rainy's luggage was sitting on the porch. The front door and windows opening toward the lake were all thrown open, and a little breeze was blowing through. She had nailed back her wall- and floorboards.

Standing at one of two large tables covered with artifacts, she glanced up, gave me a brief smile. She was sopping wet, barefoot, wearing short pants and a man's low-necked T-shirt with nothing under it.

"Evening. Been swimming?"

"I just came back up. As you see, I wore clothes this time."

"Right," I said, trying not to stare at her radiant smile or the wet T-shirt.

"I went to Spiro yesterday. Haven't slept since."

"How'd you get out there?"

"The truck I inherited."

"You don't look like somebody who stayed up all night."

"Too excited to sleep. I'm going to try tonight—which means wine. You want a glass?"

"You don't have electricity here, do you?"

"It doesn't matter. I'm used to working by lamplight."

We were soon drinking red wine from coffee cups. I asked her if the diggers had given her any trouble.

"Not after I handed Mr. McKenzie five hundred dollars. They took a real fancy to me." She leaned over the table and set one of the shells in front of me. "Look at this."

I was having trouble not looking at her. I couldn't imagine her being unaware of the effect of her appearance—her whole appearance, including the water dripping out of her black hair and almost transparent wet T-shirt. It made me feel slightly grouchy, like a man being teased. But after all, I had just shown up here without warning.

"Look inside that pot," she said, pointing at an unpainted clay pot.

I made an effort, but the lamplight wasn't bright enough to really see inside it.

"It's got about a dozen human hands in it, all broken up. Apparently most of the bones in the mound are like that, from corpses that have been taken apart—disarticulated, they call it. A lot of the other bones in the mound, from hundreds of bodies, are in groupings—skulls, legbones, hands."

"Why did they do that?"

"Do what?"

"Take the skeletons apart."

She took a drink of wine and stared for a moment at the flame from the wick. "I've heard a lot of late-night theorizing about burial methods. . . . They say that organized burial marks the beginning of civilization. Find a Neolithic corpse who's been folded up a

certain way; that implies people were appreciating each other's social roles and so forth. But then in some of the more developed civilizations, the wealthier, more powerful people started spending a
great deal on burial. Almost beyond belief in some places." She
took a cigarette from a partly crumpled pack and lit it with a
kitchen match.

"Why's that?"

She tossed her head as if shrugging. "Holding on to this life.
Trying to project this life into the next. The Egyptians had a good
time when they could, you know. If their paintings are any sign,
they drank a lot of beer. They loved the world, the pleasures of the
flesh. The rich ones had parties, big feasts, recounted on the walls
of tombs. They made themselves alluring. And in death they tried
to be alluring too. The outer appearance was everything. They pre-
served the viscera for later use—in jars packed with preserving salt.
They left the heart inside the corpse so it could be weighed for
righteousness. It invited the gods to think well of them."

She looked at the shells in front of her, smoke weaving up from
the glowing tip of her cigarette.

"The pyramids are an extreme, or they seem to be because they
lasted so well. Slaves and servants and whole treasuries of gold and
goods and artwork—all buried forever, sealed inside. I think there
are reasons beyond fantasies of an afterlife. I never thought it was
only that."

I cleared my throat. "What kind of reasons?"

"Monuments affirm the order of things, the authority of those
in power. That's part of it, I guess."

She moved one of the shells with a finger, squinting at it. A
slight breeze moving across from the window brushed smoke
through her hair. "I think people need to try to make contact with
the unknown. Maybe it helps make us human. We wonder about
what happens to us when we die. How we got here in the first
place—to me, that's always seemed even stranger. The ground of
being—is it God, your tribe, the interaction of divine mathematics,
sheer chance?

"I had a philosophy professor my last year at Chicago. He was a wonderful old relic of a man. Even his insults were interesting. There was a boy in class—a dipso, frat-boy-smug type, thought he owned the world; Smith was his name. This professor once asked him a question that he naturally couldn't answer. He gave some reply that he thought was ironic, and the professor said, 'Mr. Smith, I would like for you to try to answer a more fundamental philosophical question for the class.' And he fixed him with a look and said, 'What overcame the enormous unlikelihood of your being a witness to the world?'"

I laughed.

"Poor Smith probably went home and poured a stiff bourbon. But the starting point—how you got here, what's out there—if you absolutely refuse to think about such things, I believe the night closes in around you. You get nervous and afraid."

"Get that way thinking too much about them."

She smiled a little wistfully, still looking at the shell. "Are you a confirmed pragmatist?"

"I think about those things sometimes. I thought about them when my wife died. But I get impatient when I don't seem to get any closer to an answer."

"Yeah," she said. "But there are ways."

"How's that?"

She looked up at me now. "Oh, lots of different ways. You just haven't tried them all. Pure contemplation, pure abandonment, sacrifice. Build a mound, build a pyramid, a cathedral. Sometimes it takes hundreds of years and thousands of lifetimes of work. You sacrifice almost uncountable human effort and talent to build such a place. You build a place impressive enough to invite it in."

"It?"

"The unknown. You paint the walls, etch the shells, make statues, build shapes that are your attempt to know why the seasons are, where fire came from, who your people are, what matters the most, what happens after death. And you give it up, sacrifice it, put it in the earth. You're trying to intersect with the big secrets, align yourself with them. Looked at a certain way, it's not superstition but open-mindedness, venturing to know."

I realized I was frankly staring at her. Anybody would have stared at her—sitting there, wet, with her green eyes glowing in the lamplight. And talking as she was. She leaned over the table and pushed a shell in front of me. "But you have to start with the details. Look at that. What do you see?"

The carving on the shell was complicated and partly weathered away. "You tell me," I said, wanting just to hear her talk. "You're the archaeologist."

She dropped the cigarette into a tin can. "A man after my own heart. But come on, what do you see?"

"A bird with a snake's body."

"Right," she said. "A compound animal. Keep going."

"I see a bird's wings and feet but a snake's body and head, and I see a second one going in the opposite direction, wound up next to the first."

"Bipolarity," she said. "There is a lot of bipolarity in these images. A lot of symmetry. We've got eleven animals on these pieces, and all but one of them—a spider on one of the gorgets—is a compound animal: either a feathered snake or a cat-bird-snake or a human dragon or something else. All of the animals represented, including falcons, are predators. The clothes are ceremonial. In fact, almost everything here is ceremonial. Lee told me that, and I didn't believe him. He also told me that the mound treasures were all made from materials that came from elsewhere, far away. I don't really know enough about that yet, but I get a feeling he was right—it's all rare, expensive."

She had a complexion to go with the eyes and black hair. A dark Irish look. A drop of water plopped onto the table from her nose.

I took a large slug of wine.

"Anyway, you're learning the next lesson," she said. "You start by describing. What you see and nothing else. You try to forget all the conclusions that you can't help leaping to. People interested in archaeology used to whip up big theories about the mound builders, about how they couldn't possibly have been built by mere Indians since Indians were so dirty and unintelligent. They had to have been built by one of the lost tribes of Israel or some lost Caucasian race from Atlantis or someplace. For at least a hundred years they bandied that idea around. A lot of books were written about it—some of the all-time best-sellers of the century."

As I sat there in the latticeback chair watching and listening to her, I had the sudden urge to bolt from the place. I had no idea why—whether it was her physical presence, the way she had cohered to me as a certain kind of woman, the fear of falling into some kind of hopeless lust for her—but at that instant I wanted to run out the door. Glancing toward the open front door, seeing the convertible parked outside, I stayed quiet and remained still until my mind unclenched.

Dry mouthed, I sipped at the wine. "So you just describe the stuff. You don't come to any conclusions."

"Oh, you can't help but do that. I just try to remember that I'll probably change my mind about a lot of it."

"And what about these people? What conclusions do you come to?"

She frowned at the stuff on the table. "They were warriors and probably imperialists. They thought a lot about death. They had amazingly wide trading relationships, a well-developed culture with a strong mystical element, and what amounted to almost a written language."

Cylinder 22

"What's wrong?" she asked.

We'd been talking for over an hour at that point. Mostly I'd been listening. Then a conversational lull.

"Nothing's wrong. Why?"

"You seem distracted."

"I'm distracted by you," I admitted.

"By me?" she raised her eyebrows.

"Oh come on," I said.

For a moment she looked as if she actually was unsure of what I meant. "Do you mean you're attracted to me?"

"It's hard not to be," I said.

"Why so grudging?" she said. "I've flirted with you outrageously."

This remark hung in the air for a moment; then she added, "I'm a physically healthy woman. You wouldn't have red blood in your veins if you weren't at least a little attracted to me."

I was swallowing a drink of wine when she said this and about choked on it. "Okay, look, I'm not a masher. . . ."

She stood up and walked around the table, pushed back the shell at the edge of it, and sat in front of me on the edge of the table.

"You can look at me. Go ahead. There's no reason to be afraid of doing that."

My mind was tumbling. The honest thing to do would have been to admit that I had known her mother. She would understand my reticence and probably feel the same way. Which would have its advantages and disadvantages.

"So," she said.

"So?"

"Go ahead, you can look." She proceeded at this point to take off the T-shirt. "Why don't you take yours off?" she said.

I thought about it one more moment and decided that it wouldn't be the worst thing in the world. It had been a long time ago. Her mother was dead. I had been only fifteen. Maybe fourteen. Her mother had been twentysomething. Et cetera. I stood up and stepped toward her; she spread her legs, and I kissed her. After a couple of minutes of heavy petting I told her that we couldn't carry on because I had no protection.

"No rubbers, you mean?" she said.

"Right," I said.

"Yes you do," she said, went over to a drawer, and brought a couple of packages back with her.

"Where do we go?" I asked.

"By the window. It's too hot upstairs."

She had a little cotton mattress on the floor by the hinged window overlooking the lake. I was still taking off my clothes when she had peeled off everything and sat in the opened window with her bottom on the window seat, leaning back casually on her palms in full, luxuriant womanhood. I feared that I would last no longer than a boy with her.

I came up to her and kissed her. She was an extraordinarily fine kisser, a kisser who knew Egyptian secrets.

She nuzzled my ear, reached down, and lightly held me as if we had done this a hundred times before. She was an active explorer, her fingers playing around my body and lingering on the scars on my back. "How do you stay so good-looking?"

"Despite the advanced age, you mean?"

"Exactly," she said.

And so there we were going after it in the lamplight with the open window and lake and night behind her.

I had had sex with women who were casual about it and at least a couple who truly liked it, but never with a woman who both liked it and was so polite about it all. Sex seemed to bring out the British in her. There was a lot of "Do you mind," and "Would you please," and "That's quite all right, *quite* all right. . . ." I was in an erotic English novel, if such a thing exists, being invited in, being ridden and stroked and pleaded with—all politely and firmly and with tactful confidence. It all went on for a surprisingly long time.

At a point later in our lovemaking she said something that I paid little attention to at the moment, because it usually happened when people saw me without a shirt, and I had lived long enough to parry such questions. She said something about the scars on my back side. I made some remark about the good old days and let it go, but after we finally subsided and I drifted off briefly to sleep, I awoke remembering exactly what she had said: *You still have the scars.* It reminded me of her mother, who had seen them when they were a lot fresher and been made very angry by them.

I heard the sound of sirens in the distance as I thought about the "still" in that remark. She was curled up in the window seat above me, smoking a cigarette with her panties and the T-shirt on, a glow of sweat on her skin. She glanced down at me and smiled. I briefly thought about whether to ask her what she meant by "still" but decided that I didn't want to follow such a conversation to its logical conclusion. Besides, there were a lot of people my age carrying scars from childhood.

Getting up and putting on my clothes, I tried to locate where the siren was coming from.

"I can sleep now," she drawled. "I've wanted to get you in the sack since the first time I saw you."

I laughed.

"And you?" she said.

I hesitated. "I wanted to touch you. The night we met."

"In the car, right?"

"How'd you know?"

She shrugged. "You can see things in a person's face."

The distant siren finally stopped. Through the window I thought I saw lights playing across the hills in the direction of Hackett.

She lazily smoked the cigarette, and I felt drawn back toward the table. I went over and walked around, looking at the artifacts.

Among them was a flat, round rock about three inches wide with the carving of a man in its center. He was kneeling on one knee and his other foot was up, propped oddly on his toes. He was wearing a pointed kilt, a sash with crosshatching, and a necklace, and he had the falcon marks around his eyes. He was holding a club in one hand and in the other a human head, complete with rolled-up eyes.

A strange feeling went across me, a familiarity with this image, and I realized that the warrior in this carving looked like the man I'd seen last night, the Indian with the beaded forelock of hair and the ponytail.

She came over and dropped the cigarette into the tin and sat down on the other side of the table. "Something wrong?"

I told her about my trip to the Winding Stair looking for Levi Colbert, and told her what I'd seen, including the man on the road who'd had the same hairstyle as this guy. I pointed at the rock and she stared for a moment, a little frown between her eyes.

"What are you saying?"

I shook my head. "It's not a big deal. I just never saw that style of hair before. In the little towns you occasionally see an old Seminole wearing a turban or men with long hair. But the ponytail and the little beaded thing across the forehead—that's a new one on me."

She asked me to describe the man again, and I told her what I had noticed. She asked me to repeat the whole story in complete detail, and I did. She asked me where the mountains were, and I showed her by drawing a simplified map of the border region on the back of her notepad. "Where's Spiro?" she asked, and I pointed at a spot just north of there.

"Who lives in the mountains?"

"Not enough people to count. The timber didn't get stripped because it was too hard to get out. There's one old military road north to south. None of the mountain areas in southeastern Oklahoma and southwestern Arkansas—the Ouachitas, the Winding Stair—had many people. Except last night you'd have thought they were having a rodeo down there."

"Well, who used to live there? That was the Choctaw Nation?"

"Right. We're sitting in the old Choctaw Nation right here in this house."

"Why were there so few people?"

"The Choctaws were from Mississippi. They're flatlanders, crop growers, river-bottom types. They never cared much about mountains. Off that old road you see an occasional side path, but when I worked in Muskogee I never got sent to the Winding Stair to look for anybody. And I traipsed all over eastern Oklahoma."

She was still fixing me with the little frown. "Did you ever come across people whose tribes you didn't know, or hadn't heard about?"

I laughed. "Yeah, myself."

She leaned forward across the table. "People who lived there before Indian Removal?"

"Oh, there were several tribes who lived in the area before Removal—Osage, Caddo, a few others. After the Indian Wars they stuffed more tribes in there than anybody could count. I don't know much about that. My job was to watch over the estates of people who were in the system—mostly the ones with mineral rights. We used to argue about how many different tribes there were. Some would say about a hundred fifty, some would say closer to two hundred. Nobody ever really knew."

"So it's possible for there to be a tribe no one knows about?"

"I guess so. When they divided the land and started doing away with the tribes, they hired a bunch of clerks to work in

Muskogee. Their job was to create the rolls—to name all the Indians so their land could be cut up and distributed. I used to go to the rolls all the time for verification of inheritance. I got to know individual clerks by their handwriting. We had nicknames for some of them. They sat in a building in Muskogee trying to do a census on people scattered over fifty thousand square miles. Some of the tribes had gotten down to thirty or forty people. Some didn't cooperate, or maybe didn't get reached. Some lived on land that the government said belonged to another tribe. Some didn't call themselves the same thing the government called them, and there were divisions in the tribes that nobody at Muskogee ever figured out—whether they were the same people or different. I guess I'd be surprised if every little tribe got recorded. . . ."

I felt an odd surge of emotion and was surprised that I had to pause.

Her eyes were bright in the lamplight. "What?"

"The government was always changing its mind. Trying things for a while, then doing a complete switch. It all got caught going this way and that. The best people in the world couldn't make Indian policy work. When I was taking my degree, Indian law was the hardest course."

Seeming to be half-thinking about something else, she asked, "What about you? How do you identify yourself?"

"Generally I say hello and give my name. I was an orphan, a half-breed, left under a tree. That's all I really know. Didn't I already tell you that?"

"Under a tree? Tell me about that."

I changed the subject back to her original question. "Look, the answer to your question is yes. The agency was supposed to have the last word on the tribes, but what they knew was always limited by the job they were doing. It's still that way."

"So you do think there could be tribal people out there who still aren't known about."

"If they're small enough and in the Winding Stair, why not?"

She smashed out her cigarette and stood up. Standing by the table, she picked up a pencil and tapped it gently on the eraser, for a while not speaking. "I said Lee was something of a pest. I didn't tell you that for a while—a few days—I don't think he cared much for me either. I was the most willing ear to him, but it didn't go beyond that. He seemed wary, going on without telling me the details exactly, as though he were bursting at the seams to talk about it but didn't trust me. Then I told him a story one night. Quite idly. You know, bored, after dark, underneath a mosquito net, too tired to read. We were drinking tea. Afterward he looked at me differently. And he really opened up about Spiro."

"What was the story?"

"I told him that once, after Eric and I got married, he and I chased off to western Turkey. Some friends of Eric's thought they had found an ancient Hebrew temple in a valley of the Ararat Mountains near the upper Euphrates. It was extremely unlikely because it was so far north, and nothing ever came of it. But while we were there I met and got interested in some people around the site. They told us they weren't Kurds. We had a Kurdish translator, and they could communicate, but with great difficulty. They were talking almost in sign language. They didn't dress the same or eat the same as the Kurds around there. They called themselves Turushpah. I got interested in them and wanted to read about them. But I found that nothing had ever been written about them. Not even in German.

"Lee was fascinated. He asked me whether I wrote about them, whether I told other people. I told him I hadn't tried to make a big secret of them. After all, my husband and his pals knew about them. But I'd decided they had chosen their isolation. They must have had their reasons. Anyway, I told Lee this story, and after that—in fact, that night—he started talking a lot more directly about the artifacts."

"Did he say anything about people in the mountains?"

She shook her head slowly. "But he was always hinting at surprises, things he wasn't telling me."

Cylinder 23

I stayed at her place that night, despite the fact that there was no way for both of us to sleep on her one-person pad. Upstairs was way too hot. She had no furniture besides slat chairs and the ripped-up stuff inherited from Guessner, so I slept for the second night in a row in the back seat of a car. I left the top down and slept under the stars, mosquitoes and all. Fireflies drifted around me like shooting stars. I was unsettled. Excited. Feeling a little reprehensible. Feeling happy.

But I did go to sleep before light.

When I wakened it was with quite a jolt. Hank Twist was looming over the open-topped car. Startled, I almost pulled a back muscle.

"Sorry, Tom. I didn't mean to scare you."

He was wearing his courthouse guns. His old half-bed truck was parked nearby. "I went by your house and couldn't find you, and the judge thought you might be here."

Rainy, barefoot and wearing a loose cotton dress, wandered onto the front porch. She looked as if she had already been awake for a while. Hank introduced himself to her.

"Would you like a cup of coffee?" she offered.

"Oh, no, ma'am. I'd like to, but I'm just here to . . . Tom, I'll wait till you wake up."

I remained slumped in the dewy back seat of the car, trying to read his expression until my brain had cleared up enough to move, then finally dragged myself out of the car. "What's the problem? Don't keep me wondering."

"Well, I hate to tell people bad news when they wake up first thing in the morning. You need a cup of coffee."

I gave him a baleful look as I shut the car door.

"Okay," he said. "You know Alfred Carr in Hackett, the one who runs the store where they have court? Something happened to him last night."

"Alfred Carr?" I repeated, thick tongued.

He nodded. "Judge Stone wants to talk to you. He's in court, but you can call him out. I heard Mr. Pryor's looking for you too."

"What happened to Carr?"

"They found him dead last night in his store. Murdered."

I was used to bad news, but Hank had been right. I should have waited until I was fully awake to hear this. We had just talked to Alfred Carr.

I didn't want to leave Rainy alone, but she wouldn't leave the artifacts. We had a brief, flaring argument about it, and she was adamant. She had taken care of herself in worse neighborhoods than this, she told me.

Hank came to the rescue. He asked her if she knew how to use a pistol and offered her one of his. There was something inherently gracious about Hank. I can't say what it was, but when he offered her an ivory-handled revolver and told her it had five bullets in it, you'd have thought Tex Ritter had hopped off his white horse to protect the maiden in distress. It drew a smile from her.

Approaching the scene at Carr's store, I saw that the sheriff was there now. The mood around the place was jumpy. Curiosity seekers were huddled in groups here and there, but none very close to the building. Three of the sheriff's black Fords were lined up in front, and a couple of sleepy-looking deputies were on the porch.

The sheriff himself was sitting in the front seat of one of the cars with the door open, writing on a pad on his knee. When we came up to him, he kept writing. Eyes down, pencil still moving, he said, "I hope you already know about this because I'm sick of talking about it."

I looked down at the sheriff's bald head, trying to decide what I thought about this courteous greeting. Of course, Kenny Seabolt wasn't known for manners. He called people by pronouns—you, him, her—and more than one remark that he'd made about me had floated around in the courthouse. You expected that sort of thing in those days. But I truly didn't like looking at the top of his head.

"We can look for ourselves," Hank said.

The sheriff finally glanced up at us with his pale eyes. "Not anything to see now except the sign they left. They scraped up what they could."

"What happened to him?" I asked.

Kenny wiped at his nose with the back of his hand and glanced at me with controlled disdain.

"The girl that found him was a sixteen-year-old nigger, and she don't want to talk about it. But when my deputies got here, they found him in lots of different places in his store. Looked like a half-dressed goddamn deer."

"He was cut up?"

The sheriff looked at me a few seconds and sighed wearily. With a tired smirk, he stood up and walked over to one of his deputies and muttered something to him about half-breed. The deputy glanced up and came over to me.

"Sheriff said you wanted to know about this here," he said stiffly.

For a moment I blanked out, realizing that Kenny had told him to go talk to the half-breed. Rage played across my ribs, but I stood there and said nothing.

Hank said quietly, "What'd you find in there, deputy?"

"I wasn't the first one. Willy Kirk was the first in there. He said it looked like somebody'd took and run him through a log saw. It happened last night. Somebody heard the explosion. We called the ambulance. It's worse than any highway pileup I ever seen. The sheriff says if that sign in there is true, it ain't nothing we can do about it."

"Sign?" I said.

"It's in there," the deputy said, pointing in the door.

Hank ambled inside, and I followed, eyes adjusting to the gloom. The first thing I noticed was that most of Carr's depleted stock—which I'd seen only a couple of days before—appeared to still be in the store, although some of it was knocked around. There was a smell of petrolatum and shit in the place, so familiar to me that it was like walking into 1918.

The ceiling in Carr's store was about twelve feet high, and there was splattering on it in several places. Behind the counter on the wall, large, rough letters drawn by what appeared to be a rag said SODOMITE. I walked behind the counter and smelled it, and it had the dusty smell of blood. A sign in blood. Hank was looking around without saying anything.

"Ever been to war?" I asked Hank.

"My daddy was a miner. I know what cordite smells like."

As I climbed down the ladder, he said, "The body was here in front of the counter. That's where most of the blood is."

In front of the counter was a dented-up metal plate that had been nailed down to cover a bad place in the floor or an old coal scuttle. On top of it and the surrounding floorboards was a burst of blood.

Hank knelt down above the metal sheet. "I'm wondering how they blew this old boy up without blowing all the stock off the shelves. I guess the dynamite was under him." Hank looked up at me questioningly.

I sighed and shook my head. "This one is going to drive Don Campbell over the brink. He'll never write a report. I'll have to look at the body myself."

"Might not be much to look at."

Hank and I went around the room. In the back was a door into a storage closet that had been forced. Inside were a few boxes of canned foods and sodas. The empty shelves were uniformly dusty, as if nothing had been taken. Whoever had done this apparently wasn't interested in groceries. Through the back door, a large storage shed—about the size of a one-car garage—stood in the dirt yard with its door busted, crowbarred loose. I called Hank into the yard and stood aside while he looked at the tracks around the door. Hank knew how to track a man, with or without dogs. He walked around the yard gingerly looking at the disturbances in the dust.

"Wind hasn't filled them in," he muttered. "They're wearing round-toed boots. It looks like more than one set of tracks."

Inside the shed, spears of sunlight came through the boards. There was a well pump along one wall, a rusted bucket with a tin dipper, and the floor was damp from splashed water. There were also a bunch of shelves, all empty, but the sulfate odor of artifacts was as strong as it had been in Lee Guessner's cabin. I told Hank about it, but he was kneeling on the floor, looking at marks in the wet dirt.

"These are good prints," he said, eyes playing around the floor. "They're two-dollar boots. At least three different sizes."

"What are two-dollar boots?"

"My daddy used to wear them. All the coal miners in Moberly wore them. They're made by the McComb Company in St. Louis: good, cheap boots. You see them in a lot of company stores."

Hank and I drove into town in his truck. I felt a headache growing like a pearl in the back of my head. If I had to be in anybody's company, I was glad it was Hank's. We stopped at a place on the lower avenue for coffee.

Cylinder 24

On Mondays they cooked goat and beans at the Spot, and the air was already thick with garlic, frying bacon, and tomato sauce—smells wafting out the front door, luring the secretaries, bank workers, lawyers, and municipal cops who could afford to eat out a time or two during the week. I wasn't hungry that day. There was a pinball machine in the corner and a chalkboard on the wall that usually carried baseball scores, particularly of Cardinals games, along with messages sometimes written by regular patrons of the Spot to one another. A small-time bookie named Lyn Flower worked out of the Spot, taking bets on baseball games and Hot Springs horse races. The chalkboard had the number 700 that morning, with a big X through it; Lyn was running bets on whether Babe Ruth would make seven hundred home runs with a month to go in his career. Out one of the cafe's high, narrow windows I could see Bernie's LaSalle parked in front of the Elevator Building.

A tableful of lawyers eyed Hank and me; a couple of them raised their chins in greeting, and I could tell by their expressions that they had already heard rumors about the murder in Hackett. Smiling John Gillis was among them, in his all-white linen suit and buckskin shoes.

Nancy Petrakki came to our table, pulling a pencil out of her hair. Nancy was one of the reasons why so many people came here, particularly the men. She either threw their fresh talk back in their faces or acted openly provocative—in either case, they loved her.

"You don't look so good today, Tom."

"Give me a Greek coffee, a tin of aspirin, and an order of toast, please."

"What's Greek coffee?" Hank asked.

Nancy smiled at him and raised an eyebrow. "It's kind of like cowboy coffee, Hank. It stands up without a cup."

"I'll try some of that," he said.

After three aspirin, some toast, and a second cup of the sweet, thick coffee, the curtain on my mood was rising enough for me to tell Hank about what I'd seen in the mountains night before last. Hank was a patient listener. Over forty-some years of law enforcement and court work he'd heard it all, seen it all; nothing surprised him, he just took it in. He looked as if he was trying to suppress a smile.

"So these characters tore your Ford up?"

I failed to see the humor.

He laughed. Hank had a spontaneous but dry laugh. "Well, you've been needing somebody to take care of that car."

"I saw another man on that road. He was an Indian. Barefoot, big cut down his cheek, tough-looking, square body, wore his hair with it cut close on the side and a ponytail with a little sprig of it beaded off down across his forehead."

"Yeah?"

"A full-blood maybe—I don't know. He spoke enough English to understand me and warn me off. He wouldn't look at me directly, but I had the feeling he was really taking me in."

"Friendly?"

"Not exactly."

Hank narrowed his eyes as if thinking about something distant. "I went hunting in those mountains with some other boys one time.

This goes a way back. We were fifteen, sixteen years old. . . ." He trailed off as if unsure whether to go on.

"Didn't you chase outlaws in the Winding Stair in the '90s?"

He shook his head. "Thirteenth District was limited to West Arkansas by the time I worked for them. They didn't pay us enough to lame our horses. If there was high dollar on a man, we'd play the border sometimes, but it was too steep down there, with too much cover. Was a lot of horse thieving going on in Texas, and they'd meet in those mountains to trade horses for the Missouri market. They used that old military road going from Skullyville to Fort Towsend. But they had a regular vigilante group out of Heavener until not long ago that'd catch a few of em."

"Do you think there's any chance of people being in those mountains, hiding from the world? Maybe a tribe who's been up there and never left? Rainy thinks that Guessner knew about a lost tribe of people in the Winding Stair."

Hank glanced at me quickly, then away, a little run of sweat going down the side of his nose. To my surprise, he didn't laugh at the idea. "Don't know," he said neutrally.

"I'm trying to connect the dots here, that's all."

He took a sip from the little coffee cup and made a face at it. "You saw people on this man's property—how close?"

"It was several hundred yards and dark. All I saw were shadows in the fires. They had campfires."

While Hank and I were talking, I had noticed Smiling John Gillis eyeing us across the room, and about this time he got up and sidled over to our table. Gillis walked like he had several legs—like a spider floating on the floor. As usual he wore the malicious smile and began with the fake belly-up routine.

"Well, Tom, you beat me in court. Fair and square. I admit it. I'm down but not out." He stared out the window, shaking his head as if at that very moment accepting his fate with humility and good humor.

"That's good, John."

"This queer that got murdered last night—I hear you knew him pretty well. Wasn't his store where you held court? Was he a pal of yours?"

My heart revved up, and I hesitated before saying, "I'm not really interested in talking to you right now, John, but for the record it's the municipal prosecutor who usually handles the township courts. Where did you hear about the murder?"

Smiling John dangled his face out on the long stalk of his neck and knitted his face into an intentionally stupid smile, doing his best to get at me. "You don't need to get touchy about it. I just heard you associated with him."

Hank said, "Mr. Gillis, you must have stepped in some dog shit. I can smell it. I think you need to go outside and scrape it off."

He widened his smile. "Why, Hank, where are your big pearl-handled gats today? Don't you wear those things everywhere you go?"

To my surprise, Hank immediately stood up and with no hesitation at all grabbed Smiling John Gillis by his white lapels and shoved him backward out the screen door, where he gave him an extra shove that sent him halfway across the avenue before he fell onto his butt on the bricks. He got up quickly and seemed to consider coming back in but decided against it and skulked away.

This earned a moment of silence from the tableful of lawyers, then a nervous laugh. "Hey," one of them called. "Who's gonna pay for his coffee?"

Nancy called from behind the counter, "I will. It was worth it."

"Your boss is coming across the street under a head of steam," Hank said.

Sure enough, Bernie was coming across the avenue. The screen door slapped, and immediately he came to our table. "Was that John Gillis sitting in the middle of the street?"

I scooted over for Bernie to join us, but he remained standing. He looked tired and stiff, but he'd shaved and put his tie on straight today. The lawyers across the room waved at him with brief, false smiles. As a gentleman lawyer and prosecutor, Bernie wasn't one of the regular boys.

At this point, the sheriff drove up outside and came striding in with three deputies in his wake and, without a word to any of us, made his way to his table in the back. The lawyers made quick obeisance to him as he went by. Kenny always sat in the far back of the room, looking out on everybody else. Sometimes he sat with deputies, sometimes with lawyers and others, but he called the shots, even waving people away on occasion.

Bernie colored a little, almost blushed, as the sheriff brushed by. He lowered his tone. "Manny wants to see both of you. Our telephone lines are about to melt with calls about this thing in Hackett. Mel's been calling all over town trying to get you, and that ridiculous switchboard is jammed. She finally gave up and just went downstairs to sit at it. Mel is normally very easygoing, but she is not happy, Tom. She isn't herself. And those women who constantly come into our office to smoke and stand in the air conditioner— I'm beginning to wonder whether we should allow them . . ."

"Welcome to the office," I said.

Hank stood up quickly and said, "I guess I'd better get back to the courthouse."

"He wants to see you too, Hank." Bernie glanced toward the sheriff's table.

As we walked across the street, Bernie said urgently, "Jesus Christ, Tom. I thought you'd fallen off the edge of the earth."

"I talked to Stone last night. Didn't he tell you that?"

He looked at me suspiciously as we crowded into Thurman Gale's elevator. Mr. Gale was having a particularly lively discussion with himself today, as he always did when the building got unusually busy. On our floor two of the secretaries from downstairs were just leaving our office, both carrying little cones of water from our cooler. Inside, the air conditioner roared with cigarette smoke. Mel, who had just hung up the phone, threw me a wilting look. She was flipping a yellow Venus pencil back and forth between her fingers.

"Well, ain't we got fun. The invisible man is back. Maybe you should leave me a telephone number or a forwarding address or something. Believe me, the office needs you."

In Bernie's office, Judge Stone was sitting in one of the leather chairs in his shirtsleeves, with his arms crossed. Bernie had a Persian rug that covered most of the floor, heavily mounted paintings on the wall, brass lamps, glass-fronted bookshelves—a plush office for this old building.

Hank and I sat on the couch while Bernie remained standing, pacing, glancing occasionally out the window. We told them what we knew about the murder scene, including the sign drawn in blood on the wall.

"The sheriff is making sure everybody knows about that little sign," Bernie said, leaning on his elbows over the back of his chair.

"It wasn't little," I said. "The letters were about eighteen inches high. It said SODOMITE."

"He's telling people that the man was a pervert and it was probably just some other pervert who killed him."

"Where'd you hear that?" I asked.

"LaVerne who works in his office. That's the word she's putting out."

Hank cleared his throat. "If it was perverts, it was a whole squad of them. There were a bunch of different-sized bootprints around that well house."

The judge, who had been quiet till now and who looked as pale and weak today as he had the last day of the Goback trial, said, "Tom, what do you think?"

"About what?"

"The next step."

"I'll tell you what the next step ought to be—" Bernie started to say, but the judge stopped him.

"Let him answer, please."

Bernie, fragile and brash at the same time, flushed with embarrassment at being interrupted.

"The two murders are obviously related. I have to do some more snooping in Oklahoma. Have you sentenced Jay Goback yet?"

"No," Stone said. "It's set for tomorrow. He's been writing notes to me begging for mercy because of his back condition. For a man who beat a woman with a fireplace poker, he can get pretty eloquent about his pain."

"Can you put off sentencing? If he's in on the east-side gossip, he might know something about Jim Mackey."

"I can postpone a week."

"Hank, if there's anybody at the county jail you can trust, tell them to withhold pain medications from Goback," I said. "I want his back to hurt for a few days. We need as much leverage as possible."

Hank nodded.

Bernie's mouth had zipped straight across, and he glared at me. He was still blushing. "I feel," he said deliberately, "that something has to be done about Kenny Seabolt."

Bernie should stay completely away from work, I was thinking: three days in the office and he falls apart. Kenny Seabolt had probably personally insulted him sometime in the past, and he couldn't let go of it. But Kenny insulted everybody.

Yet in the face of Bernie's obvious sincerity, except for the clamor of the air conditioner coming through the door, the room did go silent for a moment, in bafflement if nothing else: How did Bernie suddenly become so concerned? It gave everyone pause.

Looking at Stone now, Bernie added, "Why are we putting up with him?"

The judge didn't respond right away. Eventually he took a deep breath and said with infinite tiredness, "What exactly are you proposing?"

"Something. Anything. You and I and whoever else we can trust meet with the Democratic committee and try to get him removed from the slate. That would be a start. Otherwise we're stuck with another term of him as sheriff of this county."

"That's impossible," the judge said impatiently. "The slate's already drawn up. For all practical purposes, it has been for months. Nobody gives a damn about county politics right now. It's not a good time."

"It's never a good time," Bernie said. "That's the point. Either the election is too close, or it's just passed, or it's inconvenient for some other damn reason. Meanwhile, we've got a sheriff acting like a county boss for twenty years, and everybody just swallows it. He never cooperates with this office. Tom has had to threaten subpoenas to even get him to testify in court. . . . Look, I know I don't have that much sway. If it was the sheriff versus Bernie Pryor, it wouldn't be a contest. But all three of you are in strong positions, one way or another. If you don't do something about it, nobody will."

Hank cleared his throat. "One thing about this killing last night. They made a show of it. They could have swiped the Indian stuff without murdering that old boy like they did. Even, say, if he came by the store and caught em in the act, why'd they make a big production out of it?"

Judge Stone, who was looking at the carpet, said wearily, "What are you saying, Hank?"

"Not sure. The sheriff seems to be going along pretty quick with that sodomite business. Kenny usually lays back no matter what he thinks. When he doesn't want to look into something, he just doesn't do it."

"So you're agreeing with me?" Bernie said hopefully.

"Don't know," Hank said. "Whoever did the killing might not have been the ones who made the sign. There are a lot of possibilities."

"We can't decide these things here," Judge Stone said wearily. He looked temporarily lost, but finally he gathered himself and set his eye on the prosecutor. "Bernie, one thing you need to know. The sheriff's going to hear about you dogging him. Question one person about him and he might hear about it; question three and he definitely will."

"What would you like for me to do, just say to hell with it?"

"For now, yes. We've got two murders, Bernie—two ugly murders that are going to make it to the front page of the *St. Louis Post-Dispatch* and every other place. That's the news. That's what we have to do something about."

We soon broke up. As he was leaving, Stone said, "I'm sorry about this, Tom." His eyes lingered on me a moment, and he left.

Before going back to Hackett, Hank and I stopped at St. Edward's to get a look at the corpse. A young nun directed us to a basement office, where the smell of ammonia was so strong it penetrated my skull. To my surprise, Don Campbell was there, sitting at his desk, writing on a pad of paper under a green desk lamp. Dusty jars with organs in formaldehyde sat on a table behind him. Beside his writing pad was a glass of something that looked like water but wasn't. Don would last four more years in the same pickled state, then within one week he would succumb to alcoholic degeneration, his hair turning white, his cheeks shriveling, sinking so quickly into a vodka swamp that some people held up his life as the ideal: happily drunk thirty-some years, then suddenly dead. In fact, there wasn't an ounce of happiness in him. Don was so plagued by shyness and sensitivity and the ability to see the other side of everything that I don't imagine it would have made much difference what kind of work he did. Everything he did he hated because he felt that he should be doing something else. Yet somewhere in him flowed a strong current of human decency.

He looked at us through the upper half of his bifocals. His phone started ringing, and he picked up the receiver and gently replaced it. Don was unusually peaceful today. When I told him that we'd like to see Alfred Carr's body, he said with uncharacteristic plainness that he'd be glad to describe the corpse to us. I could see his worry even as he said it. In front of the metal-strapped wooden door of the cold room, he gave us one more chance to just hear a description. Don didn't want us to have to look.

I reminded him that I'd driven an ambulance. I could take it.

Cylinder 25

When we left the hospital, Hank sat behind his wheel for a minute, quiet. I kept looking at the starter button, my mind falling into old grooves, thinking, Let's go, let's go. There were no incoming thirty-eight-centimeter shells whining like locomotives across the sky; there were no dying horses and burros screaming in supply trenches; the air wasn't foul scum; it wasn't the maze of slimy, explosion-churned roads where you were always driving to someplace puzzlingly new to collect the latest customer, who might be in one piece or might be in more than one piece, who might be smiling the goofy smile of shell shock or might be bitching about the foot fungus or might be anything; it wasn't the *poste de secour* at Haudramont, so close to the German lines that a sniper could get you going either way, but the quiet parking lot, shading off into grass, of St. Edward's Mercy Hospital, where natural death, no matter how unnaturally it presented itself, usually reigned. Still I wanted Hank to hit that button and go. His way was to sit quiet, however. He was shaken, but I could see the resolve forming in his old lawman's face, so I waited.

We were halfway to Hackett before he asked me what I thought about what we had just seen. I said that it was either a crime of hatred by psychos or high-dollar torture of an offbeat kind. Among other things, the killers had inserted dynamite into Alfred Carr's body, probably into his rectum, and blown him to pieces. Whether they'd done it while he was alive was not within Don Campbell's ability to find out or my desire to know.

It didn't take Albert Einstein to figure out that Rainy Davis should leave town, but to even get her to consider it, I had to tell her the unpleasant details about the man she'd had an RC Cola with a few days before. Rainy had been as hot as Cuba with me the night before, and when I told her she should leave town she treated me as if I worked for the Internal Revenue Service, dropping by her place for a friendly audit. Eyes narrowed, mouth turning down a little, she gave me a forty-five-caliber look as if to say watch out, buster, telling me what to do.

We were in her cabin, with the artifacts, but everything had gotten quiet after I'd given her the news and my humble recommendation.

"You want me to leave, huh?" That was all she had to say. She just looked at me as if I had turned into a statue, a likeness of doubtful validity.

Hank stood back by the door, out of the immediate line of fire, but when Rainy and I completely ran out of things to say to each other, he made some conversation about the lake, how he'd fished here before they turned it into a private club. Hank seemed to keep her from getting really angry, with his handsome old rough face and white hair and gray-blue eyes.

But under no circumstances was she going to leave town, she now told me; the diggers were pulling out stuff every day, selling it to anybody with cash.

After a few more awkward moments of conversation, I suggested that at least she try to store her collection.

"Where?"

"Mercantile Bank has a second vault they never use."

She looked at me a while, and then in an aggravating tone said, "I don't trust him."

"Who's that?" I said.

She was pacing now, smoking a cigarette. After a moment she looked up at me. "What did you say?"

"Who don't you trust?"

"Stone. He could lay some kind of injunction on it."

Now it was my turn to get mad. I argued with her.

"Look, why should I trust him if he doesn't trust me? He thinks I manipulated Lee; he thinks I'm a liar."

"Rainy, I'm not shilling for Stone, but the collection isn't my problem. For your safety, you'd better stow it. That's all I'm saying. Somebody's doing terrible things to whoever's holding this stuff. If you won't leave town, then at least store it."

"Is this the old I-know-what's-good-for-you routine?"

I took a deep breath and looked at the floor. It was what I hated about affairs, what in middle age I was happy to live without. Go to bed with somebody, or even almost go to bed with them, and within twenty-four hours you're being presumptuous with each other, or angry, or you're feeling strangely depressed, or all tangled up. The ghost of her dead husband went through the corner of my mind and winked at me knowingly.

Yes, old chap, there is another side to the story.

I gave it one last shot. In a flat voice I said, "Sign a lockbox contract, Rainy. Whatever goes into a vault is as much yours as it is in your house. The only difference is that you've got guards and you're not stuck watching the stuff. If you don't like that, ship it someplace. The point is, just don't keep it around here, or don't keep yourself around here."

"How do you know a bank will take it? Have you already arranged this?"

"Like I said, there's a bank in town that has an unused vault. I think they'll help you."

It actually seemed to allay her fears when John Wimple, an elderly vice president at Mercantile Bank, initially turned us down later that afternoon. Age had made Mr. Wimple a little loose in the ball bearings, and rather than discussing vault storage he was more interested in delivering monologues about the terrible state of things. He swiveled back and forth in his office chair and lobbed arbitrary opinions toward us like hand grenades, whatever popped into his mind—how there were too many people without property wandering around undermining our country, not enough college graduates being loyal to their alma maters, entirely too much emphasis on the expanding universe and the shrinking economy and such nonsense in the news magazines, and so on. He had a way of kicking his chair smoothly in either direction, then stopping and looking intently over the top of his glasses at others around the bank, who paid no attention to him. When Rainy or I tried to speak, he interrupted to pitch another opinion at us, eventually lulling us both into a trance. He wanted to make us sit there and listen to him as long as possible. Some survival mechanism located deep in Mr. Wimple's brain had devised an ironic smile and a trick with his eyebrows that suggested his monologues were related to the issue at hand, for those who were cunning enough to understand. He seemed always about to get back to the subject. Rainy made a few wisecracks, which he didn't register, and left it up to me.

We were in the bank for an hour and a half because it took me one hour and fifteen minutes to figure out that Mr. Wimple just needed a firm hand, someone to talk directly with him and tell him what to do: "We want a lockbox. Get out the lockbox contracts now, Mr. Wimple." This approach seemed to help him greatly. He got out the papers, and Rainy filled them in.

Until nine o'clock that night we crated all the stuff at the cabin and hauled it back to town and placed it in the old walk-in vault—with Hank's help after five o'clock. Hank and I talked briefly and firmed up plans to go to the mountains the next morning. He went home, and Rainy and I took a late supper at a barbecue and dance place called the Bluestone in the "new" black part of town. The Bluestone was a boxy two-story building, with a dining room downstairs and an upstairs bar. A weirdly beautiful man's voice, accompanied by a guitar, moaned through the floor above us. The air was tinted with smoke and Cosmoline and perfume. We had barbecue and vinegar green beans and cold beer.

Rainy asked if Hank and I were going back to the Winding Stair, and I told her yes. She wanted to go with us, she said.

"I want to see this man with the funny haircut you told me about."

"I wouldn't expect to see him again."

"I want to find out about the people living on Colbert's property. He's the oil Indian, right?"

"Oh, he's got some oil property all right."

Billy Bluestone, proprietor, a lanky man with smart, wary eyes, appeared at our table as we were finishing our food. He wore straightened black hair and a gold necklace against his coal skin. He smiled and laughed and called me "sir" and Rainy "ma'am," watchfully, and made small talk. I didn't know Billy too well beyond what I had picked up eating here occasionally. His joint was live during Prohibition—liquor could be bought—but Billy had a reputation for keeping a lid on things. I could tell by the lean of his body and the excessive friendliness that something was on his mind.

"That boss of yours workin hard. Yes sir, Mr. Pryor come a hard-workin man. He takin care of me."

"How's he taking care of you?"

"He worried about peoples comin here tryin to take money from me, think they can get protection money."

"Like who?"

"Well, you know," he said evasively, glancing at Rainy.

I asked Billy if we could talk in private, and he led me into the kitchen, where he became a lot more direct.

"He askin me about Mr. Kenny—whether he been taxin me."

"What'd you tell him?" I asked.

"Told him no."

"Is that true?"

Billy didn't answer.

"So Kenny has been taxing you. How long?"

He sighed. "Ever since I got my new bar upstairs and that range—" he cocked his head toward an impressive black Crescent range. "I thought we gon be doin good after repeal. Took a chance and spent some money. Now I be tryin to pay off with him squeezin me."

"Does the sheriff collect money directly from you?"

He nodded. "Take the cash right outen my hand. I miss him one week, here he come in four cars the next Saturday night. Bust up tables, bunch of chairs, told me next time it be worse. So I got more things to pay for."

"Anything going on here, Billy?"

Billy snorted. "You see the way it is out there tonight. Ain't exactly jumpin, is it? Well that's every night, includin weekend. Ain't nobody got no money. Ain't nothin goin on. Ain't nothin *to* go on."

"You say it's been since repeal. How'd he start taxing you?"

"See, I only been here for a little over three years. I was just food, you know, until the repeal."

"Right," I said. Billy knew I knew that wasn't true, but I didn't interrupt his story.

"A few months ago I ask the sheriff's help one time. It was a man comin by here causin trouble tryin to shake my waitress down. So I calls Mr. Kenny, and he taken care of it."

"How'd he do it? I don't remember any complaints."

"Run him out the county, I guess. Next thing, the sheriff be talkin to me about how I need to pay him against future trouble."

"So you didn't tell the prosecutor any of this?"

Billy shook his head.

"Do you want me to tell him?"

"I don't know. Don't know what to do. All I know is I can't have no sheriff bustin up my place. Insurance don't cover no raid. One more like that and I be out of bidness, trade done got so thin."

"All right, Billy. I won't say anything to him unless you okay it. Meanwhile, can you write down exactly how much money he's taking from you and when? At least we ought to have a record of that."

"I know your boss been callin round. You better tell him to be careful, less he have a sledge hammer in his desk. Mr. Kenny been around a long time. He pay his deputies extra, do em little favors, make em loyal. Be like his own army. They do what he say. Beat that nigger up, burn that nigger down, that's it. Snap. Done. Thank you, sah."

"There been any fires on this side of the river lately?"

"Enough to keep us payin," he said bitterly. "He don't always use a match. Sometime he take em across the line. Sometime he bust up the place."

Before I got back to the table I had already revised Billy's story in my head: he'd probably been paying the sheriff for liquor protection from day one. When repeal came, the sheriff came up with a different scam and called it something else.

Rainy and I left in a few minutes, walking out of the compressed air of the Bluestone and drifting slowly up Midland Avenue in the Cabriolet. It was a great night for a convertible, with the warm wind like liquid across our faces. I was preoccupied, thinking about the sheriff. Muscling restaurant and bar owners for protection money was a new one. He apparently got away with it by limiting it to black owners.

And Bernie. I kept thinking about Bernie. Naive, untested, soft Bernie, Bernie of Bernie and Berenice, Bernie of the many vacations, who talked about whatever bubbled up in his mind—what was he doing?

When we reached the avenue I asked, "You want to stay with me tonight?"

"I've got my period," she said sulkily.

I laughed. "That's not why I'm inviting you. I'm worried about you being alone at that cabin."

She sighed. "I hope you have a big fan."

We parked between my house and the shed and went into a hot kitchen. I opened several windows. Rainy at first prowled gingerly through the four rooms, looking at things but not asking a lot of questions. She seemed wary of my privacy. I had books all over the place, in stacks and on homemade bookshelves. She walked around looking at them with a little frown on her face. When people came to my house they usually felt compelled to say something about the books—Hey, Tom, startin a library?—but she said nothing. There was a snapshot of my wife in a frame sitting on the mantel above my little fireplace.

Rainy studied her and said, "She was a pretty woman. Was she part Indian?"

I nodded. "We met in Muskogee when I was about to quit the agency. She was a secretary there."

"Have there been lots of other women in your life?"

My heart rate went up a notch. Yeah, your mother, I thought. Why didn't I just tell her?

"Dozens," I said, sitting down on the couch and spreading my arms along the back of it.

She sighed and looked away. "Doesn't surprise me. My husband was like that. After he died, I found out that he once actually had a bet with a friend over who could make more different women—nonprostitutes—in twenty-four hours."

I laughed. "I was only kidding."

"He wasn't," she said. "He loved the cuties. Only he'd get confused about who was fast and who wasn't. Tried to pounce on a nurse in the hospital three days before he died. He'd stick it in a knothole if he thought something interesting might be on the other side."

"You talk about this man so much, I think you loved him."

She plunked down into a chair and got a cigarette from a skirt pocket. "Oh, I forget about him. Believe me, I do. When I'm working. Other men make me think about him. It doesn't make any difference whether they're really like him or not. Any man."

"Did he kick you around?"

She lit her cigarette. "There was some of that. A few black eyes, bruises. That wasn't really the problem. After I threw some plates at him, he mostly gave that up. . . ." She narrowed her eyes and stared. "Oxford must have been quite a place in the early '20s, judging by his pals. They showed up everywhere for a visit. You'd think you were at the parched ends of the earth and one of them would come loping out of the heat waves on a camel: drunks, transvestites, opium addicts, you name it. Lord this or that. The English are very chummy, you know. I remember sitting around a campfire in Turkey playing twenty-one, listening to them talk about how the transport strike was going to take good old England down. I remember hearing some completely dissolute man named Hugh Sykes-something spinning crackpot theories about how all hikers were socialists or all Jews were this or that—I don't know, interested in ceramics or something. Always trying to outdo each other at exotic interests, casual, useless opinions. Stay university boys forever. It makes my head spin. I was part of it. I was right there, knocking back the gin. I did it too."

"Actually sounds like fun to me."

"It had its rewards. But for some reason I don't like thinking about it."

"Well then don't. The past is gone."

She smiled at me wryly. "Do you actually believe that?"

I laughed. "I know I don't like waking up in the morning worrying about fifteen years ago."

"Never look back, eh?"

"There's nothing you can do about the past."

She blew out some smoke and stared away, above me. "Did you learn that from all these books? You don't believe that the past is important? Your own, for example?"

"My own past is not important or unimportant; it just is. But it's not something I want to relive. It doesn't fit a pattern. I figure if mine doesn't, then others' don't either. Yours, for example. You had this man who was important to you. You hate him, but he was important to you."

"Aren't we avuncular," she said with open sarcasm. "Eric was a womanizer, a dabbler, a snob—a pretentious snob who was incapable of imagining that he wasn't at the center of the cosmos. And he died very suddenly and very young. Just like that. Gone. No more Eric. End of Eric. Good-bye, Eric. He gave me the slip. And you know something? He never cared a whit for me. I was fashionable, like whiskey and soda, I was American, a little risqué. Perfect. How am I supposed to feel about that?"

She was still looking away from me, her eyes welling up. I said nothing.

"I always turn the attention back to myself, don't I? And you always turn it away from you." She brushed quickly at one of her eyes.

"Not always."

"Anyway, pardon the rambling. I guess I'm tired. Tell me more about this orphanage."

"That's too far back to remember. My life really started when I got out. When I was fifteen or sixteen I came to Fort Smith."

"I know that much." Her eyes switched very directly to mine. "Judge Stone told me the afternoon I arrived. He said rather a lot about you."

"Oh?"

"It was all about how you knew the area well, how you'd come here as a very young man—near the time my mother did, as a matter of fact."

"So . . . Stone knew your parents?"

"Yes. Particularly Mother, I think." Rainy was staring again, now at me.

The natural thing to do then would have been to ask something about her mother, but I didn't want to actively pretend, and somehow I just could not say to her, Oh, by the way, sure, yes, I did once fall in love with your mother—and around the same time I killed a man and burned down an orphanage. And yes, I loved her so much that there was room for nothing else, no friendship, no real knowledge of her beyond a vague and probably quite reasonable distrust, nothing but the sheer destructive fire of love based on nothing but itself, destined to burn out.

But apparently it wasn't her mother who was on her mind.

"You know," she said, "I think Judge Stone decided within about an hour of meeting me that he disliked me. That afternoon he picked me up. I hardly said a thing. He was perfectly nice, but I got the feeling that everything I said irritated him. By the time the rest of you got there, he seemed barely able to stomach me."

I stood up and went to the kitchen for a drink of water. I kept a bottle of water in the refrigerator, and one of my pleasures was to drink from it. I held it for a moment, grasping the cold neck, took a big drink, then came back and offered it to her. She shook her head. She was looking at me curiously, the smoke from her cigarette coming up and curling slightly around her head. I was mildly anxious and very tired, yet at the same time washed over with a feeling of intense pleasure from merely talking with her.

Her eyes still followed me. "So you can't tell me anything else about your past? Nothing about your early life. You of the fantastic memory. That was another thing that Stone said. He said you have an extraordinary memory."

I backed up and sat on the edge of the couch and rested the bottle on my knee. "What part of my past?"

"You know nothing about your origins? No clues, even? What tribe you came from?"

"There was an affidavit signed by a sheriff in the orphanage records. He said I'd been found at a place called Big Tree near Osi Tamaha. It's called Eagletown now. He thought maybe I was a Comanche or something. Or maybe Caddo. They were from around there."

"What kind of Indian do you think you are?"

I laughed. "What kind of Celt do you think you are?"

"You never were curious?"

"Oh I was. Years ago. But right now I'm not curious about anything. I'm about to fall asleep with this jug of water in my hand. Please sleep in the bed; I'm happy to stay on this couch."

"That's a love seat, Tom. There's not room for you. Sleep in your own bed—and do you mind if I sleep with you?" She grinned.

"Well, no," I said, attempting to sound hearty. "But . . ."

"I'll bet you've only got that one electric fan. One of us would swelter. Tom, after what we did the other night, don't be so bloody modest."

I shook my head and smiled at her.

She stood up, plucking a clasp from her hair that made it fall around her shoulders. "What's wrong, afraid I'll bring out the Comanche in you? Don't worry. You won't be tempted. I'm about as attractive as the back room of a butcher shop right now."

Sure, I thought, trying to keep from staring at her.

So we did sleep in the same bed, with windows open and my twelve-inch oscillating fan raking sultry air across us, and, astonishingly, I was able to go to sleep.

She said quietly, "I know about my mother and you, Tom."

Stunned awake, my heart just about jumped out of my chest. But she was breathing evenly.

I had dreamed it.

I felt a hand on my shoulder.

"Tom, I heard something outside."

This time she really had spoken. I stumbled out of bed, got a Louisville slugger that I kept in the corner, and went out the kitchen door. I walked around the Chevy and her truck and opened the panel doors. Nothing. When I went back in, she seemed to not be particularly nervous. She was standing in the kitchen in the T-shirt I'd lent her, drinking a glass of water.

"Dogs, probably," I told her. "Packs of them roam the neighborhoods sometimes."

"Cars passed on the street, and I kept waking up. Then I heard a rustling outside this door."

"Seems to be all clear."

She set the glass on the counter and frowned. Her mind was on another track.

"I keep having the oddest feeling that this is home to me. It's like something bending inside me. Even though everything's in a complete muddle. You ever had that feeling?"

"I'm glad you feel at home," I said.

When we got back in bed I didn't go back to sleep so quickly this time.

"Tom," she said, dangling an arm over my side, "where is Big Tree?"

"Southeast Oklahoma, Ouachita Mountains."

"Same as the Winding Stair?"

"Little south of there," I said gruffly.

"Maybe you're one of them."

"Who's that?"

"The ones with funny haircuts."

Cylinder 26

Tuesday was hot and dry again, and at nine in the morning Hank, Rainy, and I, in her inherited panel truck, laid a ribbon of dust westward under a pale blue sky. Hank sat in the back seat staring out placidly on the drought-blasted landscape. The emigrant wave of the previous week had abated, and Highway 9 had settled back to its normal eerie quiet. Pocola's few buildings were boarded up and abandoned except for the one gas station, forlorn of business today. I saw the running dog, prostrate, doubtless almost dead, under its tree. Dust seeped through the van's back doors as we turned into the sand dunes of the old Fort Coffee Road. Near the mound, the same trucks were parked as before, including the one from Tulsa County.

As we approached the tent, Rainy sported her usual cool and collected manner despite the temperature and the pack of dogs. I had lent her one of my Panama hats. We underwent the same routine as last week with the charging, barking dogs, and the scene there was as it had been before—the tent, the table, the mummy with his sombrero still lying in the sun on the cot—except today the table had only a few dusty things scattered across it. At the sound of the dogs one of the diggers stuck his head out of a tunnel, and eventually three others crawled out, all in their masks of dirt. As they approached, I decided to just watch and listen. They were all youngish men except one, the barrel-shaped fellow about my age who had a cigar permanently planted in his impassive face.

As before, McKenzie did most of the talking, giving Rainy a tight smile and me an unwelcoming, flat look. Hank and I made the diggers uneasy, but no more than they had been the previous week. McKenzie started bantering with Rainy about how she'd better buy that mummy and get him in the icebox before he got too ripe. His attempts at making jokes were unpleasant, pushy, as if he wanted to be friendly enough to get her money but needed to keep her in her place. She handled him smoothly, taking just enough meanness to keep him from getting hostile.

I had that plunging feeling I sometimes got on dead, blistering calm days, when there was nothing in the world but grasshoppers and heat. I walked to the table and picked up a stone mace. It was made entirely of polished rock, and I remembered what Rainy had said about all these items being ceremonial, not practical. A fighting mace, carried and used in battle, would have a wooden handle. But this one did have a cutting tip, and there was a dim but distinct stain on it. Blood? Could a bloodstain survive after six or seven hundred years? There were also two shell cups lying on the rough oak slabs. I rubbed my thumb across the dirt on them and saw the figure of a warrior wearing a necklace that radiated out to what looked like the pointed claws of a hunting bird.

Currents were passing between the treasure hunters. The one with the gun on his belt looked sullenly toward McKenzie. McKenzie's younger brother stood at a distance from all of them and kept spitting on the ground, as if the tobacco he was chewing had alum in it. Rainy pointed toward the table, frowning, saying something almost angrily.

Hank came over to the table, looking pleasantly neutral but watchful. "None of em wearing two-dollar boots," he said quietly. "You see the one in the grove of trees?"

"Nope."

"You don't have to look, but he's back there in the shade with a rifle."

"He was on the mound the other day. I guess they've got cash and are afraid of being held up."

With sweat pouring down his cheeks, Hank sighed and looked toward the men again.

Soon we were in the van, churning back along the road, past abandoned-looking tarpaper shacks. Rainy frowned out the window. "They sold a bunch of stuff today. I told them to please give me a chance to bid, and of course they promptly didn't. They sold to the first person who came along. Damn those idiots. I'm going to have to move a tent out here."

"They say who they sold to?"

She shook her head, staring straight ahead.

"Have you noticed them fighting among themselves?"

"I wouldn't be surprised if they were," she said. "McKenzie, the younger one, offered to sell me something out of his pocket the other day. They're supposed to be sharing profits. They all come out when I show up, as if they're afraid somebody will cheat them."

We reached Heavener when the sun was high. Two miles beyond the filling station where I'd stopped Sunday evening, we had what appeared to be a boil-over in the radiator. I saw the heat gauge wobbling, heading for the right peg. I made it to a little scrub shade to wait until the engine block and radiator cooled enough to pour in new water. Hank and I squatted and Rainy sat in the shade, all of us too hot to talk.

After a few minutes, Rainy cursed and brushed at the inside of her thigh; then she yelped again, jumped up, and pulled her skirt clear to the top of her thighs.

"Fire ant," I said.

"That can't be an ant!" she said, leaning down and scrutinizing her leg. Hank looked amazed, then turned away.

She saw the tiny ant and brushed it off. "That is one hell of an ant," she said.

Hank tried not to laugh, and waited until she'd let her dress back down to turn back.

"I see why you gentlemen squat," she said. "In the wrong place, that could be fatal."

Drenched with sweat, we took turns pouring out a little water from a five-gallon can that we'd brought, washing our faces and taking in handfuls to drink. After a half-hour of simmering mostly in silence, I tried to refill the radiator and saw water pouring out the bottom—a blown hose. Rainy and I walked back to the filling station, leaving Hank in the shade. We passed a house, its walls turned reddish by the dusty wind, red polka-dotted oilcloth hanging in the windows and several people asleep on mattresses and piles of rags on the front porch. The temperature was over a hundred humid degrees. The southwestern wind was picking up, rolling over the mountains and whipping down the dusty road. There was no traffic at all.

When we got to the shed-and-pump filling station, no one was there. The pump was locked. For a moment I had no idea what to do. I could form no plan. I saw the well that I'd used the other day and drew up a bucket of water and took off my straw fedora and poured water over my head. I drew up another bucket, and Rainy came up and stood by me and leaned over while I poured it over her neck and the back of her head. She reached under her shirt, took off her bra, and stuffed it into her pocket.

I walked around the closed filling station, hoping to find someone napping. Behind an outhouse, in a field of sticktights and the high-pitched striding of grasshoppers, were four wrecked cars, and I looked under their hoods. One of them had a hose that appeared to be the right size. I tried unsuccessfully to use my pocketknife on the clamp, but Rainy went off and found a screwdriver, and with it I crawled under the car and worked on breaking through the rust. I felt something on my shoulder and then on my neck and pulled off a three-and-a-half-inch grasshopper with black, leathery wings and a smaller set of vivid red wings. I'd been hearing about grasshopper attacks during the last three years—grasshoppers that would chew the binder twine off a sheaf of grain and gnaw the wooden handles of tools and eat the linseed-oil paint from houses, leaving them bare. This one looked as if he might be capable of some of those things, and I set him aside and finally broke through the rust and got the hose loose. At the well, we poured another bucket of water over our heads. I left a dollar and a hurriedly penciled note on the work counter and kept the screwdriver.

She stared down the highway toward the mountains, her face strangely pallid.

"You look a little pale," I told her.

"It's the curse," she said. "Forget it. I'm fast and furious. Turns me white as a sheet."

Our walk to the station had taken the better part of an hour, and Hank was groggy from sitting against the tree. Although we were partly shielded by the mass of mountains, the wind was kicking up dust devils, blowing harder as the afternoon progressed.

I crawled under the truck to get at the clamps. The dirt was soft and hot against my sweating shoulders. In this heat it was one thing at a time. Get that screw loose. Get the next one loose. Take a little rest. Drink a little water. Eventually I had the new hose on, and we gave up another gallon of our now precious drinking water to the radiator and drove back to the station to top it off.

"You want to go back?" I asked them. "Both of you look peaked."

Rainy squinted toward the mountains, shimmering in the burning air. "Let's go," she said. "It'll be cooler up there."

Hank glanced at me and nodded slightly.

So we went.

Just before the hills got serious, near a dry creek, was an abandoned one-room shack fifteen feet from the road with a sign painted in red on one wall: GO BACK. I hadn't noticed it last week.

We'd bounced about five miles into the hills when Hank suggested we stop soon and have lunch. He seemed to have in mind exactly where to pull over, near the base of a cliff topped by higher hills behind, where we could hear water as soon as I turned off the motor. We walked along a creek through a field strewn with room-sized boulders. Far above us was a moraine of squarish chimney-stone rocks. The little creek poured down a small waterfall into a pool. Above us turkey vultures soared on the wind.

"Where is this water coming from, Hank?"

He shook his head. "Horsethief Springs is near the crest of this mountain. There are springs scattered all around."

Rainy and I both emptied our pockets and stood clothes and all in the pool. It had a slightly mineral smell, and when Rainy picked up a handful from the waterfall Hank said sharply, "Don't drink it."

Hank had brought three cans of sardines, crackers, and apples—his daily lunch at work—for all of us. We found a rock to sit on in the shade and the cooled air of the water. Clouds were beginning to roll in.

Pulling back her wet hair, Rainy's eye played around the immediate area. "What's wrong with the water?" she asked.

"I don't know, but I've drunk it and wouldn't recommend it."

"So you know these mountains?" she said.

"I've been here a few times, but I can't say I know em."

"When did you drink the water?"

He thought a minute and said, "I hate to tell you it was almost fifty years ago."

"Fifty years ago?" She looked impressed. "How old were you?"

"Just finished school. Fifteen, I guess. We came out here, six boys, on what was supposed to be a three-week hunting trip. We had some old railroad survey maps, a wagon and team, and two riding horses."

While we loaded sardines onto the saltines, Hank told the story of coming here after they had graduated from school, of himself drinking the water coming off this hill and getting diarrhea, and another boy, named Will Clayton, on the same day that Hank drank the water—their fourth day out—accidentally shooting himself through the hand, of himself the night of the accident kept awake by stomach cramps, screech owls, and barking foxes, worried about his friend, even though it had been a clean wound between bones.

Rainy, who didn't waste time eating, loaded her last sardine onto a cracker. "What happened?"

Hank unpocketed his flask and held it out to her. She accepted the flask, took a quick sip, and offered it to me. It was a little early for me, and Hank took his after-lunch slug, washing it around in his mouth, knocking it back, his face suffusing with pleasure. Hank got more fun out of one hit of whiskey than most men got out of a bottle.

He dropped the flask back into his pocket. "We were okay until Will shot himself again."

I stopped chewing. "Again? You're kidding."

Hank went on to describe how three evenings after the first accident, about the time his and another boy's diarrhea was abating, Will Clayton was out looking for rich pine for the fire, carrying his shotgun in case he saw a turkey, and he dropped the gun, and the hammer hit something.

"It cut a half-inch-deep groove through the side of his neck," he said.

"Did he die?" Rainy asked.

Hank stood up to stretch his legs and glanced up the hill. He was noticing the weather too.

"We got out our maps and figured the best thing to do would be to go along this river valley. Then we could cut south and hit Talahina. It got too rough for the wagon, so we unhitched it. I propped Will on one of the saddle horses and rode with him, holding him up. We had to do quite a lot of backtracking, and I was still tired from the stomach disorder.

"Late that evening we met the only person we saw anywhere in these mountains. He was a Choctaw Indian, and he was walking along the creek toward us, by himself. I was real glad to see somebody. He was a grown man, strong-looking—we hailed him, asking how far it was to Talahina. I was so excited I nearly dropped Will on the ground, and he just walked by us. Didn't even act like he saw us, just went on by, like he would have walked through us if we'd been in his path, like we were invisible."

"How do you know he was a Choctaw?" Rainy asked.

"He was an Indian living in Choctaw country. I guessed he was."

"What'd he look like?"

"That was the strange part of it. None of us remembered exactly how he looked. Will figured he was a ghost."

"So Will survived?" Rainy said.

"Yes ma'am. Will Clayton survived shooting himself twice, and he survived the embarrassment of it too."

Rainy asked him a few more questions, trying to tease out a description of the Indian, but my mind went onto another track, thinking how far back Hank went.

We had finished eating when I asked him if he could think of a reason for Lee Guessner to have kept his office in the old Athenian Hotel.

Hank looked amused. "An office?"

"Hettie Weeks owns it. Guessner paid fifteen bucks a month to keep his office there."

Hank shook his head. "Wouldn't know. Maybe he used the basement for storage. All those rowhouses had good basements. They kept their liquor and money down there. Those houses had fancy liquor, you know. Men sometimes visited them just for the brandy."

"I didn't see any stairs to a basement."

"Oh, they're hidden," Hank said. "Trap doors. All of em were that way—basements better than what you'd see in the finest home. There were rumors about tunnels between them."

"What are you thinking?" Rainy asked me.

"Stone said the lake cabin was full of relics only twenty-four hours before Lee was found dead. Why would thieves pack all the stuff out, then dust shelves and sweep up after themselves? Maybe he cleaned out his cabin and took the stuff somewhere himself. Maybe to this basement—or some other place."

Back on the road, which followed the landscape, tilting in all directions, I drove slowly. Driving it in daylight, you could see where a wrong twist of the wheel would take you. Mist was beginning to lip over the tops of the ridges. The air up here was completely unlike the lowlands. It was a different country. Fallen rocks forced me to walk the car in stretches. A few miles below Colbert's property was a massive rock slide, a giant cone of rubble that had erased the road and smashed a pathway of trees below it. An entire cliff edge had fallen off. We parked and stared at it. The wind was whistling around, and pebbles and small rocks skipped down from above.

Hank picked up a rock and smelled it. "Our friend again," he said, giving it to me to smell. I gave it to Rainy, who put her nose to it and didn't even blink.

She turned her head up the hill and shaded her eyes against sunset streaming through a gap. "Somebody knows their dynamite. That's a lot of dirt."

"Have you used dynamite?"

She nodded. "In Egypt."

Hank's gray eyes played around alertly. "They sure closed us off."

"We're about an hour's walk from Colbert's place," I said.

More loose rocks skittered into the rubble. "If we leave that car untended," Hank said, "it might end up like your car did last week."

"Why don't you back away from the rock slide and park it? Stay with it and I'll walk to Colbert's. I think I can be back soon after dark."

"I'm going with you," Rainy said.

Hank looked uncertain.

"I don't know what's going on here, but there were a bunch of people on Colbert's property."

"Okay. I'll stick here. Take this."

He gave me one of his .45s, the holsters, and a handful of greasy bullets. He started the van to park it and stuck his head out. "Watch the weather," he called to us. "If it rains very much, this old road will turn into a river."

We scrambled over rocks and got beyond the slide, up the road, as banks of spectacular purple and gray clouds rose above a setting sun and mist rolled in, obscuring the sky. I was nervous about leaving Hank and taking this hike. Rainy tried to make conversation, but I was more interested in speeding up.

"I thought I was a walker," she said. "You move fast for a lawyer. I can't keep up with you."

"Yes, you can."

"You sure know how to talk to a girl."

In other places up the road there were smaller rock slides. I was trying to line up in my head how to approach Levi Colbert. Like every oil Indian, he had been harassed, sweet-talked, skimmed, double-crossed, and threatened by flimflam and con artists. Storekeepers overcharged him; his agency lawyer was milking him; his guardian was notorious. In 1922 I had read newspaper reports that he was being sued by fourteen Southern Baptist churches in Tulsa County who claimed that he had promised them money and instead given it to other, less deserving congregations. This was the everyday life of an oilholder. He wasn't likely to welcome strangers walking onto his place, trying to pry into his affairs.

Panting from the climb, I said to Rainy, "When we get there, don't ask him too many direct questions. A lot of people have tried to use him. They knock on his door, talk to him briefly, then sue him for breach of promise. Just go light with him."

She threw me a little look of consternation.

When we got to the place where I had driven off the road in my car, I was tempted to climb the hill and reconnoiter the place, but it was stormy twilight, soon to be dark, and we plunged ahead.

Cylinder 27

In the time it took us to get to Colbert's property, clouds had sealed what remained of daylight, and we smelled rain fast approaching. The gate was hanging open, and through a grove of dwarfed pecan trees we walked to the top of a low rise from where we saw a single fire not far away, sparking and twisting in the mist. There'd been twenty-three fires by my count the other night. A blast of wind came in, and heavy drops splattered in the dust. We walked on, and Rainy stopped to squint toward the fire, which was now hissing in the downpour, a single shadowy form moving just out of its light. In the fury of the storm I sensed a motion coming toward us down the drive. Headlights popped on, I pushed her to the side of the road, and it blew past us, a Plymouth, I thought, dark colored.

"That lug almost killed us," she said.

Everything was obscured by the mist, but lightning showed what looked like two rough timber roundhouses at the edge of the woods, along with a bunch of army tents scattered across the slope. A quarter-mile from the gate, on a muddy hill of dirt, stood the strangely painted building I'd assumed was Colbert's house, unlit. We stepped onto the porch, and I knocked on a door that was hanging slightly open. No response. What had looked at a distance like shutters were red-and-black designs painted on the wall. The storm now was cracking around us, blowing rain, clashing tree limbs together. When I turned to knock a second time the door was pushed open by wind. There was a sickly odor inside, and something was lying on the floor. I told Rainy to stay on the porch.

I went inside. "Hello? Hello the house?"

No response.

I walked around the room, taking baby steps, waiting for flickers of lightning through the windows to guide me, and eventually found two coal-oil lamps and stick matches on a low table and lit one of them. The thing on the floor was a woman—a young Indian woman, obviously dead, laid on her back on a woven round mat. Cleaned up perfectly, she was wearing something across her middle and nothing covering the top of her body. She was physically mature but young. There were darkened lines around her neck and wrists. She'd been dead, I guessed, a day or two. The cover around her middle was a short muslin skirt, split at the sides, with no belt. She was wearing earrings but no other jewelry, and around her head, rolled from a piece of cloth, was a simple red circular headdress. Her eyes had been closed. A fly struggled in her tightly woven braid. Some balmy herb had been spread on her skin, cutting the smell of death. Near both of her ankles were carefully severed arteries without a drop of blood beyond the immediate wounds. Rainy stood in the doorway, looking down at her.

"Stay back," I said tightly.

Rainy paid no attention to me. She knelt on the other side of the woman's body and looked at her closely without touching her, top to bottom. I pointed at the ankle cuts.

Rainy saw the other lantern and lit it. Also on the table were a circle of beads, a chunkee stone, and a wooden carving. The whole building was one large room, open to the roof. Behind the woman was a wall made of inch-thick oak boards, like a heavy stage flat, with a dark curtain hanging before it. In the shadows of a far back corner was a large worktable. Rainy stood up and walked around the girl a couple of times, still examining her.

She went to the curtain and, hesitating only to note the rod it was hanging on, pulled it aside, revealing something that caused her to jump backward so fast that she didn't seem to move but rather to be in one place, then inexplicably in another, like a figure in a broken and spliced film, for a second even ducking her head and raising her arm in front of her face as if to protect herself from what she had revealed: a shirtless man, his arms spread wide in cruciform with huge feathers dangling from several bracelets running from shoulders to wrists. He was held up by ropes that went through rings nailed to the wall. A pointed kilt made of stiff leather hung from waist to knees—that and the feathers were his only clothes. Covering the bottom half of his face was a curved, beaked mask made of what appeared to be copper. The skin on his arms sagged from age, and the eyes were circled by forked shapes of red and white paint. He was such a stunning sight, the huge feathers reaching from his outspread arms to thigh level, that he looked alive.

The worktable in the corner was covered by dark, lumpish shapes. I went toward it with the lantern, then stopped in my tracks: they were human body parts. I had seen enough. It was time to get out of there.

Rainy continued to look at the dead man, then at the young woman laid out in front of him. My heart was racing, and it was taking me a moment to comprehend certain things, like the fact that the man's head was being held upright by a wall-mounted hook inserted in the base of his skull, but Rainy went close and held her lantern up to his copper mask. A fist of thunder whacked against the side of the house, and I imagined his withered eyelids springing open. She slowly went down his body with the lantern, looking closely, actually pulling up the leather kilt and squinting under it. As her lantern descended, she studied wounds on both of his legs like those on the woman. The old man's hadn't been fully cleaned up yet, leaving his feet encrusted with blood.

"Is this Colbert?" she asked me.

Funny, I hadn't even thought about that yet. He did appear to be about the right height and age to be Colbert, and the upper part of the face looked not unlike one of the photographs of him I'd seen in the magazine.

I nodded slightly. "I think so." But I wasn't sure. I glanced through the open door and out the windows. I kept having the ominous feeling that we were being watched. There were moving forms outside, possibly only the trees blowing in the storm. With a wet hand I smudged blood from the corpse's cold ankle, put it on his forefinger and thumb, and took imprints on the only unsoaked piece of paper I could find, my driver's license. After a couple of tries I had a decent print.

"We'd better get out of here," I said. I was feeling enormously tired.

"A minute," she said, and held up the lantern for another look around the room. She held it close to the circle of beads and the wooden carving on the table, her eyes, slightly glazed, playing over them minutely. Noticing the table in the corner, she went over to it and surveyed the carnage—a human trunk, arms, legs, a head. Even then she held steady.

Finally she opened a back door and walked outside. The rain was already slowing. Behind the house was a place where fires had been built on a table rock. She shielded her lantern best she could and slogged around the mound through bulldozer tracks and mud puddles, careless of the lightning that was still tickling the sky. The house, I now saw, had been built on timbers that acted as runners and dragged onto the mound, elevating it about fifteen feet. Wet, dirty, exhausted, I waited for her as the rain came to a stop.

It had been a hit-and-run storm, which meant we did have a chance of getting out tonight if we could make it back to the truck. Hank or Rainy would have to drive, though, because I was whipped.

She came toward me and said she was ready to leave.

Coming out from behind the house to the top of the driveway, we saw the fire, which had surely been put out by the rain, blazing even higher than before, and it caused us to stop in our tracks. Somebody was tending it, and he showed no sign of seeing us walking down the hill.

He was a young man, tall, dark skinned, with his head shaved on the sides and a beaded forelock and ponytail, like the men on the Spiro shells. He wore regular denim pants with a wide sash at the waist, no shirt, and a large, flat gorget necklace. His face was painted with circles around the eyes and long, jagged dark lines down his cheeks. He turned his head in our direction but like a blind person did not focus on us. In the blowing firelight he was so still for a moment that he could have been a painted statue. I wondered if in fact he was blind. Rainy was transfixed. Somewhere behind him in the dimness I saw another man, who by the bent of his body looked older, near one of the roundhouses, lit by a flicker of lightning—also shirtless, with deep pools of red paint around his eyes. He too was aware of us but didn't show any apparent concern or interest. He was carrying what looked like a war axe. Both of them were barefoot.

Rainy started to walk toward them, and I grabbed her arm.

"Leave him alone, Rainy."

She pulled away from my grasp. "Please don't tell me what to do."

"Look at his face," I said. "He's not dressed up for a tea party. We don't know what's going on here."

"That's right, we don't," she said in an icy voice. "But I want to talk to him."

"That's warrior dress, Rainy. He'd just as soon peel off your face as look at it."

"You do have it in you, don't you, Tom? But please take your hands off my shoulders. And don't follow me. If he won't talk, I'll walk away."

I had a big urge—a spilling big urge—to try to stop her, but I didn't.

She went toward him until they were a couple of arms' lengths apart. I could hear her speaking quietly, but even with her in his face he didn't seem to notice her. The other man, in the edge of the firelight, floated a little closer, but he too affected not to see her or me. She talked and smiled and waited and gestured toward herself and toward him and did everything, mercifully, but touch him while he remained unmoved, uninterested, seeming to be off in his own world. He reached down and picked up a stick, and I stepped toward them, but then he placed it in the fire with ceremonious calm. It was one of the more convincing displays of obliviousness I'd ever seen, but I feared that at any second he was going to get fed up and jump her. There was something profoundly strange about this place, even beyond the strangeness of what we'd seen. The moon peeked out of fast-blowing clouds, and I had the feeling that I was on some vessel moving through a dangerous night sea.

She went closer to him, quite close to the fire, and I said, "Rainy, don't touch the fire; don't get too close to it."

She finally pulled back and came toward me.

As we descended through the dripping pecan grove, she said breathlessly, "You're right about the fire. I knew the minute you said it. How'd you know that?"

I didn't answer her.

"I've seen that blank expression before, but not like that," she said excitedly. "Never. He was stone. Maybe it's how they've survived."

I thought to myself, Yeah, you've got it, self-blinded, self-encapsulated, imprisoned.

Picking our way back on the slippery road, through waves of cicadas, we were blessed by enough moonlight to not have to stop. She wanted to talk, but I was too exhausted to respond, and finally we made it to the van, where Hank, in air cooled by the rain, had been having a seemingly pleasant nap in the back seat. By unspoken pact Rainy and I did not tell him what we'd seen. I completely trusted Hank, and I'm not fully sure why I didn't tell him. But Hank had good instincts. He knew I didn't want to talk, and he didn't ask any questions. He drove us out of the mountains while Rainy sat in the front seat, at first silent, then striking up a quiet conversation with him, asking him about the old days. I sat in the back, sullen, drowsing, with images that kept jolting me awake boiling up behind my closed eyes.

Cylinder 28

The heat woke me up at one o'clock Wednesday afternoon. Rainy had slept with me but had already left the house. I poured a bowl of cereal, made a strong cup of instant coffee, and sat on the front porch, watching the ice man making his way through the neighborhood. Yesterday's headache, temporarily turned aside, was coming to blurry fruition today. It felt like a class-one hangover, although I hadn't had so much as a nightcap when we finally got back at four o'clock in the morning. It wasn't going away, so I wandered off to the office.

Mel sat behind her substitute typewriter, looking unusually interested in the thing she was transcribing. She seemed hardly to notice my entrance. "'Lo," she said, her eyes remaining on her work. "You on the fritz today?"

"Can you see out the side of your head?" I asked her.

She glanced at me. "You look like one of those mission stiffs across the street. What have you been doing with yourself?"

I shook my head. "You wouldn't believe it."

"Well you got a retraction in that newspaper."

She handed me a copy of the *Sallisaw Chieftain*, where on the bottom of the second page under corrections it said:

Dale Cotton of the Combined Agency was quoted in an earlier story as saying that Tom Freshour, assistant prosecutor in Fort Smith, was fired by the agency due to his radicalism. Mr. Cotton notified us that this is incorrect. Mr. Freshour resigned from the agency.

"Make you feel better?" Mel said sardonically.

I didn't reply. I had the peculiar idea that Mel was retreating, as if her desk and she were rolling backward on wheels in an expanding room. Anger seemed to be becoming an important new aspect of my daily life. Dale Cotton. I wanted to do something terrible to Dale Cotton. My gaze fixed on the roaring maw of the air conditioner, and I remembered the black Plymouth, the one that had almost run over us the previous night.

Mel said something to me, and I had to ask her to repeat herself. Looking at me directly now, she said, "Something wrong? Your breezer is crooked. Do you need to lie down?"

I hesitated, wondering if she was taunting me. Mel never taunted. She joked around and got sarcastic plenty of times but didn't seriously taunt.

Withdrawing to my office, I just sat in my chair trying to figure out what was next. I looked through the slats of my blinds and thought about going across the avenue for a cup of Nancy's coffee, but the leering, gossipy, clientless lawyers were too much for me this afternoon. A woman with bobbed hair was standing outside the Spot, smoking a cigarette, waiting in the sunlight. Last night had made me feel unsafe, raw. I took out my driver's license to see if the finger and thumb impressions from the corpse had enough detail. I knew a little about fingerprinting because at the agency we had used them as proof of identity for probate recipients.

Glancing at the newspaper I'd thrown onto my desk, I realized that I didn't know what to do next about what we'd seen on the mountain because there was no one to trust who had authority over the east side. The LeFlore courthouse gang lived like cockroaches on bribe and kickback crumbs. The governor of Oklahoma, Bill Murray, I had met years ago, and I could probably get into his office, but he was a lame duck who wanted only to slip out of politics without suffering the fate of half of Oklahoma's governors—being run out on a rail. As for the FBI, all they'd do was sic platoons of deputies with dogs and tommy guns onto the people on the mountain—trying to create some kind of spectacle to feed a public yearning to be assured that someone, somewhere, was in control. A simple bank robber or killer, fine, call out the hounds. Whatever we'd witnessed wasn't simple, and there was no legal authority outside this office I could trust.

After sitting for a while waiting for my headache to lighten up, I made several telephone calls to Poteau trying to get hold of Bill Hagglund but had no luck. It was probably just as well. I needed to see him in person again.

There was a quick knock on the door, and Bernie stuck his head in and shot me a big Bernie smile.

"How bout that rain? Lot of sound and fury for such a little sprinkle. I think two oak trees in my front yard died of sheer disappointment."

I looked at my boss, feeling decidedly stiff and unsure of myself.

He opened the door. He was wearing brown slacks, an unmatching coat, no tie, and dirty sport shoes. Some days he was sartorially perfect, but today he was the disheveled sportsman.

"What's that?" he said, pointing at my desk.

"My driver's license," I said, offering no explanation.

He smiled at me mysteriously.

"You're chipper today," I said glumly.

His smile turned wicked. "That might just be because I have Kenny by the balls."

A week's work, and Bernie had the sheriff? Something appeared to be wrong with that picture, but after last night what did I know?

"And Berenice is coming home in a few days," he added, "maybe a week."

Ah, Berenice, now there was good news. Something about Berenice actually did warm my heart on that weird afternoon. She was solid; you could count on her: a smug, insular, superior Republican (married to a Democratic officeholder) who regarded me—the few times she'd ever directly addressed me—as a yard boy who might steal the lawn mower. A known quantity in a shifty world, Berenice.

"Glad to hear it," I said. "I know you've been missing your family. Do you want to talk about what you've got on the sheriff?"

"He's squeezing people for protection money. I have two good folks willing to testify. He's clipping them, Tom. They don't come across with the weekly sugar, he raids them, turns over tables, breaks windows, runs them out of business."

"You might want to keep a lid on that if you hope to make it to trial."

"Gotta take a chance or you'll never get anything done. Sooner or later you have to . . ." Bernie came into the office and sat down. He tried to look jaunty, but his eyes flicked around and finally settled on me. "He's been having me shadowed."

"He'll do that," I said.

"So how's his majesty?" he said.

"Wouldn't know. I haven't seen him in a couple days."

"Aren't you in constant touch with him?"

I grimaced. I didn't want to hear this. I had enough on my mind.

"Tom, there's something funny going on between our fine sheriff and our upstanding judge. Yesterday I saw Kenny parked at Stone's house. They were standing by his carport talking."

I waited for the punchline, but that appeared to be the whole story. "The sheriff isn't famous for using the phone," I said. "Maybe he had court business, an estate sale or something."

"Been talking to a lot of people around town. It's amazing how much information five bucks will buy."

I nodded at this remarkable discovery by the prosecutor.

"I dropped by the Ozark and had a heart-to-heart with Hettie Weeks."

"Missing your wife?"

Bernie didn't smile. "I went to three whorehouses, in fact: the Peach Tree Inn out by the rodeo ground, the Modern, and then the Ozark. So I'm talking to Miss Hettie and ask her whether the sheriff is squeezing her. She puffs up like an adder and starts spilling about how many respected local men make use of her facilities, warning me away, telling me to stay off her back, you know, because any trouble on her would be trouble for a lot of people. So she's ticking off her clients, and one of them happens to be Judge Stone."

"You must really have her running. What did you threaten her with?"

Bernie raised his hands in innocence. "I didn't. I really didn't. She was just nervous."

"Who cares if Stone goes to the Ozark? Besides, Hettie Weeks would lie about her mother if she thought it would save her five bucks."

Bernie in his renaissance as a prosecutor was making me yearn for the Bernie who dropped by the office occasionally to chat about whether he was shooting 87 or 91 on the golf links, or to discuss whether the once great Georgia seaside resorts were all going to hell. This new Bernie, with moral fervor shining out of his eyes, struck me as somebody who could be careless with peoples' lives.

Looking pained, Bernie said with exaggerated gentleness, "Okay, so you're saying these things are unimportant. My point is who's doing what to whom. Why did the good judge call us all together and threaten us and tell us to toe the line? Why is he so worried to find out who killed this man?"

"I wasn't aware of any threats."

"You had to call off your vacation. Remember? The one you'd been working up to for months. And he threatened me directly."

I looked dully at Bernie, suspecting that if he was sore about any vacations, it was probably his own annual "big vacation," so rudely abbreviated. But I did also remember the conversation the judge had had with me in chambers after the Goback trial—about pasts coming back to haunt you.

When I didn't respond, Bernie went on, "Remember the bit about showing me his new shotgun? Well he takes me into the back room and says, 'Bernie, if you foul this up, you are legally and politically dead. I want you to stay out of the sheriff's way, stay out of Tom's way, and do the routine work. And leave off the girl,' he said. Leave off the girl! That was what he told me. Can you believe it? Manny Stone, the little sap I used to play baseball with who couldn't catch a fly ball if it was headed straight between his eyes. He tells me to lay off the sheriff, lay off my own employee, and lay off the girl who he just met that afternoon! He tells me to go back to the office and act busy—that's what it amounts to."

I took this in. Even with a headache that made my brain feel like a wet cotton mattress; I had to admit that Bernie was right about this not quite making sense, but maybe not for the reasons he had in mind. Stone was a shrewd man. You wouldn't need to have grown up with Bernie to see what he wore like patches on his sleeves—the floating vanity and sensitivity to insult.

"Had you been badmouthing the sheriff?" I asked him.

"No!" Bernie said, taking out a Lucky Strike and sticking it in his mouth, staring at me with wide eyes. "I hadn't even talked to him for weeks. What'd he mean about any of that?"

I shook my head. "You don't know what he meant by lay off the girl?"

"Okay, okay, I was being hospitable to the new lady in town, but that doesn't mean the little shithead has to herd me into the back room and threaten me. Tom, listen to me." Bernie knitted up his eyebrows almost pleadingly. "The sheriff is as crooked as a three-dollar bill, you know that. And with Stone something ain't right. You know that too. It's not like I'm asking you to believe in the man in the moon."

I leaned back and tapped a pencil on the edge of the desk. I said nothing. It would be useless to tell him that at the agency, I'd

grown accustomed to sheriffs so crooked they could have swallowed nails and spit up corkscrews, men so blatant and brutal that
you appreciated the ones who were relatively discreet about their
crimes. Most of them were would-be mobsters, tobacco-chewing
anarchists who called themselves the law, paid by the local money
to protect the local money—state law unenforced by them, federal
law, particularly having to do with Indians, a joke to them. Some
of them couldn't read, and the ones who could pretended that
they couldn't, at least when it came to anything I ever tried to talk
to them about. Men who wouldn't talk on the phone to you, who
didn't respond to letters, affidavits, anything. Men with two faces:
wide-eyed sun-struck idiocy and pure murderousness. Walk into
their offices and tell them about a problem, and they'd raise the
corners of their mouths in tobacco-yellowed sneers and tell you
not to get your tit in a wringer. Compared to these types, our
Kenny was a civilized prince among sheriffs. He had qualities. At
least he played businessman, and presumably, when push came to
shove, you could make a deal with a businessman.

I didn't say any of this because I wasn't being paid to tutor
Bernie C. Pryor in reality. He had been raised from birth in a cap-
sule of coal-trust money, cut off from the world that was all around
him. I had learned more from a brutal schoolmaster and a herd of
orphans than he had from his preparatory school in Connecticut
and his Brown University. He expected people to be delighted
when he told stories about his dear wife, Berenice, his beautiful,
beau-besieged daughters Beatrice and Belle, and his strong,
healthy, smart son Clarke, to be entertained and enthralled by their
delightful domestic scenarios.

I must have looked as unpleasant as I felt at that moment. I said
nothing because I wasn't in any condition to control myself. The
previous night had scrambled my brains.

"What about Miss Green Eyes? Were you with her last night?"

"What are we talking about now?" I snapped back.

Bernie studied me a minute. "You know what I find interesting
about you and me, Tom? Since the first day we met, you were

straight with me. I'm going to be straight with you. Damnit, you're not a very sociable person, so you don't know how people around here regard you. They say you're a hired gun; they say you know how to deal with criminals because you're a goddamn half an Indian; they say all kind of nervous things because they're afraid of you, Tom. You are a killer in court. You have a really mean streak that is perfectly under control. When you bare your teeth, it's better than a scary movie."

Bernie went quiet a moment, then gave me a shadow of the grin. "And you've never played up to me. In fact, you usually tell me to jump in the lake, even when you are doing the regular work of this office. Unlike now, when you are doing work under the judge's direction, not mine. Do you know any other lawyer in this town who'd treat me this way?"

"Not who'd also work for you."

"And can you think of another lawyer in this state who'd do a better job than you?"

"Go jump in the lake."

The grin widened. "So tell me I'm a fool. Tell me I'm a bad prosecutor."

"I'm well aware that you're not a fool, Bernie."

"Be careful with Miss Green Eyes. And don't discount what I'm doing." With that surprisingly firm advice, he left me stewing in the headache.

Having accomplished nothing that afternoon, I went home and made a bowl of canned chicken soup for supper and sat on the front porch sipping it, floating on Count Basie for a while, then listening with one ear to a "Lights Out" story about a giant amoeba that kept growing and swallowing up whole neighborhoods. Crowds of people screamed as it rolled down an avenue eating dogs and old people.

I had my cold jug of water from the icebox. Across the street, a middle-aged man was running a boy panhandler through the neighborhood, methodically standing out of view while the boy, dressed in rags, went to every door, humbly bowing his head and

going back and forth on his feet. I had once prosecuted a talkative
bum (caught stealing jewelry) who bragged to me that he had run
a boy, a very attractive boy, through neighborhoods all over the
country, making about twenty bucks a day and even more when the
boy rendered certain services. A pretty boy is worth a fortune, he
told me, if you dress him up right and learn him how to act. He'd
lost the kid, he told me mournfully, hoping to get my sympathy.

Watching them move from house to house made me vaguely
uneasy. A prosecutor, or any lawyer, is well aware of the scheming
that can go on beneath the most sincere-appearing behavior. He
gets a bellyful of it. Bernie's dubious compliments, then his veiled
threats about me not doing the regular work of the office.

But if Lee Guessner was killed in Sebastian County, this case
was the regular work of the office, no matter what sort of feud was
going on between Bernie and the person he used to make fun of
playing baseball. As for his opinion of Stone—at least Stone had
grown up. He worked in his job. He was a good judge, while
Bernie was still a hapless silver-spoon kid, a small-town rich boy.
He finally gets interested in his job—who knows for what mysterious reason—and instead of getting his feet wet with a little everyday work he wants to ride in on a white horse and nab the sheriff
by morning.

The real problem was that I was stymied. My original reason to
find Colbert was only to ask him what he knew about his guardian's
interest in the Spiro collection. Innocent question, but as so often
happens in Oklahoma, it resulted in a tangle of other questions—
possible probate fraud at the agency, milking an oil estate, dynamiting highways, and human sacrifice and mutilation. I had no
clear idea about the killers except that more than one person was
involved, they wore boots, and they definitely were interested in
the Spiro collection. I didn't think the Indians on Colbert's property were the types to attempt to throw off a murder investigation
by writing *sodomite* on the wall.

Somehow I had to get to Mr. Oil, Jim Mackey. But he was
about as likely to give me information freely as a snake was to rise

up on its tail and play checkers. There would have to be a compelling reason for him even to talk to me. I needed something to get his attention, and I thought of Jay Goback. I gave Hank a call to make sure Goback hadn't been sentenced yet. He hadn't.

"Yeah," Hank drawled. "It's possible. Deep as he is in the east side, he might know something about Mackey."

I arranged with Hank to visit Goback's cell in the morning.

Cylinder 29

I drove the Chevy to the lake cabin at dusk. The air was a cloak of humidity. Rainy was sitting at her bare table in the big downstairs room, glowing lamps on both sides of her, working at a little typewriter. Her hair was wild, not tied back, as if she hadn't combed it, and she was wearing linen shorts and a T-shirt. She handed me the pages she'd already typed. It was a description of what we had seen the night before, all precisely described, particularly the bodies, the masks, the locations of everything, the mound being built behind the house, and the fire tender.

"You intend to publish this?" I asked.

She stopped a minute and stared. "Probably not. I don't know. . . ." She stared a moment longer and then abruptly got up.

"Tom, I'm sorry; I'm forgetting my manners. Would you like a glass of wine or tea or a whiskey and water?"

"The latter would do fine."

Pouring it, she laughed, "You are strange."

I looked at her curiously.

"You talk so formally sometimes." She handed me the whiskey, her face a sheen of sweat.

"I came to see if you want to look for a basement at that old hotel where Guessner kept his office."

"Okay," she said softly. "But talk to me about last night. The fire—how did you know about it?"

I nursed the whiskey a while before answering. "A lot of these little Indian towns had sacred fires. The fire sometimes outlives the town, with some old person keeping it burning."

"He was like a ghost," she said. "I was right in his face, and he didn't show a flicker of recognition. It was as if he was in some other time, really unable to see me. I almost got the feeling he was sick. Beneath the paint he appeared to have rings around his eyes. And the dead man—Colbert, or whoever he was—was being buried Mayan style, there's no question about that. He had wounds and infected tissue on his penis. He may have died from those infections."

"On his what?" I said.

She got a cigarette off the table. "The posture he was in, the feathers, the way he was dressed, everything looked Mayan. It was almost like a staged fresco. That's why I looked."

"I'm not getting you. About the . . ."

"Penis," she said, striking a match and lighting the cigarette. "Mayan kings did it. It was part of the job. They climbed a pyramid, cut it open, and bled for the people. That's one of the things the anthropologists don't talk about much. We walked in on a very old-fashioned funeral. Falcon mask. Sacrificed wife. Cuts on the penis. A temple mound prepared. He was being buried as the Bird King."

"Why'd they cut their penises? I'm stuck on that one."

She took a drag on the cigarette. "Nobody knows. They were obsessed by blood, death, sacrifice. When Lee and I were at Tikal, one of the other campers there was working on a book about it. He said that most of the Indians in Central America are stoic about death, quietly accepting and all that, but the Mayans were gaga about the subject, like medieval Christians. They feared it, courted it, fantasized about cheating it. Bleeding the king was either to heal the flock or to hold back illness and death. He had a theory that death-fear was the wellspring of cultural achievement. . . ."

196

She trailed off, thinking. The ceaseless bright racket of crickets and tree frogs, frantic with heat, surrounded the cabin.

"So what about the woman? Was she murdered?"

Rainy looked at the cigarette. "The woman on the floor? You saw her. She was young. I don't know if I'd call it murder, though. To them, it's sacrifice."

"Last time I checked, it was called murder in the state of Oklahoma. What about the body parts on the table?"

"The building is a mortuary. It's not a house. They're using it for burial preparations. They bury in different ways, probably depending on status. Some buried whole, some disarticulated. Buried in parts. Disarticulation is common all over the world. You saw the pot I bought from Spiro with hands in it."

"So the people on the table—"

"What I saw on the table was one body being prepared, so far as I could tell. It may have looked like more than that because it was in pieces. You can't really make any assumptions about how that person died."

"Which adds up to three corpses, anyway. . . . I don't get this. You're saying those people are Mayans? Why would Mayans be in Oklahoma?"

She paced to the window and stared down on the moonlit lake. "No, I'm not. I think they traded with Mayans and were influenced sometime long ago. There are plenty of Mayans around today, and the guy we saw at the fire didn't look Mayan."

"So who are they?"

"Maybe they're what's left of the Spiro people, inheritors who've somehow remained segregated and kept their way of life."

"Like driving bulldozers and Plymouths and wearing blue jeans?"

"I didn't see any bulldozers. Where were they?"

"They were working on the mound after dark, under headlights, when I was there last week, the night they smashed up my car."

I finished the whiskey. "If you want to check for a basement at the Athenian, we'd better go now. I'm going to be busy tomorrow."

We took the convertible. She asked for the details of my first visit to Colbert's property again, and as we rolled down her steep driveway and along the edge of the lake I told her what I could.

"So the bulldozers were probably taken away by trucks," she said. "You don't know who was operating them or who was driving either car?"

"No," I told her. "Too dark."

"Was the man who came out on the front porch the same one we found?"

"I don't know," I said, shaking my head. "Look, Levi Colbert was raised by a prosperous white family. He was educated, he went to college, he inherited record amounts of oil property. Why would he commit suicide for a bunch of backward types who don't know what century they're living in?"

"Maybe they were starving, or some sickness was going through the tribe—they needed help. He had plenty of money. . . . But how did he learn about them in the first place?"

"The story I got in Poteau was that he moved from Tulsa to the woods to escape his guardian, but the guy followed him."

She looked at me curiously. "You sound as if you're angry."

"I didn't like that place, Rainy. It gave me the heebie-jeebies. I don't see how you can be so calm about it."

"I've been dealing with burial habits for a while," she said mildly. "Big subject in archaeology."

"What we saw isn't just burial habits. I don't care if they're the lost tribe of Israel. In A.D. 1934, that's murder, even in Oklahoma."

She turned her eyes back to the road. "If they've really lived in isolation, they're not like you and me. They believe different things; different things matter to them."

This was beginning to sound like Smiling John defending Jay Goback.

"Tell it to the girl on the floor," I said. "She's maybe sixteen years old—and they kill her so the big guy can have a toss in Indian paradise?"

"You don't really know how she died," Rainy said, squinting in the wind.

We were out of the drive now, on the dirt road from Hackett to town, gravel rattling against the underside of the car.

She turned her face toward me, dash lit, eyebrows a little raised, about sixteen inches from mine. "You are being brisk with me, Tom. It's a wonder I like you.

"It really is a wonder," she repeated.

Something about that moment—the way she bounced off me, the control she kept, her tone—reminded me of her mother. Now I remembered her voice. Sam's voice. I saw her mother and me as if in an old photograph, splotched and fading, an image from a different age, quaint, ancient, gone, lost—our clothes; God knows how they'd have looked, with me barely more than a kid and she a young woman in the flush and prime of youth whose eyes, no matter how faded the print, would shine out with animal vitality. It was not altogether a pleasant thought, this imaginary photograph, this spell.

"Rainy, you're going to have to move over; you're having an effect on me. I can't drive."

"Poor darling," she said with light mockery, and moved over in the seat. "You're not that much older than me, Tom. Don't go acting stiff on me. I'm no spring chicken."

"If you like older men, at least get one who's rich."

"I'm not interested in getting any man," she said tranquilly. "And as for money, I never cared about it even when I was poor. I've got enough. It doesn't matter."

We were rolling down the lower avenue then, past dim bars and slouched forms, a small pack dawdling across the street from the Elevator Building, lazily shooting craps. A man in a ragged seersucker jacket, leaning against a light pole smoking a fag, looked up as we went by and flashed us a defeated grin. The usual gaggle hung around the charity hotel, escapees from the dollar hotels of Chicago and Hogan's flops from coast to coast, migrant harvesters with no place to go. People whose lives couldn't bear too much thinking about. As we rolled past them, I hoped that none of them heard her casual remark about money. Don't tell them that money doesn't matter. In fact, don't tell me, not when I'm a few dollars in an ammo box and an unstable boss away from being on the same street.

Cylinder 30

I pulled up at some distance from the Athenian and turned off the motor. The riverfront area was absolutely dead tonight. There wasn't so much as a breath of wind, despite the closeness of the river. As we walked across the tracks, I wondered why this old hotel wasn't used as a flop by bums. It was probably too close to the railroad storage building. Bulls would regularly check the area, and they could make an unhappy stiff a lot unhappier in about a second with their lead-weighted billys. There were plenty of hobos riding the lines who'd been knocked around so much that they were punch-drunk.

We crawled into the window on the river side, as I'd done before. I had brought two powerful flashlights, and we spotted around the back room and the room where the desk still sat.

"What an office," Rainy murmured.

We poked around all of the rooms, unsuccessfully looking for the trap door. I gave up and went outside to walk around the outer foundation, which was rock with the mortar still solid. When I came back in, Rainy was crawling on her hands and knees on the floor, knocking on the floorboards with a piece of wood. I joined her, and together we covered the whole downstairs floor—red knees, no luck. Then she studied the walls with her torch and began methodically knocking on them. In a short hallway she finally found it, an entire four-by-ten-foot wall that swung outward like a barn door, plaster, trim, and all. She glanced at me—we both smelled the copper sulfate—and without talking we felt our way down the stairs. I looked at the latching mechanism and shut the door behind us.

The air was dry for a basement. Despite everything else in the room, the first thing I looked at was the masonry work, which had been done by an artist; the floorboards above were sealed so that nothing would leak through. Hank's comment that the rowhouses had good basements was an understatement. So Guessner's "office" had really been his safe. I played the light around the room, seeing a bed in the corner, a trim little double bed with a brass bedstead, made up, complete with pillows and an old reddish bedspread.

"My God," Rainy breathed. She was flashing her light around.

The place was filled with artifacts. There were a half-dozen folding wooden tables, and things were lying helter-skelter across them and around the floor. My first impression was of cluttered piles thrown about in lumpy hempen sacks. But in them were wooden blade shapes covered with embossed copper, delicate arrowheads, shell cups—at a quick glance what looked like several hundred of them, etched with snakes, griffins, warriors, fantastic animals, and human faces eerily suggestive of real people.

On top of a table sat a row of double-stemmed pipes, sculpted in sleek, almost modern-looking lines, alongside three ornate ones, single-stemmed, with effigies of people or animals as part of the pipe's shape.

One of them, more statue than pipe, was about a foot tall, a man sitting on the ground with his legs crossed, naked except for a cape with arrows etched on it and a round hat. He had a long pig-tail coming down across his front and an arrestingly real, heavy-featured face. Sculpted into the cape over his inclined back was a burning bowl and a second chamber for drawing smoke. I picked the piece up by its two arms and was surprised at its heft. It felt almost as if it was made of lead, but in fact it was of some polished red stone. When I looked into the face a chill went through me. I don't know what caused it, exactly—the mysterious sadness of the expression or how perfectly it was made—but I felt as if I was in touch with someone or something many centuries old.

I set it down carefully and saw that Rainy was looking at a smaller thing on one of the other tables, made of cane that was bent and bound up together in perfect symmetry. Rainy was staring at it and hardly breathing.

"It's a comb," she said. Her eyes were glowing. "Look at it, Tom."

On the next table, by itself, was a box made of cedar. She went to it and carefully pulled off the top while I kept my flashlight on it. Inside, under a thin piece of mica, were four black eye masks sitting face up. They were made of some carved and polished black mineral. She picked one of them out of the box and held it in the light, for a moment looking up at me almost as if confused, and then she sat down where she was, on the rock floor, still holding the thing, staring at it.

"You okay?" I asked.

She didn't answer, and for a moment there wasn't a whisper of sound, not a creak of wood above us, not a drop of water, not the rustle of clothes, just the utter tomblike hush of twelve feet underground. I understood why she'd sat down. I had the night-sea feeling again—of being carried like a passenger on the fourth deck of a troopship with the U-boats out there prowling.

Inside one of the tow sacks was a hoard of shell cups, and I picked out one of them to look at.

When she finally spoke, she said in a small voice, "It's funny how you feel."

"About what?"

She stood up and put the mask back into the box and looked around again, sighing, almost burdened by it. "We can talk about it later, I guess. We've got to do an inventory."

"An inventory?" I said. "Can't it wait till daylight?"

"I won't leave here until I do at least a rough one. You don't have to stay."

She dictated the inventory to me to be written down later. She did estimates of some of it, but even her estimates were careful—and it soon became obvious that there were a lot more items than had been in Guessner's working inventory. Instead of seventy-five fragments of fabric, there were more like three hundred. Instead of thirteen complete fabric pieces there were thirty-three, including sashes, headdresses, and kilts, many of them brilliantly dyed with jagged triangles of color. There were about two bushels of pearls, and perhaps three bushels of arrowheads and spearpoints. There were hundreds of shell cups and fragments—too many to count—all etched with different carvings. A wooden deer mask lay casually on a stack of human bones.

While she estimated, calling out items and amounts, I was drawn again to the shells. Some were like close-ups of partial scenes, with hands going up the choosing stick and one or two faces nearby; some were mysterious creatures, fantastic animals, one looking like a microbe with a single calm eye and a wiggling tail; some were flamboyant, powerful human-animal figures; other shells had so many details that they appeared to tell stories. The etchings on the gorgets were just as varied: two-headed people; heavily garbed people holding up what looked like fans in one hand and giant steaming pots in the other; a spectacular-looking runner, made sleek by the wind; hands with crossed ovals or with eyes in their palms; and faces—faces painted like the face of the fire tender in the Winding Stair.

In the etchings there were a lot of eyes, in fact, and a lot of war, and chopped-off heads, and fantastic animals, and real animals such as hawks and snakes and falcons.

Rainy dug around, occasionally muttering to herself, and then at moments went still and quiet, just looking at something. In the almost crushing silence of that basement, surrounded by all those things, I felt strange, at once elated and depressed, fearful and hopeful, contrary moods rippling through me. Looking at the bed, I wondered what it must be like to sleep down here. It was cool but almost supernaturally isolated. Even with Rainy, I felt weirdly alone here. Had the collector ever come down here with Alfred Carr? That would have been another very good reason to pay Hettie Weeks faithfully to rent a place that no one else wanted. Because they had to be as sure of privacy as they could be—no windows; only one entry point.

I was taking one last look at the bed in the corner when I heard something above us, a scuffling that I thought at first was rats. Somebody was on the floor above us. I put a finger to my lips and pulled Rainy by the shoulder to a place below the stairs, and we turned out the flashlights. There was talking, too muffled to hear the words. I expected them to come down the stairs but began to wonder after a couple of minutes. Possibly railroad bulls, I thought. After a while they seemed to have left.

Rainy wanted to go to the cabin, to the typewriter, so we could get down the details immediately. I'd lost my headache and was hungry. On Zero Street we stopped at Norma's Restaurant, a corner joint that catered to factory workers and down-and-outers. We sat away from the other occupied table, where two women were tiredly polishing off their plates. A man sitting at the counter gave me a look of the kind I occasionally got—with my suspect complexion—when I was with white women. My wife's skin had been lighter than mine, and we'd gotten some of that.

We both ordered the two-bit plate dinner, which turned out to be black-eyed peas and a little loaf of bread wrapped in a newspaper, along with a couple of poor-looking chicken wings. Like me, Rainy didn't seem to mind what she ate as long as it wasn't moving on her plate. She'd apparently eaten a lot of camp grub. I'd been raised on poor food and occasionally actually yearned for things like shriveled cold chicken wings and fatback peas. Comfort in the known.

She ate in silence, head down. With sex she was direct and polite; with food she was just direct.

I glanced around the room. A single fan pushed air from behind the counter. The young waitress came around and filled our coffee cups with rusty-nail coffee, then went to the window and looked out the blinds nearby. We were sweaty and dirty and smelled of the artifacts, and she must have wondered what kind of ditch we'd been sleeping in. Through the blinds I noticed a black Ford go by.

The waitress went back to the counter, and we both finished, the simple food hitting the spot. Rainy left only a couple of well-picked bones on her plate. We sipped at the coffee, and I asked her what she'd thought back there.

She smiled wanly and stared off. "Lee. At Tikal. I was confident—especially at first—that I was being hounded by one more guy off his head. Another eccentric, oh so earnest but completely pegged out, full of it. Melodramatic. Making a great deal out of nothing. That's what I saw. But it was just the way the poor cush talked. He must have been at wit's end. I was the one being cavalier. And your judge, I thought he was some overexcited local arrowhead hunter."

"Easy to assume when you see what's on the walls of his den."

She made a face at her coffee.

"I've traded two-thousand-year-old papyri and probably three lorries of pyramid junk. But there are millions of Egyptian artifacts. The Rosetta Stone was cracked over a hundred years ago. Nothing like this exists. Fabrics, masks, cups bursting with information about them—all from one place. It'll be hard to keep it together. It's priceless. I guess Lee knew that. I guess it was why he was so desperate."

"Why didn't he give it directly to some museum?"

"You don't just give a collection willy-nilly to a major museum. Besides, the poor man did have to make a living."

"What's wrong with just giving it?"

"It ends up in a back room. Unless it's known goods, it takes time and costs money to get yourself—and the museum—sufficiently educated. There are important papyri all over Germany that will never be 'discovered' even though they're inside museum collections. This doesn't belong in a back room because some curator doesn't know how to label it."

"Why didn't he will it to the judge?"

She shook her head and looked away. "Experience dealing with museums? I don't know, Tom. The judge seems to be asking the same question."

When I got up and went to the register, the young waitress still looked slightly alarmed, as if she was afraid we were going to rob the place.

At the car, with no headache and some food in me, I felt human for the first time that day. Rainy seemed to feel better too. "Sit close to me," I said.

"Why should I, after what you said earlier?"

"Did you notice how dirty we are? You have it on your face."

"So you'll accept my affection now? You find a dirty face attractive?"

She bantered with me, then scooted over. I wondered if Rainy was free-acting like this, physically self-confident, because men were only part of the score for her, down her list, and she could take us or leave us, except possibly for her dead scoundrel of a husband. The thought was strangely comforting.

I shifted down to third as we passed through the dark streets. The slaughterhouse smell had made its way to west Fort Smith tonight. Passing a domino and pinball parlor, we heard the monotonous ding of a ball hitting the pegs. One of the sheriff's Fords was lurking in front of the parlor, and he drove out and smoothly latched onto us, but as soon as I braked he turned off onto a side street, here and gone as fast as a bad thought. If Kenny knew that the prosecutor was after him, he naturally assumed I was too. He was sending his boys around—warning shots to make me nervous. That was his style. They'd probably been the ones searching around the Athenian. They'd seen our car and done a casual search.

We headed down the dusty road to Hackett.

When we got to the cabin, Rainy lit a couple of lanterns and we started getting the inventory on paper immediately. I dictated it to her from memory, and she sweated at the little typewriter, whacking away at the keys with two fingers, x-ing out mistakes with no concern for neatness. I sat directly across from her, listing the stuff. The window and door were open, but there was no breeze tonight and no coolness reaching up from the lake. When we'd finished, she spread out the three pages and frowned at them for a while, wiping her face with a handkerchief.

I paced, went out on the front porch a while, and came back in. She stood up and stretched. "Another whiskey?" she asked.

"Reached my limit," I told her. "Look, I'm about to melt. Maybe we'd better go back to my place. At least I've got an electric fan."

"Nonsense," she said. "Come with me."

I followed her down to the lake, and we ended up in the overflow pool below the dam, with a two-thirds moon hanging above us in a clear night sky, our bodies entangled in lilies in cold water. The cool water of the spring ran over the dam, refilling it constantly. We'd been hot so long that a chest-deep ice-water bath felt good, but I did hope the copperheads were asleep. We sat across from each other, and she picked up one of my feet and started rubbing my toes, telling me a story as she did.

"I had a professor at Chicago, Oriental Institute. A bit of a sot but a good teacher. He was the person who interested me in archaeology. He'd march into class and start lecturing before he even put down his briefcase. Short little bulldog of a fellow, dynamic— he's digging now at the palace of Sargon II, where there are winged sphinxes, centaurs, mermaids. Grand stuff. In fact, I was in Chicago before coming here, trying to get on that dig."

She was working on the bottom of my foot, then slowly up to the ankle, not in a hurry. I was hearing what she said, watching her remember, but with other things billowing up in my mind, like the thought that you live somewhere for years, you occupy it mostly in stupefied partial awareness, time going by at a certain dull pace.

And then this feeling comes along and wakens you and puts you completely there, in the heart of a place.

She sighed. "Anyway, this was before, when I was a student. I've forgotten a lot of what he taught in that course, but I remember his two lectures on the mounds. He spent one class talking about their discoveries and what they looked like. Not a word about what they meant or anything about their significance, just a lot of places and names and how they were first described. Marquette and Joliet first describing Cahokia, and so forth. It was rather dull. The next day he came in holding up one of those pulp magazines—*Amazing Tales* or something like that—bright colors, ten cents, Martians and spaceships on the cover. And he said, 'American archaeology arose from science fantasy writing very much like the material you read in this magazine. Set forth in some of the greatest-selling books of the nineteenth century. Plenty of quite serious minds subscribed to it then, and plenty still do.' . . ."

She let go of my leg. "Do you like what I'm doing to you?"

"Yes," I said.

"Please do it to me. My feet are dead from last night."

I did so happily, and she lay back and groaned. "That's it, my dear. That's it. The toes."

"Quite serious minds," I said. "Is that the end?"

"There you go. You can move up the leg, if you like. In fact, I invite you to do what you're doing to my entire body. What did you say?"

"Serious minds subscribed to it, you were saying."

"Yes," she said, with her head back and her eyes closed. "And one of the reasons they did was that all those impressive eastern mounds I've been telling you about appeared to be largely empty, with only bits and pieces and an occasional remarkable single item—here and there a pipe, a statue, little to go along with it, nothing to build a context. It allowed the fantasy writers to run wild. They could imagine anything, and naturally they imagined that no mere Indians could have been the first great American engineers. Instead, all kinds of people—Vikings and people from

Atlantis and outer space, some great white master race—these were the original great Americans, you see, not the ancestors of the shabby, poor, dirty Indians who stood before their very eyes."

I was so absorbed in watching her, with her head back and neck exposed, that I didn't respond. I'd dropped one leg after reaching the lower thigh and was working up the other one. She seemed happy with what I was doing.

Our bodies had eventually come closer together in the water, although she was still lying back, eyes almost closed, legs actually spread, with me and several lily stalks between them. I had a momentary fear, a shudder that went through me, the source of which I couldn't identify, but I looked around, along the top of the dam, as far as I could see into the moonlit forest, and the feeling passed, and I was as erotically charged as ever in my life.

She scooted backward out of the overflow pool onto the ground and to my surprise presented herself up on all fours, like an animal. But it was only where we started, because there were rubbers in her cabin, and a small mattress, and we did have the pool to wash in and cool ourselves off, mosquitoes be damned. Rainy was wanton, giving herself to it entirely, asking me to do things to her in ways that I had never encountered before.

Twice in the cabin, very early in the morning, she woke me again. And in the dreamy melancholy that finally ensued, when the two of us were dozing on the tiny mattress, only a couple of things slightly bothered me: the British phrasing she fell into in her most unguarded moments—dear and indeed and oh my—and knowing that in a way I was, to her, the ghost of a dead man and she, to me, that of a dead woman.

Cylinder 31

I got up the next morning and wrote her a note while still three-quarters asleep. The Chevy, covered in heavy night dew, glowing in the reddish early morning light, looked almost like an imaginary thing that would disappear if I looked away and then back again. Driving to town, I started thinking about the fact that this car was stolen, that I'd gotten it, technically, by armed theft, and this thought must have excited what little Presbyterian was left in me, because then I thought about a whole trail of other sins and breaches and failings.

I had a half-hour, so I stopped at the Spot and got a quick breakfast. Babe Ruth's changing home-run record was still the big item on the chalkboard. For a few precious moments I read a *Post-Dispatch*, which had enough disaster and uncertainty in it to have been written by Old Testament prophets. Nancy had the radio turned on low, mumbling music behind the counter, then the unmistakable voice of the *Jerry Custer News*.

News on the radio was hardly an innovation in 1934, but Jerry Custer was the first local radio newsman in Fort Smith. He either didn't know how to use a microphone or trusted it so little that he figured he had to yell to make sure he got out the word. What he called news was usually him reading from some newspapers, crinkling and refolding them noisily, and adding a few useless local odds and ends when they came his way, with a strong preference for cheerful items about garden clubs and golfing tournaments and visiting families. Jerry was emotionally and philosophically opposed to the Depression and therefore avoided any news having to do with it unless it was banner-headline material like the bank closings, and even then he would read about it only briefly, desultorily.

Nancy was just about to turn him off when something in his tone caught her ear. Casual pioneer though he was, Jerry Custer did get excited when he actually had some juicy local item. At his first enthusiastic mention of a house fire, I guessed the rest of what he would say, so it later seemed: ". . . on Free Ferry Road, and that entire house is burned down this morning. Gone completely. Mr. Bernard C. Pryor, and I believe he is a local officeholder at the courthouse, if I am correct about that. I repeat, the entire house, and, boy, it was a big one, totally flat as a fritter, a smoking bunch of sticks. Fortunately the family was not at home at the time, thank the Lord for that. . . ."

As I stood up, Nancy and several others in the place looked at me. Leaving money at the table, I saw Hank coming out of the Elevator Building and walking fast across the avenue. He was chewing a matchstick, something he did when he was nervous.

"I've been looking for you," he said.

"Where's Bernie?" I said.

"He's holed up in his office, Tom. He's got the door locked, and he says to leave him alone for now."

"So he got out okay?"

"He wasn't in the house when it happened. He was in his office, working late. Time he got home, the fire was already out of control. They were just trying to keep the woods from catching and burning down all the neighbors."

I hesitated, wondering whether to go up now and try to talk to Bernie.

"So you went out there?"

"I was there before sunrise. The judge called me. I looked around the place. It smelled like whoever burned it used both gas and kerosene. You want to see it?"

On Free Ferry, we passed Judge Stone's house and, within a few hundred yards, turned left up the graciously curved driveway that had led to the Pryor house. Jerry Custer had it right. Except for a couple of smoldering interior walls and the stone work, it was flattened. Some of the oak trees nearby had caught fire, but the firemen had at least managed to keep that part of the blaze contained. The petroleum odor was so pungent that we could smell it almost from the street. A couple of awestruck neighborhood boys were the only people at the place besides Hank and me.

"All this gasoline smells like they used a tank truck," Hank said as we walked around back, where the swimming pool was a black swamp of greasy soot and debris. The separate garage had burned and collapsed around Berenice's seven-thousand-dollar Lincoln.

Being in the presence of arson made me uneasy, given my part in having once lighted up a large building full of children as young as four years old. Now a prosecutor, a discounter of excuses, I had once done something so heinous that it sounded like the first line of a joke. And I'd never gotten a conviction in an arson case. Very few prosecutors did in those days. We would kick the charred timbers and walk away thinking, Oh well, the only people who ever win these are insurance companies.

Hank and I retreated to the tennis court to survey the scene from there. Even the net on the court had caught fire, and it smelled as if somebody had actually walked out here and taken the trouble to douse it with kerosene.

"They weren't exactly trying to hide the arson, were they?" I said.

Hank stood with his arms crossed, staring across the ruin, still chewing the match. "Damn place smells like an oil field. This is a grudge fire or a scare fire. They wanted him to know it."

"You think Goback had it done?"

Hank shifted the match to the other side of his mouth and frowned. "He is a burner, but he'd be a bigger fool than I thought to order up something like this before his sentencing."

As we drove toward the jail, I felt myself turning inside, getting ready. In situations like this, one makes calculations fast, and I did hope that the man already in jail was responsible. If he wasn't, that left one suspect.

Hank was shaking his head. "I don't know why he'd torch Bernie's house when you were the acting prosecutor. Bernie wasn't even in town until they read the verdict."

"But he is the prosecutor. Maybe Goback figures I'm just working for him."

Hank took a deep breath and gazed out the window toward the old gallows standing half-rotted near the building. It was the old Parker courthouse and jail, still being used for overflow county prisoners. It had been the headquarters of Hank's early career, but he didn't look as if he felt very nostalgic about it. Beyond the gallows, smoke rose from a shantytown called Coke Hill. There, near the site of the original Fort Smith stockade, above the confluence of the Arkansas and Poteau Rivers, people lived in homemade shelters of scrap wood and tin. It was a somber, hopeless-feeling place.

As we walked toward the jail door, Hank pulled a weighted black glove out of his back pocket.

"This old boy's a rough customer," he said. "I watched him in court. Only one language he understands."

The two deputies in charge of the overflow jail sat playing cards at a beat-up desk with a black Toronado fan moving back and forth between them. They had recorded four visitors to Goback until a couple of days ago, when they'd gotten the word not to allow any others. I looked at the list of names and recognized two who'd been character witnesses during his trial. Hank suggested that the guards go take a smoke while we visited Mr. Goback. Hank had a kind of reputation that defies explanation except to say that it derived partly from his past, from long service often in hardship and danger. I knew few details of his career as a lawman because he didn't talk about it much. To him, the mythologized outlaws were mostly drunken lowlifes who'd gone on one too many killing sprees, and he'd sooner talk about baseball.

The deputies took a walk.

Everything about the old courthouse jail was dismal. It consisted of three tiers of jail cages and catwalks. The windows had been boarded up, and light was limited to two windows. The place smelled of unflushed toilets. Somewhere a radio was on, and a country whine echoed off the old rock walls.

Hank's only weapon was the glove on his right hand. It was padded with iron filings along the knuckles. He had once told me that he used that glove—or used to—when he was called to break up fights, because if you used a sap or a club, somebody else might turn on you or you could kill a person.

Hank's eyes had taken on a hard, fierce light, and when he turned the big key in the lock, Goback looked up from the single bunk in his room straight at the black glove, as if by radar. His cell was a dank six feet by ten, located in a corner of the building.

"What d'you want?" he said, standing up as we came in. When Hank gave him two quick ones in the gut, his eyes just about popped out. Back against the wall, he gasped, "Whatchu doin? Gotdamnit!"

"Did you set a fire last night, Goback?" I asked him.

"What the hell you talkin about? I been in this lousy hole—"

Hank gave him a couple more quick ones in the ribs, back against the wall. I watched his eyes, looking for some sign that he knew why we were here. When Hank had finished with him, he was sitting on his bunk with spit dripping down his chin. He tried to shoot me an angry look after he'd stopped coughing and gotten his breath.

"You ought to be able to take that," I said. "Your wife did plenty of times. You've got one chance of not getting life without parole, and that chance is gone if you lie. A place was burned down last night. Do you know anything about it?"

He shook his head. "Hell no."

"There was gas and kerosene all over the place. We have a lead on the car that left the scene. I'm going to check it, and if you ordered the burn, you'll get the maximum sentence for attempted murder. If you do confess to the arson, and give me the details, I'll prosecute you for arson but recommend leniency in both cases. You'll do a nickel on each, with a chance of parole. That's a lot of difference."

"I didn't . . . order up no arson," he said, wiping at his chin.

"I know you're a burner. You've bragged for years about how many people you ran out of the cattle auction business. I want to save myself some trouble, but I'd just as soon do it the other way. I'll give you a couple of minutes to think about it if you need to. If you were responsible for the incident last night and don't confess, you'll die in Tucker Prison Farm. I personally guarantee it. Confess and you'll get a better deal."

"You tryin to get me to confess to somethin I didn't do?" he said.

"I'm trying to get you to tell me the truth. Whichever way it is, you'll be better off not lying."

"I didn't do it," he said flatly. "I didn't have nothin to do with no burnin."

I told him that we had a list of the people who had visited him in jail, and I was going to question them. If any of them seemed suspicious, I'd run them to the ground; I'd offer them deals. Did he understand me?

"I didn't do no goddamn arson," he repeated.

"You've done it before, haven't you? Tell me you haven't, and we'll know you're lying."

He looked at me with hatred glaring out of his eyes. My face felt hot.

"I never burned nobody that didn't deserve it. And I ain't never burned in this county."

I told him he could revise his story until we left this cell. Once we were gone, that was it, the deal was off.

"Plus I never used kerosene," he added. "Don't need to. That's askin for it."

"Thanks for the tip," I said. "But now I need another piece of information. What do you know about Jim Mackey out of Tulsa?"

Goback's expression, the look of his eyes, positively billowed up with hatred toward me, but prudence reigned for the moment. He was too miserably sober to imagine that he could fight his way out of this.

"Owns the sheriffs, I know that. All over the east side. Owns the sheriff here too."

"Where'd you hear that?"

He laughed bitterly. "Everbody knows it."

"We run in different circles, Jay. Where'd you hear it?"

"S'pose I could get some whiskey now?" he asked.

Hank answered him. "I'll get you some whiskey. Tell him where you heard it."

Goback gazed now at Hank, the man who'd just knocked the breath out of him, as if he were suddenly his best friend. You could almost feel sorry for Goback, for how quickly he had collapsed from windbag bully to abject, dry drunk.

"This between us?" He lowered his voice.

"Don't worry, all I want is information. Anything you tell me is just what I heard on the street."

He took a deep breath. "An old boy name of Jelly Nash holed up with me a while. Stayed at the stockyard. I didn't have nothin to do with him cept to let him stay there. I paid him to wrassle cattle for a couple weeks, but he wasn't no good at it; then I heard he was tryin to set hisself up fencin bonds."

"From bank heists?"

"Don't know where he got em. I just know he was puttin' out the word he'd pay twenty cents on the dollar for what he called bear bonds."

I glanced at Hank. We both knew of Jelly Nash, a holdup artist who'd been convicted several times and kept getting out on parole to do it all over again. One of his partners in crime had been Al Spencer, locally notorious for managing one of the last train robberies on horseback, near Bartlesville, in the early '20s. Nash had been arrested in Hot Springs only the year before and transported through Fort Smith to Kansas City, where somebody had opened up on him in Union Station, stacking up five bodies before it was over.

Goback had stopped talking and was looking at Hank's midsection, as if calculating. "Reckon I could get a drink of whiskey now?" he said. "Clear my head? Help me remember."

Hank pulled out his silver pocket flask. "Keep talking."

Staring at the flask, Goback said, "Look to me like Jelly Nash was gettin in over his head with these here bonds."

"So he did fence some of them?" Hank said, slowly unscrewing the cap.

He licked his lips. "I didn't have nothin to do with him, but I heard he was. And he got a telephone call." Goback held out his hand and looked at Hank like a whipped dog hoping for a friend.

"From who?" Hank said.

"Reckon I could get this nip?"

"Two swallows. Take more'n that and I'll knock it out of you."

Goback's big paw reached out and snatched the little silver flask, and he slammed down two of the biggest, fastest drinks I've ever seen, his eyes watering with happiness. He stared at the scratched silver flask and burped slightly. "God damn, that's purty," he said.

"Who was the call from?" I asked.

"They sent somebody after him. Taken him to Tulsa, and he come back and told me Jim Mackey would give him protection for a cut. Said he had all the sheriffs on payroll, includin the one cross the river."

"Did he name the sheriff in Sebastian County?"

"Said he wouldn't give Jelly Nash no trouble if he cut Mackey in because he had him on his payroll. Seabolt. Kenny Seabolt."

"What if he didn't cut him in?" I asked.

Goback shrugged his shoulders. "Earn hisself a new assole."

He handed Hank back the flask and turned his eyes to me. He was a whipped man, but the whiskey made him feel good enough to say to me, "Looky here, you think my wife didn't have nothin to do with it, well, you ain't seen that bitch in high gear. She changes mounts faster'n a rodeo rider. You'd get sour too."

Outside the jail, Hank waited until we were back in the car to say, "A big old thick, brawling son of a bitch like that, you'd think he was honest. Looks like he'd be too stupid to be anything else. The man doesn't have an honest bone in his body."

"What do you think about that Jelly Nash and Mackey story?" I asked him.

"Wouldn't be surprised if it was partly true. Little too fancy for him to make up on the spot." Hank got out his flask and tipped it, then looked at it and laughed his dry laugh. "One thing he knows how to do—drink a half-pint of whiskey in two swallows."

"Do you think he paid somebody to do Bernie's house?"

He shook his head and sighed, staring at the gallows. "You're the lawyer."

"If you had to guess."

He glanced over at me. "If I had to? I'd say he didn't. But mainly because he hasn't been sentenced. You write down those four names for me. I'll find em and talk to em."

I found a piece of paper and wrote them down immediately.

"I'll go to Moffitt and start checking these men this afternoon," Hank said. "I'd just as soon do it on my own. Drop me at my truck."

Cylinder 32

"'Lo," Mel said.

On the surface, the office was ominously normal: Bernie's door shut, no visiting secretaries standing in front of the air conditioner at the moment. For me, though, this place seemed slightly less familiar every time I came here, like entering a fading memory. I was a little shell shocked by the avalanche of events. For a long time things here had been routine, even boring. Now, in a very brief period, everything had turned upside down.

The Pryors' house getting torched rattled me. I had mixed-up feelings about Bernie: I liked him, appreciated him, envied him, and despised him; I disliked his wife for being a cruel, self-satisfied, small-town relic, but I was glad she was around to give me an excuse to feel sorry for her husband. I envied the fact that they had three fine children. And the house itself—I had joked with him about its showiness and yet secretly admired it as one admires a nice church. Emotions are seldom simple, but my feelings about Bernie were a particularly tangled web.

"You're supposed to say, 'Hello there, Mel.' And you better close your mouth or you'll catch a fly."

"Sorry. I was thinking."

She gave me a look and a gesture of the head to get me outside the office. I walked with her down the hot hallway to an open window overlooking the avenue.

"How much do you know?" she asked.

"Burned flat," I said. "Bernie was in the office working when it happened. Nobody killed. Definitely arson."

"There are a couple more details you should know before you talk to him. Bernie was having a small dispute over the insurance rate on his house. Because he's a prosecutor, they kept upping his rate. He was holding out on them, trying to negotiate a better deal. He hadn't paid in two months, and they're telling him that it's his problem."

"You're kidding."

"It's a total loss, Tom. The other thing is that he called his wife and she told him she isn't coming back, and isn't bringing the children back, until he's gotten the situation straightened out."

"Straightened out? What the hell does that mean?"

"You'll have to ask Berenice about that. But considering this crusade he's on, it's probably not a bad idea for his family to stay out of town. Just be nice to him, Tom. He's been getting hit every way he looks."

"Why wouldn't I be nice to him?" I dabbed at my forehead with my handkerchief.

"One other thing you ought to know. He was going to file charges against the sheriff today. Word of that may have gotten out."

I groaned. "Gotten out how?"

"LaVerne maybe. She was willing to talk to Bernie at first because I think she's disgusted with the sheriff. He called her at home trying to get information from her. She may have cut and run. Maybe he told her a little too much about what he intended to do. Maybe she leaked it to Kenny. I'm just guessing."

"And Kenny goes and torches Bernie's house, bam, just like that?"

She shook her head. "I don't know. But I'm checking my own house insurance. It probably wouldn't be a bad idea for you to do the same. And I'm moving my mother out for now, sending her to her sister's."

Mel turned and went back into the office, leaving me sweating in the hall, contemplating what she'd just said. Despite all the crooks and bootleggers and woman beaters we'd prosecuted, and all the threatening telephone calls we'd received over the years, I'd never heard Mel express concern about her own safety or that of anybody else in the office.

I drank a couple of cones of water before going to see Bernie, who surprised me as much as Mel. I expected him to be half nuts, but in fact he appeared to be doing the opposite, acting more sure of himself as the heat went up.

When he let me into his office, he looked weary but less fidgety than usual, as if getting his house torched was just the thing a person needed to focus his mind. He sat there with a cigarette smoldering in his hand and reported plainly, without apparent anger, what he knew—which was little more than I knew. I told him about Hank and me talking with Jay Goback in jail. He was shaking his head before I even got to the punchline.

"I wouldn't think he did it," he said. "You're the one who got him convicted."

I told him what Goback had claimed about Jim Mackey paying off the sheriff, and he looked interested.

"I've heard of Jim Mackey," Bernie said. "My father had some run-ins with him."

"About what?"

He shook his head slowly and tried to remember. "Mineral rights, I guess. I wouldn't have paid any attention except that he actually scared my father. Anybody do that, I figured he must have three heads and ten arms. I remember him saying that man has a pharaoh complex. I was eighteen years old and fascinated by the idea of somebody who could scare my father. But Jim Mackey's over in Tulsa, isn't he? What's his involvement here?"

"I'm following leads on it."

"And you aren't going to tell me a thing, right?" Bernie said.

My impulse was to change the subject, but at that moment Mel knocked and opened the door. I waited for her to say something, but she didn't; she just leaned in the doorway, looking at me.

Despite the fact that she was twenty-some years younger than I, there was something about Mel that could sometimes affect me, influence me, like the older sister I'd never had. Having never had any female influence in my childhood, I can't claim this notion as fact, but there was something about Mel. Men in offices say patronizingly that their secretaries keep them in line. Mel couldn't have cared less about keeping anybody in line, but I always watched her face to see what she thought about things.

And so there the three of us were, in silent conference. Bernie, with his palace burned to the ground, crushing out his cig, Mel just standing there with her arms crossed for some reason, and me, as usual, initially thinking how I was going to give Bernie the brush-off. I raised my eyebrows at Mel as if to ask, "Did you want something?" and she merely raised hers back at me. Maybe she'd heard us through the door and come in to remind me to give Bernie a break: he'd had a bad day and was taking it like a stand-up guy, so give him a chance; fill him in on something.

There hadn't been a lot of times when Bernie had cared about what was going on, but he did seem to now. And he was getting knocked around, taking big blows, and showing class. So I went ahead. I decided to tell him.

"It's still pretty hazy," I said, unsure whether this was a good idea.

Mel left then—uncrossed her arms, walked out, and shut the door. I told him what I knew and what I was working on. I even gave him a short version of the trip to the mountains, which he asked so many questions about that he got the whole story.

"You didn't even tell Hank about this?" he asked.

"Not about the people. I don't think those Indians killed Lee Guessner or Alfred Carr."

Bernie turned his chair toward the window for a moment, looking through the blinds.

"Why not?" he asked, clearing his throat.

"I just don't think they're the kind to drive over here in a car, blow somebody up, and write *sodomite* on the wall. That's white-man nasty."

He turned his chair back around. "I thought you believed in the equality of the races when it came to crime."

"Nobody has a corner on it," I allowed.

"But you believe these primitive types wouldn't be capable of such a thing, even though they do appear to sacrifice young women?"

"Look, I don't know anything about those people. Not really. It's all speculation. I don't have any opinions yet. I'm still turning over rocks."

"Don't get angry," he said. "You must have asked yourself the same question."

"I'm not angry."

"You sound angry."

"I just don't really know anything yet."

Our conversation fell into a lull. I was thinking that I shouldn't have told him. A lot of things were going on in my head just then, which I can't sensibly explain even now. I somehow felt implicated in his house getting torched.

"You mentioned them shooting a flare at your car," he said. "Do you know where they use signal flares?"

"I saw a lifetime supply in France," I said.

"Another place they use them is oil fields. My father . . ." Bernie hesitated, the vague look he often got when talking about his father drifting over his face. "He drove me around to a bunch of fields when he was making a stab at getting me interested in the business. He told me they used flares to communicate when they needed something at a drill site. Pipes, whatever—different colors for different things they needed."

Actually, I hadn't known that. I'd been around plenty of oil fields and never picked it up.

"Did you check the ownership on that convertible you're driving?" he asked.

"There's no license plate," I said.

"How about calling dealers in Oklahoma?"

"You can't be sure they'll tell you the truth. Not if it's guardianship money."

"I'll find out what I can," he said. "Don't worry about it."

I made a face and shook my head.

"You just lost your house."

He snorted. "Did I ever show you the third floor in that place?"

"I was never in your house, Bernie."

"It had a little schoolroom, complete with desks and blackboards. I don't know who my father thought would go to this school. Between you and me, I never really liked the baronial style. Oh, my wife liked it." He took a deep breath and smiled ruefully. "She's upset. It'll be quite a nick, especially with the stock market swooning again. Afraid our next house won't be up to her standards. . . ."

He tapped a fingernail on the desk. "By the way, I found out why the sheriff was visiting Manny Stone—possibly why. Manny was apparently collecting money from the neighbors and paying the sheriff off. He never asked me for any money, so I didn't know about it."

"Paying him for what?"

"To keep people looking for a handout off our street. I don't know if they had some kind of disagreement or if the neighbors weren't paying or what happened, but the sheriff stopped patrolling. Also, Tom, you'd better know I was going to file extortion charges against the sheriff today."

"Did you talk to Stone about it?"

"I mentioned it to him a couple of days ago. He said he didn't think I had a case."

"Did he try to talk you out of it?"

"He gave me a lot of chaff, but he didn't outright tell me not to file."

"Who else knew you were going to file?"

"The only others who even had an idea were the witnesses, Mel, you, and LaVerne over in his office."

"One of your witnesses could have flipped on you. How many complainants do you have?"

"Three," he said. "Maybe. At least two . . ."

I leaned forward. "I still think you ought to hold off on it."

"Why?" he said flatly. "Because he burned down my house?"

"No," I said. "I think the sheriff is somehow involved in this Spiro business. I'm talking out of instinct, but I think you ought to lie back at least for a few days."

"Give me a better reason, Tom. Because Stone doesn't want me to? Because see, that's not enough."

"No," I said. "Because he does want you to."

Cylinder 33

I really had two other reasons for asking him to hold off.

The first was simple. Bernie had little trial or trial-prep experience. He seemed to fancy that if he'd gotten a couple of complainants to promise to testify, that was it, he had the case made. But extortion against Kenny would be hard to win in the best of circumstances. The crime itself was a fuzzy offense. In the mental arithmetic of a lot of juries, a sheriff demanding payoffs from black clubs was understandable since everybody knew what happened at those places.

A puny crime, a puny case: two or three nightclub owners or liquor dealers who'd said they'd testify, assuming they hadn't heard about the Pryor house fire and weren't already packing their bags to leave the county. Billy Bluestone hadn't sounded to me like a committed witness but rather an understandably nervous potential witness, at best. Bernie might file charges and be stuck with one poor man being taken apart on the witness stand for vague, nefarious Negro crimes, or he might end up with no witnesses at all. A weak prosecutor, a vague crime, a powerful sheriff—it wasn't promising.

The other, far less certain reason was an impression I was getting that he was being led into this. Bernie hated to be told what to do by people he considered to be authorities. This was a handicap in a job where the first thing you did on a work day was stand up when the judge walked into the room, and I had kidded him about it a few times before he let me know to lay off. It was one subject that made him sore.

Now he had been told by Judge Stone—a shrewd man who'd known him since childhood—to fill out forms and do nothing important and certainly not to engage in a campaign against the sheriff, a man whom he intensely and instinctively disliked. Surprise. He had gotten himself busy doing exactly what the judge told him not to do.

Bernie didn't say anything for a while. He let it soak in, brow furrowed a little, eyes focusing as if he was looking inside himself.

"Wants me to? Why me?" he asked. "Why not you?"

I shook my head. "I have no idea. Maybe the sheriff's squeezing him somehow; maybe he's desperate for somebody to run a little interference, and he's calling on you to do it. You told me something was going on between them."

"Why wouldn't Manny talk to me directly about it? Why would he tell me not to prosecute him?"

I just looked at him then, and, again to his credit, Bernie figured out the obvious.

The two of us talked a while longer, and he agreed to play possum, at least for a few days. He would try to trace the Chevy. We would work together.

Leaving the office, though, I still wondered whether I'd made a mistake by telling him everything.

All that afternoon I couldn't find Rainy. She'd left her cabin without a note. My note to her was still lying on the table. I hung around trying to decide what to do, then went back to my house, then the Athenian, then the Goldman. I stuck at home that night, hoping she'd show up. *Chesterfield's Music That Satisfies* didn't satisfy me, and two nightcaps didn't put me to sleep. I had to leave for Oklahoma the next day but now was considerably worried about her. My other, nagging concern was that while I had a small handle on Jim Mackey, courtesy of Mr. Goback, it was hardly enough to get his attention, meaning I had no clear plan about going to Tulsa.

I wasted time the next morning, then at noon met Hank at the Spot. He hadn't seen Rainy either. He'd been in Moffitt talking to Goback's jail visitors, who all worked at the auction barn in Moffitt. They'd denied any involvement, of course, and Hank seemed to believe them. He just wasn't buying Goback being that stupid before his sentencing.

I pushed aside my partly eaten lunch and watched the street. The sheriff wasn't here, but a couple of his deputies were at the sheriff's table back in the corner.

"All these things at once," I said. "We've got two murder cases, and now arson, and I don't feel like I'm getting anywhere. You've been around longer than I have, Hank. Give me some advice."

He snorted. "I haven't been around that much longer."

Hank had ordered a Greek coffee, and Nancy brought it over and set it down. "There you go, Hank. We'll have you drinking ouzo next."

"Ouzo," he said. "What's that?"

"Soon as you get used to that, I'll take you on a vacation to the Mediterranean," she said.

"Break out the ouzo," he said wistfully. Watching her walk away, he said, "What is that? Ouzo? It sounds like something you'd put in your transmission."

"It tastes like it."

"Whatever it takes." He sighed, gazing after Nancy, and took an appreciative sip from the tiny cup.

I glanced back at the deputies and asked quietly, "You think Kenny's fool enough to torch the prosecutor's house?"

Hank rolled the coffee around in his mouth and just shook his head. "Don't know, Tom."

I stood up and counted out fifty cents. "Look, I've got to find Rainy. If you see her, tell her I'm looking for her. I'm going to make one last run to her cabin. If she's not there, I'm going to Spiro."

Cylinder 34

It was a gruelingly windy day, with so much blowing dirt that I stopped partway there and put up the cloth roof. The isolated showers in the mountains hadn't fallen here. The weather had a relentless, ominous feeling. I drove through the ghost town of Pocola and turned off to wallow through the mounting sand of the old Fort Coffee Road, under the dust-hazed sky, the wind, the heat.

My first thought on getting to the mound was relief at the sight of Rainy's van. The van was alone in the parking area, the artifact table was turned over with one of its legs knocked off, and the tent that had sat behind it was gone. In the rough field, obscured by dried weeds and wind-created dunes, I noticed pieces of shell scattered around the ground. The sombrero that had been on the mummy by the tent was anchored somehow in the ground. I pulled on it, and a skull appeared in the sand.

I called out Rainy's name and, getting no response, approached warily. At closer view, it was apparent that the main tunnel into the large mound had collapsed, the dirt slumped around it, and there was a crack above it, a blowout, in the central cone. A dynamite charge had been set on that end, probably from inside the tunnel. As I walked around the large cone Rainy appeared, standing alone in the field. I called her name and walked over. She hardly seemed to notice me. She was wearing her desert clothes, loose cotton shirt and pants, canvas shoes, and a fedora-shaped hat with her hair tucked into it. She had a few pieces of shell in her hand and seemed to be wandering around in a daze. In that heat, I wondered if she was okay.

She tried to give me a little smile but clearly wasn't in a smiling mood.

"They blew it up," she said thoughtfully.

"I can see that. How long have you been out here?"

"There are fragments all over this field," she said.

I nodded. "You aren't looking too good. Want to sit in the shade a while?"

We got her bottle of water from the van and sat in the Chevy, which wasn't quite as hot as the van. She drank and handed me the jug. "Why would they do that?"

Sitting in that field looking onto the desolate mound, with the forlorn wind whistling through the cracks, I glanced around. The weather seemed unaccountably malicious, sand ticking against the car, the canvas roof rattling. I didn't want to sit here very long, nor add to my growing list of unanswered questions, but we talked for a brief time and made a plan to see what we could find out.

She followed me into the little town of Spiro, where I knew a man who ran a gas station.

Elvin Purl was a rangy, sinewy half-Cherokee in his sixties who looked and talked like a hill-country white. He'd been raised at the edge of Cherokee country in the Boston Mountains. When we drove up, he was lying on his back on the hard-packed, grease-soaked dirt floor of his garage, with only his legs and patched shoes visible. When I called him, he wiggled out with black on his face and the stub of an unlit cigar sticking out of his mouth. Mr. Purl knew me because I had once looked him up to tell him that he was owed money—a small annuity from a mineral claim inherited from his mother that he had long assumed was worthless.

Mr. Purl was a good wind-up talker, but he became strangely shy when you tried to converse with him. When you asked him particular questions, he tended to get confused and worry about exactly what you meant, a fact that I remembered and Rainy sensed after we'd asked him a few questions about the treasure diggers. We stood in his junky office drinking six-ounce Cokes from his icebox, watching through his oily, cluttered front window a growing darkness on the horizon, a dust storm running west of there.

He took the cigar out of his mouth, revealing a groove in his lower lip.

"Oh yeah, they'd blow in here for gas, but none of em ever said much to me. Wasn't the kind to set and shoot the breeze. Not what I'd call friendly, even with each other. All of em had fancy new rigs, pickups. They was haulin in the money sellin them old Indian treasures. The newspapers come out here and everything. The crew boss did the talkin and kept the other ones quiet. I heard him one day with one of the newspaper men, and he could sling a line of bull, all right. He'd try to act keen with me, tellin me to hurry up and all. I told him if he'd like to get out and crank the pump that'd be just fine. Save me the trouble. I guess he figured I was so bad off I'd put up with his mouth. Other one of em was so dumb you coulda toed a line in the dirt and he'd stand there lookin at it until you clapped your hands and told him to stop. Somebody asked me this mornin if I knew about em clearin out. Believe it was yesterday, they set off a big charge. Must have been a lot of dynamite because it carried all this way. Caused that muffler nearly to jump out the window."

He nodded at a rusty muffler propped in the corner of the window. "Now, I can tell you a little somethin about that mound. Aunt Rachel Brown owned the land it's on, and I promise she's turnin over in her grave. Long as she lived, she didn't let nobody tear into it. They come out for arrowheads, she'd run em off. She put in cotton around it, but that was all. She told me one time she seen a man that told her not to let nobody mess it up."

"Did she ever describe this person to you?" Rainy asked him.

Her question flustered Mr. Purl. "Well, she was just a old nigger lady. I mean, she was a good woman. . . ." Mr. Purl got more flustered at this point, actually blushing.

Rainy smiled gently and had enough sense to wait until he decided to talk.

"Well, she was here fillin kerosene, told me a man come in her door, which usually, you know, they'll holler first, and it was evenin, not dark yet but the sun was down, and this old boy worried her because he had paint on his face, and there he was standin in her door, and she went back far enough or maybe had heard stories, like he might be comin to git him a scalp. Said it was like a dream, this here painted Indian standin in her doorway. Or maybe he was a angel, way the sky was gold behind him, come to take her off, and that was fine, she said, the Lord call, he could send a well-favored-lookin angel like that anytime he please, which is her word, not mine. Wasn't none of her business whether it was a Indin or a white man or what.

"Whoever he was, he made like for her to go outside and took her round the corner of her house, and he knelt down on the ground and drew a shape like the mound, which was right there in front of em, and he pointed at it, and he drew a circle around that shape and touched her on the shoulder, kind of took her by the shoulder and give her a look. Said that man only studied her once, rest of the time he looked away, but when he drew that circle and stood up and looked her in the eye, it put a chill to her spine. Said she got the message, wasn't no question about it, wasn't a word spoke, just that circle and touchin her and lookin at it a while, and then he was gone quick as he came, trotted right on off across that prairie like killin snakes. Didn't waste no time. Can you imagine such a thing?"

"Yes I can," Rainy said. "Did she describe this as something that really happened?"

"Yes, ma'am, she told me like it was a fact. But people around here call it Aunt Rachel's vision. I don't know why."

I asked Mr. Purl, "Did these miners use dynamite before yesterday?"

He looked puzzled. "Why sure they did."

"Where do you think they got the dynamite?"

Mr. Purl looked uncertain. "Where they got it? You mean where they bought it? Be hard to say. Mr. Matthews used to sell it over here to the hardware store. But when the mines went down, he quit. He don't stock it. Now, I do remember one time, that old hombre out of Sallisaw that worked with em, I seen him put two stout wood boxes like the ones that carry dynamite from his truck into that crew boss McKenzie's."

"Can you describe him?"

"Well, I don't know. . . . What do you mean describe him?"

"What he looked like, the one from Sallisaw."

"I wouldn't know," Mr. Purl said with sudden finality, as if it would be shameful to describe somebody upon demand. I had encountered this before with witnesses, and it drove me nuts.

He plugged the cigar back into his mouth and, talking around it, added, "Do know he wasn't in their regular crew. Come out of Sallisaw, or drove that way. They was all from the other direction. He'd carry that rifle. Like he was a guard or somethin. Hard-lookin' old hombre, best I could say."

"Was he from Sallisaw?"

"Wouldn't know."

Cylinder 35

We left the Chevy at Mr. Purl's, filled the van with gas, and drove together south to Poteau. On the way there Rainy asked me how far it was from the mound to the Winding Stair, and I told her I guessed seventy-five miles. She was pensive a while and then said, "Does it rain more there?"

"I guess it does. It generally rains more in the mountains."

She stared out on the devastated landscape. "When was the last time there was a drought this bad?"

I told her I had read in the newspaper that the heat and drought were the worst in written record, which around here would be a little over a hundred years.

"I wonder if this is what happened when the mound was abandoned," she said.

"You think the Spiro people left here because of a drought?"

"That's the most obvious explanation. It's right in front of our eyes. A tribal culture couldn't live through this."

As we headed for Poteau, Aunt Rachel Brown kept floating into my mind. It was her house where I'd knocked on the door the first time we went to the mound. An old woman—black, Indian, and probably illiterate—why would she have been so careful with the mound? And had an Indian come out of the mountains to tell her that it was sacred to him? Had he really? Why?

In Poteau I found Bill Hagglund's truck at Martha's Roadside Diner. I'd been trying for days to get him on the phone. Bill wouldn't want to be seen hanging around too much with somebody from the Sebastian County prosecutor's office, or with some striking-looking woman from who knew where. In the weird, ingrown little world of county courthouses, questions arise, rumors start. In our conversation the week before, Bill had sounded as if he was already worried enough about his position in the current pecking order under Judge Spellman.

Rainy stayed in the van while I went inside and bought some chewing gum. After I was sure Hagglund had seen me, I left, and he eventually followed. We ended up at his house in an old residential neighborhood, a little box-and-strip bungalow with a clump of still living blackjack oak shading it from the dust-reddened afternoon sun.

Mrs. Hagglund was apparently used to her husband showing up at home for business. Like a lot of shoestring lawyers, he had no office except the courthouse lobby and the cafes. Mrs. Hagglund handed Rainy and me glasses of lemonade, complete with mint and big chunks of ice, and offered us food—deviled eggs and leftover potatoes and ham—which we gladly took. For some reason, I was impressed by how easily Rainy accepted the food. She was hungry and happy to eat. The shade trees and fan kept the temperature from being intolerable, and sitting on their old couch drinking Mrs. Hagglund's lemonade and enjoying her food, one wouldn't have guessed that the world outside was falling apart, despite the echoing gloom of a country radio announcer reading the prices of cotton and corn and cattle.

Out the small front window I saw a darkness still in the northwest. A dust devil kicked along the street, stirring the curtains of a nearly paintless house opposite the Hagglunds'. I fell into a mood, thinking about this neighborhood, where the better houses with all taxes paid were worth seventy-five or a hundred dollars and where you were in the solid middle class if you had a kitchen stove and something to cook on it; where the lucky ones were just hanging on, and there was danger in all directions, and beyond the danger seemingly a great indifference. It felt like war, the baleful news flaming up from newspaper pages, burning houses, dynamite explosions, the black wind cutting paint from houses. In my childhood I had imagined shining cities somewhere in the distance, perhaps in other countries, but now I knew that there were few shining cities in this whole great, wide, terribly connected world. I had the latest news out of Berlin from only a couple of days ago, and I had no trouble imagining what it implied.

After we'd finished our little repast, Mrs. Hagglund disappeared into the back yard to work on her garden.

Bill said, "She goes out there every day to keep the sand from packing the roots. I tell her she'll get blistered under that sun. Then she waters it in the evening. The cistern's dry, so she hauls it from the well. As long as it still has water in it, she'll put it on the garden. She doesn't worry about when it'll run out. When it does, that'll be that; she'll probably have us moving to California. What the heck, maybe I'll go out there and get in the movies. I know an old boy that ain't half as good-looking as me, works as an extra in the movies, says you sign up at central casting and when they need you they pay you ten bucks a day."

I brought up the subject I'd hoped to discuss and didn't get very far at first. Hagglund seemed to like Rainy okay, but he wasn't comfortable talking in front of her. He was an accomplished small-town scrounger, a survivor, and one of his first rules—right up there with payment on delivery—was not getting caught with his tongue wagging against whoever was in charge at the moment. For fifteen minutes we talked around this and that, and only after Rainy got up and went to the outhouse in the back yard did he say he had done some looking around and found out a couple of things for me. But he seemed hesitant, and at first I thought he was fishing for how much it might be worth to me.

"I was gonna drive over, but this is pretty ticklish," he said, and glanced through the kitchen toward the back yard, where Rainy was now standing in the shade of a sassafras tree talking to Mrs. Hagglund.

"So you didn't find Levi Colbert?" he asked.

"Had car trouble. Never talked to him," I said.

Although his reluctance seemed genuine, Bill could put on a show in hopes of a higher fee, and I thought I'd better lay that question to rest.

"I can't pay you any more than last time, Bill. I'm working out of my own pocket now."

Bill raised his eyebrows in comic disbelief. "What happened to the coal trust?"

"His stock's down right now."

"Yeah . . ." He fiddled with his glass and looked back at me. "That's not the only thing of his that's down today, is it?"

"So you heard about the fire—where—on the radio?"

"I heard it before the radio. That ice in your lemonade comes from Ward's Ice Plant in Fort Smith. Young Italian stud that brings it always has a little gossip. This morning he had big gossip."

Bill glanced out the back door again and sniffed. "Okay," he said, "I'll tell you this, but if it gets back to me I won't need to wait till the well gives out to have to leave town. And this lady out here, I don't care if she's your long-lost whatever, she doesn't hear a word of this and neither does anybody else in a way they can trace back to me. Got me on that?"

"I got you," I said.

"After you walk out that door, I won't talk to you about this, and if you ask me I'll call you a liar. We straight?"

I nodded.

"So you didn't talk to Mr. Colbert?" he asked me again.

I shook my head, thinking but not saying, and I never will.

"Well, this is what it says in the records. This is the official story: Levi Colbert requested that his guardian cash out his assets. Jim Mackey resisted but finally gave in, with the agreement of Colbert's probate lawyer at the agency."

"Dale Cotton," I said.

"I don't know his name. I'm just telling you what I heard. He did it, anyway. He sold out."

"Sold what?"

"The land, the mineral rights. Everything. The whole kit and caboodle. His entire estate."

I sat for a moment with what must have been a disbelieving look on my face. "They couldn't do that," I said, as much to myself as to Bill. "They couldn't get away with it."

"Well, I don't know if they got away with it, but they sure as hell did it. The sale was made at the courthouse here in Poteau. It's a done deal. It was done six months ago."

I leaned back in the couch and just tried to take this in.

"First time I ever saw the wind knocked out of you, Tom. And I haven't even got to the good part."

I waited for him to go on.

"What do you reckon that land was worth? How many million on a bad day? They had em a fire sale, it seems. Eleven thousand dollars."

"Who bought it?"

"Jim Mackey."

I sat there shaking my head slightly. It was improbable not just because of the amount but because of the high profile of the Colbert estate. And a guardian buying the estate of his own "incompetent" raised red flags that would have been seen all up the line, even if the probate lawyer was in Jim Mackey's back pocket. The agency director and the Department of Interior in Washington couldn't help but be aware of it.

"What's your source?"

"County clerk," he said. "The one that you rented the keys from last week. James Cross; his wife died four, five years ago, and he's got a closet full of gin bottles. He's sore at the judge for not giving him a big enough cut on the deal. Spellman threw him a tip like a short bit to a shoeshine boy while he took his loot to a bank in Kansas City. Cross wouldn't mind Spellman getting caught—if he could just figure out how to get it done without himself getting caught too."

"Why did Cross tell you about this?"

"Just what I said. He'd like Spellman nailed. But he's a drunk, Tom. He don't know what the hell he's doing."

I thought about the piece of paper I'd snatched from Dale Cotton at the agency. The amounts that I'd guessed were kickbacks to him for sweetheart lease arrangements—too low even for one-year leases—were apparently the numbers they'd cooked up to sell the land. I hadn't tallied them exactly but guessed that they amounted to a little over ten thousand dollars.

In the back yard, Rainy was still keeping Mrs. Hagglund company. She had evidently sensed that Bill wanted to talk to me alone.

"Is this all from Cross?" I asked him. "Did you see any of it on paper?"

Bill shook his head. "I didn't see paper, but I have a pretty good nose for bullshit, and this old boy ain't known for being creative, drunk or sober. It was a whole deal. They put in records that the Indin had requested the sale and Mackey as guardian had denied it, but that Colbert kept after him and threatened to take him to court. They built em up a little file, took their time; somebody at the agency was on the payroll helping em, I guess. Anyway, they got it through probate there, went ahead and sold at what they called distressed prices."

"A guardian can't buy his own incompetent's assets," I said. "It's flat against the law."

"There's where you may have him, if you're fool enough to try. Cross said Colbert sold it to a dummy buyer, then Mackey bought it from him. He claimed he didn't know who, but it was somebody in Fort Smith."

I finished the rest of my lemonade. "You think he really didn't know the name?"

"Claimed he didn't, and I believe him. You stay away from Cross, Tom. Don't go knocking on his door."

"Is there any possibility that Colbert really did request that sale?"

He snorted. "You're kidding. For eleven thousand dollars? If he did, he deserves what he got."

I recalled the painted, costumed man nailed to the wall and wondered if Bill had any idea of what was going on at Colbert's place.

"Something else I wanted to ask—"

"Jesus, ain't that enough!" he said, laughing. "You probably ought to be getting along. I don't want anybody to notice you here."

"One other thing. Last week you told me there were strange people living on Colbert's property and it was dangerous in the mountains. What exactly did you hear about that?"

"Now you're making me nervous, Tom. I feel like I'm on the stand."

Rainy took a couple of steps toward the back door, then stopped for a last word with Mrs. Hagglund.

"Whatever you know," I coaxed.

"It was a bunch of Indins, full-blood types. And they were doing stuff, ritual things, I don't know what. And I guess Mackey's boys never were too far away. I don't know what they were doing exactly."

"Did you hear this from James Cross?"

He shook his head. "It was just gossip in town. There was a bulldozer operator working in the mountains; believe it came from him. I never talked to him personally. I think he was from Tulsa, but I guess he came here sometimes when he was working in the mountains."

"Do you know where I could find him?"

"Yeah, but you won't find him." Bill stood up as Rainy walked back through the kitchen.

"Where?" I asked.

"He had an accident. Dozer flipped on him or something. He's dead. Anyway, that's the word."

Cylinder 36

Rainy didn't question me about what Bill had said. As we started out of Poteau I told her she needed to get back to Fort Smith, find someplace safe, and if possible get out of town tomorrow. I had something to do. Staring ahead, she murmured that she wanted to go with me. I glanced in the rearview mirror, stopped the van right there on the highway, and said, "I have to do something illegal, Rainy. I have to break into a place. There's no reason for you to be with me."

She sighed wearily, like a wife who was sick of a husband. "You don't get the message, do you?"

"What message?" I said.

"I don't need to be looked after by you, and I don't need your advice. I care about this. I trust you. I want to go with you. I don't want to be anywhere else."

"That warms my heart," I said. "You trust me. That's just what I want to hear. It'll help me a lot. Look, you don't know where I'm going."

"To hell with you," she said, her eyes flashing. "You don't know where I've been. And I have as much right to care about this as you do."

"It'll be hard enough," I said.

"If we get in trouble, I can handle myself. I can help. I've got some money. If it's necessary, I can pay lawyers."

"Lawyers?" I said, laughing. I started to turn the wheel for Spiro, but she reached out and clutched my arm.

"Tom, please. Just please. I don't trust you, okay? Is that what you want? Whatever. Just please. Let me stay with this."

"Look, we're burning up here. Why can't you go back to town, find someplace safe for the night, tomorrow arrange for the artifacts—"

"It's the people. I want to know more about them. Talking to that man in Spiro was worth a sack of artifacts. Hearing Hank's story about hunting in the mountains was worth another sack. Think of where we've been, for heaven's sake. Every day I'm with you—"

"We aren't going back to that mountain," I said. "I have to go to Muskogee and Tulsa."

"All I mean is that I'm learning more than I would in a year of puzzling over those things. And fortunately I'm not a bloody academic who has to worry about the niceties. I can play the field. I've been in the Valley of the Kings; I've been in Sumeria and Turkey; I've been all over the Mediterranean, the jungle, you name it. But this is where I can actually do something important. It's what I was meant to do. Let me stay with you. Please."

"Shit," I said ungraciously, and turned toward Muskogee. "You don't know what I intend to do. You just want to be with me?"

"I can tell by the look on your face that *you* don't know exactly what you're going to do. Why should I quiz you if you don't have an answer? Tell me whatever, whenever you feel like it. I've been finding out things every day I'm with you. You're a world-class guide, and you don't even know it."

I grunted.

We drove then for miles almost without talking. The world-class guide had a distinct suspicion that we were being pulled in a fast current toward a roaring sound.

It was a three-hour drive, northwestward into flatter landscape, bleak on that afternoon, with the darkness of a dust storm ahead of us, passing occasional box houses in soil rippled by the wind. Drainage ditches filled with sand. A few gaunt cattle. A woman putting clothes on a wire between her house and a dead cottonwood tree, pausing to gaze at us as we drove by.

Brain in slow working order, I was thinking over Bill's story. He had of course taken the ten dollars I'd slipped him before leaving but surely had another reason for telling me, and I suspected that, like the county clerk, he wouldn't mind seeing Randy Spellman get caught. The picture was filling in, anyway. Mackey's involvement made better sense now. He had taken the trouble to buy and hold guardianship over Levi Colbert not just to milk his estate but with an eye to stealing the whole thing. And the artifacts were only a means, an entry point, a way to get to Colbert or to somebody else. Somebody in Fort Smith.

It was after five o'clock when we got to Muskogee, so we had time to kill.

I stopped at a gas station and looked up Dale Cotton's address in a telephone directory and then headed there through cicada-buzzing streets. Cotton was my best bet, really. He was a crooked office-mole lawyer who'd probably made a killing for himself. He wouldn't be surrounded by toughs, like Jim Mackey, and if he had a gun he probably wouldn't enjoy using it, even on me. Going by the house, I saw a for-sale sign. A neighbor was sitting on his front steps in his boxer shorts and T-shirt.

I pulled over and got out and talked to the neighbor, asking him about the house for sale. He told me that the owner must have come into an inheritance, the way he was buying things over the last year, and now he was moving to California.

"Land of milk and honey," I said.

"Musta been oil," the man said, staring away. "Lot of them get rich on oil, you know. Don't even turn a hand. Government gives it to em."

The "them" the neighbor in underwear was referring to, with dainty ugliness, was Indians, a statement made as if he was oblivious of me. For a moment I could almost feel sorry for Dale Cotton.

I was acquainted with enough people in Muskogee that I feared being recognized, but I knew about a fairly safe place we could hole up. The town is at the confluence of three rivers. In the old days Tulsa was about as far north as the riverboats went up the Arkansas, and there was an old "port" area. Not far from there, down a little dusty path, shaded by trees that were kept alive by their closeness to a feeder creek into the Arkansas, was a stone motor court with eight cabins, which in high water times flooded but always got reopened. It wasn't the kind of place where I was likely to bump into somebody I knew. We drove there and rented a room and a fan.

The people staying there were mostly residents paying by the week, some of them near the end of the line with money, and there was also a Mr.-and-Mrs.-Jones trade, which I knew about firsthand from my younger years in Muskogee. Occasionally families went to this funny little motel for vacations, a place to just get away. Some past owner had been a nut about water and had drilled his own deep well and installed a gasoline pump and large tank.

I took a cool shower, and when I came out Rainy was sitting on the bed looking at me curiously, and she said, "Tell me about my mother."

Just like that. "Tell me about my mother." That was the moment she asked it.

It felt like a ceiling beam had fallen on my head. I quickly finished putting on my pants and shoes and, shirtless, walked out the door of the cabin. It was all I could think about doing. Just walking out.

I went up the road toward the riverbank hill. She called after me and, getting no reply, eventually followed. There was an old river lookout spot under the crest of the hill, and that's where I ended up. The sun was behind us.

"I didn't mean to trick you," she said. "I saw the scars on your back when you went into the shower. It reminded me of what she told me about you."

"Damnit, Rainy," I said, shaking my head. "I can't talk about this. I can't do it now. Just consider me a rat. Consider me a rat and don't ask me any questions because I cannot talk about it."

"Why?" she said.

I looked at her, amazed.

"Yeah, why? Because you think you were wicked to succumb to my charms? Tom, I seduced you. I chose it. That is not a question. And I am the daughter of Samantha King and Clarence Pierce; that is a fact. And you knew my mother; you knew her briefly, and I remind you of her. Okay? Done. Big deal. How old were you? Seventeen? And how old was my mother? You were only one of many notches in her stick, I assure you; does that make you feel better?"

I had the urge to hit her in the nose just then. But I stood there looking into her eyes until I found the words to ask, "Why did you wait until now to talk about this?"

She broke eye contact with me then. "Talking to that woman today in her garden. For some reason, she reminded me of my mother. I don't know why. I didn't intend to talk about it at all. . . . I wasn't waiting to do it. At first you were just a marvelous curiosity to me. A fiction come true."

"What does that mean?"

She raised her eyebrows. "Don't get on too high a horse. You could have brought up the subject as well, you know. I gave you a couple of very big opportunities to do it, in fact."

"I know that," I said. "Believe me."

"Stone hinted that you and my mother knew each other, as I already told you. Of course, I would have known you anyway. I knew your name. I knew who you were from the moment you walked in his door."

"What do you mean I was a fiction?"

"Oh Tom," she said, her eyes welling up slightly, shaking her head.

I stared at her. "What?"

"Poor Tom," she said, one or two actual tears popping out of her eyes then. "Poor Tom. Poor Mother. You were the love of her life. Nothing ever matched up to you." She turned and looked out across the river.

I sat down then. I had the choice to either sit down or fall down, so I chose to sit down. The breath was knocked out of me.

Still standing, her leg almost against my shoulder, she said, "Mother's death wasn't easy. I was with her in Memphis for her last six months. I grew to love her. We hadn't gotten along so well before then. But she told me these things; she talked about you. You were a story to me, my mother's hero. An incredibly vivid story. I know it all. I never expected to see you. But then I did, and it went on from there. I didn't have evil designs on you. This whole thing has been remarkable to me, starting with meeting a man on the top of a pyramid who willed me his estate. Who would believe that?"

I still couldn't quite speak.

"Forgive me. I didn't know that you felt as strongly as she did. How could you have? You were so young."

"Sit beside me," I eventually managed to say.

She did so, and after a little while put her head on my shoulder, which was too much for me. I felt as if I'd sink into the earth. I just sat there with tears running down my cheeks, drinking in her presence. It is hard for me to describe this even now, but I have practiced: the sun was going down. The only sound was wind coming up over the hill behind us. After a while I wanted to say something to her but knew that I wouldn't be able to speak of her mother, that I couldn't, but I wanted to tell her something. Anything.

"See out there. Across the river. That was the old Fort Gibson. Ten thousand Cherokees gathered there in 1895 to get their allotment payments for the Cherokee Strip. It's quite a historical place, this town. . . ."

"Tom," she said gently, raising her head and looking at me, "it's all right to have your own history, your own life. It's not excessive or foolish. And for people you've known to still mean something to you even if they're gone. I think it's a fine thing to have a love. For one time to be purely in love. A wonderful thing. No matter how deluded you were, or young, or how hopeless it was. And whether they're around—they never are, really. Only briefly. If you knew them for two days. Many people don't. Ever."

I bowed my head. "Is that the third lesson?"

"If you like," she said.

"I can't talk about her."

"Well then, don't, that's fine."

"You're too young to be so understanding."

"Would you please give up on the too-young business? I have gray hair."

"Where?" I said, looking at it.

"Oh shut up," she said.

Then, more seriously, still looking over the river, she said, "I guess I have traveled a way emotionally. Been around. And I do think about these things, after all. My husband accused me of being clouded, melancholic, having a lot of peculiar thoughts that were irrelevant to 'the field.' That's what he called his work. He could be an utter prig at times. It was a little hat he put on when he began to feel ashamed of himself. I'd tell him that if you didn't think out your relationship to your own past, you certainly couldn't make sense of archaeology. He said that was a lot of bosh. His own past, public school, Greek and Latin, complete bosh, he said, couldn't remember a word of it. Old fools for parents—"

"You loved him, didn't you?"

"Oh, I did," she said, with a quick smile at me before looking back across the river.

I watched her face.

"I do let myself think about the bastard. I do talk about him. I talk to him sometimes. He's still in my thoughts. The way he died. He asked for my forgiveness when he died."

That stopped her for a minute.

"He was just so hapless. All his pals goaded him about his interest in the Jews. They called him the Ancient Jew. He didn't have enough sense to quit drinking and leave off the girls. That's what I wish, that he'd had a chance to get a little older and wiser. I think about him, yes, I have the feelings. I try to let them arise and just . . . let them arise. What else can you do? I don't try to lock him away. And you mustn't do it either—with my mother or Laura or anyone else who matters to you."

"You remember her name?"

"Laura? Of course. I've been paying great attention to you, Tom. I'm not a dumb girl."

"Was your father okay?"

She gave me a quick glance. "'Clare,' we called him. Yes, he was okay, not the greatest but okay."

There was a strange telepathy in this answer, as if she knew that I really didn't want to know too much.

We walked back down the hill to the cabin, where I still had a few hours to wait, and the telepathy continued. I felt unexpectedly relaxed with her, considering what we'd just talked about. I flopped down on the bed and wasn't concerned when she did likewise. She took off her shirt, which in that heat was only realistic. I had mine off, and it was still sweat-running hot. The mattress was a little rank, but it had sheets on it. The ceiling was made of cedar boards.

I began trying to plan what I had to do, where I'd park the car, how I was going to get into the agency building. What I wanted to find.

Through the noise of the fan, we could hear an occasional sound of children playing outside. Of course I was aware of her beside me, but she was different now. The cat was out of the bag.

She said, "So what did you think when you first saw women?"

I laughed. She really did know the story—that fresh from a childhood spent in isolation, I had never talked to a woman under sixty or seventy years old until the day I met her mother and in fact had seen only a few of them.

"Seriously. Tell me."

"What did I think of them? I was scared, and interested. I love women," I added impulsively, then realized how absurd that sounded and said, "It was natural to be interested. I believe I was actually about fifteen."

"Yeah," she said, rolling onto an elbow and smiling at me. "I can just see you, with your glancing eyes and nervous, sensitive ways. What did you love about women?"

I snorted and glanced at her slightly disapprovingly.

"Why do you think one holds things like that so dear?" she asked.

I understood what she meant.

"Not a single reason, I guess. Things conspire. When I met your mother I was a little like . . . I don't know what. Like someone raised in a closet, or in another world. But educated in a way. A funny mix. And Samantha was a lot like you."

"What do you mean like me?" she said.

"Don't make me talk about her," I said.

"So talk about me."

"Spectacular," I said.

"Oh? You find me spectacular?"

"Don't give me that," I said, attempting to sound irritated.

"Can I ask you one question?" she asked.

"The answer is yes, I did. I killed someone. The assistant prosecutor is a killer."

"Another thing held dear," she said gently. "But that wasn't what I wanted to ask."

"I can't talk about Sam. Anything about her is between you and her. I guess you had plenty of time to talk."

"I know she came to Fort Smith to find her father."

Lying there looking at her, I had a weird thought, and she read it in my expression and smiled. "Don't worry," she said. "I'm not your daughter. I was born almost two years after they married."

"I wasn't thinking that," I lied.

"Just making sure you knew," she said lightly.

She lay back down, and we were quiet for a while. I had a deepening sense of her presence beside me. Our shoulders were touching. I began to feel that talking was a good idea.

I said, "What's the one thing you wanted to ask? Maybe I'll answer it."

"Did you really take care of Mother when she was sick?"

"That's what you want to know? Yes, I helped a little. We were staying in the same boarding house. I took her food at night. It was only for a week or so."

"And when you finally left her, she said you were together on that old bridge, across the river—"

"This river," I said.

"And you rode away, into the territory. Where did you go when you left her?"

"That's two questions."

"Don't be stingy."

"I just knew I had to go. I had nothing for her. I was a killer. A half-breed kid. Gallows material. I had to get out of town. There was no choice."

"But where did you go?"

"I went to a place called Osi Tamaha."

"What did you find there?"

I laughed. "That's three questions."

She was quiet, waiting for my answer.

"I found a job clerking in a store. Just a normal job. I worked for two years before making my way to Norman."

"But that's where you had been left as a baby. Big Tree, right?"

"It was a name on a map, Rainy. I just went there."

"Did you find out anything about your past?"

"No. The Indians, the nomadic ones, had quit coming through there. The Comanche had been moved west. People didn't like to talk about them. They'd stolen livestock, taken slaves, killed people. It's a wonder whoever found me in the first place didn't slit my throat."

"So there really is a big tree."

"It's a bald cypress about fourteen feet in diameter and two thousand years old. It was on the old military road from Little Rock to Fort Towsend. It also happened to be on the property of a kind man named Jefferson Gardner. I told him that I'd come to see the tree, and he ended up giving me a job."

"That man who walked out of the mountains to Aunt Rachel's house, he was doing the same thing. Where you come from does matter. It's part of what makes you human."

"He didn't come from an Indian mound."

"Don't pretend to be dumb," she said, suddenly irritated. "They get their identity from their ancestors, and their ancestors are represented by the mound."

"How do you know that?"

"Oh go off," she said.

She sounded genuinely perturbed, and I said nothing else about it. We remained beside each other, unmoving.

She was quiet a while and eventually said, "I read an article in *Life* magazine by some scientist who said that love is just a form of brain chemistry. He had it all figured out. What do you think it is?"

"Divine madness," I said, no joke intended.

"A stinging sense of the present," she countered. "And of the possible."

"The world opening up," I added, smiling at the ceiling.

"I think it is chemistry. I think it's inheritable."

I noticed myself still smiling. It was extremely pleasant being beside her.

"Do you wonder why I haven't taken a shower?"

"No," I said.

"It's because I actually like sweating. Do I stink?"

"Oh no," I said quickly.

"Don't be afraid. I won't rape you."

"I'm not afraid," I said, taking my turn to sound irritated.

"Well here I am. Honor thy mother. Cherish her memory. Do as she would. She's gone, as I will be, as you will be. If she were here now, she'd approve. She had a very broad mind, you know. For someone who never found another person to match some kid she'd met years ago. She even had a sense of humor about it. An odd one, she was. Almost European, and living in Memphis. Oh she had a full life, believe me. She was never pitiful about anything. She just had these clear and rather dramatic ideas. And you were one of them."

"You have a broad mind yourself," I said.

"Broader than yours, Mr. Small Town."

"I'm not small town," I said, laughing. "I'm a citizen of the world."

Silent a while, she said, "Spectacular?"

I didn't respond. I wanted to just lie there. I had slipped into a mood of extraordinary peacefulness. Yet at the same time I was quite aware of her half-naked presence beside me. "The other night at your cabin, I thought I would have to run out the door, I loved being with you so much."

"Emily Post doesn't cover this situation," she said after a while.

"True."

"I'm certainly not going to take off your clothes and climb onto you and make you do what you did before." She sighed.

"Right."

"However, if you took off your own clothes. I mean, you don't have a lot on, really. And I have only this pair of pants and underwear. You could do it in probably ten seconds by the clock. Take them off. Both of us."

"Yes," I said.

"But you would have to do it yourself. And there we'd be, quite available to each other."

"By the river," I said.

"The very same," she said.

Cylinder 37

At ten-thirty I left Rainy at the motel and drove to a place below Agency Hill, parked the car, and blundered up an old path, some distance from the road. No one appeared to be near the building, but I didn't have time to walk all over the hill looking for possible parked lovers or sleeping cops. I just had to break the window and get on with it. I did it, hating the sound of the beautiful old blue-tinted imperfect glass shattering. The master files, located in an open room, were like a card catalogue in a library telling where other files were kept. They did have fingerprint records, however, and when I found Colbert's file, I took out my driver's license and looked at the print I'd made on the back of it. It looked the same.

I heard a noise and switched off the flashlight. But it was just the moaning wind that always took me by surprise in this building, even though I'd heard it so many times working here. When the wind was high and coming from a certain direction, the sound could almost run you out, like a chorus of lamenting spirits. I memorized the number of the estate-detail file.

The detail room was at the back of the second floor, and I reconnoitered from the front window, still seeing no cars, before going down the hall to its door. The janitor, Peely, sometimes used to forget to lock doors, but tonight he hadn't. The door was solid walnut that opened outward, making it impossible to break in. There was an adjoining bathroom with a door that was nailed shut. My only hope to get into the room was to crawl through the transom in the bathroom. Its riser was rusted into place, and I took off a shoe and beat on it with a heel to knock it loose. I stood on a sink, but getting through the transom opening with my flashlight wasn't fun. I held on to shelves to pull myself through and break my fall.

The big stand-up library table that used to be in the room was no longer there, and two new rows down the center of the room had been installed to accommodate all the files. The guardianship business was booming.

There were four detail files on Colbert, and I spread them on the floor and started leafing through them under the flashlight beam. In the most recent file I noticed some typical red flags, such as six new cars bought over the last two years for a total of eighteen thousand dollars from the same car dealer in Tulsa. Included among them was a Chevrolet Cabriolet, bought for about five hundred dollars above even its Blue Eagle price. Expenditures also included one thousand acres of land in the Winding Stair Mountains bought for two hundred grand, which was probably twenty times its market value. There were records of bulk foods purchased, but only dollar amounts were given, not vendors. Payments of five grand each had been made to two unnamed bulldozer operators. Rounded numbers, unnamed recipients, padded figures—the file had obvious pointers to a guardianship out of control. Mackey had been paying himself thirteen hundred dollars a month for cashing Colbert's royalty checks and managing his assets.

Royalty check amounts showed a dramatic drop-off only a few months after Mackey had taken over. Previously running over sixteen thousand dollars a month, royalties had plunged, according to the monthly numbers penciled onto the cards, to about one-tenth that much. I had been away from this place a long time and was out of touch with prices and fields, but common sense told me that the market, and these properties, had not dropped tenfold in this period. I could check by looking at royalty amounts on contiguous properties, but in order to do that I'd have to break into another room.

The requests to sell assets that James Cross had described to Hagglund were in the file, as he'd said—and the letters did mention declining royalties as their reason. There were three letters, good forgeries of Colbert's handwriting, but the language in them was filled with intentionally misspelled words and awkward-sounding language that didn't match Colbert's writing style in earlier documents in the file, which was school English. Mackey's forgers had apparently not bothered to notice Colbert's style, only his hand. Anybody reviewing this file up the line should have questioned it.

It wasn't hard to believe that a guardian would do such things. In that room I was surrounded by thousands of files full of this sort of theft on a smaller scale. The hard thing to believe was that the asset sale had made it through the channels. It had to involve wheel-greasing up the line. With this much at stake, I supposed, a lot of grease could be bought.

Kneeling there on the floor of the detail room, flashlight in hand, with the wind keening through the building, I got that old feeling again. I remembered why I had quit this job: because it was a swamp. It was a hang-yourself-in-the-shed job. You couldn't win. Go out there and try to deal with it. Go to the oil towns, talk to people about chiseled deals, stolen land, forged documents, kickback sales. Forget it. It wasn't just whites and Indians. It was the whole situation. You might as well stand in the yard and yell at the wind. I shuffled quickly through the rest of the papers. I didn't even need to read this. I was about to shut the file, almost forgetting one of my reasons for coming here, when there it was, an affidavit recording the purchase of 313 oil properties in Creek and Tulsa Counties, dated April 25, 1934. It was signed neatly, in perfect handwriting, by M. Parfit, purchaser. Signed at the courthouse in Poteau, notarized by a clerk there.

My heart beating faster, I stared at that signature, which I knew well, running through possible implications, flipping through them almost as quickly as I'd been looking at these pieces of paper.

Whatever came next, I had to decide whether to take this file. If Dale Cotton's neighbor was right, Dale had taken his money and run. But I didn't know who was working here now or how far they could be trusted. I decided to take the fourth file. I swiped an accordion holder and put it inside and pitched the whole bundle through the transom into the bathroom, hoping it didn't fall into a urinal.

I stacked up some files and managed to lever myself back through the transom and step down onto the sink. I went to the front landing again and stood for a while at the window, watching for cars, letting myself calm down. I decided to put away my impatience long enough to find out about contiguous properties. I fetched a tall, heavy, cylindrical ashtray from the hall and walked past the director's office to the map-room door, which had a pebble-glass window. I took a deep breath and with the heavy base of the ashtray ruined some more federal property.

I lost track of time, running back and forth getting numbers, essentially trying to build a case in record time. My flashlight burned out, and I just started turning on lights. Hours later I'd gotten enough. Oil revenues on contiguous properties had fallen, but not tenfold, and deeper drilling in some cases was resulting in higher outputs. There was so much reference in the files to uncertainties and changes in the law that I got curious about what was going on in Indian Affairs.

I threw caution to the wind and broke into the director's office. In his cabinet I found a file labeled *Indian Affairs* and in fairly short order learned that Hoover's appointee had been a man named Charles Rhoads. I had heard his name but knew little about him. The letters from him were interesting—in fact, would have been shocking ten years before. He was clearly friendly toward establishing or reestablishing tribal authorities and equally clear about his unhappiness with the situation in Oklahoma.

A recent letter in the file was from Roosevelt, introducing his appointee, Charles Collier. The president's letter was brief, merely stating the appointment and the fact that he had the full faith and support of Secretary Ickes.

Dated in early July was a single letter from Collier, and if Rhoads had been shocking, Collier was a bomb blast: "I regard the destruction of tribal governments and severality as an ill-conceived and ill-executed blunder. My office will encourage native arts and religion, preservation of group relationships, and tribal governments."

Standing with his letter in my hand, I didn't know whether to laugh or cry. Oops, Mr. Collier was saying, we've been coming at this wrong for the last forty years. There I was, in the very place where I had toiled to execute a policy that they'd finally figured out in Washington wasn't working too well. I was getting it from the horse's mouth.

There was a sound in the building. I put the letter back in the file and went out to the landing and looked down. I saw moonlight on a car parked in front, and I turned in time to see him hit the stairs, fumbling with a pistol. It was one of those moments when curiosity almost exceeds the instinct for self-preservation, because certainly I should have run. He wasn't a killer, he was a lawyer, but he was pulling back the hammer and was clearly distraught.

"Hey there, Dale. I thought you went to California."

"You've broken in here!" he said. "You were snooping around my house, and now here! You son of a bitch."

Dale was working himself up, trying to convince himself that he could shoot me without getting into trouble for it, but he was shaking so much that the little man inside me, the observer, had the irrelevant thought that he was going to hurt himself. The little man also wondered what I was doing just standing here at the top of these stairs as he stumbled upward with a cocked pistol. He made it to the top, and there we were together, two old coworkers, standing not ten feet apart on the landing, near the window, with the dry wind ripping the sky outside.

"I guess that was you the other night in the mountains. Boy, that was quite a scene, wasn't it?"

Dale pulled the trigger then, but not until the barrel, as if of its own accord, had pulled to the side. The noise was considerable in that big, echoing room, and we doubtless both jumped. The bullet ripped into the walnut paneling. He tried to cock the gun a second time but was shaking too hard. He cursed weakly when I took it away from him. Dale wasn't cut out for this kind of thing. He started to turn to go down the stairs, but I told him to stop, which he did.

"I've been reading the latest directives coming down from Washington, Dale. It sounds like they want to bring back the tribes. They don't like what's going on here in Oklahoma. Wouldn't know anything about that, would you?"

Holding on to the banister, he finally turned and stared at me, as if he couldn't quite focus. He was bent over as if he had a stomachache. I was still holding the pistol by its barrel, and he was probably trying to calculate how threatening I was. He hadn't responded, so I tried a direct tack.

"So tell me, blood. How much did they pay you?"

"I'm not blood!" he said with horror.

That was a curious moment—one of the few sincere exchanges I'd ever had with Dale Cotton, despite having worked with his sorry ass for years.

I shook my head and laughed and maybe felt a little stab of pain somewhere. "You look like one to me, Dale. But I know what you mean. I do. You and I both . . . Anyway, we're lawyers, aren't we? We can make a deal. You're going to tell me what you know."

"I've got no reason to talk to you."

I nodded my head slowly and changed my tone of voice and used a few trial theatrics to menace him. Dale hadn't had much court experience, and he obviously hadn't had a real night's sleep in a while, and he smelled like a whiskey mill. His nerves were frayed. I threatened and cajoled him a little, and before he had left the landing, before he had even moved a step, he started talking. He talked the best he could.

Cylinder 38

Dale Cotton was in deep. You could read it in his face and the tone of his voice. If anything went wrong, he might as well get his affairs in order and report to One Mackey Plaza in Tulsa. Going to California—which in fact he had been in the process of trying to do—wouldn't save him. I convinced him that I was interested in only one thing, murder in Sebastian County. I convinced him that if he worked with me, I'd try to keep him alive and, depending on how much he cooperated, out of jail. Both were reckless promises, and he must have known it, but he wanted to believe. He was ripe for conversion.

Mentally filtering what he told me, and filling in some blanks, I got the sense that Hagglund's story about Colbert going to the mountains to escape his guardian was true, although Dale wasn't very forthcoming on this subject since he had been on the payroll, helping Mackey get the guardianship in the first place and then helping him keep it.

He claimed that Mackey's guardianship fees and kickbacks were on the high side, but the whole thing didn't go crazy until after Colbert requested a big asset sale to buy land and run some kind of rescue mission in the mountains for full-bloods. Not long after moving into the mountains, Colbert gave up on being emancipated from his guardian and began to just play the game, making his requests like a good boy for monthly allowance increases and individual expenditures. Dale claimed it had all seemed pretty innocent at first. He first heard about it from a letter Colbert sent to Mackey asking for the asset sale. Mackey himself had brought the letter to Dale at the agency and asked him what he knew about the fullbloods and the property, and Dale had told him he knew nothing. He was only the probate lawyer on restricted property; he wasn't following the old man's daily business.

Dale claimed he was never trying to hide anything. He had even talked to the director about it. He said there were other oil Indians running relief missions, and the agency was bending rules for them. It seemed to him like a good use of the money.

"You mean the property sale was okayed by the director?"

"He never wrote it down, but I talked to him about it. He said if the old man was worth millions, why not put some of it to work feeding hungry people? It made sense to him. That's what he said."

Dale really didn't want to talk anymore. He was like a clock that was running down. The thought that talking to me was a mistake kept flickering across his face. I asked him if he knew where there might be a drink in this building, and that seemed to give him temporary hope.

Dale had a pint bottle in his otherwise cleaned-out desk. He slumped into his chair, I sat in his client's chair, across the desk, and we passed the bottle as if we were old friends. I put the gun on his desk. Looking at it seemed to make him more uneasy than watching me hold it, and I wondered if he hadn't been lingering too long over the suicide stories in the newspapers.

He claimed not to have seen Colbert's property until last Tuesday night, although Mackey's foot soldiers had apparently been crawling all over the place keeping an eye on Colbert and also delivering the bulk foods there, hiring bulldozers—doing whatever the old man wanted.

"Why was Mackey still watching the place?" I asked him. "The property was sold six months ago."

"He was still the old man's guardian," Dale said. "He was taking food up there and such."

I looked at him. "Come on, Dale. He'd gotten what he wanted. Why didn't he just leave the old man alone?"

"I don't know what all's been going on!" Dale said, again trying to sound defiant. "All I know is that he's been squeezing me, threatening me, telling me what to do. That son of a bitch starts wrapping the ropes around you . . ."

"Were you there when the land was sold?"

"No," he said flatly. "Why should I have been?"

"Do you know anything about the buyer?"

He shook his head.

"You don't know if he was a shell buyer?"

"All I had to do was get the sale approved. That was it." Dale was looking down at his desk again.

"But you had to get it approved at certain amounts. Why so low? With the changes in Washington, wasn't that asking for trouble?"

He stared at his desk. "It's trouble one way or the other once you talk to Jim Mackey. Do one thing for him. Light his cigarette for him. Then it starts."

"Good Oklahoma businessman, huh?" I said.

Dale smirked briefly. He was holding on to his whiskey bottle, tightly.

"Colbert's estate is worth millions of dollars," I said. "Why didn't Mackey make the price less of a red flag? He could have worked it out with the shell so it was mostly play money. Eleven thousand dollars is ridiculous, Dale."

"You seem to know all about it," he said disconsolately. "You tell me." He turned his eyes up to me. "See, you don't understand, Tom. Mackey doesn't believe in red flags. He doesn't believe in the Indian office. He thinks it's a joke. He thinks I'm a joke. He doesn't believe in the goddamn federal government. Hell, he doesn't believe in anything but what he can get. And he doesn't spend any more money than he has to to get it."

"Why were you up there last Tuesday?" I asked him.

"A man running a bulldozer was killed in an accident. I'd gotten him the job in the first place. Name of Cooper, from Tulsa. I heard about the accident from O'Brien. He told me to call the man's wife. I went up there to see what happened."

"O'Brien worked for Mackey?"

"O'Brien and Stahl," Dale said tiredly. "They were the ones always coming here, running Mackey's messages, telling me what to do."

"They push you around?"

Dale didn't even bother to respond to that question. He only stared at me.

"So did Mackey have Levi Colbert killed?"

Dale just shook his head. He didn't know. That's all he knew. He was completely drained. He looked like his head was going to fall over on his desk. I asked him whether he'd known anything about the artifacts, and he responded no, except that he knew Mackey was giving them to the old man.

"Giving them?"

"O'Brien said Colbert was a fool for those old Indian curios. Said it was better than whiskey to keep him happy. Old man claimed he wanted them for the full-blood types living on his property."

"Who are those people?" I asked.

He shook his head again. "Bunch of crazies. I don't know. I never had anything to do with them."

"In the file, the requests to sell his property are forgeries. Who put them in there?"

He glanced at me quickly, obviously surprised that I knew. For a moment he seemed to think about lying; then he looked down at the desk.

"Stahl and O'Brien brought them. They made me put em in the file."

"If Levi Colbert really did ask for an asset sale in the first place, why'd you replace the original request with forgeries?"

"Because he wouldn't have liked the price. The old man had a pretty good idea what he was worth. I guess they wanted letters in there that made him sound crazier."

"So somehow the purchase got effected anyway. Somehow he signed the bill of sale even though the price was completely out of whack?"

"I guess so. I told you I wasn't there."

"Who was the bulk-food supplier?"

"General Distributors and Purveyors. Tulsa. I think Mackey owns it."

Cylinder 39

Dale had to leave. He didn't want to talk to me anymore. He didn't want my help or advice. He was sour and drunk and whipped. He just wanted to go off somewhere under a bush. As he wobbled down the stairs, holding to the banister to keep from falling, I looked after him, wondering whether something like this would have happened to me if I had remained here. I like new cars. I like a good restaurant dinner. I like a lot of things that cost money. Jim Mackey was only one of many smiling sharks ready to come around the Indian office, wanting to be pals, offer little tidbits, make promises.

It was exactly five o'clock when I left the agency with the Colbert file. Rainy had slept well at the River Inn. She could see that I was a little worse for wear and didn't ask me any questions. She drove us to Tulsa. I lay on the seat beside her, taking what was for me a very solid car nap, complete with a couple of 180-proof nightmares.

"What on earth?" she said, startling me awake. I sat up quickly.

"Sorry," she said. "Is this Tulsa?"

We were entering a forest of wooden derricks. "It's the Glenn Pool," I said, blinking at the sunlight. "We're close to Tulsa."

The Glenn Pool wasn't the first thing I wanted to see when I woke up. It had bad associations for me—with a job poorly done while working for the Indian office, with the churning mechanized destruction of wartime. That old dirty, nervous feeling. Black slag pools, smoking motors, mazes of roads and trails, earth scraped and plowed and stained where bulldozers gouged slurry pools and flattened places for drilling, alarming combinations of smells, traffic jams, piles of busted-up machinery, dirty, sometimes angry men with their eyes in fixed stares. Men gathered around somebody who'd been injured. Jury-rigged wires snaking across the landscape. The shack and ragtowns scattered around oil fields reminded me of wartime too, of the R-and-R depots where soldiers were sent to avoid going nuts in the trenches—except in oil ragtowns there were no Red Cross tents and no delousing vats, and the whores were more expensive. Here the towns were mostly saloons or clubs, gathering places for sneak thieves, pickpockets, grifters, pimps, and organized mobs with names like the Curbside Boys and Kelsy's Rats that hired out to the highest dollar.

We both wanted a cup of coffee and something to eat, but I saw a truck belonging to Blackwell Rigging and Drilling turn onto a side road. I asked her to follow it. He drove about a mile into the field and stopped between a rig and a tin shack. As soon as Rainy turned off the motor the *whump* of a nearby explosion of dynamite caused the ground to shake and a rain of curses to come down from a pipe puller hanging from the top of a rig.

"You ignorant educated goddamn college fuck, stop doin that without warnin me!"

Sitting at a card table was a young man with a geophone, not paying much attention to the pipe puller, somehow reading his information in a havoc of noise. Cable rigs whammed at the ground not far away, trucks crawled across the hills, diesel motors rattled, pipes clanged together.

Rainy stayed in the car, and I went to the tin building and rapped on the door to avoid startling anybody. The mood in the fields could get pretty edgy because of theft, intimidation, espionage, and the simple danger of the work.

John Blackwell was facing the door at a little rough table. He was busy with paperwork and a little vexed-looking, but he remembered me. We had once been on the same side of a lawsuit. He had been drilling for a company whose lease was challenged, and I had helped his side by supplying documents and testimony verifying that the owner actually held the rights. It had been a messy Tulsa County affair in which the claimant came to court so soused that he could barely talk. Blackwell and I had gotten acquainted over several days, but it had happened twelve years before. He had struck me at the time as a hard-driving but honest driller.

After we'd gotten through the obligatory weather talk, I told him I was working on a criminal case in Arkansas and trying to get general information about what was going on in the field these days.

"General information?" he said skeptically.

"That's right, John. It's been a while. I guess there've been some changes since the early '20s."

Blackwell took me outside the tin shack. He nodded at the young man at the card table. "See that doodlebugger?" he said, voice raised above the clatter. "The boys make fun of him, but he can set off a charge and find oil. Beats hell out of the old witchin days. They've got college boys studyin drill cuttings under microscopes, lookin for fossils that go along with oil. That's the biggest change. They're better at findin the right formations. That college boy is keepin me in business, and I never thought I'd say such a thing. Hard damn worker too. He's been settin on this hole for three weeks straight. Sleeps in the shack. Wasn't for him, I'd probably have to move on."

"Why's that?"

"Jobbers are hangin on by their fingernails. We'd be workin for less than the cost of bits and labor if it wasn't for men bein so hungry they'll work for nothin. I've been patchin together old cable rigs out of junk to save money on Hughes bits. Tool pushers been workin for me fifteen years I'm payin half wages to. And you better believe I've got some wives to answer to. We're drillin deeper for less. This tin shack, the man I'm drillin for came here the other day and asked me if I really had to have it. He said the rent had been raised on him to three hundred a month just for the shack. Three hundred a month for me to lock away equipment and set in a chair out of the dust. And I'm runnin six holes. I told him hell yes, I had to have it, unless he wanted to buy all the equipment they stole from me. Anyway, that's it: rents and leases are risin, if you can believe it. We're workin seven days a week. We're bein squeezed on both sides."

"What's an acre going for?"

"Could be anything, but six to eight hundred is about typical."

"How can they be raising leases in a mature field?"

"Consolidation. You're dealin with big boys now, and most of em white men. They know what they can get. Lessors didn't know how good they had it when the owners were mostly Indians. I reckon you'd appreciate that."

"Who owns this piece?"

Blackwell was eyeing someone on the rig and growing distracted. "Don't know. Man I'm drillin for never talks about his business, but I hear Jim Mackey owns a big chunk of the field now. He's big in the Seminole too. People like that, you can't fight em. They set the price. You don't like it, there's more where you come from."

Blackwell broke off and stepped forward. "Hey, Jimbo! I need to see you in the shack."

"One more question. Do you know a bulldozer operator by the name of Cooper here in Tulsa?"

"Cooper?" He frowned at the ground. "There's a Wayne Cooper used to do some dozer work here now and again. Seems to me like I heard he got killed."

"Does he have family in Tulsa?"

"I know he's been around a while. Wouldn't be surprised."

As I was turning to leave I noticed Blackwell's boots—new ones. "Like your boots," I told him.

"Yeah," he said, glancing down. "Somebody's sellin em up on the highway. Everybody's wearing em."

I thanked him and snaked the van out of the field, past an old ragtown of tents at its border. The Green Lantern was a big tent with the skirts folded up around the edges, fans blowing inside, and several men sat hunched forward over beers around a spool table, wearing fedoras or straw hats, sweat-stained white shirts, and shoulder holsters. They watched suspiciously as we drove by. Men like John Blackwell hated the oil-field mobsters who hung out at places like this, but fighting them only resulted in feuds.

I maneuvered us on dirt roads out of the Glenn Pool to intersect with Route 66, which had just been opening over the last five years, a smooth concrete ribbon that slashed southwestward across Oklahoma on its way from Chicago to Los Angeles. The traffic was unbelievably heavy for a Saturday, particularly going toward Oklahoma City, with cars so close together that it looked as if there was some infinite funeral in progress. The wind was kicking up, blowing straight into the face of the westward traffic.

Cylinder 40

Before getting onto the highway we stopped at the Rocket Burger and had burgers and malted milks, then coffee. It was a new, fairly large highway restaurant of the kind that was springing up along Route 66—smoky, loud, jammed with people, a lot of whom were counting their money and studying menus. We sat in a corner booth, and I gave Rainy the basics of what I'd learned last night and today. She wanted to know what Dale Cotton had told me about the Indians living on the mountain, and I said he didn't seem to know much about them or about the artifacts except that Jim Mackey had apparently used Levi Colbert's interest in them to maneuver him toward a property sale. She asked me who the property buyer had been, and I hesitated a minute but told her.

She stared at me for a while. "You're kidding."

I just looked at her over my coffee cup.

"The officious one who first called me in Chicago? Does that mean Stone is involved?"

"I doubt if Mr. Parfit is a big risk-taker with his own money. He lives on a secretary's salary. And he does whatever the judge tells him to do."

"Why would Stone want you working on this if he was implicated?"

"His friend was murdered. Maybe his conscience got him. The day you arrived, that morning, he called me to his office. He was in a funny mood, talking about rumors, reputations, the past. He wanted to remind me that I had my own skeletons in the closet. I got a feeling he'd made some kind of big decision."

"What?"

"Maybe it was to get the man who'd killed his friend, no matter what the cost."

The waitress, a speed demon with a ponytail, ran by and splashed more coffee into our cups.

"Why didn't he just tell you what he knew?"

"Because he wasn't sure who did it. There's a chance it could have been somebody else. Stone's enough of a poker player not to throw everything away for no reason."

Rainy took up her coffee, frowning at me. "If Mackey's such a bad character, why would a judge get into a deal with him in the first place? He's not a fool."

"Doctors get sick, judges get conned. Everybody's got a weakness."

She grimaced. "Right-oh. And dirty hands make clean money, and short visits make long friends. That's no explanation."

I moved my butter knife to the middle of the table. "Okay. At first Lee Guessner is collecting from the mound; he's gotten in early and stuck with it, travels out there every day buying things off the table. Manny Stone, who's been arrowhead hunting around here for years, is interested too. He visits Guessner's cabin, buys a few items, and they become friends, start talking about keeping the artifacts together in a single collection."

I picked up her knife and set it alongside the other one. "Levi Colbert, in the Winding Stair, is also interested because the people he's living with consider the mound sacred or whatever. Maybe he's deluded, playing his own little guardian game. We don't know how he connected with them in the first place. Hagglund thinks he moved to the mountain to escape Mackey, which is possible."

I picked up a salt shaker and put it between the two knives. "Jim Mackey. He's milking good money out of the old man, and he learns about his weakness for the artifacts and the people living on his property. He starts buying pieces at the mound, muscling in on the dig, taking dynamite to them. He learns that this guy Lee Guessner has already got a big collection of artifacts, and pretty soon he's playing along with his and Stone's idea about a trust. He promises them the moon and stars, fifty thousand dollars over five years for helping him with a land sale."

I crossed the butter knives by the salt shaker. "He sets them up, invites them to the courthouse to sign papers. Parfit is the shell buyer. Mackey needed a shell buyer because he was the old man's guardian and the title couldn't transfer directly to him. The old man and the collectors both think they're getting what they want."

Rainy frowned at the knives, shaking her head slightly. "But they want the same thing. The artifacts."

"They both want money too, large amounts of it, and that's where he's got them. Mackey's not above anything. He'll lie, switch documents, forge signatures, change dollar amounts. He lives on that kind of thing. He gets in, finds out what you want, makes deals that implicate you. If necessary, he either finds out dirt or gets dirt on you. Truth is irrelevant to him. He scratches the right backs, and the system lets him do it."

"Sounds fairly involved."

"When you consider the stakes, it's simple. He played it by ear. Let it develop. First, he was just looking for artifacts to butter up the old man. It went on from there."

"Why was Lee murdered?"

I stared at the V of skin above her blouse and thought aloud.

"Lee eventually figured out that Mackey had poleaxed them, that he'd gotten what he wanted and there was no fifty thousand dollars. The deal had blown up. Lee tried to sic the judge on Mackey. Maybe they threatened to go public on the land fraud. Then Lee met you, remembered you from Egypt. He desperately needed someone he could trust with the collection. He was trying to get out of this mess he'd gotten into and came up with the idea of willing you his estate. He was trying to hide the Spiro goods when he was killed."

Cradling her coffee, she shook her head once, slowly, her eyes focusing on the highway outside. "So Alfred Carr was murdered for the same reason Lee was? Because he knew about the land deal? But they stole artifacts from his well house."

"Mackey couldn't care less about artifacts. They're currency to him. The torture and the blood sign on the wall were warnings."

"To . . ."

"Stone and his secretary, the other ones who know about the land deal. I've never seen Stone act like he has been lately. He doesn't want to tell me the whole story because he knows the game will be up if he does. This is one of the biggest property heists I've ever heard about, and I've seen some fast real estate. Around here they set the standard."

She leaned back, shoulders slumped in thought. "We saw two men dressed as warriors. The one I approached, the man at the fire, the look in his eyes . . . First, I thought he was avoiding me, like Hank's story about the Indian fifty years ago. The way he stared through me. I keep seeing that look, wondering what was on his mind. He was in another world."

"The one I saw on the road that first night acted like any man. Not that he didn't scare the hell out of me, but he did speak a few words, in English. He warned me away from the place."

"An outlyer. Every group has them. Living on the edges. Maybe there are others," Rainy said. "I have to go back there."

"We're in Tulsa now. You insisted on coming with me. I'll put you on the train—"

"Oh shut up," she said, standing up. Rainy had told me to shut up three times over the past few days, and every time it had caused a little irrelevant surge of lust in me.

The restaurant had a telephone booth, and I made a collect call to Mel in Fort Smith. She answered the phone quickly, a little breathlessly. I asked her how it was going.

"Bernie's going in all directions again," Mel said.

"What do you mean?"

"He comes in the office, shuts himself in, and stays there for two hours; then his door flies open and he disappears for who knows how long. He's got me typing up these affidavits on the sheriff. He doesn't know how to use the dictating machine—he bought it with his own money, and he can't figure it out—so he paces around my desk dictating like a madman, tells me to get it done, full report, and shoots out the door like a torpedo. I think he's going too far, Tom. What's happened to him? Why on earth is he doing this? Has he had some kind of religious conversion? His house, this sheriff thing—"

I laughed but felt a little twinge of envy at her admiration. "I hope he's not there right now," I said.

"No," she said glumly. "He's not here."

"Where is he?"

"The judge called. I think. I don't know. I don't know what's going on half the time. And of course the sheriff's cars are prowling all over town like a bunch of nervous tomcats. And these women with their Spuds, can't they smoke anything better? I'd rather smell a nice cigar. Barbara Jean absorbs all the cool air; she puffs away like a paint-factory chimney, and the whole office gets hot within five minutes. Oh, and my typewriter. My Burroughs latest greatest Electric Carriage Return typewriter. The repairman brings it all the way here, swears to me it's fixed, I turn it on and hit the carriage return, and it nearly jumps off the edge of my desk. If it hit your wrist it would break it. So no. I have to honestly report that things aren't hunky-dory. Not entirely. When are you coming back?"

I started to answer her, and she added, "And he moons at me. Tom, he *moons* at me."

"Do you mean he's bothering you?" I asked.

"No. Well, yes, he is. He only moons at me slightly. He's being a good soldier about that too. I just can't stand it."

She sounded as if she was on the verge of tears. "Explain what you mean, Mel. You aren't making sense."

"Oh, go figure it out yourself."

"Is Bernie bothering you or not?"

"No," she said. "That's the problem."

I was silent on the line a while until the light bulb went on. Finally I was getting it. I'd never known Mel to act so upset, but then I'd never known her to be in love with a married man either. In fact, I'd never known her to be in love at all.

"He needs me. He's upset. I'm worried about him."

There was static on the line.

"Mel, can you hear me?"

"Yes," she said.

"If you do stay in the office, get Hank in there—him or somebody he trusts. Don't stay there without him. And if you've got affidavits on the sheriff, be sure you have copies at other places. Take the yellow sheets and stow them somewhere outside the building."

"You think they'll burn us out?"

"Just be careful, Mel. I'll be back tomorrow, I hope. One other thing. Call Judge Stone. Tell him I suggest he make himself scarce for a while."

"And when he asks why?"

I hesitated, looked at my fingernails, thinking of exactly how to phrase this. "Just tell him that with all the current disruption, Tom has a hunch that it would be a good idea. But be firm, Mel. As firm as you know how to be."

On Route 66, Rainy and I drove by diners with neon cowboys on their signs and streamlined gas stations and motels busy even in the middle of the day, on across the river, pushed by the wind, into Tulsa, the city that oil built. In my lifetime, Tulsa had been a rough little Creek Nation cow town of a couple hundred people, one of the more reliable places in the Indian Nation to get killed. It was still a good place to get killed, but the downtown was full of shiny buildings now, twenty-nine stories here, fourteen stories there, towers decorated with colorful terra-cotta tiles, monoliths designed by big-time architects.

We stopped at the new Union Depot, which today was surrounded by freshly plastered Klan posters. There'd been a race riot in Tulsa in the early '20s, with over a hundred people killed, and racial unrest had simmered ever since. I separated from Rainy and went looking for a man who worked in the station as a porter. In one of the depot's large rooms, a dance marathon was under way, the frenzied sounds of a band echoing sadly through the big terminal. As I walked by, people were slumped against each other, dragging each other around a gritty floor.

The man I was looking for was a light-skinned Negro who went by the name of Pale. Pale acted oblivious of people and their doings, but he was one of the more observant men I'd ever met. I knew him for the same reason that I knew John Blackwell, but in Pale's case I had been a direct advocate for his family. His grandfather—and his father as a young child—had been Cherokee slaves who were granted tribal land rights as freedmen. I'd gotten them a change of venue for a land case that they wouldn't have had a chance of winning in Tulsa.

I found him and managed to get a couple of minutes of his time between trains. He knew a place to stand where no one would overhear us. The wall behind us was resplendent with art deco sunbursts and chevrons. Pale maintained a flat expression on his face so that anyone watching from a distance would have thought we were talking about some trivial subject. When I asked about Jim Mackey he got a vacant look in his eye for a minute, but I saw him decide to tell me at least some of what he knew. He told me he knew Mackey was in town now because there were some Indians who'd arrived by train yesterday, about a dozen of them up from Oklahoma City whom Mackey's men had picked up with fancy cars and girls.

Pale dropped the innocuous expression and said, "His boys knock around the porters. Yell at em, tell em they ain't going fast enough, kick em in the butt."

"They kick you?"

"Oh, they got better sense. They do it to the younger boys. It's just a little show for the Indians with the oil. Kick around the niggers."

I smiled. "You think they get what they deserve?"

"Who?" he said.

"The Indians with oil."

He laughed. "Surprised to hear you say that. Oh I guess they get it when he finish with em. I used to think everybody get what they deserve. But you probably seen the posters outside this building: join the cause. I give up worryin about what people deserve; figure some get more'n they deserve, some get less, least for a while. I have to put my faith in the Lord's justice."

As sometimes happened, I was momentarily lost in that simple declaration. Whenever someone spoke of the Lord's justice, I envied them. I envied their having a resting point, even if justice seemed to me to be a primitive human approximation of anything God might be interested in.

I asked Pale where Mackey took the Indians for entertainment, and he told me the oil man was having a barbecue tonight. He had an annual barbecue at his ranch north of town, near Sperry, celebrating his first oil find.

I found the addresses of Wayne Cooper and of General Distributors and Purveyors in a phone book. Going through town, Rainy craned her neck to look around at all the concrete, the polychrome roofs and terra-cotta panels, the zigzag lightning bolts, the sphinxes.

"This place looks like ancient Egypt," she said, dabbing at her sweating face with a shoulder.

Wayne Cooper's address was in the West Bank of Tulsa, which was the other side of the coin from downtown. Among haphazard, potholed dirt streets and bedraggled houses we found the dead bulldozer operator's house. A large woman in a plain white housedress was just going in the front door with a mop and bucket, and I drove down the block to park.

I turned the motor off and sat a minute, trying to plan what I'd say to her.

"Something tells me this woman isn't going to trust me. Her husband was working among Indians, telling her God knows what."

"I'll do it," she said without hesitation.

"What'll you tell her?"

"What would you tell her?"

I blinked at her. "Damn if I know. I know she doesn't want to hear about prosecutors and crimes and all that. Her husband was just killed."

"I can handle it," she said.

Before I could say anything else, Rainy hopped out the door and walked down the street to the house. I watched in the mirror. It took a long time—forty minutes, forty-five, but I just kept my eye on the street and the house, making sure no one else went in. I checked the glove compartment for Hank's pistol. I sweated. I worried. It was almost an hour before she walked back out and down the street toward the van. I noticed her stumble slightly and saw the look on her face.

Cylinder 41

Working at the agency and prosecuting, I thought I'd seen it all, heard it all. What might seem revolting to an outsider would be a mild case to me, all in a day's work. Anything Rainy might tell me she'd learned from the bulldozer man's wife I could put into perspective. She was dismayed, you could see it in her eyes, but I wouldn't be.

She was still absorbing the meaning of what Mrs. Cooper had told her as she stepped into the van. She gave me the basics, and we sat there blinking at each other, silenced.

But it was the kind of story that makes you want to go somewhere else. Just about anywhere else. Get away from it like a bad odor.

I didn't want to go to a bar, so we ended up on a bank of the river, in the shade of a warehouse. The nearest people were a couple of fishermen on the water. Across the depleted river with its oily scum were the new city's shining towers. A little way down, on our side, a group of about twelve people was being baptized, even though it was Saturday—and I wondered, irrelevantly, if they were a sect who ascribed to the Old Testament sabbath. The men had on ties, the women their best dresses, but the water they were entering looked for all the world like a sewage ditch.

Our conversation became desultory as we both tried to comprehend Mrs. Cooper's story. My observer, my little man who pops up with a gag, was off work today. He'd had to work all night in Muskogee. He was asleep.

Wayne Cooper had been worried about what he was doing for Mr. Mackey, and he had talked to his wife about it. And poor Mrs. Cooper, herself confused, grieving, had talked openly to Rainy, a stranger who'd just walked in her door. Rainy had introduced herself as a Christian lady who was recruiting for a church and shared one of the great trials of her own life, a husband who had died young while researching the holy land—so close to true that it must have been easy to play the part—and then Rainy had given out the hints that inspire others to open up.

Mrs. Cooper, who had so recently endured the death of her own husband, had opened up, and now we were sitting by the river trying to digest it, the need to find some answer to this, do something, clearly shared and weighing on both of us. I panted in the heat like a dog, watching the people as they walked into the river, holding hands to support each other, all looking solemn.

"Can he get away with that kind of thing?" she asked me.

"As long as he's throwing around big money, this town belongs to him. He can get away with just about anything."

She sighed, pressing her lips together and squinting toward the line of Christians.

I put my head between my knees and shut my eyes. I had a lifetime of training in calming down, not getting in an uproar, not succumbing to crazy urges. But I had a sound in my ears, a humming, a distant roar, I don't know what, and it didn't help to analyze and weigh and put in perspective. The greed was old hat. The legal shenanigans—outrageous though they were—weren't new. Oklahoma was a legal cesspool. But the casual disregard of a whole group of people, and the way it was delivered—as food, as sustenance, as help, as bait—that got to both of us.

"Did she say what these packages looked like?" I asked. "Did she use a word like *barrels* or *boxes* or anything to say what they were in?"

Rainy sighed, a faraway look on her face. "They had her husband pick up packages of food, which included meat. He didn't have an icebox, and they didn't give him one. They told him these people wouldn't eat food that had been under ice."

"Packages?"

She nodded. "He took a bunch of loads of it up there. He drove back here on the weekends. He told his wife that a lot of the people were sick. Some of them were dying, and he was worried that the food he was taking was part of the problem. He said that over one week about ten of them died. He was there, working, when they died. He went to this distributor again, and they said he didn't have to worry. He wouldn't be taking food there anymore after one last haul. All he had to do was deliver it and pick up his machine. He dropped by to tell his wife that he was finished after one last run. He was happy to be finished with the job. Then they told her he was killed in a trucking accident. He went off the side of the hill, and they didn't find him until a day later."

I watched the people in the river, now being baptized, one at a time going under the water and being brought up by a person on each side.

"Why would they keep eating food that was making them sick?"

She shook her head. "He told his wife he saw them picking over the food and throwing some of it away. I guess they were trying to eat only what they thought wouldn't kill them. They must have gotten worn down. He told her that some of them were going blind—even the young ones—and their skin was darkening."

"What?"

"That's what he said. Going darker in the skin—around their eyes. He was afraid of them. He just wanted to get his job done and get out of there."

I recalled the smell I'd noticed the night I went to the mountain alone.

"Where the hell was Levi Colbert? The man was educated, for Christ's sake. Was he senile? Why would he let them—?"

"You don't have to be educated to know not to eat rotten food, Tom. Those people lived without refrigeration."

"So what the hell happened?"

"Maybe they were collapsing. At the point of no return. It happens in epidemics and famines. Towns, cities, whole civilizations can collapse."

"But what was he doing up there?"

"You mean Colbert?" She blinked at me.

"Yes," I said.

Rainy picked up a stick and scratched in the sand. She shrugged a little. "You saw him. Maybe he'd given up. He tried to keep them fed, tried to give them a safe place to live, tried to return their stuff. He tried to build a mound to rebury it. If your ancestors are important, if you believe that your identity comes from them, destroying the physical emblems of them weakens you."

"Horseshit," I said, speaking out of frustration more than anything, but it made her mad.

She stabbed the stick in the sand and looked at me with fire in her eyes. "Have you ever lost anyone you cared about?" Our eyes locked, and we each knew what was going across the other's mind.

"If you can't think about it any other way, think of it that way. That's what it's like for some people. I don't mean educated, modern, up-to-date people like you."

"And you know how they feel, huh?" I said, now angry myself.

"Not fully. But I can find analogies, I can put two and two together. Their ancestors matter like personal relationships matter to us. Losing contact with them, defiling them, is a terrible blow. How would you feel if a committee of men came to your house, found all the mementos of your wife, set up a table outside, and sold them to passing motorists, or they dug up her bones and set them out on a table with a sombrero over her skull? And the people were sick, Tom; they were hungry. They were falling apart. Maybe Colbert finally chose the old way, their old way. Maybe he physically sacrificed himself."

"Oh, that's great," I said.

She gazed back out at the river. "You think that's foolish?"

"I think he should have gotten them to goddamn town and gotten them something to eat."

"Maybe he tried and they wouldn't go. Maybe those guys were guarding the road. Didn't you say there were guards all over the road the night you went there? Then the road was dynamited. Maybe they were too weak to walk out by then."

The baptizers were making it down the line, one after another plunging all the way under the brown scum. At that moment I was boiling inside. I felt a little knocked around by Rainy saying I couldn't put myself in the place of the people on Colbert's property. I had spent a good many years working for the living Indians, and it was frustrating, grief-inspiring work. It was work for people who had given up, or wanted to give up, war-blasted cynics, existentialists, or people like Dale Cotton. Poor Dale Cotton had sold his soul and wasn't even enjoying it. Clients who sat in their houses, as useless as the leeches who were sucking out their blood, clients wasted by booze who didn't bother to farm or anything else. People with income—more income than their neighbors—who were so disorganized that they lost their teeth by thirty and died of cirrhosis at thirty-five, clients for whom the money only hurried along the rot. The money wasn't it. Not all of it. Not really. Maybe the new boys in Washington had something. Maybe it was a good idea to give up on integration. I'd been among the first wave, trained so white I didn't know how white I was. I was so white I could talk white circles around most white men. But I had been born an Indian and raised in a shithole Indian orphanage, and I had lived in one of the most Indian places in Oklahoma for several years and clerked for a wonderful man who had been a chief of the tribe. In my life I had witnessed the whole spectrum of this cursed place.

What had she done? Dynamited a few pyramids, read some books, pranced around the Mediterranean with a bunch of British dipsomaniacs. I said nothing, though. It was too complicated. It wasn't the time. There were more immediate things to deal with.

The sun-glazed surface of the Arkansas River looked as if it would catch fire. I sat quiet a moment, thinking, trying to put what Mrs. Cooper had said into the story I already knew.

"Okay. Mackey screwed the old man out of his estate two months ago. That was a done deal. Why would he do this now? Did Mrs. Cooper say anything else?"

"It may have taken that long to get it finished," she said grimly. "He wasn't using a fast method but a slow one. And if you think about it, it's ingenious. Devious. How do you prove that food wasn't safe?"

"That's all she told you?"

"That was all. Believe me, I squeezed her like a dishrag. Her husband didn't like talking about it. He was getting paid a lot of money. But he was having nightmares, she said. He just wanted to finish the job and get out."

"Does she suspect he may have been murdered?"

Rainy shook her head. "Not that I could tell. She was crying, upset. They only told her about her husband's death on Wednesday. She's a decent, open woman, but she isn't brilliant. She didn't seem to be trying to hide anything."

"When did he leave here?"

"Sunday. We were there on Tuesday night. So he delivered the last load of unrefrigerated food two days before we went. They may have been trying to break camp when we saw them, the few who were alive. Maybe they were making a last effort to get away. They might have killed Cooper, you know."

We watched the newly baptized walking out of the river, again all holding hands. The white dresses and shirts were dyed now with mud and petroleum.

I heard the humming again, the roar. If I turned tail, I'd never have another decent night's sleep. Going back to Fort Smith and informing someone about this would be completely useless. It would just alert Mackey to cover his tracks.

We drove to a sleek gas station on the highway, where we both drank water and went to the bathroom. Thoughts were streaking through my mind like comets. I bought a tin of aspirin and took about three of them.

When I walked out, Rainy was already outside in the blazing sun. Around her, heat shimmered off the asphalt, making her seem to rise in the liquid air.

We drove to General Distributors and Purveyors. It was a one-story building in a neighborhood of oil-field-supply businesses. The idea I had was to search for some kind of evidence, some proof of what Mrs. Cooper had told us. Or to find somebody who could be threatened into being a witness. I asked Rainy to take the driver's seat and keep the motor running. I thought of taking Hank's pistol, putting it into my belt, and buttoning my coat but decided against it. I wiped the sweat off my face and got out.

Cylinder 42

I don't know whether I was lucky or unlucky to walk in the door and find four of Jim Mackey's men sitting there. I guess it was lucky because they were just finishing lunch, a couple of them already smoking cigars, and they weren't inclined at that moment to be nervous with four of them and only one of me.

Four men sitting around a cheap table with ashtrays and the remains of food on it—one with a hat knocked back on his head, one with an old-fashioned mustache, one with fuzzy, receding red hair that was cut in a perfect flat-top, which made him look a little like a fright mask. The other was a tall, powerful-looking man with a bony face and broad mouth that reminded me of Abraham Lincoln's but eyes that were yellow and depthless, like a goat's.

As I walked in, the fuzzy-headed one was just saying something, and the others were chuckling. I stood at the small counter and smiled. "Good afternoon, gentlemen. Is there a Mr. O'Brien here?"

"Depends who's askin?" said the fuzzhead with a quick, weirdly puckered smile. His hair looked a little like Harpo Marx's, but the grin was all wrong.

I gave a fake name and told him I represented Central Wholesale Supply in Kansas City and wanted to give him prices on our line of products.

Fuzzhead didn't respond. The older man with the mustache yawned, eyes still on me. Still none of them responded.

"Who may I talk to?" I asked.

"Who may he talk to?" fuzzhead mocked, casting the puckered smile around the table.

None of them seemed inclined to answer my question. After waiting a moment, I said, "Is there a Mr. Stahl here?"

I saw fuzz and yellow eyes exchange quick, sharp glances.

The older one stood up. "Name's Katawski. I'm in charge here. Leave your price sheets. I'll let you know if we're interested."

"Glad to meet you, Mr. Katawski." I smiled and held out my hand. He took it for a brief handshake. "My job is to give you a better deal than you currently have. We are aggressive marketers, Mr. Katawski. If you can give me a look at your current line, I guarantee that we'll do better."

Katawski sighed wearily. "You give me the sheets. I'll see if we have any reason to talk."

"That's perfectly all right. If you can't give me information about your pricing, can you tell me what products you currently run?"

"The usual," Katawski said. "Meat, vegetables, fruit."

"We are the best in the central states region with meat," I said enthusiastically. "Our office is within a block of the Kansas City stockyards. I can almost guarantee you the best prices, plus packaging to fit your needs. If you'll show me your packaging needs, I can make a proposal that will please you."

I noticed fuzzhead and Abe Lincoln exchange another glance.

I was making this up as I went along, probably not using the right buzzwords, but Katawski didn't seem to notice. He looked bored and sleepy. "Go ahead," he said. "You can look in the warehouse and see what we sell. I don't have nothin written out. Just keep your hands off the food. You'll have a hell of a time beatin our meat prices. We're gettin it for nothin. We might could do better on vegetables."

As I walked toward the door, he said, "You need somethin to write on?"

"No sir," I said. "I've been in groceries since I was fifteen years old. I have a great memory for food." I pointed at my temple.

In the stockroom, I walked between unpainted pine shelves stacked with cans. Katawski watched me for a moment from the doorway, then disappeared, and I went toward the back, where there were food-preparation tables along one wall and four large coolers. I was beginning to doubt this visit was going to do any good, but at least I knew who Stahl and O'Brien were. I had them identified. I looked quickly in one of the coolers, then shut the door, and my eye was caught by three gallon-sized, yellow-labeled cans under one of the preparation tables. My heart was beating hard before I even fully grasped why.

I recognized the can and label, with its black skull and cross-bones, from seeing one in Don Campbell's office at the hospital. Arsenic was a good murder weapon, Don had told me, because it was used in embalming fluid, making it impossible to detect in a corpse past the undertaker. You could kill somebody slow or fast with it, he'd said, and it took very little to do the job.

I opened the door of the meat locker and stood inside for no good reason. I just stood there thinking. Bad meat hadn't been enough. It was taking too long.

What next?

As I turned and walked through the swirl of mist back into the stockroom, Stahl, the man with goat eyes, was standing there, ten feet from the locker door, with his hand inside his coat.

"Why'd you ask for us?" he said.

"I beg your pardon?"

"Why'd you ask for me and O'Brien? We don't work here."

I started to lie to him, but something stopped me. Then I started to tell him the truth—that whether he worked for this place or not, he did work for Jim Mackey and had helped to murder a large number of people. The thought of giving him a precise and lawyerly response actually went through my mind—but instead I just went for him, knocking him at the throat into nine-foot-tall pine shelving, cans and bottles of food raining down around us. He was squirming around, pulling out a pistol, when I picked up a gallon-sized bottle of pickles and bashed his head with it.

Katawski appeared at the warehouse entrance but didn't make a move to come in. Then O'Brien was at the door with a sawed-off shotgun. He discharged one barrel, and I felt stinging in my shoulder and arm; food containers started leaking all over the place. I tried to get the pistol out of Stahl's hand, but he went into a seizure, his body partly raised, shuddering, grasping the gun in a steel grip and unconsciously firing it into the wall. Apparently unsure where the shots were coming from, O'Brien ducked back into the front office. I kicked at the gun in Stahl's hand, but he held on to it, making an unearthly low *huh-huh-huh-huh* sound. I went for one of the yellow-labeled cans of poison and the back door, which was locked. The truck entrance was a big double door, and I managed to push it open and slip out before O'Brien let off his second barrel of lead, some of which splintered through the wood.

I ran behind another building and up the street, then doubled back to the van. Rainy was there, motor running, wide eyed, when I piled in. "Go!" I said.

By the time we hit the highway, O'Brien and Katawski were in a car behind us. I told Rainy to head out of town so we wouldn't get stuck in traffic. Katawski looked scared and O'Brien appeared mad, his fuzzy hair sticking up above a livid face. O'Brien was a comedian, a Marx brother; Katawski, with his mustache, a common hardworking man past his prime, getting old and stiff. Yet if our car stopped, either of them would walk up to this van and kill us and never get into a bit of legal trouble over it.

"What is that?" Rainy asked, nodding toward the yellow can I'd put on the floor.

"Tell you later. Just don't stop the car. Don't get into a traffic jam." I had taken out Hank's pistol, made sure it was loaded, and collected the extra bullets in my pocket.

We were going thirty in traffic, and O'Brien rode up and butted into our rear. He was driving a newish Pontiac, which was considerably lighter than our van, and his car took the worst of it. To my amazement Katawski, the older man who'd acted half asleep at the warehouse, dangled himself out the window and shot at us, ripping a hole in the top of our back doors.

"Are you hit?"

"No?" she said, as if she wasn't sure.

"Fast, Rainy. We can't let him get that close. He's going for the tires."

The sawed-off shotgun was wholesale deadly at close range but probably wouldn't blow out a tire at a hundred yards. The car in front of us turned left, and I told Rainy to go faster. We were up to about fifty on a flat, straight road. I was in such a state that I didn't even know where we were headed except out of town. He was bearing down on us. He had more motor and less weight than we did.

Katawski hung out the window again and blasted away. Something about being shot at does it to me. It scares me, yes, but mainly it makes me hate.

Katawski ducked inside and reloaded, then again dangled out the window, aiming toward us.

"He's coming," I said. "Get down in the seat and hit the brakes."

"What?" she said.

"Let him hit us." I squeezed down to brace my neck, and she imitated me.

"Are you sure?"

"Yeah!" I said. "Hit the brakes!"

She did so at the same moment that the entire rear window blew out from a shotgun blast, showering us with glass. Our tires howled, and they rearended us. Crunched in the front, the Pontiac veered off to the left over an embankment. I sat up in the seat, watching her, ready to grab the wheel.

"Are you hurt?"

"Good God! Can I stop?"

When we'd pulled over, she felt the back of her head, nervously picking at her hair.

"What is this?"

"Safety glass," I said. "Brand new for 1933."

She didn't see the humor. "Jesus, what are those people doing? Good God!" She went on for a while, letting off steam, while I sat still trying to figure out what to do next.

"Tom, you're bleeding."

I unbuttoned my shirt and saw some pellet holes in the shoulder and one that had hit me in the chest and seemed to have bounced off a rib. A car slowed down, then hurried by, and with Hank's pistol I got out and walked across the highway to check the Pontiac. It had run off the roadbed and squarely into a three-foot-thick cottonwood tree. Katawski had been thrown fifteen feet and appeared to have broken his neck. O'Brien was slumped in the seat with a crushed face.

I felt another surge of adrenaline and pent-up anger. It just came up again and washed over me. I don't know why. There was nothing moving, only the desultory sound of wind rustling weeds and a few midday grasshoppers. When I got back to the van Rainy was standing outside shaking the rest of the glass out of her hair.

"Come on," I said as calmly as I could. "I'll drive."

As we drove back into town, she said, "You need to go to a hospital."

I shook my head. "It's okay. They're just pellet wounds. It'll stop bleeding."

She looked down at her feet, at the yellow can I had gotten from the warehouse, now on its side. "What is that?"

"Arsenic," I said.

She looked down at the skull-and-crossbones label, at first blankly. She started to say something but stopped.

I had the half-baked idea of going to the Mackey Building and just confronting him, but as we approached the building I remembered what Pale had said. He wouldn't be here. It wouldn't work anyway. I was feeling lightheaded.

We were in the middle of town, driving past the Mayo Hotel, when Rainy said, "What is it for? Did they put that in the food?"

"I don't know," I said. "I'd like to ask him."

"Tom, you need to go to a hospital. Your eyes aren't right."

I finally had enough sense to pull the van over. "We can't go to a hospital. Not in Tulsa. I've got another shirt in that little suitcase in back. Could you get it for me? And something to wipe this off." The sunlight was buzzing in my eyes.

She started to do as I asked, but the look of concern deepened on her face, and she began to recede. I noticed myself slipping into a strangely pleasant remove from the situation, like someone reading a book, or remembering reading a book as I was going to sleep, idly wondering about a certain matter in the story—if it was possible that one of those pellets had made its way someplace important and the man—what was his name? Me?—was bleeding significantly inside.

"Okay," I said, with what she later called a ghastly smile. "Let's go to a motel instead." Then I took a nap—from my perspective a pleasant sort of half-doze, during which I gave the world up to others, let it go entirely, and became happily uninvolved in its poor struggles. Although part of me was aware of this person feeling my pulse, looking at my color, then finally shoving me across the seat, I had no name for any of these actions, for I was basking on the balmy, tropical beach of the shocked.

I fainted, is what it came down to, and Rainy didn't.

While I dozed she swallowed what must have been an overpowering urge to find a hospital and instead went to a motel, rented a room, and somehow managed to drag me inside. She also fetched—with the help of the motel manager and luxurious tipping—a doctor who came to the motel, examined my wounds, listened to my ticker, and pronounced me not likely to die.

She had cleaned up most of the blood before he arrived, so the wounds didn't look quite so fresh. I did hear him ask her how I'd been wounded because by then the doc was dripping a salt-and-sugar cocktail of some kind down my throat and I was coming around, beginning with the tongue. Still half in dreamland, I heard her respond with an amazingly well-performed lie. She sounded irritated and British. She'd just arrived here from Chicago; this man had been sent to pick her up and drive her to Oklahoma City. The poor chap had been hunting with his brother, and his brother had accidentally sprayed him with pellets.

She sounded unpleasant, mildly sneering, playing the part of someone you might not want to get too involved in helping.

"Can you believe it? He manages to get me and my suitcase out to the car, and to tell me his little hunting story, and then puff, end of driver. I guess these poor people are so desperate for work. They should have kept the man in Oklahoma City and sent someone else; that's what I think. He gets me to the car, sits behind the wheel, and faints. And I pay his medical bill. That's a fine welcome. I'll pay your fee, but I bloody well assure you I'll get my money back."

I heard the doctor ask her something, and Rainy answered vehemently and unpleasantly, "I hate hospitals. I do not patronize them. My husband died in a bloody rancid hospital, and as far as I'm concerned they kill people. Whatever else happens, I won't be responsible for killing their incompetent man. No, I'll drive him back as soon as he comes round. I'm quite able to handle it, thank you."

Cylinder 43

Whether because the doctor had given me some sleeping potion, or because I needed it, or because I felt completely safe in Rainy's hands, I ended up drifting back to sleep and woke up, to my astonishment, to find Hank in the room with us. Rainy had had the further presence of mind to call my office, and Bernie had sent Hank in his LaSalle. He had made it in a little over three hours and was exhilarated by the experience of driving the big car.

"Damn thing flies," he said. "I had it up to eighty on the straightaways."

With Hank there, Rainy took the opportunity to disappear into the bathroom and take a shower. I got up and walked around the room, trying out my legs. I told him the situation, pretty much spilling the whole sack of beans, including the poisonings and the fact that Stone's secretary was implicated in the land deal.

Hank, sitting at a little table with his silver flask in front of him, grimaced slightly at this information, turning his eyes to the floor.

"Something was going on with Mr. Parfit this morning," he said. "He didn't show up at work today. Judge Stone had me go to his house, but either he wasn't at home or I couldn't rouse him. The judge was pretty upset. I think he called Mr. Pryor too. Parfit hasn't missed a day of work in fifteen years. Rumors were starting at the courthouse."

"Did you go inside his house?"

"Locked. I checked through the windows and didn't see anything. I figure a man missing work one morning wasn't cause to bust down his front door. If I'd known about all this, I'd have gone in."

"I called Mel and asked her to mention to the judge to lay low. Is he doing that?"

Hank shook his head. "Don't know. I think he called me from his office."

"What about Mel? Has she got somebody with her in the office?"

"Right now, I don't know."

Rainy appeared at the bathroom door, combing her hair, and she eventually came over and lay down on her back on the bed and promptly shut her eyes. Hank glanced at her and put his hand over his mouth and lightly cleared his throat, as if being in a motel room with a horizontal woman with wet hair made him a little self-conscious.

"Shouldn't they be taking care of this in Poteau?" he asked.

I gave him a skeptical look. "Come on, Hank."

"Mm." He reared his head a little, as if he didn't need any more convincing. "I guess you thought about the FBI."

"The chance of the FBI doing more harm than good with this kind of thing is—what? Three out of four?"

"Nine out of ten," he muttered, frowning and narrowing his eyes. "You have a plan?"

"Haul him to Fort Smith ourselves."

"What'll you do with him if you get him there?"

"Prosecute him for two murders in Sebastian County."

"In Stone's court?"

"We can worry about that when the time comes. I think we'd have Stone's cooperation."

"Even though he's implicated in this?"

"That's right."

"He couldn't try the case."

"Maybe not, but I think he'll do the right thing. Change the venue. Resign. I don't know."

"So you figure to kidnap this man, illegally extradite him, and prosecute him yourself in a court where the judge'll have to resign. . . . I ain't a lawyer, but—"

"No. He's in Fort Smith, and you happen to see him and arrest him. We get out the warrant, maybe predate it."

"I'm not a good liar," Hank said flatly.

"So we handcuff the son of a bitch to a light post. If a warrant's out on him, anybody can arrest him. I'll get a municipal cop to do it."

Even as I said it, I knew Hank was right. It wouldn't work.

He was shaking his head. "The guy can afford to hire a pack of lawyers from hell. And with Kenny working for him . . ."

"Got any better ideas?" I said impatiently.

He thought a while and eventually just shook his head. "Don't know, Tom. I really don't."

There was a long silence, except for the whisk of cars going by outside, until Rainy's voice came from the bed.

"Why don't we take him to the mountain and show him what he's done?" she said.

Hank and I traded glances, at first equally blank, and both looked at her. She was lying still, arms at her sides, staring at the ceiling.

"They were his victims," she said. "Put him face to face with them."

"Face to face with some corpses. He'd cover his nose, say he was innocent, and have us killed."

"I think there are some left." She turned on her side and propped her head on her elbow. "Like the man you met on the road on your first visit. The outlyers."

Hank shifted in his chair and unscrewed the cap on his flask. He took a slug and handed it across the table to me. "I turned some bad actors over to the locals," he commented. "Of course, this was a while back."

"What locals?" Rainy asked.

"Whenever we came out here, we were out of our jurisdiction. The tribes had courts. Sometimes they wanted to handle cases. We almost got into a fight over one man because we'd put in so much effort getting him. There was a reward on him."

"Who?" she said.

"Name of John Pike, worked as a bartender and bouncer, set himself up in business as a hired killer. He lived by the old Chickasaw line in one of those little towns that's gone now, where you'd ride in Friday night and have a fifty-fifty chance of getting out by Sunday. He killed a man with a baseball bat on the river ferry into Fort Smith, and Sheriff Bill Tilghman sent us after him. He told us to follow him wherever we had to. It was probably two hundred miles out of our jurisdiction. He wasn't hard to find when we got there. He had an office along this row of saloons with a sign in the window advertising his occupation. He gave out business cards that said 'John Pike, Hired Assassin, 7 Cents a Mile Plus Bounty.' I kept one around the house for a memento until my wife threw it away. He told me he'd killed forty-seven people, mostly Indians. After we nabbed him, the local guys, lighthorse, heard about it and came looking for us. There were twelve of them and three of us. They got him."

"That's forty years ago," I said.

"Yeah," Hank allowed. "A little over."

"And even if there are people still on the mountain, they aren't going to have any judicial—"

"They've been managing all this time; they must have some way," Rainy said.

"But they aren't managing now, Rainy."

"Put him face to face with it, Tom."

"What's the purpose? Why not just kill him?"

"Because you aren't totally sure," she said. "You've got all kinds of evidence, but it isn't conclusive. He did most of it through employees. You need to find out how much he knew."

Still holding the flask, I was pacing now, shaking my head. "It's not a good idea."

"Then you trust the law, turn him over," she said. "You've got the file from the agency."

I stopped and looked at Hank.

"What do you think?"

He tossed his head. "Hard part would be snagging him. He's probably got a lot of men around him."

"He has a hell of a lot around him tonight. He's having a big barbecue at his ranch."

"It might be the best time," Rainy said. "We could melt into the crowd."

Hank gave her a little half-smile.

"Do I get a drink?" She held out her hand toward the flask.

That wasn't the end of our discussion. My chest and shoulder had begun to ache. I kept checking out the window, looking at Bernie's LaSalle. We finally all got bored with talking and agreed on a plan, a thin one, of making a pass at Mackey's ranch and casing the joint, at least seeing what the place was like, possibly going to the party if there was a big enough mob there. If it looked too dangerous, we wouldn't push it. We didn't talk any more about trying to kidnap him. It was just a reconnaissance. That's what we had agreed to do when we left the motel. I drove the van to a dirt street several blocks from the motel, left the key on the floor, and took the gallon can of arsenic to stow it in a corner of the La Salle's trunk. Hank and Rainy picked me up, and as we drove away from the van I began to feel a little steadier.

Hank, chewing his matchstick now, drove us through town, and Rainy found a clothing store open until six o'clock while Hank and I drove down the block to fill up on gas. The LaSalle attracted attention from everybody. I bought some candy bars.

Inside twenty minutes Rainy walked out of the clothing store carrying two sacks that she dumped onto the back seat when she stepped in.

"Party clothes," she said.

Hank laughed. "How'd you do that so fast?"

"I hate to shop."

It was after seven o'clock when Hank pulled down the driveway of an abandoned house on a highway north of Tulsa, and we got out, ate the candy bars, and put on the new duds. For Hank, who already was wearing a cotton coat, she'd bought a string tie and a ten-dollar Stetson hat. I got a clean shirt and ready-to-wear white serge summer suit. She tied my tie and helped me on with the coat. Hank and I turned our backs while Rainy got into her clothes.

Nearby was an abandoned sod house with powdery sand climbing the south side and spilling over what had been the roof. The trunks of two dead trees were also buried. The low, rolling country was normally hay and cattle land, but this year the crop was sand dunes and grasshoppers. Sirius was setting with the sun.

"Why would somebody have a party in dog days?" Hank asked.

"Celebration of his first well, I heard."

"Okay, boys."

We turned and saw Rainy in a tawny, slim-waisted dress with a demurely high neckline. It wasn't flashy, just plain, thin wool, but it showed all her bones and curves, from her clavicle down, and with the fake diamond necklace, some lipstick, and dressy shoes, Hank and I were doing double takes.

Hank cleared his throat. "What do I owe you for the Stetson?"

She just threw him a smile. Her devil-may-care attitude made me start worrying again. Hank seemed to be almost enjoying himself.

In twenty minutes, approaching Sperry, Oklahoma, we quickly found ourselves in traffic, driving alongside a painted white wooden fence marking off fields that were magically green. The cars began to sandwich in behind us, and we were headed for a gate with four uniformed, armed guards.

Cylinder 44

"Looks like they're checking invitations," Hank said.

I was about to say we should pull out when Rainy pushed open her door and hopped out. "I'll take care of it," she said. She approached one of the guards, put a hand on his shoulder, and invited him away from the others. The guard walked back with her, leaned in Hank's window, and glanced around the car.

"You can pull out here, take the lady right on to the door. Park back up on that hill."

"Thank you," Rainy said, with a little smile of apparent embarrassment.

"What'd you tell him?" I asked as we pulled out of line and drove in.

"That I was desperate for a bathroom."

Hank shook his head slightly, glancing at her in the mirror.

"It's all in the presentation," she said.

Hank took her to the house, where she went toward the open double doors and moved quickly between groups of people drifting around the front porch.

The parking spots were on an elevated place, and we could see over a hundred people drifting around the back of the house, where a stage and large tent were set up. We shut the door and looked down on the place—a sprawling house, a barn as big as a large hotel. In the darkening green fields were haystacks three stories tall. Mackey had a water tower and irrigation pipes running through the fields, and some not far from the house were spraying water high into the air, air conditioning the very sky. No telling how far he'd had to drill to get that kind of water, but then who could afford to drill deeper than this man?

Hank looked at me and said, "Well, I'm the driver; who are you?"

"I guess we should have thought about that. Just call me Chief Tom."

"Chief Tom who?"

"That's all you need to say. I've got a half a quarter-section of prime oil land just outside the derricks south of Oklahoma City. If you have to make conversation, tell them you just moved from Fort Smith and fell into the job. Easiest damn job you ever had. I'm talking Indian half the time, and you don't understand me. That, and act like you don't like me. Stay away from Mackey's men, if you can."

Hank took a deep breath. "All right. So we're casing the joint?"

"I guess so."

We approached the ranch house, and Hank split off to a group of what appeared to be drivers near one of the outbuildings. I went around, avoiding entering the house, to the food and music. There was a big tent, where the food was being served. It looked like a mostly rich crowd, Oklahoma and Texas rich, and they were dressed in a wild clash of styles, some wearing denim and others looking as if they'd come for an evening at the country club. For a moment I almost forgot myself in the pageantry of it: beefy, red-faced men braying laughter, some dressed like bankers, some like dude cowboys with fringe and Stetsons, women dressed and coifed and bejeweled Texas style, embroidered jackets, flame-colored dinner dresses with fluffy sleeves, wicked necklines, bows, puffs, crinoline. A few pale flappers stood around with their hipbones sticking out, flicking their cigarettes, their beaux lurking nearby knocking back the drinks. By the body language, I got the impression that the heavy hitters were dressed down, the less secure dressed up.

A banner stretched across the bottom of the stage: FOUR-TEENTH ANNUAL THIEVES AND CROOKS REUNION.

The country-music band, led by a skinny lead singer, was one I had heard both on KVOO, the Voice of Oklahoma, and on network radio out of Los Angeles. The musicians played smoothly and grinned tenaciously. A movie cowboy, a dashing villain who rode black horses in the serials, stood near the stage fingering his pencil mustache with what looked like genuine uneasiness. From the outfits some were wearing—blue jeans with chaps and six-guns, flouncily dressed women—I wondered if other actors had been hired for flavor.

The Indians, though, were real, clustered by one end of the stage near a table. There were about a dozen of them. Some of them wore traditional turbans—Seminole, the tribe Mackey currently needed to make deals with. A couple of them were sitting on the ground, drunk. Apparently they hadn't been allowed to bring the girls who'd been provided in town, and they didn't quite seem to know what to do, so they just remained in a clump, as if protecting the ones too drunk to stand, making what looked like occasional attempts at conversation. Waiters circulated with trays of drinks.

Central Oklahoma hadn't been part of my beat, so I didn't know many Seminoles. I was less concerned about being recognized by one of them than by the oil people, the lawyers, the bankers, or the guardians, many of whom I'd made unfriendly visits to while working probate. Here and there, around the edges, were suited men whose eyes played warily over the crowd, but I saw no one from our run-in that afternoon.

I got the feeling that the party wasn't really going well. The mood wasn't right. Where was Mackey?

And where was Rainy?

There were several cooking fires being tended, roasting corn and potatoes, and a cooking pit for the meat. Vinegary, sweet barbecue smells mixed with perfume and talc and bay rum and nervous sweat and the slightly rotten, iron-smelling odor of water being sprayed into the air. Water-cooled or not, it was still swooning weather. Tables were lined up for a sit-down dinner, and a few people were bringing out plates. I decided to go get food in order to have something to do.

By the entrance to the tent stood a thin woman wearing a poison-green dress that bared her skinny shoulders, with a veil of tulle around her chin and mouth. I was wearing my most blank, least inviting expression, but she spoke to me. "Hello, young man, are you here with the others?"

I looked at her and said, "Which others?"

"Our . . . friends by the stage?" she said, smiling enough to show me her teeth. I guessed, without knowing, that she was a relative of Mackey's, wife perhaps, posted for some duty at the food tent. She was in her forties and smiled like someone who didn't particularly want her "friends by the stage" to be going into the food tent.

There was a loud clattering, and a cowbell rang over the public address system. A man with a white hat pulled strangely low over his forehead stood at the microphone.

"Howdy, ladies and gentlemen. Welcome tonight to the fourteenth annual thieves' reunion. Before I introduce tonight's guest speaker, Hollywood actor and star Rafe Woods, I want to say a word for Mr. Mackey. He won't be speakin tonight on account of showin respect for three of his employees that was killed in an accident today."

"Who's that?" somebody asked from the audience.

"We haven't got all the facts yet, but we heard it was a gang of coloreds of some kind. They tried to rob a place; our boys ran em out and was about to catch em when they had the accident. We're takin care of it. Don't worry. You're here to have a good time. Mr. Mackey did want me to say on his behalf that he's proud the Oklahoma primaries are windin up and it's official: the Reds ain't takin over after all. Five out of nine representatives who voted for the New Deal will be out of office come the next Congress."

A woman said cheerfully, "Well that didn't take long, now, did it?"

There was a smattering of laughter and applause.

"Now here's tonight's guest speaker, Rafe Woods."

The movie villain came up to the stage and pulled out two guns and shot them into the air, which turned out to be the high point of his appearance. He holstered his guns and unfolded a piece of paper and began reading from it. Anybody who went to movies in the '20s spent a good many quarter-hours watching Rafe Woods, glittery-eyed and vicious in silent serials, but tonight he had a thin voice and looked a little pickled.

"Our host, Jim Mackey, is happy that y'all could come. As you know, old Jim pulls out all the stops, so loosen your belts and enjoy yourselves! This party's held every year to commemorate the first Mackey oil strike at Red Fork. I'm told that some came to the first reunion by horseback and wagon. Now times have changed, and some of you even flew on private aeroplanes all the way from Texas."

"And Colorado!" said a drunken voice from the crowd.

"Hey Blackie!" someone yelled. "Where's your damsel in distress?"

The actor tried to think of an off-the-cuff reply but gave up and went back to his script, and during the rest of his speech the audience steadily lost interest.

"Jim especially wants to welcome his friends from the Seminole Indin tribe here tonight. He hopes y'all enjoy yourselves."

"What's this guy talking about?" a man said through a cloud of cigar smoke.

As the noise level increased, the movie villain glanced up anxiously from his speech. "Now, gettin on to the festivities. I hear there have been a number of crimes committed around here lately, and Judge Mackey will be holding his annual kangaroo court after a while, and there will be strict fines levied on all those who have broke the law. Last year he fined the governor of the state two dollars, so y'all can be darn sure I'll be makin myself scarce. . . ."

A few were listening, even trying to laugh politely and applaud at the right places, but the crowd noise had gotten too loud, and he read the rest as quickly as possible. Some man kept erupting with a shrieking, hysterical laugh, and the woman who'd questioned me at the tent entrance plowed through the crowd toward him and escorted him to the house. The annual thieves' reunion was feeling a little ragged around the edges. Before the actor had announced dinner and fled from the stage, people had already begun pressing into the tent.

Rainy hadn't shown up outside, and I skirted the crowd and went toward the house. The living room was as big as a hotel lobby, with huge flagstone fireplaces at each end and lots of taxidermy mounted on the walls or standing on display shelves—several fish and bucks, an elk, a stuffed bobcat, and a stuffed mountain lion. I saw Rainy talking to someone near the entrance to the hallway.

The party inside was on a more even keel, and I got the impression that this was the better half. There were big bowls of apple cider, but guests were going down a hall to the den for the real drinks. The temperature was cooler inside, the cigars Cuban, the perfume subtler. These were the bigshots, the guardians, the real oil and money men, the better-off judges and politicians and their wives, women who spent a lot of time playing bridge, perfecting their appearance, being entertained. But still the mood was just a little off key, anxious—probably because of the "gang" attack that day. I picked out at least two guards eyeballing the crowd. The man with the laugh had been ushered to some back room, but his hysterical cackle still floated down the hallway.

"It's one of the Kaisers," drawled a heavy-lidded woman in jodhpurs. "You'd think with all that money he'd know how to laugh."

She was talking to me, unfortunately. Ten feet away was a man whom I had once given a lot of trouble on behalf of an estate. All he had to do was turn and he'd recognize me. I went to the serving table and accepted a cup of cider, stiffly handed to me by the black waiter.

I moved toward Rainy, who was acting animated. Jim Mackey was the man she was talking to—which somehow didn't surprise me—and I drifted close enough to hear them. Mackey looked unchanged from photographs I'd seen of him years ago. He had a knowing, ironic half-smile, neatly oiled and parted hair, and what could almost seem like a friendly face. He was wearing a plaid cowboy shirt with a red bandanna around his neck.

On the table were artifacts—Spiro artifacts—and Rainy was probing him, questioning him, but in a kind of breathless, flushed state, and Mackey's eye was traveling over her quickly. He had amazingly active eyes, as if he was taking in everything. I couldn't hear everything he said, but I did hear him say that he had always been interested in Indian history, and he was giving a lot of these curios to the Seminoles as party favors, tokens of his friendship. He picked a feathered cape off the table and put it over his back, chuckling.

Rainy sounded very British and excited. She reached out and stroked the cape. "My heavens, where did you get these things? They're quite charming, really. Do you have others? I'd love to see them. I must say that things like this positively arouse me. I've spent hours in the British Museum. Particularly things with feathers. These things have an effect on me."

One track of my mind was thinking, Oh, she doesn't know; she has no idea. She's underestimating him. This man is not an idiot. Another track was thinking, "party favors"? I didn't have the feeling for these things that Rainy did, or the judge, or apparently poor Lee Guessner. But "party favors"? My blood pressure up, I stared out the front window and told myself to relax. But I had the mounting feeling that I needed to get out of this place.

I was about to give Rainy the eye when the woman in tulle I'd met at the door of the tent went by, ushering the hysterical laugher back outside. She was looking severe, and Mackey glanced after her with a smile that became slight distaste after she went by. His eyes darted back to Rainy, standing before him, all flushed with her green eyes and exposed bones, and he said something quiet, questioning, and she followed him down the hall.

I hesitated as Jim Mackey's wife ushered this person by. He was someone who was apparently too important to their finances to simply kick out of the party. I wavered, looking after her, and at that moment the woman in jodhpurs walked over, smiling. "Do I know you? You do look awfully familiar."

I tried to extricate myself by telling her I was from Arizona, where I worked for a pipe-manufacturing company, but she acted quite interested in pipe manufacturing.

Rainy had just gone to the den for drinks, I told myself. But after several minutes they hadn't come back. I left the woman in the middle of a question and went down the hall, and they weren't in the den. I pushed through the smoky, boozy, crowded room, and they were absolutely not here. I tried other doors—bathrooms, bedrooms. In one large bedroom I heard a thumping and grunting sound from the shadowy bed and waded toward it until I caught sight of a red dress on the floor.

Other doors, no good. Going through the hallway and checking them again, I tried to slow down so I wouldn't attract attention. In the master bedroom a second time, I found a door leading outside that was cracked open.

Outside, the chauffeurs were around a little fire, thirty yards away, and Hank, bless the old hunter, saw me and made immediate eye contact. He chuckled at something someone said, then ambled down the road, away from the house. I followed. Approaching an outbuilding the size of a small barn, he broke stride and rushed the open door.

When I got inside, one electrical bulb revealed sacks and boxes of artifacts and Rainy in the dirt, with her one free hand hitting at Mackey, who was still wearing the feathered cloak, while with his right fist he hit her in the jaw and quickly drew back to do it again. Hank was closer, but I was madder, and Mackey connected with her about the same time I struck a glancing blow against the side of his

head. He tumbled off her but quickly got up on one knee and lev-
eled his eyes on me.

"Scum," he said, and started yelling for help, but I wasn't the
right person to be called scum, not by him, not at that moment. I
connected with the front of his face in a way that damaged his nose
and made him hit the ground like a sack of potatoes. It also left my
knuckles and wrist numbed.

"Jesus Heavenly Christ," Hank said.

Rainy was dazed, her jaw bleeding from a cut from his diamond
ring.

"So what do we do now?" Hank said.

"I'm afraid that's been decided for us," I said, rubbing my hand.

Cylinder 45

Hank went out and moved the LaSalle close to the little barn. People were walking by on the driveway within twenty yards of us, and we turned off the electric light. Hank had brought handcuffs, and he put them on Mackey and gagged him, and we got him into the trunk without anybody seeming to notice. He was knocked out clean, his nose was still bleeding, but he'd be coming around soon. We'd be lucky to get out the gate.

"We have to take the artifacts," Rainy said.

"No," I said. "We'll be lucky to get out of here alive. We have to leave."

We had a fierce, whispering, ugly argument, which ended with me eventually threatening to throw her into the trunk with Jim Mackey and her—infuriating, indomitable, with fake passivity—saying go ahead and do it, then. Hank and I could go if we wanted to. She would not leave these things here. In light playing through the cracked door, our faces were nearly touching. I was spitting angry; she was bleeding from the gash in her cheek, wobbly but completely sure of herself, immovable: she would not leave these things here. She was careless of consequences. I wondered if she was in shock, just doing what she automatically did without understanding. She certainly had no idea of the danger we were in.

Hank finally suggested that we'd probably save time by just loading some of it and getting out. The LaSalle was a big car, but there was no way that we could get all of it inside. We stacked it everywhere, including the trunk, and used two saddle blankets that we found in the barn to cover what we could. Rainy continued bleeding, and my right hand was numb but working. I was frantic to leave by the time we piled in and Hank took the wheel.

Rainy and I sat in the back seat, separated by piles of artifacts on the seat and floor, and as we approached the gate I saw three men in the gatehouse. The area was well lit.

"Rainy, cover your cheek," I said.

One of the men came out of the gatehouse and up to Hank.

"Headin back early?" he said.

"Yeah," Hank said. "We're going all the way back to Oklahoma City tonight."

Something thumped in the back of the car. Mackey had rolled over.

"Well, I hope everybody enjoyed themselves," the guard said.

"Oh, we did," Hank said. "Good-night."

The man took a step closer, looked down, and saw the piles of stuff. He did a double take. "Uh, sir, could you—"

Hank pretended deafness and pulled out. I didn't look back but noticed that Rainy's face wound had dripped blood onto her dress.

"Don't know," Hank said, glancing in the mirror. "Reckon I ought to hit it?"

I looked around and saw that both other men had come out of the gatehouse and were looking after us.

"So far they're just talking. Hold back. I'll tell you when we're out of sight."

When we were, Hank cranked us up to sixty miles an hour on dirt. He gripped the wheel tightly for the sandy spots, which with all that weight made the car pitch and yaw like an overweight ship in a storm.

"Too fast?" Hank said. He was chewing a matchstick.

"Do what you can. Go north, away from Tulsa."

We drove through Skiatook before slowing down a little and turning back eastward toward Claremore. Nobody appeared to be following us. Rainy's cheek looked as if it had been sliced with a razor, and I took off my new coat and had her press it to her face to try to stop the bleeding. I kept asking if she was okay until she finally said, "Relax, Tom. You're the one with the bullet holes."

"I know a doctor in Muskogee. We can stop there."

Eventually I slipped into a trancelike state, not sleep, not napping, but a sort of nervous resting state. Our rider started rolling around in the trunk, thumping and kicking at the back seat, but we put up with it for the time being.

"Are you awake?" I kept asking Hank.

He glanced back at me, chewing his matchstick. "Tell you when I'm not."

"He's breaking artifacts with all that kicking," Rainy said.

We went through the lights of Claremore, home of Will Rogers, the sign told us, briefly on pavement. Across Route 66 the traffic thinned to almost nothing.

"So we're going to Muskogee?" Hank said.

"I know a doctor."

"All right," Hank said. "And then where?"

"We can talk about it after we see a doctor," I said.

Mackey continued rolling around and kicking, knocking at the back seat, and Rainy kept worrying.

"He's breaking stuff, Tom," she said.

"We've done everything your way, Rainy. It's my turn for a while. I don't want him in here."

Mackey kicked spasmodically at first, then started kicking regularly.

I hoped the doctor I knew in Muskogee was still practicing. He would be in his sixties or seventies. His house and office were on a dead-end street near the agency. We parked some distance away, and I went to his door alone, heartened to see that his sign was still up: Dr. P. C. Rider, General Practice.

He came to the door blinking, in a house robe, but he was used to being waked up.

"Yeah, I remember you," he said pleasantly enough. "What can I do for you?"

Dr. Rider was a short, neat man, and I had visited him with my complaints when I lived here. He was an old-fashioned doctor who knew what he could and couldn't do and, without seeming in a hurry, dispensed medicine and comfort with little wasted effort.

"I've got three or four pieces of shot in my shoulder."

He held up both hands. "Let's take a look at it."

"I've got somebody with me who needs you to look at her first. She's got a cut."

His eyes rested on me just for a moment. "Bring her in while I wash my hands."

When Rainy and I walked into his office, he turned from the sink and focused immediately on the cut. He picked up a bottle of disinfectant and asked her to sit down. He didn't say a word as he swabbed the cut. It was about two inches long, a bruised gash. He asked if she wanted morphine, and she declined.

"Okay, then," he said. "You're going to have to lie back and hold still. I have to suture it up close or you'll have a scar."

"Are my looks ruined?" she said gamely.

"Not if you hold still. Change your mind about the morphine, tell me."

She stared at the ceiling and didn't move when he pierced her skin with the needle. When he was nearly finished, he said, as if casually, "You all are mighty dressed up. Party get out of control?"

"It's a long story," I said, hoping to close the topic.

"Didn't rob a bank, did you? Last time I sewed up some bank robbers, they nearly threw me in jail."

"Unh!" Rainy said through her nose.

"Sorry," he said.

"How many bank robbers do you see?" I asked.

"Oh, they haven't been too bad here lately," he said, deadpan.

"Two or three a week. Okay, young lady. You can sit up when you feel like it. I'd rather leave that unbandaged for now if you can avoid hurting it again. I want you to blot it with alcohol at least twice a day—or any time your face gets dirty."

She sat up and smiled at him from one side of her face. "That hurt."

"Good," he said. "That means your nerves are working."

He got me on the bench, shirt off, and poked around in my shoulder and had me move my arm around and tell him what feeling I had.

"Those pellets aren't close enough to the surface for me to just pick out. Better to do that in daylight. Plus you're going to lose some blood with me messing around in there. It probably won't hurt you to carry them. You live in Fort Smith?"

"Yeah," I said. "How'd you know?"

"I read the Fort Smith paper sometimes. You're working for the prosecutor. I thought about you today."

"Really? Why?"

"Did you hear about that fellow—he worked here at the agency? Cotton, I believe, Dale Cotton."

"Yeah," I said. "I remember Dale Cotton."

"Came out in the paper this afternoon that he had a car accident. Apparently he was driving at such a high speed they couldn't get his car unwrapped from a tree."

"When did this happen?" I said.

"Early this morning, I believe. He was by himself."

When we walked back to the car, Hank was leaning against the driver's door. All the windows were up, but I could hear Mackey kicking at the back seat, methodically kicking and yelling.

I was weighing options. It was my call. Even if we got away with arresting him in Fort Smith, I'd still have to build a case against him, with a diminishing supply of witnesses. At the moment the only ready case was against us—Rainy, Hank, and me. We'd be a cinch for a Tulsa prosecutor. What Mackey had done—something having to do with a relief effort for indigent Indians, some business transaction concerning land sales—would be deemed minor compared with kidnapping.

"What about you two taking a bus to Fort Smith?" I said.

"I'd just as soon see him delivered," Hank said.

Rainy was very tired. She just shook her head. "I'm going, Tom."

"Okay. Let's let him ride in the back seat," I said.

Cylinder 46

I asked them both to step back from the trunk so he couldn't hear us and said to Rainy, "If he gets a handle on what you want, he'll just feed it. He'll try to make you think he holds the key to what you want to know. He'll lie anyway, but we'll get more out of him by not asking questions. Hank, do what you have to to control him, but don't answer any questions and don't let him get to you. It's midnight now. I figure we've got the night. They'll be looking for him tomorrow. I know the roads down here. I'll drive. The rule is silence."

When we opened the trunk, he looked up at us. He actually grinned—the mean little small-town-boy-made-big smile, dried blood from his nose around his mouth. I had to hand it to him.

"Finally got on your nerves, did I?"

"Yeah," I said neutrally. "Finally did."

"Just tryin to breathe. Where do you think you're takin me?"

Rainy sat in front with me while Hank put Mackey in the back seat, with his cuffs secured by a strong hand pull on the back of the front seat. He complained, but Hank convinced him to give it up.

This was my first time to drive the LaSalle, and sometime in the first hour behind the wheel I drifted into a philosophical moment. The car itself was just a car, of course—heavy but smooth, with nice instruments and comfortable seats—but driving it made me think of how life can so outstrip the wildest imagining, how the most free-wheeling fantasies are dishwater beside what the future can offer. When I was a young man growing up in this neighborhood, un-comfortably close to where we were, in fact, at that moment, and headed closer, if someone had told me I would one day be a driver of self-powered vehicles picking up sick and wounded and dying men in a roaring, rat-infested suburb of war, where men sometimes fell out of the sky in flying machines and others rushed out of trenches to strip souvenirs from them, I wouldn't have believed or disbelieved such a prophecy because I couldn't have imagined it.

Or closer to now—say, three weeks before now—if someone had told me that within the cycle of the same moon I would be driving the LaSalle through the country that I loved and hated most in the world while Bernie was back in town trying to put away Kenny Seabolt; that riding along in this car would be the sultan of the Glenn Pool along with a trove of Indian relics and Rainy, daughter of Samantha King—and it could go on. Beside the mar-vels that unfold in time, even the most fevered dreams are pedes-trian.

"You all from Fort Smith?" Mackey asked.

I didn't respond.

"Saw the Arkansas plate. Couldn't be too many of these cars from Fort Smith. Must not be more'n two or three in Arkansas."

He stayed quiet for a while. I could hear the gears in his mind going through options, alternatives, trying to figure out the best ap-proach, the best way in, how much to threaten, how much to cajole.

After about five miles, he said, "Cat got your tongue?" He looked at me in the mirror, and when I didn't answer he glanced at Hank. Hank said nothing. The busy eyes went back to me in the mirror.

"Hey, you got a pretty good punch, you know that, buddy?" he said enthusiastically. "Your lady friend here, though, she takes the cake. Regular cat. I'd hire her to run a drill crew if I wasn't afraid she'd bust their balls. Where'd you learn how to fight, lady?"

When no one responded, he added, "If this is about these old Indin things, you can save yourself the trouble. I don't give a damn about em. You want em, you can have em. I'll give em to you. You let me out at the next town and drive away. I won't bother you one way or another. I've got better things to do."

When he still didn't get an answer, he said, "You people are in trouble, you know. Ain't no way you can get away with it." His frustration was rising, but he controlled himself. "Two things can get you in trouble: liquor and women, my old daddy used to say. I guess he should have said liquor and women and Indin curios."

Failing to get a response, he said, "So what's your game?"

I held his glance in the mirror for a second, long enough to let him know I was listening.

"I know where we are. We're in Latimer County. I don't have nothing to do with Latimer County. If you put me to some kind of harm, don't matter where it is, you'll get caught. All the cars that come in that gate was checked by license plate, both ways. They're already lookin for me. My boys, every sheriff in Oklahoma . . . Ain't like it used to be, you know." He glanced around, trying to pick up clues about who we were.

"Like I say, you can have these damn curios. I just collected em for some friends of mine. I ain't got any use for em now. I was givin a bunch of it to my Indin friends."

I kept eye contact with him.

He said, almost hopefully, "Look, you do know who I am?"

Mackey leaned so that he was looking at me squarely in the mirror, and he gave me the banker's grin. A cowlick of hair stirred across his forehead. "You don't work for yourself, do you? This car is too fancy. Whoever it is, I could put em in my pocket. So what do you want out of me? You set the price. Figure it out. Take your time."

Through the great emptiness of Latimer and Pushmataha Counties we drove on, for a while spared from Mackey's nagging. At the farthest point south, not far from Texas, we were close to the place where I'd grown up—Bokchito, the Armstrong Academy, out there somewhere, a burned hulk of building then being reclaimed by the bottoms. I still feared that place, although it was dust. Like all the sites of woe and self-inflicted human agony, let it disappear to nothing.

Passing through the orbit of Bokchito, I had another glimpse of the fact that I couldn't get rid of my past even if I wanted to. That I would always meet myself coming and going, and trying to avoid such meetings would just amount to bleakness, forever bleakness. The ghosts, and the people, would always be there. I looked over at Rainy, who'd now leaned the other way, over a sack of artifacts, with her cut and bruised face under the dim glow of the electric clock.

Then Mackey started talking again, nagging, threatening, bullying. He even tried direct verbal assault. He called me a nigger. An Indin. Which was it? he demanded. "Nigger? Indin? Both? What the hell are you?"

I watched him in the mirror as he said this, possibly even showing some disappointment in my eyes. I had imagined that big-time guardians like Jim Mackey were chess players, adepts, maestros of a certain sort, even if the people they hired to do their work, the ones I had mostly dealt with, were punks. When you've lost most of your battles, you hope you've been fighting worthy opponents. But in the face of simple silence, Jim Mackey showed himself to be no more interesting than the people he paid. Against silence, he was a fox without a nose.

The territory we crossed inspired changes in his monologue, his busy eyes noticing when we turned back eastward, through the sleeping town of Idabel, where our headlights cut across families scattered on quilts in their yards. Past Eagletown, as we headed northward into the high mountains, my shoulder was stiff and my mouth sour, and I was glad when Hank handed his flask across the seat. I took a sip and washed it around my mouth. Rainy had awakened and lit a cigarette. Everybody in the car was awake when we hit the first patch of mountain fog.

"I know who you are," Mackey said. "You're working for that judge in Fort Smith. Before you do anything to me, you might tell him we know who he is and what he is. The sheriff over there has pictures of him, and my boys have copies. If something happens to me, they'll go to every newspaper in this area, I guarantee he'll be ruined.

"You understand me? You want a guarantee?" he blustered. "What kind do you want? You name it. You want photographs of me lying with a dark-skinned man, that's fine, I'll pose em. I know he don't want that no more than I do. You can call it blackmail, but he's the one doin it. I didn't ask him to. Your judge is a homosexual. You know what that is—a queer? Sheriff found it out. You can check with a woman name of Hettie Weeks if you don't believe it. One of em was dumb enough to tell her all about it. We've got the record on him, not just the pictures. His own goddamn sheriff has him under surveillance. He was a queer in the army; he got in trouble in the service in England; it's in his record; we got the whole deal. It'll all get out if you hurt me."

After another mile or two, Mackey was still talking, saying things like, "Look, you don't want to line yourself up with people like that."

Still getting no response, he decided to slow down and control his tone. "If you want somethin out of me, you're gonna have to tell me what it is or you'll never get it. Take money from the queer or take better money from me. If you like a thousand bucks of queer money next to fifty of mine, that's up to you." He leaned away, as if trying to set the hook.

"And if your judge sent you to the place where the old Indin used to live, he's sendin you to hell, because the only ones left up there are killers. Savages. They don't know you from me. The ones left are the worst. If he told you you'll be gettin money from Levi Colbert, he lied to you. He's dead. My boys was watchin the place. There was a plague of some kind that killed most of em off. I know because I was Colbert's guardian. I know all his business down to the gnat's ass. He didn't have a cent when he died. He used to have money. Used to, not now. His property got into such a mess that he had to sell what was left of it.

"I was the man's goddamned guardian. Do you know what that is, mister? Do you know what I'm talkin about? I was in charge of his estate."

He leaned toward me in the mirror, desperate to get me going, and not answering him gave me a momentary sense of giddiness. If I could stay silent then, I could handle whatever he said.

"He went senile or something. He got in with these bare-assed Indins. They're all crazy as bedbugs. They'd as soon kill you as look at you. You can't do nothin with people like that. Old Colbert couldn't hardly talk to em himself, but he was bringin em food. He figured he'd be the one to rescue em. They had malaria, and I got the quinine for him. He was always callin on me to get things. They wanted these relics outa Spiro. They wanted food. They wanted one thing and another. Bulldozers. He thought that'd help em. You couldn't keep em happy. Hell, they was livin up there without nothin, and as soon as you give em one thing they want ten more of somethin else. They don't know how to live. Wanted to dig a big mound and put these things in it. That makes sense, don't it? Spend a bunch of money diggin somethin out of the ground and then put it back in the ground. But I was goin along with it. I shouldn'ta done it, but I did. . . ."

Mackey rattled his handcuffs against the seat handle as he babbled. Our nerves, all of our nerves, were at the breaking point. I got a feeling that he half-believed his story, that if he lived beyond tonight, given a few years, it would be the story. It would be what had happened. And that was the thought that almost got to me. Or maybe it was what made me carry on.

"Look, you have made your goddamn point. What do you want to know? I'll tell you anything. I'll give you anything."

Rainy glanced at me, and I just shook my head slightly, passing up the opportunity to question him. He was frantic for one of us to talk to him. He might have even told us something we didn't know. But for this man reality was plastic, fluid, ever capable of being re-molded to suit his needs. He was a pragmatist of a high order. He snatched words and intentions from you and started bending them to his shape. Whatever worked. If he figured out that the murders in Sebastian County were our concern, or my concern, my official domain, he would merely start generating clouds, lying freely, half-believing his lies.

I stopped the car and pulled on the emergency brake. "Be back," I said to Rainy, and went to the trunk, where I had stowed the can of arsenic trioxide. Following a premonition, I took the feathered cloak from the trunk and put it on a rock beside the road. I took off the party shirt that Rainy had bought and used it to grasp the can of arsenic, which I brought around to Mackey's door. I set it in his lap and slammed the door.

By the time I got back into the driver's seat it had fallen to the floor between his legs, but he had seen the label. I was surprised to see him grinning again in the mirror—a rattled, tentative grin, but still a grin. He thought he had a handle on us now.

"You work for them, don't you?" he said. "I don't know how good you know em, or how they hired you, but you can't trust em. You're probably from Kansas City, right? Well, you won't get nothin out of them people. You may think they're givin you a bounty, but they won't do it. Them people ain't like you and me. I know. They don't follow agreements. You've got your curios. If you have to take somethin, take them. Hell, leave me tied to a tree. I'll give you fifty thousand dollars. Be more than what they'd give you, I promise you that, cause they ain't got shit, I know that for a fact."

And on Jim Mackey went, trying angles, offering deals, again growing uncertain against our silence.

We bounced in ruts, near precipitous edges, where for long stretches there was no way to turn around. We hit patches of deep fog. Twice we had to stop while Rainy walked ahead, testing the edge of the road. Crossing a ridge line, we descended through a stunted oaken forest. Scattered along the wet road were glowing green things, some as long as two feet, and only the rule of silence kept me from asking Hank if he knew what they were. I was afraid I was imagining them. Later I learned that they were exactly what they appeared to be, giant glowing worms that lived in certain places in these mountains and came out in the wet fog or rain.

I was weary of maneuvering this ocean liner. Would we ever get there? Was this even the right road? My eyes were itching with fatigue. I couldn't focus on what Mackey said any longer. His deals, his denials, his moaning and pleading became unpleasant background noise. I probably should have stopped and let one of the others drive, but I felt locked in, bound to complete the journey.

Rainy was walking along ahead of the car through fog, watching the edge, when Hank said, in a remarkably calm voice, "Somebody looking in the window here, Tom."

"Oh God, oh Jesus," said Jim Mackey.

I looked in my mirror and there he was, with his face briefly very close to the window. He made no gestures of either friendliness or unfriendliness; he just looked, noticing what and who were in the car. There was no recognition on his face, no sign of what he thought. It was not the knife fighter, but this man had appeared the same way, not there, then suddenly there, and he walked the same way, with the ease of someone who always walked, in mountains, over rocks. I stopped, and after a moment Rainy turned and saw him. He remained near my window, stopped with the car.

"Oh God," said Jim Mackey.

The man was in deerskins—no blue jeans for this one. In my childhood, I had once been given a gift of skins, a beautiful fancy fringed set of a kind that during those days only the Creeks around Muskogee made. It was the first gift I ever received in my life, other than the friendship of Rainy's mother. I was actually wearing those skins when I last saw her. And so at first, amazingly, it was the skins I noticed—not the knife, or paint, or forelock, and not his eyes, which could have been the eyes of a panther. I felt a strange emotion, completely unidentifiable, perhaps only the result of adrenaline and fear, but it felt like a kind of giving up, like a person must feel when he is dying. I don't know what I was giving up, except it felt as if it had to do with the past, my own past.

Rainy didn't look fearful, but she had enough sense not to confront him, not to get friendly. She stepped back to the car and got in.

"He's not sick," she said.

"Goddamn it!" said Mackey. "Keep the doors locked. For God's *sake*, turn around."

"I hope we're close," I said.

We were, it happened. In fact, we were within a few hundred yards, but by the time we made it to the gate there were others walking with us. At first behind the car, then around us. There were eleven or twelve of them, and they followed and led the car, in cortege fashion, without impeding us. There were no women among them. Their faces were painted in different ways, in white, red, and black, but all of them had jagged lightning shapes coming from their eyes. At first I hesitated at the gate, but they continued to move around us as if to encourage us up the driveway.

"You're crazy," Mackey said. "You don't know what you're gettin into. If you go through that gate, they'll cut you all to pieces."

"What do you think, Hank?" I asked.

Hank said, "Might be right, Tom. They ain't here to play baseball."

"Hell yes, I'm right!" said Mackey. "You don't know. You don't know."

I looked behind me, and Mackey was cringing, getting as low as he could with his hands cuffed to the handle and the artifacts on the floor, for some reason clawing at the red bandanna that was still around his neck, trying to get it off.

I looked at the men outside, trying to gauge their mood, but couldn't. They were simply here, obviously aware of us, looking at the car but not at our faces. It was as if the car had no one in it, or as if we were simply part of the car. They were wearing different kinds of clothes, some shirtless, three in skins, some with denims like the man I'd seen the first night, a few barefoot, others wearing boots.

"We're here now," I said. "We might as well carry through. Mackey, I believe in the law—"

"Believe in the law!" he said. "You think I don't believe in the goddamn law?"

"You have corrupted and ruined lives and murdered people and stolen property."

"Who the hell are you?" he shouted at me, suddenly looking up, red faced, lunging at me in the mirror. "My fuckin goddamn judge and jury? If you think I've done somethin wrong, turn me in. You're gonna get us all killed. This lady. You're gonna kill her."

"We're wasting time listening to him," Rainy said.

"Be humble," I said. "Hank, follow my lead."

I left the motor running and left the lights on and got out and stood looking at them, showing that we had come here intentionally. The rotten odor was high but acrid now, charred, and through fog walking along the hill I saw that the roundhouses had been fired. They had burned the corpses. There was no way to guess how these men had survived, but clearly they hadn't eaten the poisoned food. Maybe they had kept their code while others took help from Colbert. For whatever reason, they were tolerating our presence for the moment, but I knew that I'd better convey why we were here as quickly as I could.

I turned back to the car and pulled out the sack that had been sitting beside me and walked over and placed it on the ground in front of the man who appeared to be the oldest. The lights of the car reflecting off the fog illuminated his face. It was hard to tell beneath the paint, but the shape of his face gave me the impression that he was in his late thirties. He made no gesture or sign to me, although he was clearly aware of the artifacts. The others circled closer, but I could tell nothing about their moods either. They didn't talk. They moved, changed places, in a silent almost-dance, without telling gestures or emotions. While their arms were held loosely at their sides, some turned either one or both of their wrists outward, then turned them back. I couldn't tell if this was a nervous gesture, communication, or just some shared trait.

I asked if anyone spoke English. Eventually the older one looked up, but his eyes fixed on some spot beside me, as if he was looking at an image that wasn't there. I said hello in Choctaw, and he didn't respond. From my days of working at Gardner's store I remembered the Caddo hello, and it merited a slight but unreadable change in his expression. That was all the response I got. Hank brought over another sack of artifacts. They didn't open them, or look among them, or show pleasure or displeasure, but stood around, not speaking to us or to each other. Not engaging our eyes. We weren't of their world. Through frayed and agitated nerves, I felt a tremendous sense of loneliness. They showed no fear, no evasion. They were plainly responding to our presence; they just acted unaware.

I was about to go back to the car for another sack when suddenly two of them picked up the ones we'd already put on the ground and went up the hill toward the mound. The others surrounded the car again, as if to encourage it to move. They wanted me to drive it to the mound, and I did, with them walking, again, behind and in front of us.

As we drove up the hillside, Mackey, with shaking hands, was still trying to dig the bandanna off his neck. He knew what he had done. His terror was the final indictment.

The LaSalle was able to make it up the driveway to within a few feet of the mound. I parked and turned off the motor.

"It's all going back," I said to Rainy.

"I know," she said, and got out.

We opened all the doors and watched them take out the relics and carry them up the mound's slope. They didn't want our help now, so the three of us stood outside the car.

Mackey whimpered when he saw them reaching into the car. When one of them saw and smelled the gallon can of arsenic, he hesitated, his nostrils dilating. His eyes narrowed a little, and he left it there. I saw him go quickly to the mound. For the minute they were all gone, Hank and Rainy and I were alone, standing outside the car.

Hank had one of his pistols, but he'd had enough sense not to take it out. He said, "Look, Tom, there's a dozen of them. I don't like this."

"Let me take care of it, Hank. Don't reach for any guns unless you have to."

Before I'd finished saying it, they were coming together down the slope, all of them. The car was empty now, and the men were approaching, the white on their faces floating toward us. Jim Mackey had gotten off his bandanna, and for some reason the poor man had put it over his head as if to hide. It was probably fortunate that my brain was flickering, almost ready to shut down. I knew that these seemingly dreamy, inaccessible men could act quickly. And I knew something of their way—not their words or exact gestures, but their directness. Maybe I knew it from the first three years of my life, when I was a bare-assed Indian myself; maybe from reading books. I'll never know and don't care to.

They had made a decision. Several of them were carrying what looked like tools.

"Unlock him," I told Hank, taking out the bone-handled pocketknife I carried. "Turn your back, Rainy." Hank unlocked Mackey's shaking hands, and I reached in and grabbed him by one of his ears, roughly, and he said in a surprisingly quiet voice, "Okay, okay, look, you can't hurt me, they'll kill you faster—"

I dragged him out the car's door.

After I'd pulled him to his knees, I cut off his right ear.

His scream echoed off the rocky hills, and he just knelt there, holding the side of his head, blubbering, repeating, "You can't do that to me."

I spotted the older one and held out the ear to him. He didn't take it or say anything, but I was sure, in the lights coming from the opened doors of the car, that his eyes focused on mine for a moment, the panther eyes, and even that he gave me the ghost of a smile. I threw the ear into Mackey's lap, which made him scream again.

With the things they had brought—crowbars, a huge monkey wrench that looked like it was meant for bulldozer treads—they began to destroy the LaSalle, as they had destroyed my Ford. One of them knelt in the back seat and started taking it apart by neatly slashing it down the middle with a knife and pulling out the stuffing. I remembered the neat slash down the center of the mattress in Lee Guessner's house at about the same time I saw the trademark MCCOMB on this man's boot, and I realized—quite suddenly, given what was going on—that if my job was to nail everybody responsible for the two murders in Sebastian County, I had probably failed. I knew that the whole story of those murders would never be known. Whether Mackey's men had hired some of the stragglers of this group—men like the knife fighter I'd met the first night, who spoke a little English—or whether some of these men had walked the largely uninhabited forests between here and Fort Smith and killed the despoilers of their mound, I wouldn't ever know, but I was finished with it.

Jim Mackey was guilty of worse crimes, and we'd brought him to the right place. He was begging now. He had tried everything else, but even now he couldn't stop blaming it on others.

"Outa hand," he panted, "my boys sometimes get . . . they're the ones . . . please don't do this."

The LaSalle was solid, heavy, double welded, double bolted, more like a tank than a car, but they demolished it as methodically as scavengers taking apart a deer carcass, taking what parts they could into the mortuary house. They disregarded Mackey until he tried to move, at first on all fours, then up and stumbling, and one of them followed him, in no apparent hurry.

"Let's get out of here," Hank said, and he herded Rainy and me like stunned cattle down the driveway. I could walk, but I was numb, not exactly awake. I would later see, and of course dream about, what happened next, as I assumed we all would. My eyes had adjusted to the darkness well enough to see in outline in the moonlight. The man who was following Jim Mackey eventually caught up with him and—we saw and heard—pulled his head back and cut his throat, and within a moment lifted his head into the sky and took it to the mortuary and threw it onto the porch.

We all remained conscious and on our feet. Rainy went into anthropologist's shock, thinking she wanted to stay and see what happened next, to see them cart Mackey's decapitated body along with parts of the LaSalle into the mortuary house, but Hank made us go.

Cylinder 47

After all, it was what we had intended, what we had planned to do. No justice was more deserved. He was guilty. He had done it to the people in the Winding Stair, and he had paid for it. Looked at a certain way, what we had done was a stroke of genius—swift justice for a man who otherwise would not even have seen a courtroom for his crime. We had done the right thing. We truly had. But brutality is a destructive force. It knocks people apart. In unpredictable ways, it realigns things.

We saw the fire behind us in the still black sky, with the house that Levi Colbert had built and Jim Mackey's corpse and the prosecutor's work car burning together. The people of the Winding Stair—what was left of them—had once again sealed themselves off from the world, however briefly.

We stuck to the road and walked southward, toward Eagletown, in the direction from which we'd come. I noticed the rock where I'd put the feathered cloak, and picked it up. After a while, how far I don't know, I could go no farther. Hank, who had more than fifteen years on me, could have walked on, but I was cooked. We lay down in dry grass, and my brain immediately turned into an anvil, dead to the world but with alarming noises coming from somewhere, clanging.

We made it out. Thirty or forty miles down the road, late the next afternoon, we got a ride with a man who was scouting softwood for Dierk's Lumber Company. We went to Eagletown, where there were still people I knew. Jefferson Gardner's son and his wife, along with several kids, were still living in the big house, and he put us up.

After a good night's sleep, Rainy and I walked over to Big Tree. In a way it was my mother, this tree, sentimental as that may sound. I had come to her before. This time Rainy went with me, and there was a certain miracle in that. But something was wrong. Something was gone. I wasn't able to appreciate it. I sat down and leaned against the 150-foot tree and was numb, barely aware, scarcely hearing the river nearby.

The thing that's terrible about war is that it takes something out of you. You're never quite sure what, but something is missing, and you can't put your finger on it. To some extent, that's what happened to Rainy and me in our own different ways. We were knocked out. Hank was hanging in there. I hadn't known how tough Hank was until that night. Three weeks before, I had known him as an acquaintance, an occasional beer-drinking pal, an old guy, a courtroom functionary with an interesting past. I knew him better now.

Rainy talked to me—under the tree and later that day—about the people on the mountain, but there was something gone from her expression. She didn't have the same clear light of curiosity, as if seeing them had whetted her appetite and somehow slaked it, both at once. With what interest I could muster to listen to her, I wondered if she hadn't been changed forever.

We had more immediate worries. Making it back to Fort Smith. Dealing with the rest of this.

She had to leave the area and, if necessary, come back at a later time. There were three people involved in the kidnapping and disappearance of Jim Mackey, and one of them was a woman. One of Gardner's sons drove us to the train station in Little Rock. While we were there, we talked about when she would come back. I told her I'd try to make sure the artifacts in the basement of the Athenian were safe.

When she got on a train for Chicago, the feathered cloak was the only thing she carried. Our departure from each other was muted, dazed, emotionless. We had a lot to worry about. Short of disaster, we would see each other again, but we both suspected that this was the end of the personal affair.

Hank and I got a six o'clock train to Fort Smith. We talked unenthusiastically about our story. We decided not to ask anyone else to lie for us. We'd say that we'd tried to investigate Mackey, he wasn't around, and we drove back. We'd wrecked the car, totaled it, on the way home. Period. We knew nothing about any kidnapping. The story was flimsy but simple, and we had each other to back it up. We could only hope they hadn't taken down our license-plate number at the gate. Our guess was that they hadn't when we were driving in but might well have when we were driving out. We had one thing on our side: everybody was going to assume either that Jim Mackey had been kidnapped for ransom or that he'd gotten killed because of an oil-field dispute.

Hank tried to cheer me up.

"That was the best cross-examination I ever saw you do, and you didn't say a word."

"Right," I said, giving him a smile.

Hank leaned his head back in the seat and said, "You know, I saw a man poisoned with arsenic one time. He knew he'd been dosed and for some reason came to the courthouse instead of the hospital. I guess he figured he was a dead man. He walked into the office and wrote down a name, and then it hit."

"You're lying," I said.

"No, I'm not. It happened the first summer of Prohibition. His brother-in-law did it to him. Turned out he'd poisoned his own wife a year before and gotten away with that. It was some kind of insurance deal. This guy calculated he'd get rich knocking off his family."

"What happened?"

"A couple of us drove him to the hospital, and we saw the whole show. It took him about an hour to die." Hank turned his head and looked out the window at the river valley rolling by, then looked back at me. "And let me tell you, that man was lucky."

"Who?"

He narrowed his eyes a little. "That old boy we took to the mountain. He deserved worse."

We rode a while in silence, and eventually I said, "I keep wondering about those people. Why they're living like that."

Hank raised his eyebrows but didn't answer.

"They can't close their eyes. The world's coming to them. Timber companies snaking up those hills. They get into a scrape with a logging outfit, they'll be wiped out. . . ." I broke off, not sure what I was trying to say.

"What are they supposed to do, go to Tulsa and starve in the streets?"

I had no answer for that.

"I kind of like the idea of them being up there, long as they can."

"Right," I said. "The only problem is that in about a year that whole mountaintop will belong to Mackey's wife and heirs, who-ever they are."

Hank sighed. "Can't fix everything at once."

After we got to Fort Smith, Hank let me drop him off and bor-row his truck. I went home and took a bath, swallowed some aspirin for the pellet wounds, and sat for a while on the front porch with a bourbon and water, my radio turned on for background music. I decided I wouldn't be able to sleep until I'd seen Manny Stone.

Mrs. Stone met me at the portico door, worried-looking but, as always, cordial. Manny and I sat together in his den, amidst his ar-rowheads. At first he was grim, dignified, almost his courtroom self. He could read my face as well as I could his. He knew I knew things. He also knew I'd been in some kind of trouble in Tulsa. Bernie had told him.

"You're holding yourself stiffly," he said.

I wanted to say a lot then, but didn't. It wasn't called for. I kept it straight. "Is Parfit all right?"

The pain that shot across his face looked almost physical, as if I'd punched him.

"He went to Fayetteville. He has relatives there. He left town a while. He's all right. He's quite all right."

"Well, that's one man who isn't dead," I said.

He just looked at me now, waiting for the rest. But I didn't speak. He was going to have to be the one to talk.

"What do you know?" asked Judge Stone.

"I know about the land deal."

He nodded once and looked away.

I looked up at one of the panels of mounted arrowheads. "Was it just for the artifacts?"

Mrs. Stone came to the entrance of the den and said anxiously, "Would you gentlemen like me to bring you a drink?"

"No thank you, Elizabeth," he said.

She quickly disappeared. The level of tension in this house, I realized, was high.

He fixed his eyes on me and said, "Tom, what's happened?"

"You don't want to know everything that's happened. But you're going to have to talk straight to me."

After another hesitation he said quickly, "Lee Guessner and I had a special friendship. He had gotten into a mess with this oil man, and he asked me to help get him out. I couldn't say no. You already knew that."

"Special friendship?"

Stone looked at me searchingly for a minute, then nodded, looking down.

"Has the sheriff been watching you?"

The judge was ashen now. He was taking shallow breaths. "Tom, did you ever do anything you can't talk about?"

"I think you know I have. I think you know exactly what I've done. You've made it pretty clear that you do."

His face struggled. "Then maybe you can understand. Samantha King understood. I knew her, Tom. Sam was the best friend I ever had. She was the only one I ever told about myself. And she didn't condemn me. She accepted me."

"Then we have something in common," I said. "What about your wife?"

"She knows but doesn't want . . . to talk about it. We have an agreement."

"Is Kenny Seabolt blackmailing you?"

He looking down again, his eyes playing around the figures on his Brussels carpet.

"So it started with you going after Mackey for your friend. Mackey hired the sheriff to get dirt on you, and he hit the jackpot. Bingo. But for something that good, the sheriff figured he ought to pull down a little for himself. Then your boyfriend was murdered. And you conned Bernie into going after the sheriff to get him running scared. And Alfred Carr got dynamite put up his ass and blown to hell. And Bernie's house got burned down because the sheriff didn't like the heat coming from him. And Dale Cotton committed suicide. Did it ever occur to you that maybe you ought to come at this a little straighter? Maybe tell somebody the truth. Maybe not have everybody else running interference. I've been in your courtroom for seven years, and I've never seen a better judge. Why this?"

If I hadn't known better, I would have thought that the look Manny gave me then was a long Stone minute. It looked much the same. Solid, handsome face. Penetrating gray eyes. Not letting anything by him. To his credit, he didn't remind me again of what I'd done when I was fifteen years old. He understood that whatever had happened that many years ago was between me and my conscience.

"What do you think it's like being a homosexual in a town like this?"

"I wouldn't know. Probably not much worse than being a half-Indian. A bum deal, but not terminal."

"At least yours is on the surface."

I laughed one bitter snort. "My what?"

"Your . . . difference."

"In your courtroom, you taught me that the buck has to stop somewhere. I knew it before, sure, but you taught me the practice because you're a smart man. You have discernment. If what you are doesn't work here, go somewhere else. Go where you can live with it. Just don't wind other people up like little toy soldiers to run interference for you."

"Manny?" It was Elizabeth Stone, standing in the doorway again, now looking terrified. "What's happened?"

He shook his head. Tears were coming out of his eyes. "Go, Elizabeth. Go."

I stood up. "No, don't go. I'm leaving."

Stone looked up at me. "Can you at least . . . can you at least sympathize?"

I was a little dizzy. My shoulder hurt. "Yeah," I said. "I sympathize. But you've got to do the right thing."

"What?" he said.

"Admit the land deal. Write a letter to the superintendent of the Indian Agency in Muskogee. Copy the letter to the agency in Washington so there can be no mistake. His name is Charles Collier. If you have to resign the judgeship, do it. This little town isn't the only place in the world."

Cylinder 48

I still have no adequate explanation for how a man who had been on an unhappy vacation most of his adult life suddenly became a hardworking public servant. But then, I've come to believe that there are no odds against change. The past had held Bernie in its grasp until he was middle aged, seemingly set in his useless ways, with almost grown kids, and then suddenly, casual as a pagan god, it put him down and let him stumble off to find his way. He didn't have to learn that he was dying, or that one of his children was sick; he only had to be conned a little, swindled, and have his house burned down. As for the divorce from Berenice—which took a while—I wouldn't exactly call that a disaster either.

Despite his reputation of being a country-club golfer and not much else, Bernie did have social authority. He was a rich man, after all, or had been rich by local standards, second generation, and although it would be a long time before people stopped making ironic remarks about him at the local coffee shops, Bernie still could get into any living room in town. And unlike a lot of people, rich or poor, he started putting his frustrated idealism to work, beginning with the prosecutor's office.

He didn't get Kenny Seabolt for arson. He didn't even try. He stayed with what he'd started, against my advice. He indicted

Kenny for the relatively small crime of knocking protection money out of restaurant and bar owners. He held on to his witnesses in ways that I had never used, and never could have used with Bernie's style. He visited them at home. He called them every day. He got four witnesses lined up and only lost one to a last-minute move out of town. The case was holding. He called the sheriff's office and told him that if anything happened to any of the witnesses, he'd indict Kenny for murder.

Like a lot of bullies, Kenny couldn't take his bluff being called. When he tried to scare the witnesses, Bernie got a newspaper article written about it by a reporter who was young enough, dumb enough, to take a chance. The editor tried to pull the article, but Bernie talked the owner of the paper into letting it run. Kenny tried to pull his trump card then: he directly threatened Judge Stone. He told the judge he would send the photographs he had to newspapers unless Stone called Bernie off.

The next day Manny resigned his judgeship, and in record time he and Elizabeth moved away from Fort Smith. Without the judge to threaten, Kenny didn't know what to do with his dirty pictures, and he ended up doing nothing with them. Before the trial, he made a deal with Bernie: the charges would be dropped if he resigned. I was not present at this negotiation. Bernie Pryor sat across the table from Sheriff Kenny Seabolt, who had burned his house down and had done God knows what to whom, and he backed him down.

The missing Jim Mackey remained on the front pages of the Oklahoma papers for over a week. People at the party described an attractive woman with a foreign accent, but that was as far as their clues went. The men who'd been at the gate turned over their list of license plates but admitted to seeing nothing unusual, either coming or going from the gate. Nobody working for Jim Mackey wanted to admit screwing up.

Within a month of his disappearance, suppliers and drillers in the fields began to sue for nonpayment. A newspaper article revealed that he had sunk even more dry wells in the Seminole fields than anyone had thought. He had been in the process of trying to find outside investors for his oil company when he disappeared. The Mackey empire turned out to be severely overextended. There was speculation that he had committed suicide, and the articles quickly disappeared from the front pages. His wife couldn't sell his holdings because she had no right to do so until he was declared dead. When that happened in September, his property went to probate, at which point creditors all over the east side and central Oklahoma began clawing over the remains.

But something else happened that I didn't know about until five years later.

It was about two weeks after the Nazis smashed Poland and the rayon factory in Fort Smith blew up, causing rumors to start flying that Nazi sympathizers had done it. We were headed for war, as a lot of people had been fearing for years. Bernie Pryor was now working in Little Rock as an area director for the WPA, and I had gone on to other things myself, working as an investigative lawyer out of Fort Smith but traveling some.

Melody Parker Pryor and I met at Franke's Hotte Shoppe on West Capitol in Little Rock. Mel and Bernie had been married three years by then, and they had a girl—Bernie's fourth child, her first. Mel and I were sitting by a window. Outside three young men with duffel bags waited for a bus. It was late afternoon, and fall leaves were blowing down the street. Mel told me that her stepson, who had just graduated from Dartmouth, was hot to join the army. She searched my eyes, but we knew each other well enough that I didn't have to say anything. We both ordered coffee and egg-custard pie and sipped and savored as we fell into talking about that summer five years before, and Mel told me the thing I hadn't known.

A week after we got back from our trip to the mountain, she had gotten a call from the sheriff's office in Tulsa and was asked if Bernard L. Pryor had a LaSalle automobile.

That one stopped me chewing.

"Did they have a license-plate number?"

She shook her head. Just the car.

"What did you say?"

"I didn't. I gave the phone to Bernie. I was watching him try to figure out what to say. The guy on the other end asked him if he'd been at Jim Mackey's party, and it gave him time to think. I saw it happen in his eyes. He said, 'I used to have a LaSalle. Unfortunately it burned, along with my entire house, some time ago. You can read about it in the papers.'"

"And they didn't check on the car?" I asked.

"I don't know if they checked or not, but Bernie then went around casually mentioning that the LaSalle had burned in the fire. I heard him tell it to several people on the phone. They'd ask if he was doing okay, what with the house fire and all, and he'd say yeah, but he had no wheels."

"But people had seen the car after his house fire. And Berenice—"

"He was willing to take the risk."

Mel had finished her egg-custard pie. She put down her fork. "What happened over there, Tom?"

"Give it a few years, Mel."

She looked through the window as the three boys outside hopped their bus.

"You may not know this, but Bernie really likes you. He's always liked you. We talk about you a lot. I think he's unhappy that you didn't get to be closer friends."

I laughed. "Well, you know how it is."

She sighed. "Yeah, but it's a bum deal. What's going on, Tom? What happened?"

Mel looked at me searchingly, and I knew she was asking about something else.

"What's Bernie talk about these days?" I asked, changing the subject.

"Privies," she said.

"Beg pardon?"

"Privies. Toilets. Concrete toilets. They've put in over fifty thousand of them. He's ruined more than one social occasion talking about them. He's become a work fiend."

She took a last sip of coffee and shook her head slowly. "How these changes work. It's beyond me. Oh, he's still Bernie. He still gets impatient; he still flies into confusion. But now it's privies and hookworm."

"So you're in high society now?"

"High society? In Little Rock?" she said, laughing. "Not if you work for the WPA."

"Do you drive a fancy car?"

She snorted. "Try my Chevy. Bernie spends everything on his kids. Now his girls are in college. And we've got our baby."

I gazed at her. "You know what your Chevy reminds me of? The morning—"

"The morning I picked you up for the Jay Goback trial in my yellow skirt."

I laughed. "How'd you know that?"

She grinned at me. "You're not getting off the hook, buster. What's the situation?"

"What situation?" I said.

"Don't give me that," Mel said.

"You aren't referring to my love life, are you—or lack thereof?"

"You know, Tom, I used to be your secretary. I'm not now. We're sitting here. We just had the best custard pie maybe in the United States. God knows what'll happen between now and the next time we see each other."

Mel tossed her head slightly toward the window, where the sun was turning the sky rose over Capitol Street.

She added, "I gotta go back to my baby; she's a sweet kid, but she's a kid. So give me some grown-up gossip. You're one of the people in the world I care about. Don't give me the runaround."

For some reason this caught me off guard, and I may even have had tears in my eyes for a moment. Mel had always been bold but, I thought, emotionally shy. She wasn't now. She was out there.

So I told her some things about my personal life and about Rainy. Rainy had come back to town on several visits. She had spent five months working as a volunteer on the WPA–University of Oklahoma dig on the Spiro site. She had taken part in the effort to get the legislature to pass a protection law for Indian artifacts, and they had passed one—the first archaeological protection law in the nation, and the state of Oklahoma had passed it. Rainy had tried to find a good home for Guessner's Spiro collection. A man in Britain had wanted it, but she hadn't trusted him to keep it together. Eventually she sold the whole lot, minus three keepsakes, to a university museum for a modest fee and a covenant not to resell.

Mel knew about the people in the mountains. Bernie had obviously told her, and sitting there with her at Franke's—after what she'd said—I didn't think it was necessary to pretend he hadn't.

I told her that Rainy and I had never again spoken about those people. We occasionally looked at each other, as if to bring it up, but something held us back. We did things together whenever we found time. Rainy was in a period of change over those years. She seemed less brash, less sure of herself. She talked about her dead husband less often. He was an absurd man, a scoundrel—but she'd say it with a fond smile, as if to invite no further discussion of him.

"And you didn't want to go with her, Tom?"

"She's too young, Mel. I'm over fifty. She has worlds to conquer. She's in Central America now. She wants to write a book about the connections between the Mayans and the Spiro people."

She raised an eyebrow. "Keep talkin."

"We're friends, Mel. When she's in town, we spend time together. At her cabin maybe, or maybe she drops by my house. We sit on the cliff at her place and let the wind blow through the trees. We go swimming. Time moves on. I hope she finds a man more her age. When she does, I will gladly give her away in the courthouse."

"So," said Mel, looking at me with consternation, "a lone wolf. Is that what you're gonna be? A lone, lost wolf?"

I grinned at her. "I don't know about the wolf part, but yes to the lost. I like being lost."

"What do you mean?"

We were standing up now, and I gave her a kiss on the cheek. "Ask Bernie," I told her. "He'll know what I mean."

Acknowledgments

The central characters in the novel are fictional, as are most of the immediate plot details concerning the murders.

However, descriptions of the Spiro Mound itself, its exploitation and destruction, the items in the mound, Oklahoma history and geography, and other details, such as the operation of the courts in Fort Smith, are taken from history. Description of the so-called guardianship system in Oklahoma is particularly influenced by Angi Debo's classic *And Still the Waters Run: The Betrayal of the Five Civilized Tribes* (Princeton University Press, 1940), a balanced but still shocking chronicle of embezzlement, forgery, conspiracy, and acts of violence.

Some details of this novel are fictions arising from historical facts—for example, the facts that in the 1930s the tribal people living in isolated places were in dire straits; that certain well-off Indians devoted their estates to famine rescue efforts; and that the Winding Stair, particularly the area near the headwaters of the Kiamichi, was the home of the Caddo tribe, which is among the definite successors to the Spiro people.

Unlike some finds, the Spiro Mound was well known during the period when it was being exploited by the "Pocola Mining Company," due to widespread publicity such as the *Kansas City*

Star's front-page article headlined KING TUT TOMB IN THE ARKANSAS RIVER VALLEY. Dealers became interested, and as the quality of the artifacts became widely appreciated, some even began to forge and sell fakes. *Spiro quality* became a term used by collectors for artifacts having nothing to do with the Spiro culture. According to Forrest E. Clements, the affair turned into something like "a minor oil boom."

Due to the level of interest, and to the dynamiting of the mound (which one archaeologist calls a tragedy equal to the destruction of the Aztec Codices), the conservation of what remained of it was left in the hands of a few area people with limited resources. Forrest Clements of the University of Oklahoma and S. C. Dellinger of the University of Arkansas gathered significant collections. Mr. and Mrs. Henry W. Hamilton of Marshall, Missouri, devoted sixteen years to tracing the scattered items that had been sold, gathering information to make reassembly of the collection possible.

Rainy's speculations about the mound reflect the thoughts of several anthropologists and archaeologists since the '30s on such matters as the description of individual artifacts, the overall significance of the etched shells, Spiro's remarkably wide trading network, its cultural connection with Central America, and the possibility of a culture-killing drought cycle sometime in the 1300s.

Early theories about the Spiro people focused on connections with Central America and with other temple-mound people in Alabama, Georgia, and western Illinois. Their art seemed morbid and haunting to some, representative of a culture obsessed by death and military dominance. By the 1940s these notions had cohered in the idea of Spiro as representative of a "Southern Cult" ruled by messianic warrior-priests who were threatened and stimulated by an agricultural or military crisis. Anthropologists described this Southern Cult as having spread northward from the shadowy Toltecs and Mayans. However, more recent dating indicates that the Spiro people probably preceded other North American temple-mound cultures, and some now describe their art as influenced by, but not derivative of, the Mayan, celebrating harvest and renewal as well as military dominance (thus Rainy's discussion of the shift-ing significance of symbols).

I am particularly beholden to books and journal articles by Forrest E. Clements, Robert Silverberg, Philip Phillips, and Steve Wilson as well as to interviews with Dennis Peterson, superinten-dent of the Spiro Mound, and Michael Hoffman of the University of Arkansas.

In a University of Arkansas vault, near a storage area contain-ing dozens of boxes of the famous etched shells, resides the famous effigy pipe, described briefly in Cylinder 30, nicknamed "Big Boy." Big Boy is regarded by many as the best single piece of Native American statuary; it is too valuable to be on exhibit without guards and climate control. The effigy is fashioned from reddish, ex-tremely dense Missouri fire clay. Although only ten inches tall, the piece is breathtaking, its workmanship and melancholy expressive-ness the equal of any art I have ever seen.

The future of the Spiro treasures, which are distributed among several museums, is in question because of the Native American Grave Protection and Repatriation Act of 1990. The three tribes with kinship or claimed kinship to the Spiro people are the Caddo, the Wichita, and the Tunica-Biloxi. They, along with the Oklahoma Historical Society, have discussed the possibility of re-burying all human remains and building an expanded holdings and visitor center at the mound. However the issue is worked out, I be-lieve that it would be a wonderful end to the story if others could have the chance to see Big Boy as well as the other priceless arti-facts of Spiro.

Thanks also to Henry Koch for oil-field details; Mary Sue Jones, Sebastian County circuit court deputy; Lem Bryan, who was a city prosecutor in Fort Smith in the 1930s; and my mother, Betty Speer Morgan, who, as I discovered—to my amazement, after starting this project—worked as a secretary in the city prosecutor's office.